DEATH'S ANGEL

A CHILLING ESSEX MURDER MYSTERY

DS TOMEK BOWEN CRIME THRILLER SERIES
BOOK 6

JACK PROBYN

CLIFF EDGE PRESS

Copyright © 2024 Jack Probyn. All rights reserved.

The right of Jack Probyn to be identified as the authors of the Work had been asserted him in accordance with the Copyright, Designs and Patents Act 1988. Published by: Cliff Edge Press, Essex.

This is a work of fiction. Names, characters, places, and incidents either are the products of the author's imagination or are used fictitiously. Any resemblance to actual persons, living or dead, businesses, companies, events, or locales is entirely coincidental.

No part of this publication may be reproduced in any written, electronic, recording, or photocopying form without written permission of the author, Jack Probyn, or the publisher, Cliff Edge Press.

eBook ISBN: 978-1-80520-056-7
Paperback ISBN: 978-1-80520-057-4
First Edition

Image Copyright: Dawid Glawdzin

Visit Jack Probyn's website at www.jackprobynbooks.com.

ABOUT THE BOOK

Every angel deserves their wings...

When flight attendant Angelica Whitaker is reported missing after a night out at one of the most popular nightclubs in Southend, the case is handed to DS Tomek Bowen for the first time in his career.

As soon as the investigation begins, the finger is pointed at the man she danced with at the club, but when her body is later found in a church, posed like an angel, the same fingers begin to point towards a calculated, composed, and sadistic killer.

But as the investigation progresses, and as Tomek delves deeper into the victim's life, it becomes clear that there is no shortage of suspects, and everyone's got their secrets — some more than others...

JOIN THE VIP CLUB

Your FREE book is waiting for you

Available when you join the VIP Club below

Get your FREE copy of the prequel to the DS Tomek Bowen series now at jackprobynbooks.com when you join my VIP email club.

JOIN THE VIP CLUB

Your FREE book is waiting for you

Available when you join the VIP Club below

Get your FULL copy of the prequel to the DS Tanesh Bowen series now at bit.ly/enovabooks.com when you join my VIP email club.

CHAPTER ONE

Her body rippled and swayed in time with the music, her hips rotating elegantly, shoulders flowing freely, head lolling about as the chemicals and substances percolated through her bloodstream. She had her eyes closed so she could lose herself completely, let herself become one with the sound waves. She ran the fingers of one hand through her hair as the heavy bass shot through her core with every beat.

Around her, eyes still closed, she could hear the noise of people, dozens, hundreds of them, screaming, shouting into each other's faces in an attempt to converse, flirt, and hopefully by the end of the night, if their luck was in, fuck.

She had been approached by a few already, drunk, alcohol steaming off their breath, the smell of their heavily applied aftershave lodging itself down her throat, all hoping to chance their luck. And there had been a few that she'd taken an interest in, spoken with for over thirty seconds before she'd inevitably turned her back on them and continued dancing. For those select few, their luck had been in. Half-luck, mind, as she had only gone so far as to hand out her number. If they wanted the full deal, they would have to put in more work, more effort than that. They had to earn it.

She continued dancing, swaying, her body and muscles relaxing, succumbing to the trance the music had put her into. All of this was a learnt sport, an art. In the past few months she had learnt to let herself really go, to free herself of the constraints and anxieties she placed on herself, to enter a different state, one that was ethereal and almost out of body.

Suddenly, in the middle of the dance floor, she became aware of the urge to drink, to replenish some of the fluid she was constantly peeing and sweating out, and with her cup firmly in hand, eyes still closed, she raised her arm to her mouth. It felt like an extension of her body, as though someone was doing the movement for her, and for a few moments, her lips searched for the straw, tongue poking out of her mouth like a turtle's head breaching from its shell. A second later, she felt the straw being inserted into her mouth. She opened her eyes and saw a man standing immediately in front of her, guiding the straw with his fingers, a warm smile on his face. She half recognised him. James? Ashton? Percy? Or some other weird name? It was one of them. Coming back for round two. Putting in the hard yards, really trying to leave the club with more than her mobile number that would immediately block any number or call made to it twelve hours later.

The man leant closer to her, placing a hand on her waist. As he did so, she caught a whiff of freshly applied aftershave, thick, gagging, yet one of the more enjoyable, tolerable ones. Perhaps he had applied it in the bathroom and been charged a fortune for it by the toilet attendant. She wondered which one he'd gone for: Armani, Yves Saint Laurent, Dolce & Gabbana, Boss? She was familiar with them all, but this one was lost on her, yet the recognition of it lingered in the back of her mind.

'Can I buy you another drink?' he shouted, his words barely audible.

Before she was able to answer, she felt another hand on her. This time from her friend, Elodie, grabbing her arm and pulling her away. She was reunited with her trio of friends a moment later.

'What'd you do that for?' she asked, surprised to hear how slurred her words were.

'He was trying to put something in your drink earlier,' Elodie replied, leaning into her ear. 'I told him to fuck off when he bought you the first one. I told the bar staff to replace it.'

She looked down at her drink, wondering if she would see any indication that it had been spiked, but then remembered what Elodie had just told her, that she was looking at the wrong cup.

'I told you, you need to be more careful,' Elodie lambasted as she placed a hand on her hips. 'You need to be more vigilant, girl.'

She swatted away her friend's hand dismissively, then turned her attention back to the man, who had been lingering sheepishly on the outskirts of the group, dancing, shuffling his feet together out of time to the music, pretending not to hear any of their conversation though his body language suggested he'd heard the whole thing. Then she shuffled towards him, her legs and knees faltering. She'd been standing in her heels for too long. Either that or it was the alcohol coursing through her veins. She didn't know how much she'd had, but she was experienced enough to know that she was still in control of her body, still in control of her faculties. And as she approached the man, she passed him her drink to hold for a moment, then shimmied her skirt down her thighs till it was at a responsible level. Once she was happy with it, she took the drink, turned her back on him, and began dancing on him, gyrating, their bodies separated by less than an inch, gradually coming closer and closer into contact, until she felt his groin against her backside. She could feel the warmth and stench of his breath on the back of her neck. She also sensed hesitation, a brief pause as he waited to put his hands on her body. First, one on her waist, then the other wrapped around her chest, as though she was his possession, his trophy for the evening. He had claimed her, and she was happy to let him think he had.

Let him think that his luck was in.

As they danced, she began to feel his semi-erect penis pressing harder into her, prodding her like a child trying to wake a sleeping dog. He could prod and poke all he liked, but she'd decided this dog would remain asleep.

She made eye contact with her friends, enjoying the comfort and security of her new companion. Occasionally, he tried to kiss her neck, and even shoot his chance on the lips, but each time she would pull away, continuing to tease him. Revenge for trying to spike her drink. She knew what her friends would be thinking right now: that she was stupid, reckless, that she wasn't in control and didn't know what danger she was putting herself in. But she knew, all right. She'd experienced far worse than this. On the balance of things, dancing with a man in a nightclub was tame compared to what she'd seen, been through, experienced. Her friends weren't ready to hear about that.

Maybe one day. But not now, not when her closest friend was eyeballing her every movement, trying to summon the courage to intervene.

She and her new companion stayed like that for the next ten minutes, their bodies locked together, each enjoying their time for very different reasons. Until, eventually, after seeing enough, Elodie told her it was time to go. They had an Uber waiting outside for them, and they didn't want to miss it.

As she was pulled away, the man, who was now hungrier than ever, chased after her, followed her like a child, holding her hand towards the exit.

'Leave her alone!' Elodie yelled in the man's face, trying to tear them apart.

'Can I come with you?' he asked.

The tone in his voice was beyond hopeful, almost to the point of begging.

'Fuck off,' Elodie replied.

'What about you come back with me?'

Desperation laced his words. His last attempt at getting lucky.

She decided to dangle the carrot in front of him.

'You've got my number,' she said, as she was pulled away from the club. 'Text me.'

As the cab door closed behind her, she watched the man dig into his pockets and pull out his phone.

CHAPTER TWO

Even in a deep sleep, she looks beautiful. Gentle, elegant, angelic. Her eyelids flutter softly as her eyes move beneath them, the only sign of life in her otherwise lifeless body. Even her chest movements are barely noticeable beneath her skin-tight black dress.

I crouch down beside her onto my knees, my feet flat against the surface, so my knees are at a forty-five-degree angle, tucking my elbows into my hips, leaning forward, hovering my ear over her mouth and nose, listening to the faintest whispers of breath as they caress my cheek. Then I run the pad of my index finger over her neck, moving from the side opposite all the way towards me, feeling the cartilage and bones move underneath. I stop when I feel the pulse, the only thing keeping her alive, moving the blood from one part of her body to the next. Weak, yet steady, rhythmic. In the silence, it's amplified, drowning out the sound of my breathing, the sound of the street below.

Dum-dum.

Dum-dum.

Dum-dum.

All it would take is one nick of the blade, one deep laceration into the vein, into the tunnel of life, to send all that beautiful, perfect blood spilling from her body.

But not yet. There are things I must do first. Things I must experience. Before I progress to the next stage in our time together, I want to take in a final mental image of her in this state. Dirty, filthy, unclean – whorish. That will all have to change. I must return her to her angelic state.

I lift myself away from her body and roll her onto her front. The back of her dress is fastened with a zip, the hem cutting into her flesh. But there's hardly any body fat on her so it doesn't spill out of the sides. Slowly, I lower the dress all the way to the small of her back until it becomes loose enough to free her from it. Delicate, gentle movements are required. Nothing too rash, too drastic. Time, more than anything, is the most important. I want to enjoy this, revel in it, remember it for the rest of my life.

Once I've carefully removed the dress from her body, neatly folding it into a small square and placing it next to her high-heeled shoes, I look at her figure. Tonight she has chosen not to wear a bra and has let them all hang out. But I'm pleased to see she is still wearing underwear – thin, lacy, almost nothing to it – that she has saved some dignity at least. I remove what's left of her clothing and place it beside the dress. Now she's completely naked, glowing beneath the lights. I bathe in the sight of her petite figure, fully formed and proportionate in all the right places. Her breasts list to one side and now I can see the rise and fall of her chest. Everything about her is perfect. Her toenails, her feet, her thin calves, her thin thighs, her vulva, the two poles of her hip bones sticking out, her small, neatly tucked belly button, all the way up to her visible ribcage and collar bones. It's all on show. And it's all for me.

But it's not perfect-perfect.

There are a few niggles, a few minor defects. Like the two-day stubble on her legs and armpits. Like the small patch of hair on her pubic bone. The thick black hair on her forearms that she's always been self-conscious about. All the way up to the thin white hairs that have formed on her neck and top lip. The chipped finger- and toenail varnish that desperately needs replacing. The lazily applied mascara that needs to be removed. These are all just blemishes and irritants that diminish her beauty.

There is still a lot of work to be done until she can become the angel she was always meant to be.

Fortunately, there's plenty of time.

CHAPTER THREE

Tomek nursed his second pint of the evening, snapping his mouth open and closed to savour the taste. Tonight he was trying a new beer. Some IPA, hipster, fruity-flavoured bullshit made with love and an admirable yet naïve company ethos that planted a tree with every order. But despite his snobbish attitude towards anything that wasn't a pint of Heineken or Guinness, he found he quite liked it. He'd broadened his horizons slightly, and he was enjoying it. Though he didn't want to get ahead of himself and try everything on the menu; he'd only tried the planet-saving beer because Abigail had recommended it. Tonight was her special night, and he didn't want to upset her. So much so that he'd booked the venue she'd asked for, drunk the beer she'd recommended, and worn the outfit she'd chosen for him. His original plan had comprised a smart, blue-and-pink striped shirt with a pair of cream chinos, to which she'd said, 'You're not fucking going out looking like that.' Much to his dismay; it wasn't like he hadn't bought the outfit especially, like he had put no thought into it. There was a half an hour in M&S he would never get back.

In the end, she had selected a plain white T-shirt beneath a high-collared jumper for him. It was horrendous and itchy, and he felt like a twat – an *uber* twat – sitting there in the middle of the restaurant, looking like he'd come directly from the eighties. But it was her special night, and he didn't want to say anything.

As he set the beer on the table, he rubbed the itch on his neck with his finger, and turned his attention to Kasia. Tonight she'd put on her nicest pair of jeans and a small satin shirt, accompanied by a full layer of make-up.

She was in the middle of texting someone, a friend presumably, and had been lost in the device for the past ten minutes.

'How was school today, Kash?' he asked.

'All right.'

As always. Either that or it was "fine". The vernacular of a teenager going through a turbulent and tumultuous time. Tomek thought he had probably been as opaque as her at that age.

'What classes d'you have?'

'The usual.'

'Great. Which ones?'

She finished sending the text message – or Snapchat, or Facebook, or Instagram, or TikTok; whatever it was she was using – before giving him her full attention.

'Erm... maths, chemistry, biology, physics and PE.'

'Wow. That's a full-on day. Especially with all those boring subjects.'

Now he understood why she wasn't in the mood to discuss it.

'Yep.'

Tomek sensed he wasn't going to get anything else out of her no matter how much more he tried, and so he left it. Abigail, his girlfriend of four weeks, decided it was her time to weigh in.

'Your dad tells me you'd like to own a coffee shop one day.'

Kasia returned her attention to her phone. 'Yeah. One day. Maybe.'

'Well, I think that's a great idea. But it's a lot of work. Do you think you're up to the challenge?'

More monosyllabic answers. More staring at her phone.

'I think you've got it in you,' Abigail continued, holding the stem of her wineglass in her fingers, spinning the base of the glass with her other hand. 'If you ever need someone to help you write a business plan, I'm your gal!'

Kasia slowly raised her head. Tomek could see on her face what she was thinking – "You might not be around by the time I get to that point in my life" – but fortunately she didn't say it. Instead, she replied with a stunted response: 'Yeah. Okay. Maybe.' Then she turned her attention back to the black mirror in her hand.

Before Tomek could intervene, the food arrived. Lamb shank with plum sauce, sautéed potatoes, and fried veg for him. Beef wellington served with onion and truffle in a red wine jus for Abigail. And a chicken burger and chips for Kasia. The staple of any teenager who was going through their fussy stage. Tomek didn't remember going through his, but he'd heard stories from Nick about his three children going through similar phases. Refusing to eat because they weren't hungry, detesting the sight, smell and taste of anything healthy, always going for the greasiest and most calorific thing on the menu, resorting to frozen chicken nuggets and chips every meal of the week. At that age, though, as was the case with Kasia, it didn't affect them; thanks to their hypersonic metabolisms and constant movement at school and extra-curricular activities outside it, they were constantly moving, constantly doing something, burning off the fat. Even so, Tomek had decided to keep a keen eye on it in the background. The concern with her was that it might develop into an eating disorder, a complex. She had been through so much in the past few months that he would be lying if he said he wasn't worried about the societal pressures she was being placed under at school. And because she wouldn't open up to him about it, all he could do was let his thoughts run wild with one another.

But this wasn't about Kasia. This was about Abigail, about her big night, her cause for celebration.

Beside him, Kasia reached for her knife and fork, showing no regard for etiquette. Tomek stopped her. He raised his glass, then waited for the girls to do the same.

'To Abigail,' he said, lifting it slightly higher, 'the new editor of the *Southend Echo*. To Abigail.'

'To Abigail...' Kasia said half-heartedly.

'To me,' added Abigail with the smugness of someone whose ego was currently as high as the moon.

Normally that type of behaviour would have grated on Tomek. But not tonight. It was her special night, and she deserved it. She had put in so much hard work over the past few months that it was nice to finally see it pay off. Several weeks ago, the founding editor of the *Southend Echo*, one of Essex's largest and most popular newspapers, had been arrested for sex trafficking. He, along with a handful of other members of Southend's political elite, had found themselves on the wrong end of a criminal investigation that had seen dozens of lives affected. As a result, the position of editor had become available. At first, it was a position that nobody had wanted, as if it were tainted by the former editor's behaviour, his scent enmeshed in the fabric of his seat, his prints all over the furniture, an indelible stain. But then Abigail had had the brilliant idea, and the courage to go with it, of applying for the role. She had sat Tomek down one evening and explained to him why she was fit for the job. A mini interview. By the end of it, he'd advised her she should go for it, that she had nothing to lose. In his mind, she was the right fit for the job, even though he wasn't the one she needed to convince. That burden fell on the newspaper's board of directors, and so ensued a lengthy process of coming up with a three-month, six-month, nine-month and twelve-month plan on how she was going to incentivise revenue and increase the reputation of the business. If local businesses didn't want to advertise with them, then there would be no money coming in. If there was no money, there were no jobs, no colleagues. In the end, the board of directors had liked her plan and offered her the role.

'What's the first thing on your to-do list as the new editor-in-chief?' Tomek asked as he began to dig into his food.

'I need to let Sami and Khalid go.'

'Ouch.'

'Yeah. Really putting me in at the deep end.'

Not as deep as they're *gonna be when they find out they can't pay their rent next month.*

'Rather you than me,' he said.

'But look on the bright side, you and I are going to be working a lot closer. A lot more back-scratching going on...'

'Eww!' Kasia dropped her knife and fork onto the table. 'Not this again! I've had enough of you two talking like you're in some porno!'

'How do you know what porn is?' Tomek asked, eyeing her suspiciously.

'We've been over this! I know about these things! And I don't want to talk anymore about it!' She pulled her napkin from her lap and slammed it on the table, then climbed out of her chair, the sound of wood scraping along ceramic echoing across the restaurant.

'Where are you going?'

'To the toilet, if that's *okay* with you?'

Tomek let her go without answering. The restaurant they were in was far too nice for them to create a scene. High end, luxury, and with an expensive bill to match. When she was out of earshot, he returned his attention to his food.

'Maybe let that conversation topic evaporate,' Abigail said.

'Why?'

'Because it's not worth it. It's old ground. We've been over it before. Let it go.'

Tomek glanced at the bathroom door, making sure that she wasn't coming back anytime soon.

'What did you mean about us rubbing against each other?'

'I never said anything about rubbing against each other,' Abigail replied. 'You've taken my words out of context, and I don't appreciate that. I was talking about us, you and I, the newspaper and the police.'

Right. Of course she was. Leverage, that was what it all came down to. She would want to use her power as the editor of the newspaper to get information out of him about the latest case. While he admitted that it had happened in the past, it had been done without the power dynamic changing between them. Before, they had been on a level playing field. They had both done it to further their respective careers. Now with the difference between them, that would undoubtedly change. It was impossible for it not to.

Tomek glanced at the bathroom door again. It had opened, and Kasia was sauntering back towards them, taking her time.

Before she made it to the table, Abigail leant forward and lowered her voice.

'Though if you did want to rub up against one another tonight, I wouldn't object to the idea.'

It was her special night, after all.

CHAPTER FOUR

The rain lashes at my face so hard that it gets into my eyes and forces me to blink. I try to swat it away, but it's no use. My hair is soaked, my trousers stick to my thighs, and my socks are quickly getting wet despite my school shoes supposedly being waterproof. But I ignore it and continue. Adrenaline courses through me like a potent and violent drug.

Adrenaline and fear.

Laced with a hint of anxiety.

I'm late. And Michał is waiting for me. Brother Michał. My older, bigger, stronger brother who always beats me in an arm wrestle or an actual wrestle.

I've just crossed the road. Over the other side, a hundred yards away, I can see the kids outside the off-licence. They're there as usual, loitering, hanging on the handlebars of their bikes, opening their energy drinks and dirty magazines. I think one of them is even unloading a cigarette from the carton, the little fucking idiot. Probably thinks he's the hardest kid to have ever walked the planet. Little does he know he's a fucking bellend.

Ignoring them, I turn my attention back to the park. A few hundred metres up the road, on the right-hand side. The same entrance I've gone in dozens, hundreds of times before and after school – and thousands of times since. Outside the entrance is a single, lonely street lamp, gunmetal grey and rusty, covered in dogs' piss, its dim sodium light leaking onto the ground. But none of it is strong enough to spill into the park. It's enveloped by darkness. A thick, cloying, ominous darkness that reminds me of the nights back in Poland, during the blackouts.

I come to a rapid stop outside the park. On the ground, a small puddle of mud has formed. Over a metre wide and a metre long. In the centre is a metal gateway, covered in rust, its paint falling away. I latch onto it with my hands and, using my toes, propel myself into the air and over the puddle. I narrowly avoid the mess, but my efforts are in vain. The whole place is fucking filthy and covered in mud everywhere. I might as well have rolled in it before I came in; it wouldn't have made a difference.

I'm looking down at my shoes when I hear it. The sound, coming from my right. The whimpering, the groaning, the giggling. I look, but I can't see anything, just the outline of the playground. The swings, the slide, the seesaw and merry-go-round. And the figures standing in it.

Then I begin to focus, to narrow in. The sound of tyres rolling along the tarmac gradually begins to dwindle, and the noise of rain slapping into the mud begins to fade, until all I can hear is the sound of my breath. Laboured at the running I've just done.

Slowly, sensing what's in front of me, I lower my gaze a fraction and see the body lying in the debris, crumpled into a heap. My brother. Michał. Then I lift my gaze, and in the darkness I can see his killer, his eyes, yellow and piercing like a cat's. Nathan Burrows, standing over Michał.

But there's a problem.

It's just him.

Alone.

No one else.

Just Nathan and Michał. One killer, one victim.

I try to move, but I'm frozen to the spot. There's something holding me back. Like someone's wrapped their arms over my shoulders and is keeping me there, like the time Dad bear-hugged me to stop me from chasing after Dawid in the garden. Even though I was smaller than him, only by a few inches, I was still prepared to give it to him as good as he gave it.

Just like now.

I'm fired up. I need to know what's happened to Michał. I need to know why he's not moving.

Eventually, after ten, twenty seconds, I feel the restraints begin to release, their grip loosen. And I step forward. I move closer.

One step becomes two.

Two becomes three.

And before I know it, I'm running, sprinting, charging towards Nathan Burrows. As soon as the little fucker sees me coming, he turns and sprints away. But this time I give chase. I follow him to the back of the playground, through a small, bush-lined alleyway. Brick and rubble from the construction work that's been going on nearby litters the ground. Canopies of brambles and vines dangle from above. The sound of his footsteps followed closely by mine echo down the path. At the end is a soft, dull, pathetic sodium glow. Otherwise, we're covered in darkness, relying on the abilities of our eyes to see through it all, to make out the fuzziness and shapes.

But Nathan's quicker than me. He's pulling ahead. I have no chance. Five, six years he's got on me.

At the end of the alleyway, he makes a left turn. Before I get to it, I trip, my foot snagging on an upturned slab or piece of stone, my body going arse over tit, destroying my lunchbox and water bottle in the process. But I don't care about any of that. I need to follow him. I need to chase him.

After I haul myself to my feet, I stumble to the end of the alleyway, feeling pain swell in my knee and hands. It's nothing compared to the pain Michał felt, I tell myself. But by the time I get to the street lamp, Nathan Burrows has gone, disappeared, vanished into the half-light of the street.

It doesn't take me long to think of Michał, so I turn and head back towards him. For a moment, I wish I hadn't. I wish I'd stayed where I was. I wish I hadn't even left school.

I wish I hadn't been late in the first place.

He's lying there on the ground, coat off, shoes discarded, trousers down by his knees, bag thrown to one side, its contents upturned and littered about the tarmac. My eyes move from the top of his body, down. Large chunks of his skull are missing, and his thick blond hair has become matted with the colour crimson, the white chunks of his exposed brain and bone matter glistening damply in the low light. His eyes – his fucking eyes – have been bashed in with bricks and battery acid poured into them. The evidence of it is sitting on his face and in the crease of his chin. Two of them, dented from where they'd been split open by a rock or a brick.

The top half of his body has been left alone. It isn't until I get to his lower half that I want to be sick. His penis – something I've never seen before, except for when we used to share baths together as toddlers – has been hacked at, maimed with a knife. Blood continues to trickle from it as though it's the last piece of him that's alive.

Tears begin to well in my eyes as I look down at my dead brother, the images of his body slowly becoming ingrained in my mind, open to thirty years of torment and interpretation. I want to look away. I know I should, but I can't. Something, like my father's arms around me in the garden, compels me to stay, to look. To soak in the debt I owe him. To absorb the nightmares and guilt I know will haunt me for the rest of my life.

I was too late.
I could have saved him.
I should have saved him.

CHAPTER FIVE

Tomek pulled the covers off his body and swung his legs out the side of the bed. On the bedside table next to his head was his phone, plugged in and charging. He prodded it with his finger, saw that it was a little before four am, and unplugged it. Sleepily, yawning and scratching his armpit, he headed towards his wardrobe on the other side of the room. Abigail was fast asleep, the gentle sounds of her breathing (you could never call it snoring, *never*; she refused to believe she did it and had done all her life) expelled through her nostrils. She looked so peaceful when she slept, but he knew she could wake up at any moment. She was one of the lightest sleepers he knew. Subtle movements were important.

Planting both feet firmly on the carpet, in the spaces that didn't contain any creaking floorboards, Tomek pinched the handle with his fingers and gently caressed it open. Now and then – at twenty degrees, forty, eighty – the hinges screamed at him. Each time, he glanced back at Abigail, but she remained asleep, undisturbed by the sounds. The IKEA wardrobe was a mess: at least a dozen pairs of shoes chucked in the bottom playing their own game of Jenga; pants and socks messily crammed into a small cubbyhole; too many hangers and clothes for the rail that ran across the top. But what he was looking for was in the top cubbyhole, shoved in firmly at the back. He'd put it there for safekeeping. Out of Abigail's and Kasia's prying eyes. He fished inside the hole and removed the item. Then he took it into the living room, being careful not to crash on any of the floorboards. At the dining room table, he pulled out a chair and sat, placing the item on the surface.

It was a thin envelope: a letter from HMP Wakefield, a letter from

Nathan Burrows. It had come that morning, during his day off, while Kasia was at school. He'd held it for ten minutes, staring at it, deciding whether to open it, the words of the first letter he'd received playing in his mind. In the end, he'd left it. It wasn't worth ruining Abigail's big evening. He hadn't wanted to be distracted. But after the nightmare he'd just had...

He was sure there was a connection: the second killer, the one who'd been locked inside Tomek's brain since that afternoon thirty years ago, had been missing from his nightmare. Just as Nathan had said it would.

There was nobody else there, Tomek. I killed him all on my own. You've been imagining it this entire time.

Tomek inhaled deeply before turning the letter over and opening it with his thumb. As soon as it was out of the envelope, he held his breath and wasted no time in reading it:

Deerest Tomek,

Please axcept my apologees for the delay. I have been bizzy here in Wakefield. They have opened up a new bizness learning development corse and I have gone to a few of them to try to learn about bizness. But I've been struggling with the reading materials. I'm slowly learning, and I hope you can foregive me. Please be patient. I have my cell mate who helps, but sometimes he is just as bad.

Anyway, how are you? How is Kasia? How is Abigail? I saw in the news about her promotion. Please tell her I said congratulations. I bet she is very pleased and proud. You should be as well.

Last time, I meant to ask how your parents are doing? How have they been keeping? If they would like to come visit me, they are more than welcome. I'm not going anywhere! Perhaps you could all make a nice family day out of it. Don't forget to invite Dawid along as well. Did Dawid ever tell you that he came to visit me once? It was many years ago now. We talked, we discussed. There were *things he wanted to know, and so I told him. Don't worry, I told him the same as I told you. That I'm sorry to say I killed Michał alone. There was no one else with me. Sometimes I think it would be better if there was, you know? So I could share some of the guilt I feel for what I did to your brother with them, but I will never have that luxury. I am sorry that you thought this for so long. It must have been so painful for you all this time. I want to make it up with you. That is why I wanted to open the dialog. Please reply. I do hope that you can find the time. I know you are a bizzy man but it would be nice to speak with you again. If you ever would like to talk over the phone, as it can be much much easier, I have just got a new number - don't tell the guards! Ha ha! I have put it on the back of this letter for you. Please do not lose it. I miss your voice and would like to hear it again.*

Thinking of you.
NB

BENEATH NATHAN'S initials was a signature, and sure enough, on the reverse was a mobile number. Eleven digits, written in the neatest possible handwriting so there could be no confusion, no possibility that Tomek entered the wrong number in his phone.

Cunt.

Cuntcuntcuntcuntcunt.

So many thoughts, so many emotions rattling inside his head. He suddenly felt sick, a deep knot tightening in his stomach (and it wasn't the food). Then the sensation passed almost as quickly as it had started, and he was greeted by an old friend: rage. The same emotion he'd had when he'd read the first letter. He'd wanted to leap into the document and strangle Nathan as he wrote it. He'd wanted to tear his eyeballs out and shove battery acid in them. He wanted to get retribution for the atrocious things he'd done to his brother.

That reminded him.

The other one.

Dawid.

That little fucker, visiting Nathan without telling anyone. What had they discussed? What had Dawid asked Nathan? And why had he kept it from them for all these years? Had he expected nobody would ever find out?

Tomek had the sudden urge to pick up the phone and ask him, to find out the answers to those questions and more. But it was too early, still dark outside. It would have to wait, a conversation for another day.

He looked at the letter again, reading it through once more. He was concerned by three things: one) Dawid's secret meeting with Nathan Burrows, two) how Nathan had known about Abigail's promotion when the news had only broken the week before, and three) that he was starting to believe Nathan. He was seriously considering the possibility that there hadn't been another killer, that he had imagined it that afternoon and in the thirty years since.

He closed his eyes and cast his mind back to the nightmare he'd just had; it had been so vivid, so visceral. It had been one of the clearest nightmares he could ever recall. And yet, had any of it been true? How much had been fact, how much a fiction created by his brain and subconscious? All this time he'd pictured a second killer there. But perhaps there was a reason why he'd never been able to see the face clearly. Perhaps there was a reason the police had never found a second killer or any evidence suggesting someone else had been present. What if Tomek's fractured and fragile mind had conjured him up, a literal figment of his imagination, an innocuous and generic shape his brain had warped and manipulated into a figure? It was a question he'd wrestled with countless times over the years, and now his latest, his clearest nightmare to date, was pulling him in the other direction. Away from his identity.

And the name, Charlie, the name he'd heard during a nightmare once that had sparked renewed hope – what if that was wrong as well? More recently, that was a question he'd tried to grapple with, one that he had a little less faith in, only because it was the same name as someone who'd been involved in a murder investigation at the time, and he had convinced himself that it had been his subconscious calling out to him. Why, after thirty years, would a name come to him all of a sudden? It didn't make sense. He knew the brain worked in mysterious ways, but they weren't that mysterious. There was usually something behind what went on.

He was beginning to think that none of it had been real at all.

As he was about to tear the piece of paper in half, he heard a sound; the living room door creaking open, followed by the sounds of nails scratching on wood. Tomek swivelled on his feet so fast he felt his spine buckle under the pressure.

'What— What're you doing awake?' he asked Abigail, as her head peeked through the gap in the door.

'I got cold. I couldn't feel you next to me.'

'So you woke up?'

'I didn't have my snuggle buddy.'

Tomek cringed. 'I'll be back in a sec. Just give me a minute.'

'What are you doing?' she asked.

'Writing in my diary.'

It wasn't a complete lie. But it wasn't exactly the whole truth, either. Right now, he didn't want her to know. Not because he didn't trust her with the information, but because he didn't want her to panic over the fact Nathan Burrows, a murderer serving a life sentence, knew intimate details about her.

'Did you have another nightmare?' She cautiously approached and placed a comforting hand on his back.

'Yeah.'

'A bad one?'

'No,' he lied. 'But it was more confusing than the others.'

'You can tell me about it later. For now, you need to go back to bed. You've got an early start in the morning.'

CHAPTER SIX

Tomek failed to stifle the yawn as he left the courtroom. The night's disjointed and fragmented sleep had left him feeling tired and groggy, like he was a teenager again, wanting to stay in bed until lunchtime. It was his third visit to Southend's Crown Court in the past three days. He had been attending as a witness in relation to the murder of a man on Two Tree Island, a small salt marshland situated in Leigh-on-Sea. The victim, Reece Cartwright, had been bludgeoned in the back of the head and left for dead by the very eyewitness who'd claimed to have found him. According to his confession, which had come shortly after the team had found the murder weapon discarded in the undergrowth nearby, the victim had stopped the killer in the middle of the path and begun harassing him, drunk, and under the influence of something else. When the victim's advances hadn't abated, the cyclist had struck him over the head in an attempt to deter him, but had in fact killed him. A simple act of self-defence had now turned into a murder investigation and what was soon to be imprisonment. The question the jury now faced, however, was whether it was murder or manslaughter. Tomek, in all his years of experience, sensed the man would get manslaughter. Not only was there no evidence to suggest that the two had ever come into contact with one another before that fateful moment, but the nature of the killing suggested it had been an accident in some way, a one-punch hit gone wrong. It was an unfortunate end for a man who, according to his friends and family, was going through some of life's lowest moments.

The beautiful thing about attending court was that it was only thirty seconds away from the office, so within half a minute, he was back in CID headquarters, making his way to the incident room. When he got there, he headed straight for the kitchen and started to make a cup of coffee. DCI Cleaves, the head of the team, had recently managed to find enough money in the budget to purchase a top-of-the-range automatic coffee machine – equipped with digital interface, twenty-litre coffee bean capacity, and sleek finishes – that required a technician from the company they'd bought it from to clean and service it on a fortnightly basis. It was, in short, one of the greatest things Tomek had ever seen, one step removed from the fancy, over-the-top coffee machines you saw in the likes of Starbucks and Caffè Nero. Except better. There was no need to froth the milk or clean the jets of water after every use – the machine did it all for you. Shortly after its arrival, there had been a clamour, a feverish excitement, and queues of his colleagues had formed, each impatiently waiting to use the machine. On a couple of occasions, Tomek had been forced to intervene and separate some of them, wedging himself between them so that he could break up an altercation before it got ugly, and then at the end of it, skip the queue. Despite it being two weeks old, the team's fascination with the coffee machine hadn't subsided, and there was still a queue in front of him when he returned. DC Nadia Chakrabarti, the team's HOLMES inputter and actioner, responsible for managing everyone's tasks during the various investigations they had going at any one time, was in the middle of placing the mug under the nozzle, when Tomek asked, 'Need a hand with that, Nads?'

'I'm pregnant,' she snapped. 'Not a fucking invalid.'

Eight months, to be precise. About to burst. Well overdue her maternity leave. Various members of the team, including HR, had suggested she make the most of the time before the baby came, to relax, to settle a little, but she'd said she didn't want to be bored, that she didn't want to stay at home doing nothing all day except wait for the moment to come, not when there was still a mountain of work that needed doing. A mountain of work that, despite her intelligence, now included learning how to use the coffee machine properly; Tomek watched her struggle for a few moments as she placed one hand on her stomach while the other searched for the right button to press.

'You sure you couldn't do with a hand? Baby brain again?'

She huffed, looked back, and glowered at him.

'If you mention baby brain one more time, I'll smash your head in so *you* have baby brain.'

'Halfway there, mate. Think my parents and brothers did most of the job for you already.'

Another huff, another glower. Tomek paid it little heed, then slipped past three members of the civilian support staff, apologising with a polite whisper the way British people did, and stopped beside Nadia. Cries and boos came from behind him.

'She's pregnant! I'm just helping someone in need.'

'You'll be in need if you carry on,' she said, then looked back at the buttons.

'Tough decision,' he said, 'going for the same one you always have.'

The look on her face suggested she wanted to smack him, but didn't have the energy. Instead, she let out a long exhale, and eased the tension in her body. 'Fine. You do it. Hot chocolate, please.'

'One hot chocolate and flat white coming up!' he said to another chorus of groans and cries. He turned to face the crowd. 'Hey! None of you were willing to help this *pregnant* woman. It's only fair I get my just rewards.'

'You're such a martyr, Tomek,' Nadia jibed. 'It's a wonder you haven't been given a knighthood or CBE – or one of the other ones.'

Pointing to the crowd behind him, he said, 'I do it for my fans. I don't do it for myself.'

'Pah! And I've got the body of Kim Kardashian.'

Within a few moments, Nadia's hot chocolate was finished, and as he was about to hand it to her, he placed his mug underneath the nozzle and pressed the button for his own drink. As he turned back to Nadia, he found her looking at him, bewildered, eyes as wide as the rim of her mug. And then he looked down at the floor. She had dropped the drink to the floor, spilling the contents onto the tiles, smashing the mug.

But that wasn't the only liquid he saw. Her trousers, her thighs, were darkened.

'Nads...?'

'I think my waters have just broken.'

CHAPTER SEVEN

Tomek had been less than useless, flapping about like a pigeon on cocaine, shoving team members aside and causing accidents as they bashed into the cabinets and banged their wrists on drawer handles. But the worst of it had been when he'd started screaming. His orders – at least, that's what they were to him – were nothing other than incoherent wails, the sort you might hear from a beached seal trying to call for help. He was a nightmare, and at one point Nadia had stopped in the middle of the office, grabbed him by the shoulders, slapped him across the cheek, then told him calmly and coherently to "sit down, shut the fuck up, and breathe.". She was the one who should have been freaking out, losing her mind, not Tomek. It was a terrifying ordeal for him. Give him a serial killer or a high-speed pursuit – either in a car or on foot – any day of the week and he'd be as cool as you like, but this... this had felt like meeting a girl for the first time; he couldn't speak properly, he couldn't stop sweating, and he was sure there was a little bit of pee as well.

It had come as a massive surprise then, when Nadia had granted him permission to drive her to the hospital. In a situation like this, she'd said, where she needed to get there as fast as possible, it was the *only* time she trusted him to do anything regarding her pregnancy (even though it would technically be the last thing he could do, bar delivering the baby; he decided not to mention it). Instead, Tomek had nodded absent-mindedly, uncertain, a dozen thoughts and images and scenarios racing through his head as he'd sat there in the office, listening to her voice and following her breathing exercises. But all that anxiety and doubt disappeared as soon as he'd felt the rigid leather seats of the pool car hug his body.

After he'd switched on the engine, he turned to face her and said, 'Nadia, it is my honour to drive you in your hour of need.'

Panting, her face scrunched against the pain, she had turned to him, bared her teeth, and screamed in his face, 'Drive! Or I'm fucking doing it myself!'

For Tomek that wasn't an option, and so he'd hurtled through the traffic, jumped a couple of red lights (he'd bill her husband for any of fines later) and skidded to a stop outside A&E at Southend Hospital. There, he'd commandeered a wheelchair from a corridor and, feeling like Jack Reacher tearing his way through a city, leaving no prisoners behind, Tomek charged through the corridors and got her seen to as fast as possible.

Nadia's husband, Sharif, arrived half an hour later. By that point, the baby was well on its way, and Nadia had been sent to one of the rooms along one of the many corridors. The man had been panicked and exasperated, and Tomek had tried his best to allay his fears and calm him down, but when he hadn't exactly been the hallmark of relaxation himself, there had been no conviction in what he'd told Sharif to do. The last he'd seen of the man, before he'd gone running into the birthing room, was a look of shock and fear on his face, as though the realisation of what was about to happen in the next thirty minutes – and the next thirty years of his life – had suddenly dawned on him.

Tomek had decided to stay. Not because he wanted to see the baby, but because he'd been so overwhelmed with it all that the sudden rush of emotions he'd felt in the office had come back, rooting him to the spot. For some inexplicable reason, he felt impacted by the baby's birth, and as he waited, he decided that was an avenue of thought he didn't want to venture down just yet. Or maybe ever.

One was enough, thanks.

A little over an hour later, Sharif returned to the waiting room, charging through the doors. As soon as he saw Tomek, he paused.

'What are you still doing here?' Sharif asked before addressing his own family, who had trickled into the waiting room during the birth.

Tomek climbed out of his seat and clasped his hands together. 'How is she? How's the baby?'

'Fine. They're both fine. Both mum and son are healthy and happy.'

The news was met with a chorus of cheers from Nadia's and Sharif's families. Hands were shaken, bodies embraced. It was a pleasant, wonderful experience and a sight to behold that brought a smile to Tomek's face. Then he realised that he was the odd one out and had no reason to be there.

'I'll pass the news on to the team,' he told Sharif softly as he made to leave.

Just as he was about to open the door, Sharif called him back and asked if he'd like to see the baby before he had to go. Yes, Tomek had replied without thinking. But as he wandered along the corridor, moving closer and closer to the newborn baby, Tomek began to understand the way Sharif had felt. A knot had formed in his stomach, a lump in his throat. The lights in the corridors seemed to dim, and the walls seemed to close in on him, as though he were in a horror movie. But as soon as Sharif opened the door for him, that all disappeared, and the room was filled with a brilliant glow that accentuated even the bleakest of colours.

Tomek hadn't been present for Kasia's birth. Namely, because he hadn't known anything about it. He hadn't seen her be born. He hadn't held her in his arms for the first time. He hadn't experienced any of it. The same applied for the first thirteen years of her life. But here, now, now he was experiencing it by proxy.

Nadia, dressed in a hospital gown, was sitting high in the bed, cradling the baby.

'Tomek,' she said, glancing between Sharif and himself, 'you're still here?'

'I... I'm sorry. I couldn't bring myself to go back. Not until I knew how everything was. How is he?'

'Good as gold. Adorable. No issues at all.'

Tomek approached her cautiously, lest any sudden movements disturb the peaceful, resting baby. When he reached Nadia's bedside, he leant closer to inspect the baby. The little thing was nestled in a blanket, save for his face that was topped in a thin head of hair and some bodily fluids that were still drying on his forehead. His eyes were scrunched and his little lips were moving rapidly.

'He's gonna be a talker, that one,' Tomek said. 'Guarantee it. Do you have a name?'

'Not yet.'

'What about "Tomek"?'

'Why would we do that?'

'Because without me you wouldn't have given birth to him – not here, anyway.'

Sharif and Nadia shared a glance.

'You're joking?'

Tomek was unable to pull his gaze away from the baby. 'I feel like I've been a part of his birth. I feel like I had *something* to do with it.'

They shared another glance.

'Yes,' she said. 'You're right. It was fifty per cent me. Forty-nine per cent Sharif. And one per cent you for getting me through the doors. We really couldn't have done this without you. Between the three of us, we've had a baby. Congratulations.'

Tomek was so overwhelmed with delight that he paid Nadia's jibe no heed.

'But I don't think we're going to call our baby Tomek,' she said, sterner this time.

'Why not?'

'Because if *you're* anything to go by... I just don't want the hassle.'

Tomek understood that, appreciated her candidness. 'How big is he?'

'Nine pounds and nine ounces,' Sharif answered.

'Bloody hell, Nads. What you been feeding him?'

'A strict diet of frogs' legs, caviar and mushrooms. What do you think?'

It was then that Tomek saw Nadia in her rawest, most vulnerable beauty. Her hair and face were covered in sweat, and the bags under her eyes looked about ready to be checked in for a first-class flight to the other side of the world. Yet she looked glowing somehow, as though she contained all the joy in the world, captured in her expression and smile. Tomek didn't know what was going on in his mind – was this what it felt like to be broody? – but he didn't like it.

'He'll be the one pushing you through the hospital doors next time,' he said. 'But at that point, you'll be sick and infirm.'

The glow on her face dwindled slightly. 'I might be on a lot of medication and painkillers right now, Tomek, but I *will* throttle you if you say one more thing that might upset me. And don't think I won't just because you're my senior...'

Tomek raised a hand to his head in mock salute. 'Yes, Captain. Understood, Captain. And on that note, I'll leave you to it.'

There were no objections from either Sharif or Nadia. And he couldn't blame them. He'd already outstayed his welcome, and the last thing they wanted while they shared this precious moment with one another was him loitering around, reminding them of his one per cent contribution to the happiest day of their lives. A one per cent that he would try hard not to dine out on too much over the coming days.

Before he left, he kissed Nadia on the cheek, stroked the little guy's forehead, then shook Sharif's hand.

As he got to the door, Nadia called him back.

'Tomek?'

'Yes...'

'If you tell anyone at the station about how bad I look, I will set fire to everything you love.'

CHAPTER EIGHT

Tomek hadn't been able to come up for air in nearly twenty minutes. As soon as he'd set foot through the doors to the major incident room, he'd been surrounded by his colleagues, badgering him, bombarding him with a dozen questions a second. They were like a ravenous pack of hyenas, desperate, and Tomek was very much their prey, and the information they wanted was the meat on his bones. He had begun to understand what it was like for celebrities being hunted down by paparazzi, having almost every aspect of their life scrutinised. His colleagues, Rachel and Martin in particular, had wanted moment by moment updates. The three words, "And then what? And then what? And then what?" had been promoted to the barred list in the office. He didn't want to hear, see, or even think about those words for a long time.

After he'd satiated the hungry crowd with his slightly embellished story (taking the one per cent up to an agreeable four or five), he headed towards his desk. He made it as far as placing his hand on the back of his chair when he heard Detective Inspector Victoria Orange call his name from the other side of the office.

Sighing heavily, Tomek took a moment to compose himself before making his way over.

'If I have to explain what happened one more time, I'm handing in my notice,' he told her.

She hovered in the doorframe, arms folded across her chest. She was dressed in a pair of smart trousers and a bright orange floral shirt that illuminated the room. 'I've already heard,' she said.

'How?' He tried to hide the surprise and slight disgust in his voice, but it was unsuccessful.

'Sharif,' she answered. 'He called me from the hospital to tell me that both mother and son were fit and healthy.'

'So you knew, but didn't want to say anything to the rest of the team?'

'Not when I knew how much they'd eat you alive when you got back. I must admit, it was quite the watch.'

Tomek glared at her.

'Anyway, come in. There's something I think you might want to hear.'

As Tomek crossed the threshold into her office, he was hit in the face by a wall of cold air. For some ungodly reason, she had her air conditioning unit on in the middle of March, when it was still below ten degrees outside, and had been for the past few weeks. He shut the door behind him and hovered, balancing his weight on his left foot.

'What have I done?'

'It's a shame that's your go-to response, but I can't lie, even I'm surprised that I've not called you in for some misdemeanour or for your ill-fated behaviour.'

'This must be serious then.'

'Quite the opposite.' Victoria rounded her desk and sat, brushing her hair out of her eye line. 'This morning, while you were gone, a woman came in. A woman called Rose Whitaker, with the rest of her family. They've come to report a missing person.'

'Right.' He braced himself for what was to come, fearing the worst, even though he knew from the context of the conversation so far that, on the balance of things, it wouldn't be.

'There's no need to look so afraid. I'm not giving you the sack.'

'Couldn't even if you wanted to,' Tomek said defiantly. 'Only my mate, Nick, can do that.'

Victoria shook her head. 'Now I'm starting to have second thoughts. Maybe this wasn't such a good idea, after all.'

Tomek pulled out the chair opposite and sat. 'No, no. I'm all ears. Shoot it, sister.'

The finger gun he fired at her didn't land. She sighed heavily through her nostrils, and leant forward, resting her elbows on the desk.

'I was going to instate you as SIO in the investigation.'

'Me?'

'Yes.'

'*Me?*'

'Yes. Are you deaf?'

'Why?'

'Because you've repeated yourself twice now.'

'No, I meant why me?'

'You're doing it again. You keep saying the word, "me".'

Tomek opened his mouth to correct her, but then he saw the smug smirk on her face, and understood. He feigned a laugh. 'I get it. You're being funny.'

'Taste of your own medicine. I'm sure you would've done the same if things had been the other way round.'

Tomek chose not to respond to that because she was absolutely right.

'I think you've earned the chance to have a go at managing an investigation like this on your own. You'll be SIO, and that means managing everything that comes with it. Nick and I decided it's about time. But we'll keep a close eye on you, make sure you don't fuck about with the budget and everything.'

'Budget?' Tomek's eyes illuminated. 'I get to play around with all that money?'

'Fucking hell,' she whispered with a shake of the head. 'What have I got myself into. I—'

She stopped as soon as she saw the smug smirk now on his face.

'Touché, Bowen. Touché. But you won't get much of it, I can tell you that for free. And I can only give you a reduced team as well.'

'Why?'

'Because there are other responsibilities. There's too much going on right now to give you a full outfit.'

'Fine. Who do I get?'

'That's your choice.'

'How many?'

'Two... at a push, three.'

Tomek didn't even need to think about that. The names appeared in his head instantly.

'Chey and Rachel.'

'Why don't you think about it?'

Tomek sensed the reticence in her voice.

'I've made my decision. I want Chey and Rachel, please.'

As though they were players in an NFL draft pick.

She sighed slowly, trying not to let on that she was discontent with the decision.

'Fine. You can have them. Now get out of here. The family's waiting for you downstairs in meeting room one.'

CHAPTER NINE

Tomek had felt like a teacher running late for a parents' evening with the smartest kid in the school. As he entered the room, the Whitaker family looked up at him, deeply unimpressed, as though they'd been waiting for hours and were wondering what their taxpayer money was going towards.

As he entered, he set a notebook on the table and introduced himself to the family. There were three of them in total. Rose Whitaker, a woman in her thirties who looked as though she'd taken fashion advice from Kate Middleton and the various tabloids that documented her every outfit choice, with the exception of the various bits of jewellery on her body. Her fingers were covered in diamond-emblazoned rings, a bracelet on each wrist, a large necklace with a heart-shaped pendant that dangled between the buttons of her shirt, and a pair of earrings that Tomek considered much more muted than the rest of the ensemble. Tomek didn't like to guess at how much it had all cost, as it would have likely been more than he had in any of his bank accounts, and he was having such a good day already he didn't want it to be dampened in any way.

Accompanying her, he quickly discovered, were Rose's mother- and father-in-law, Daphne and Roy Whitaker, a couple in their late fifties who looked as though they'd been married for the past thirty years, and only some of those years had been enjoyable. They too looked as though they were wearing more than Tomek had to his name, except it was in the form of their designer clothing. Bizarrely, Tomek's eyes were drawn to the man's cufflinks: a pair of blue and red, diamond-encrusted commercial planes. Roy Whitaker looked like the type of man who was fairly easy going but had the capacity to switch at any moment, and not many people would like it when he did. Daphne Whitaker, on the other hand, sat upright, her lips pursed, a look of silent judgement drawn across her face. Tomek got the impression she was the mute master of the family who controlled them all with a flick of the head or a narrowing of the eyes.

'So...' Tomek started, suddenly feeling slightly intimated by them all. 'I understand you wanted to report a missing person?'

'Yes,' Roy answered as he placed a hand on his wife's lap. 'Our daughter, Angelica.'

Tomek made a note of the name.

'She's our precious little angel,' Roy continued.

'I'm sure she is. When was the last time you saw her?'

'We haven't seen her in the past couple of days,' Daphne answered, her voice thin, measured.

'And you think she's been missing this entire time?'

'No.' This time the question was answered by Rose, who was leaning forward in her seat. She looked at Roy and Daphne before continuing, almost as if seeking approval. 'I last saw her yesterday afternoon. She works for me in my jewellery shop on Leigh Broadway.'

That explained the dazzling amounts of diamonds on every part of her body. And now that she mentioned it, he noticed the jewellery on her in-laws. That they'd all probably been gifted them over the years made him less than impressed about them anymore.

'Do you own Whitaker's, just next to Tangerine, on the Broadway?' he asked.

Rose nodded, her face filling with pride. 'Guilty as charged.'

'Ah, nice. I've seen it, often walk by it, but never been in. Always been a bit put off by the...'

'By the prices?'

Tomek turned shy. 'Yeah. And the fact, until recently, I've not had anyone to buy for.'

But now Abigail had come into his life, now she had just been given her big promotion, and now she had a birthday coming up in the next couple of weeks... he might have to change his habits.

'It's not *that* expensive,' Rose explained. 'We cater to all kinds of budgets. You should come in sometime, and if you can help us find Angelica, I'd be happy to give you the same discount I've given the rest of the family.'

Angelica.

The name appeared in his mind in bright red letters.

'Angelica. Right. Where were we?' He consulted his notes. 'You were in the middle of explaining why you were the last person to see Angelica...'

'Because she works for me,' Rose explained, stroking the hair tucked behind her ear. 'She works with me during the off season.'

'Off season?'

'During the winter months, when they don't need her as much. She's a flight attendant. For TUI.'

Tomek scribbled the note in his book.

'A flight attendant?'

'Yes,' answered Roy with a semblance of pride. 'She was incredibly good at her job, but with companies like that, their busiest months are in the summer, so understandably, when things are quieter, they don't need a lot of the staff so they have to let them go. It's not a completely reliable income, and it means that six months of the year she's out of work and needs a job, but we're fortunate to have Rose in the family who is kind enough to give her a job for the rest of the year. We have tried over the years to convince her to move companies, move to a more... respectable, and secure line of work in the industry...'

'...but the competition for those roles is so fierce that only a handful of people get selected every year, as I can attest,' added Daphne. As she said it, her back straightened, and her crow's feet disappeared as her expression was replaced with self-pride.

Rose leant forward and pointed to her mother-in-law. For Tomek's benefit, she explained, 'Daphne was a flight attendant for BA her entire career, and Roy was a pilot.'

'That's how we met,' Roy added.

Tomek's eyes fell to the man's cufflinks, which he rubbed absent-mindedly with his fingers.

'Of course, we would have loved for her to join the family tradition, as it were, and for her to join the BA crew – I even reached out to a few of my former colleagues to see if they could put in a good word or bump her up the list – but she refused. Said she wanted to do things her own way.'

Tomek was reminded of a conversation he'd had with Kasia a few weeks before. The two of them had been in a café, enjoying a spot of breakfast and a coffee, when Tomek had joked about her powers of deduction and becoming a police officer. She had then point-blank told him no, and that her dream was to one day open a coffee shop. Tomek had no problem with that. It was her life. She was free to make the choices she made – within reason, of course – and if she needed to make mistakes along the way, then he would always be there for her. But for the Whitaker family, Tomek sensed it wasn't the same. He sensed that they'd had many arguments over Angelica's choices, and that she had constantly felt as though she hadn't lived up to her parents' expectations. Tomek didn't want to have the same relationship with his daughter.

'Can you walk me through what happened when you last saw Angelica?' Tomek asked, directing the question at Rose.

'Of course,' she said as she brushed a piece of fluff from her skirt so that it looked almost immaculate, brand new. 'We were working in the shop. It was a quiet day, as were the last couple, and so I told her she could leave a few minutes early. She was going out last night, and she wanted to get ready. Besides, there isn't much for me to do at the end, anyway. The longest part is taking all the jewellery out of the windows and putting it all in the safe.'

Tomek nodded, but he didn't care about any of that. He asked where Angelica had been going the night before.

'Out with a group of friends.'

'How many?'

'Four of them in total, including Angelica.'

'Do you know their names?'

'Only first names. Bit weird if she'd been talking about them in their full names, don't you think?'

'Quite. Did she tell you how she knows them?'

'From work. They're all flight attendants,' she answered. 'They all met at TUI, but I think she said something about them all working for different companies now. They got split up over the years, but they've all managed to stay in touch with one another – if I'm not mistaken, one of them may have been a friend from school as well.' She turned to Roy and Daphne. 'Elodie... I think her name was. Does that ring a bell for either of you?'

Their expressions were blank. They looked at one another, then shook their heads slowly. It was clear to see that they knew very little about their daughter's life, that perhaps they had shunned her for her choices, and that Rose was, out of the three of them, the person who knew her the best.

'It's not a problem,' Tomek continued. 'I'm sure we can find them somehow. Did she tell you where they were going?'

'Memo Night Club in Southend. Do you know it?'

'I might be old, but I'm not that old. I've arrested a couple of people outside there as well, so I know it fairly well.'

While the club might have changed a bit on the inside since Tomek had last been, he was almost confident that the type of male customer that attended it hadn't.

'When you said goodbye to her last night, how did she seem? Angry? Upset? Excited?'

'Excited, hundred per cent. She was really looking forward to seeing her friends. Said she hadn't been out in a long time, that it was their last hurrah before the season starts again.'

Nodding, Tomek continued to scribble in his notebook.

'And when did you notice something was wrong? Presumably when she didn't show up for work this morning?'

'Correct.'

'Has she ever done anything like this before? Has she ever called in sick, turned up late?'

For the past few minutes, Tomek had been directing his questions at Rose, completely ignoring Angelica's parents as though they weren't even there, and out of the corner of his eye, he saw Roy bristle with deep frustration.

'Our little angel is a very respectable, prompt, and agreeable individual. She would not have just called in sick or done a runner without genuine reason for it. It's not like she's having a lie-in – we've checked her house, and she's not been there. No, something has happened to her and we demand to know what. We need your help to find her.'

That had answered one of Tomek's next questions: whether anyone had been to her place of residence to verify she wasn't there. But that still didn't answer his original question. He turned to Rose, waited for her to respond.

'She's... sorry, Roy... she's been late a couple of times, from when she's gone for nights out, but it's never been *too* bad – twenty, thirty minutes here and there. Forty-five *tops*. She's never taken the piss like this. Never given me any reason to worry about where she might be. This morning I think I must have tried her mobile about fifty times, and there was no answer. She's usually glued to the bloody thing. That was when I knew something was wrong, as Roy said. That's why we're here.'

'I get it,' Tomek said. 'So would you say this is uncommon for her?'

'Yes.'

'What type of person is she on a night out? Or in general?'

'Why's that important?' Daphne asked.

'Well...' Tomek paused a beat. 'If she's gone out to a nightclub with friends, and she's got talking to someone at the bar, then she might have gone back with them.'

'Oh, no. No, no, no. Not our Angelica. She's the life and soul of the party, yes. Very outgoing, always talking to people, always wearing a smile on her face – it's a part of the job, it gets ingrained into you – but she's not *easy*.'

'Nobody's implying she is, Mrs Whitaker.'

Daphne slapped her husband on the arm. 'Tell him, Roy. He's got it wrong about our Angelica.'

Roy looked down at his lap, spun the plane cufflink a handful of times, sending it into a downward spiral, before replying. 'Absolutely,' he said, though the intonation in his voice belied his choice of words. 'Our daughter was a saint... she was an angel.'

'You wait until Johnny's back,' Daphne added, as she began wagging her finger at Tomek, as if he was the one she should be pointing her anger and frustration towards. 'He'll be able to tell you all about what she's like. He'll tell you the same thing as we have.'

'Who's Johnny?' Tomek asked with a shrug. His patience was beginning to run a little thin.

'Angelica's brother, my husband,' answered Rose.

'Where is he now?'

'Away for work. Dublin. He's on his way back this afternoon. He managed to get an early flight back to Southend Airport after I told him what's happened.'

Tomek offered her a thankful smile. Of the three of them, she was the one who most wanted to help, who was prepared to be honest about Angelica and what might have happened to her. Whereas her parents were blinded by their own relationship with their daughter. Tomek knew which of the family members he would lean on for information going forward. At the end of the meeting, he informed them of the next steps: that they would send a team out to her home; that they would monitor her phone; and that they would speak with her friends and anyone from the night before. But more importantly, he told them he'd keep them in the loop. They would be on a need-to-know basis, and as SIO, only he would choose what information they needed to know.

CHAPTER TEN

Tomek took the mug of coffee with thanks and set it on his knee delicately. He wasn't in the mood for it, but had just accepted it out of politeness. Out of the two of them, it was the person he'd come to meet that needed it more. Elodie Locket's first words to him had been, "Fuck me, I'm so hungover." And she looked it with the haggard face, the burst blood vessels in her eyes from lack of sleep, the messy hair, the colour that had washed out of her face thanks to the dehydration. If that wasn't enough, then there was still last night's make-up on the twenty-nine-year-old's face, clumpy and streaked. He didn't want to know what her pillow looked like, though in the background, he heard the sound of a washing machine mid-cycle and presumed she was already one step ahead of him.

Elodie was dressed in a pair of fancy, strawberry and banana-emblazoned Primark pyjamas, with a knitted shawl wrapped around her. She lived in a house share with two other girls and a man, all of whom had let them use the living room for their discussion. The place gave Tomek student house vibes, with the scuff marks on the walls, the yellow recycling crate filled with empty vodka and beer bottles, and the mould in the corners and on walls that none of them had been arsed to do anything about. The house was a state, but Elodie, on the other hand, wasn't. Beneath the hangover and clumpy make-up, she looked well put together, and from the way she was perched on the edge of the sofa, and wrapped the shawl around herself, was trying to come into contact with as little of the furniture and atmosphere as possible. Tomek got the impression she didn't want to be there any more than he did. And he was willing to bet money that hers was the cleanest room of the lot.

'I'm here to speak with you regarding your friend, Angelica Whitaker,' he started, setting the coffee down on the floor. As he pulled out his pen and notebook, he saw an insect crawl towards the mug from beneath the sofa, like one of the toys from *Toy Story*, lurking in the shadows.

'Angelica? What's happened to her?'

'She hasn't turned up to work at her sister-in-law's this morning. Her family has reported her missing. I just want to ask you a few questions about last night, and about your relationship with Angelica. Plus anything you can tell me that you think might be important.'

As he spoke, Elodie's hand flew to her mouth, and she began to breathe heavily, her small frame heaving with each breath.

'Oh, my God. She's missing?'

'We're trying not to jump to any conclusions,' he answered. 'In most scenarios like this, the person in question usually turns up at some point, unharmed and safe, if not a bit confused.'

'But you don't think that about Angelica, do you?'

Right now, Tomek didn't know what to think.

'What makes you say that?'

'Because you're speaking to me. Because of last night. You think something might have...' And then she broke down in a flood of tears, her body shuddering and convulsing – and not because the heating was off in the house. Tomek leapt off the sofa and hurried to the bathroom, immediately wishing he hadn't. He yanked the toilet roll from the holder and hurried back, passing it to her, apologising for not knowing where the real tissues were.

'There aren't any,' she said, sniffling.

A minute or two passed as Elodie cried into the tissues, smearing the tears and make-up across her face. When she was finished, she looked like a female version of the Joker; black smudges the size of oranges surrounded her eyes, and traces of lipstick he hadn't noticed before smeared her cheeks. He was starting to have doubts whether she was as put together as he'd originally believed. When she finally calmed down, she leant forward, resting her elbows on her knees, staring into the toilet paper in her hands, playing with it, tearing it apart in her fingers.

'Tell me about last night,' Tomek said gently. 'Take as much time as you need.'

'What... what do you want to know?'

'Everything. Start from the beginning.'

Before she did so, she snorted the snot away from her nose, cleared her throat, and sat upright, composed.

'Come on, El,' she told herself. 'Come on. You've got this.' She gave a shake of her head, slapped her cheeks a couple of times, and then suddenly her face fell flat, as if she'd become a different person. The shuddering had stopped, the rapid breathing, the tears, the sniffling – she had even stopped playing with the tissue paper. Somewhere in her brain, she had flicked a switch and now she was the epitome of calm and resolve. 'We'd arranged it ages ago. It's one of our things. Right before the new summer holiday season starts, we spend the couple of weeks beforehand going out and celebrating, enjoying ourselves because we know we won't be able to for the next couple of months. The season's so full on that we aren't always able to catch up or meet up, and it's even more difficult when some of us are in different countries. We have these nights as our last hurrah, if you want to call it that. And last night was no different. It was me, Ange, Xan, and Zoë. The four horsewomen, we call ourselves. We've been together for years. Ange and I went to school together and went into the industry at the same time. Then we met Xan and Zo when we were working with TUI. Fortunately, most of the time we're all based at Southend Airport or Stansted, so we're never too far from one another during the off season.'

'Where did you go last night?' Tomek asked.

'Memo, in Southend.'

'What time did you get there?'

Elodie pulled out her phone and unlocked it. For a few seconds, she scrolled through the device, searching for her answer. 'Ten fifty-three,' she said. 'Zoë and I went in first to get the drinks while the others wanted to get cash out.'

'What time did you leave?'

More checking of the phone. This time, she flipped the screen round to show him. 'One fifteen am,' she said. On the screen was her Uber app, with the name of the driver, the exact time they'd been picked up, and the route they'd taken home. Tomek reached out for the device and took it from her. He observed the map, noting all the local landmarks and the points at which they'd stopped.

'Am I right in thinking you dropped Angelica off first?'

Elodie nodded. 'She lives closest.'

'And the rest of you?'

'I'm the farthest away. Well, actually, no, that's not true. Xanthia lives the farthest away, but she stayed round Zoë's last night because she's all the way out in Chelmsford and none of us earns enough money to be able to pay for the cab all the way back to there.'

Tomek passed the phone over to her. He wondered how Chey and Rachel were getting on, speaking with Angelica's other friends.

'Were your friends all as drunk as you?' he asked.

Elodie slotted the phone between her leg and the side of the sofa and wrapped her shawl around her tighter.

'We were all pretty drunk. We'd had a couple at the Last Post before going to Memo. But out of all of us, I'd say Ange was the drunkest. I mean, I've seen her at her worst, and she was very near that.'

'At her worst, how?'

Elodie's eyes fell to the floor, where she hesitated, lost in thought. 'These guys just kept buying her drinks. About four or five of them. I'd lost count at one point, stopped caring. But she was all over them, grinding, dancing.'

'Does that happen often?'

'Like you wouldn't believe. She always gets the most attention on nights out. It's like all the men just flock to her, like she's got some sort of cock signal that calls out to all the arseholes. But she never does anything with them, never kisses them or anything. She likes to tease them. She'll let them buy her a drink, and then she'll move on to the next one. It's a cheap night out, but it's also stupid. I've warned her so many times about the dangers of it. That's why we always go out together and look out for each other.'

Tomek sensed there was something Elodie wasn't sharing.

'How do you mean?'

'Well, last night, there was this guy, right? Tall, dark and handsome – her type, down to a T – all covered in sweat and his eyes as wide as the fucking DJ's decks, right? He comes up to her at the bar and tries to spike her drink. I didn't see it, but Xan did. We tried telling someone but nobody listened to us, so we moved to a different part of the club. He found us a couple of minutes later and went straight back to Ange. He was besotted with her, like he had a hard-on and wanted to rub it out against her.'

'But you didn't let him?'

'I wish. We told her he'd tried to spike her drink earlier, but she didn't care. She told us to trust her and then she went off with him, dancing with him, grinding all over him.'

Tomek tried not to imagine the twenty-nine-year-old Angelica gyrating her hips against a man off his face, because he was afraid the girl would transform into his daughter. While she was still only thirteen, he didn't want to think about how that might be her someday – in as little as five years – putting herself in danger, at the mercy of disgusting men like the one Elodie had just described.

'Did anything happen between the two of them?' he asked.

'No. We pulled her away and then we went home before anything could.'

'How did he react?'

'He followed us out of the club.'

'Did he follow you in the cab?'

Elodie paused, staring into the carpet again. 'I don't know. I didn't see. We were so focused on getting ourselves out of there that I kind of forgot about him.'

Tomek made a note to visit the nightclub. They had a long time until it opened, but he could guarantee there would still be workers setting everything up for a Saturday night of alcohol-fuelled debauchery and antics.

So far, everything had made sense to him. The group had gone out, they'd had a good time, they'd come back home, and then in the time between getting out of the cab and turning up to work in the morning, Angelica had gone missing. She had left her home, and not returned.

'Has she ever done anything like this before?'

It didn't take long for Elodie to respond. 'Loads of times.'

'As in, she's gone home, left the house shortly after in the middle of the night, and then no one's been able to contact her?'

'Oh! You meant that?' Elodie scratched the back of her head. 'She's only done *that* a couple of times. Sorry, I thought you meant whether she'd danced with guys in the club before, because she's always doing that. She's always the one to make conversation with guys on a night out – it helps that they always come up to her in the first place, like I said, but she loves it.'

'When has she gone out in the middle of the night in the past, Elodie?' Tomek asked, trying to get her back on track.

'With a couple of her exes. Crawling back to them for a quick one-night stand, even though we'd warned her not to.'

Tomek was beginning to understand that this was a woman who did what she wanted, ignored her friends' advice even though it had been in her best interests, and didn't seem to care about the repercussions. Quite the opposite of the angelic image her parents had of her.

'Is it possible she did the same last night?'

Elodie considered a moment. 'Possibly. But she's not been with Sammy for a couple of months now.'

'Sammy's one of her exes, I presume?'

'Yes. And then you've got Cole before that. They're the most recent two that she's had in the past year or so. They don't tend to last very long.'

'Why not?'

'She gets what she wants out of them and then moves on. Sometimes they take it well – only because they're after the same thing and they're glad she's the one to call it off, that way they don't look like arseholes – while some don't.'

'And which categories do Sammy and Cole fit into?'

The sides of her mouth lifted as she stifled a laugh. 'Sammy is very much in the second category, while Cole... he couldn't have cared less about the two of them breaking up. Fairly sure they were both just fuck buddies for each other.'

Tomek peered down at his mug. By now a thick layer of grime and soapy residue had formed on the top. He eyed it suspiciously as it moved and shimmied against an invisible breeze, as if there was so much bacteria and mould in it that it had started a life of its own.

'Sorry about that,' she said. 'I've told them so many fucking times to stop using my mug, and then when they do, they don't even have the decency to fucking clean it properly.'

Tomek could relate. He'd stayed in various shared accommodations during his mid- to late-twenties. Not because he enjoyed staying with people, but because he couldn't afford to move into a place of his own. He'd left home at eighteen, and had later been booted out of an ex-girlfriend's, whom he'd been living with at the time. From there it had been a string of sleeping on friends' couches, trying his best to be as clean and respectful as possible, followed by a multitude of spare rooms and shared flats, until eventually he'd managed to get a place of his own. It had been so precious to him that he'd stayed there for just over a decade until a few months before, when he and Kasia had been forced to move out due to lack of space.

He picked up the mug and handed it back to her, a look of pity on his face.

'Is there anything else you think I should know?' he asked as he rose from the sofa. 'Anything else you saw last night? Anyone following you at all? Anything you think might be worth looking into?'

Her eyes fell to the carpet, and her leg bounced up and down. It was then that Tomek noticed her painted toenails for the first time. Red, seductive. There had been a time, only a few years ago, when he would have found himself in bed with a woman of her age, someone considerably younger. Some women he'd been with liked him for his age, while others liked him for his job, and the fantasy that came with it. But it had all been superficial, physical, the coming together of two horny individuals desperate for another's attention. He'd been happy to give it to them and they'd been more than happy to receive it. That had all started to change since Kasia had come into his life, but there were times, moments, when he felt the urges smother him, blur the sensible, logical part of his brain, and make him regress. He was sitting firmly on the fence, only a breath or two away from going back into his old life, one where he'd found fulfilment and nourishment in the touch of a younger woman. That same sensation rushed into his bloodstream now as he surveyed her red toenails, his eyes moving farther and farther up her legs.

In that moment, Elodie noticed his gaze crawling up her, but she made no effort to stop him or cover her leg. Instead, she stroked her hair behind her ear again.

'No...' she said slowly. 'There's nothing else I think you should know.'

CHAPTER ELEVEN

Memo nightclub had been a staple of the Southend high street and underground club scene – literally, because the club was situated down two flights of stairs – for over thirty years, since the early nineties. The owner, Jimmy Rayner, had designed and built it, and despite a turbulent and rocky past, it had continued to survive while the rest of the high street and other nightclubs had crumbled. Over the years, it had been on the receiving end of several nicknames. Some positive, others pejorative, from the likes of Messy Memo to Mandy Memo, which had followed a weekend of proficient drug taking, and had resulted in tighter restrictions and larger bouncers on the doors and on the dance floors. The club was famous for its Monday Night Memo, or MNM as it quickly became known, and had once been the host of such stars as Danny Dyer, Professor Green and pop boyband JLS in the late noughties. Going to Memo was a rite of passage for anyone either living in Southend or within a ten-mile radius. And when they needed somewhere that had plenty of late-night kebab and pizza shops open, with easy access to cabs and transport home, it was the perfect place. And at the height of the nineties rave and dance culture that had gripped and bled through every twenty-year-old that was part of that generation, it had offered the perfect mix. Tomek had been there countless times in the past (countless, namely because he'd been so drunk he hadn't remembered many of the nights), and had even made out with a few of the girls from his school there. By and large, he had fond memories of the place.

Despite the club being there so long, none of it had changed. The entrance to the building was still a hole in the wall that was entered via the same wooden doors, padlock and chain, which Tomek remembered from his first visit. It was a miracle it hadn't been broken into or vandalised more times over the years. Above the doors was the club's name, spray painted on the wall, presumably to stop people from damaging the signage or it becoming a hazard. Even the smoking area, delineated by metal barriers that had been welded into the ground, was as small as it had been twenty years ago. Nothing about its exterior had changed. But that was what made it so beautiful, so historical. Like a castle, or Buckingham Palace, a place of local historical significance. It was too beloved to modernise it or update it in any way. It was a part of Southend's heritage, a part of its history, and nobody dared touch it.

The downstairs was the same as the outside. Old and untouched, still sporting the same circling stairs he'd once plodded down, swaying, holding onto the banister for support; the first bar that frequently bottlenecked and caused one too many arguments as egos collided; the stickiest dance floors known to man; the DJ booth at the back of the dance floor, with podiums on either side, and another set of bar areas in the same corner; the second dance floor that played a different type of music, catering to a different consumer.

It all came back to him as he stepped off the final step. Dressed in his smartest shoes, the baggy jeans, the tight-fitting Topman V-neck that showed more chest than it ever should, his mates by his side, alcohol coursing through his veins already, his body would vibrate along with the music. Men and women would be everywhere, dancing, having a good time, a thick layer of smoke hanging in the air and rapidly filling his lungs. The queue for the toilets that never seemed to go down, but that was okay because you always made a new best friend while you were waiting for a piss – or even when you were standing next to someone mid-flow.

Tomek had made the most of those days in his twenties, and some of it had spilled into his thirties. While there were parts of him that missed it, he realised he was far too old for anything like that now. He was forty, for fuck's sake. Nobody who was any way respectable should still be doing that at his age.

At the bottom of the step, he made his way through the large archway that connected the first dance floor with the second. In there, the lights were on, and he saw the interior of the club in the flesh. It unnerved him. It was like walking into a brilliantly lit cinema. Disorientating and confusing. The seats and floor were grimier than you first thought, covered in popcorn and sugary drinks, and it just felt wrong being there. Waiting for him behind the bar was the manager, Marcus

Rayner, Jimmy's younger brother. The word that immediately sprang to Tomek's mind was *Oasis*, one of the world's biggest bands. Marcus looked as though he was still stuck in the nineties, with his long sideburns, his bowl haircut, parka jacket and circular sunglasses. The only thing that was missing from the Liam Gallagher homage was a more prominent monobrow.

'You the detective that called?'

'Definitely, maybe.'

'What?'

Tomek sighed deeply, unable to hide his disappointment.

'Yeah, I'm the detective. You prepared what I asked on the phone?'

'I got the tapes, but the guy's shift don't start till ten.'

'So could you give him a call and get him to come down earlier, like I asked?'

The Liam Gallagher impersonator raised his chin in an act of microaggression. Tomek was the one with all the power, and he knew it.

'That'll fuck up my shift pattern. I'll be one short tonight, on a Saturday too – our busiest night.'

Tomek shrugged. 'That's not my problem. I should think that, given all the club's gone through in the past, you'd be used to doing everything you can to help the police with their enquiries.'

Tomek was referring to an incident that had occurred at the turn of the millennium. A girl had been sexually assaulted in one of the men's toilets. It had been a quiet night, and the attacker had dragged her in, closed the door behind them, and proceeded to change her life irrevocably. It had been one of the darkest days in the club's history, but not nearly as dark as it had been for the victim. A boycott had followed for approximately two months, before it had become forgotten about and people came to the realisation they still needed a place for a night out and London was too far.

'We cooperated fully during that investigation,' Marcus said.

'Nobody's saying you didn't. All I'm saying is, now, something like that has happened again and we need your help.'

'But it didn't happen on our premises, I wanna make that abundantly clear.'

Abundantly. Tomek laughed at the word choice. As though it absolved him of all guilt, like when a politician washed his hands of the blood of innocent victims and children because he didn't pull the trigger, just sold the machine guns and explosives to the person that did.

'I know that,' Tomek responded, 'but you have a duty of care over your customers and one of them, the girl we're trying to find, was almost spiked last night, but her mates saw it and rescued her. Now, are you going to make the call or not?'

Tomek shot the man a hard, impervious stare. Marcus held it for a good two seconds before eventually relenting and reaching into his pocket for his phone. Less than a minute later, Marcus confirmed the staff member who'd been working on the bar last night would come straight in to talk with Tomek. He was only ten minutes away.

'That wasn't so hard, was it?'

Marcus said nothing as he turned his back on Tomek and opened a door that looked as though it had been painted on the wall. In all his years of going there, he had never seen that before. It was like something out of a science fiction film the way it cut a hole into the wall.

Tomek followed the man in, trying to contain his excitement.

'So this is where the magic happens,' he noted.

'No magic. Just business. No magic whatsoever. I'm not having you guys come in and drug test the place.'

'Well, you see, now that you've gone and said that, all I wanna do is bring some guys and see what sort of classes we might find.'

Marcus's eyes turned beady.

'I'm joking. Just show me what you've got and then I'll be on my way.'

Marcus didn't need telling twice. The small room was an office, complete with oversized desk, crappy chair that had more holes in it than a cheese grater, a computer, two monitors and a small shelf containing overflowing folders that balanced precariously on the edge. It was cramped, confined, yet oddly cosy. Tomek wondered how many one-to-ones and personal reviews Marcus had conducted in there – either to intimidate or make a move. Shortly after, Marcus woke the machine, logged into his account, and waiting for them on the screen was a moving image of Angelica Whitaker on the dance floor, talking to a man, his face pressed right against the side of her head. Tomek recognised her instantly. Prior to his arrival, Chey had confirmed that they'd found Angelica's social media accounts. She had three personal ones across the various platforms and an extra Instagram account she used as a travel blog, documenting her adventures across Europe for work. Each account had thousands of followers, with hundreds of likes on each post, and dozens of comments beneath. It would take a long time to sift through it all, and with a reduced workforce, Tomek had started to wonder whether things would fall behind. Or perhaps they might not need it. Perhaps right now he was looking at the person who knew where she was – the man touching Angelica's waist, moving his hands lower and lower, until she shimmied away. Tomek felt a knot form in his throat; he always got an eerie feeling watching the moments before someone's death or disappearance, as though he had the benefit of hindsight to do something about it. Sometimes he just wanted to scream at the screen. 'Don't go that way!', 'Don't go home, go back to your friend's house instead!' It was like watching a horror movie where you questioned the token blonde victim's idiotic decision to enter the dark room alone, and rolled your eyes whenever she was chased back out, later falling victim to a knife-wielding maniac in a costume or clown mask. Except this was different. This wasn't entertainment. This was real life.

And Angelica Whitaker was still missing.

Tomek spent the next five minutes watching the footage. Of Angelica dancing, grinding with the man, just as her friends said she had. Of the man holding her close against his body, his hand hovering over her drink on several occasions. Then of her being pulled away from the creep, and the creep following her up the stairs like a lost puppy. Outside, the cameras had shown the girls leaving, getting into the back of the Uber, while the man had stayed put, left behind, abandoned. Tomek asked Marcus to focus the cameras on him as he'd headed back inside the club. The footage then showed that he'd stayed in the club for the next hour, stumbling across the dance floor, leering over the women, selecting his next victims, right until the lights came on and those he'd been dancing with realised what a mistake they'd made. Once everyone had made their way to the exit, the man stumbled down the high street, eventually disappearing out of sight. By the end of it, Tomek didn't think the man was worth pursuing, but there would be no harm in sending someone along to speak with him. The only problem was finding his name and address.

'How did he pay his entry fee?'

Marcus shrugged, unhelpful. Tomek told him to rewind until they saw the man arrive at the club. Together, they watched him pay with a debit card. Tomek made a note of the timestamp and asked to see his entry from a different angle. This time, it showed the man going up to the bouncers, handing across his ID, and the bouncer scanning it under a blue light. A second later, an enlarged version of the man's driver's licence exploded onto the screen, with a green tick overlayed on it. Tomek told Marcus to pause the footage and zoom in. For CCTV footage, which was famously of a lower resolution than televisions from the 1950s, this one was surprisingly high-tech, and Tomek was able to make out the man's name with ease: Adam Egglington.

He took a photo of the man on his phone just as the employee turned up, hovering in the doorframe awkwardly. His cheeks were flushed and hot air expelled from his mouth and nose rapidly.

'Here you go,' Marcus said to Tomek, pointing to the young man who was no older than twenty-five. 'He's all yours.'

Without saying anything, Marcus pulled out a memory stick, copied the footage onto it, and passed it to Tomek. Before Tomek could thank the man, he ushered Tomek to the bar, and said, 'You need me, I'll be in here. Hopefully, you've got everything.'

Tomek sensed the manager wanted to add, "Because if you haven't, you'll have to come back another time."

With that, Marcus shut the door firmly, leaving Tomek and the bartender alone at the bar. The young man's name was Adrian, and he had worked at Memo for six weeks.

'Thank you for coming down,' Tomek told him.

'I'm still under probation. I didn't have much choice. Plus, you're the police... so it must be serious. Has something happened?'

Tomek explained the situation. Adrian's eyes widened as he listened, and he suddenly looked afraid, as though he was being the one accused of having something to do with Angelica's disappearance.

Tomek showed him a photo of Angelica that Elodie had sent him, followed by another one that they'd found on Xanthia's social media. It was a photograph of all four girls, posing and smiling at the camera, in the middle of the Last Post, their last stop before making it to Memo.

'Do you remember seeing this woman in the black dress?'

Adrian took the phone from Tomek and inspected it. His lips pursed and his cheeks tightened. 'Sorry,' he said. 'But she doesn't ring a bell. I mean, I served a lot of people last night.' His hands shook nervously as he passed the phone back to Tomek. 'They... they all sort of look the same, and we were super busy. I don't remember serving her specifically.'

Tomek tried to calm the man's nerves with a warm smile, but it was clear to see he was shaken up by the news that she'd gone missing, as though he was somehow responsible and was supposed to carry the burden of finding her.

'What about this bloke? He was seen dancing with her and buying her drinks. It was also reported that he tried putting something in one of them.'

This time, Adrian recognised the man's face instantly.

'Yes. I remember him. Two girls came up to me with a drink I'd just poured and told me it had something in it. I didn't know what to do so told one of the guys on the floor, but I don't think they did anything about it... I got distracted by some other customers and completely forgot.' He placed his hands on his head. 'Oh God! I fucked up, didn't I? I really fucked up. Fuck... I knew I should—'

Tomek placed a comforting hand on the man's shoulder. His rapid breathing immediately stopped, and he seemed to come to momentarily. Once he had controlled his breathing, Tomek said, 'It's okay. She wasn't hurt. He didn't hurt her. And he didn't hurt anyone else. You did your job. Just... let it be a lesson for next time.'

'Fuck...' Adrian continued, still lost in his own thoughts. 'That's it. I'm gonna fuck up my probation. I'm gonna need to find a new job. I—'

Tomek placed a hand on his other shoulder. It was the best he could do to not slap the twenty-five-year-old across the cheeks.

'Your job's fine. If my interaction with Mr Rayner is anything to go by, I don't think he cares all that much about what you did or didn't do. Your job's safe. You've got nothing to worry about.'

CHAPTER TWELVE

A check on the police's internal database back at the station showed that Adam Egglington had previous. In the last two years, he'd been arrested for drunk and disorderly behaviour along Southend high street, with a further arrest for the same charge along the seafront, except in the latter he'd been found naked from the waist down, lying on the beach, staring into the moonlight, wiping sand out of places it was never supposed to be. And so the arresting officer had added public indecency to the charge sheet. The most recent arrest had come six weeks ago, and assuming he hadn't moved in that time, Tomek hoped he was standing outside the right flat.

He knocked on the one-bedroom maisonette in Lee Chapel South, a short walk from Basildon Hospital, and waited. When there was no answer, Tomek took a step back from the porch, onto the overgrown front lawn, and looked up at the bedroom window. The curtains were closed, obstructing his view, except a small window had been left open at the top.

Tomek tried the door again. This time he peered through the window beside it, cupping his hands to his face, squinting. But it was no use. In one last attempt, before moving along to the neighbours, he crouched down, opened the letterbox, and just as he was about to scream Adam's name, a violent, pungent stench assaulted his senses, knocking him backwards onto the slabs of concrete. The smell was so strong it stuck in his throat, and for a few seconds afterwards Tomek tried to cough it up but ended up gagging and dry heaving on the porch. It was the smell and taste of vomit, vomit that had been stagnating, putrefying, congealing for the whole day.

Tomek didn't like the thoughts that were percolating, and decided to call for uniformed support. The dispatch controller over the phone told him it would be at least five minutes before they arrived. Five minutes too long.

Deciding he wasn't going to wait around, Tomek banged on the front door one last time, and when there was still no response, he knocked on the neighbour's door. The woman who answered was frightened and cautious of him, but as soon as he'd shown her his ID, she relaxed a little.

'Don't suppose you have a key, do you?' Tomek asked. It was a long shot, but sometimes the simplest options were the ones overlooked.

The neighbour shook her head.

'What about a hammer of some kind?'

The woman looked at him aghast, eyes beady. He glanced down at her hand, saw a ring, and asked, 'Married?'

She nodded, eyes still wild, as though she was having an out of body experience. She was experiencing fight or flight, and right now she was doing neither, absolutely fucking nothing.

'Does your partner have anything we can use?'

'He... he's not home.'

Tomek swore. The last thing he wanted to do was spend time tearing through a complete stranger's house and garden shed.

And then it came to him.

The garden!

Without asking, Tomek shimmied his way past the neighbour, and hurried towards the small set of patio doors at the back of the house. The neighbour, in her bewildered state, was a few seconds behind, the cogs in her brain taking time to adjust and come to terms with what was happening in her home.

'Key,' he said to her, agitated. 'I need a key. I need to get into the garden.'

She pointed to a small pot that was wedged into the corner of another windowsill. Tomek reached for it, grabbed the key, and let himself out. The garden was in its early spring state. The flowers were beginning to blossom, the grass was overgrown, and life was coming back to the trees. And the air was filled with it. It would have been a pleasant experience, sitting out there, had it not been for the hospital round the corner, and the sound of sirens firing off every two seconds.

Tomek turned his attention to Adam Egglington's house. The two were almost identical: the kitchen door, the patio doors that opened onto the garden, the window above. It was like looking in a mirror. He paused a moment, surveying his options. The way he saw it, there was only one: he was going to have to break in and deal with the consequences later.

Before hopping the fence, he searched the neighbour's garden, looking for anything heavy enough to shatter the glass. He found it in the form of a brick that had come loose on a small bed of flowers. He bent down to pick it up, and just as he was about to lob it over the fence, the neighbour called out to him, 'What are you doing? You can't take that.'

Tomek observed the object in his hand. 'It's a brick. You really gonna miss it?'

Then, before she could respond, he lobbed it over the fence in front of him. It wasn't until he squared up to the fence that he realised he'd thrown it over the wrong one. The neighbour had distracted him, and his body had been facing the opposite direction as he'd chucked it.

'Oh, for fuck's sake! Sorry!'

Another bend, another brick, using more force to yank it from the ground this time. Now he owed her and her husband two bricks. He threw it over the correct fence and, using a bird bath for support, propelled himself into Adam's garden. The landing was soft, his body barrel-rolling across the overgrown grass and weeds. After a few seconds of searching, his fingers trawling through the undergrowth, he eventually found the brick. As he charged towards the house, cocking his arm back, ready to throw the object, he stopped when he saw a man appear from the cloud's reflection in the window. Adam Egglington was lying on his sofa, flat on his back, his face and neck covered in vomit. His chest wasn't moving, and when Tomek knocked on the glass, there was no response. Tomek cupped his face to the window and peered through. In the fading light, he could see the man's face, a pasty white beneath the thick splatter of vomit. He was fully dressed and still in the same clothes from the night before. He must have come home, passed out on the sofa, and been so wasted he'd choked on his own vomit. Seeing it reminded Tomek of the time he'd nearly suffered the same fate. He'd been nineteen, gone out for a big night with his mates, and woken up on his side with a pool of vomit beside his head, crusty on the outside, soft and spongy on the inside, like a bodily fluid flapjack. For days afterwards he could still smell the stench of it hot in his nostrils, but what had really stuck with him had been the near-death experience, the unshakeable fact that he could have died if his body had been rotated another ninety degrees. That was it, all that had been between him and death. Something as arbitrary as a ninety-degree angle.

Before he could ponder it anymore, the sound of sirens grew louder, and he realised it was the backup he'd called for, pulling up outside the house. He vaulted the fence, raced back through the neighbour's kitchen, and found them in the front garden. He was met by a duo of confused faces.

'No, you're not in the wrong place,' he told them. 'But I've found him. He's in the living room at the back of the property. Have you got an enforcer?'

One of the uniformed officers nodded, then turned towards the vehicle. He returned with a large battering ram in hand.

'Great,' Tomek said, then watched as the man proceeded to batter the heavy-duty metal object into the weak, wooden front door. It didn't stand a chance, and after one hit, it buckled and gave way.

But Tomek couldn't follow the men in. Something held him firmly rooted to the spot, keeping him outside as the wind began to pick up and wrap itself around him.

He couldn't bear to look at the man lying in a pool of his own vomit because, before he'd pulled his eyes away from the image a few moments before, all he'd been able to see was himself there, slightly longer and larger, taking up more of the space, covered in his own sick. He couldn't bear to look and be reminded of what could have been.

CHAPTER THIRTEEN

The image was still in his head when he entered the major incident room. He'd been unable to shake it the entire time the SOCOs and uniformed staff had processed Adam Egglington's body and removed it. Ingrained, indelible. Each time seeing his own face instead of Adam's.

Waiting for him in the MIR were Chey and Rachel. Tomek had told them to ready their information ahead of the meeting. Usually, an inspector would require a written report from each member of staff actively working on an investigation, someone who was out there on the frontline. But Tomek didn't like reports. They were a constant bugbear of his, and it wasn't the way he wanted to manage the investigation. If he couldn't be arsed to write them in the first place, you could sure as hell bet he wouldn't be arsed to read them either.

'What you saying, Sarge?' Chey asked in a spritely tone.

'I'm saying nothing at all, because for the next ten minutes I want to be doing all the listening.'

'And maybe have a little nap as well, by the looks of it,' added Rachel unapologetically. 'I've seen single mums look less tired than you.'

A smile flashed across Tomek's face. He could always rely on his team – especially those he'd specifically chosen – to raise his spirits. The banter between the three of them was arguably the best in the office (Tomek's argument, only) and that was part of the reason he'd selected them: some light in what he sensed would be an otherwise dark and depressing investigation.

Tomek pulled a seat out from beneath the table and dropped himself into it. It was only the first day of the investigation, and already he was feeling deflated. Like he had nothing left to give. Was this how Nick felt twenty-four seven? Was that why he always sighed, because he'd had enough twenty years ago and was now just hanging on by a thread?

'Where would you like us to begin, Sarge?' Chey asked.

'From the beginning. Do we have any idea where she is?'

Chey shook his head. 'Her phone's still off, and has been since the early hours of the morning. I've contacted her service provider for more information, and I should have it by tomorrow morning.'

Tomek spun on the chair and looked at the wall of whiteboards that ran along one side of the room. The notes and images from a previous investigation had been left up there, waiting to be pulled down, and Tomek found a small empty section of the board beside Chey and Rachel. He grabbed a pen and wiped clean a small smudge from the surface.

'What's the timeline?' he asked, writing on the whiteboard. 'Her and her friends left Memo at one fifteen. According to Elodie Locket's Uber account, Angelica was dropped off at her flat at precisely one twenty-eight, thirteen minutes later.' Tomek recalled all of this from memory, while the other two searched through their notes, cross-referencing the information they had versus what he was telling them. 'She was due at work in Leigh Broadway by nine am.' He drew a line between the two times, going over it repeatedly, leaving enough space to fill in the gaps. 'That leaves us a seven-hour window for her to go missing. What can you add to that?'

Chey consulted his notes. 'The last ping from her phone to a cell tower was at one fifty-two in the morning, which is...' He paused as he calculated the time difference. 'Just over twenty minutes after she got home.'

Tomek noted the time and action on the board. 'Right. So she either switched it off herself, it ran out of battery, or someone else switched it off for her. Do we have any eyewitness reports of her leaving the house at that time?'

Rachel shook her head. 'Nothing yet. From what I've collated with uniform, and from the neighbours I spoke with myself, nobody saw her or heard her. It was the middle of the night. Everyone was asleep.'

'Right. And what about home security footage? Anyone come forward with that?'

Chey and Rachel shook their heads in unison, wearing the same apologetic look on their faces.

'Anything else?'

Another synchronised shake of the head.

'So she just... disappears?'

Tomek ran his fingers through his hair and scratched the back of his head, acutely aware that both had their eyes on him, him in the driving seat, leading the investigation. Two pairs of expectant eyes waiting for him to tell them what to do. He wasn't sure he liked that. He didn't have any ideas. Before, when someone else had been running the investigation, he'd been able to come up with the answers, with the solutions without issue. Possibly because he hadn't had the burden of someone's life on his shoulders – that he in some way felt one step removed – or possibly because it had been an ego thing, a chance to prove himself to Victoria and Nick. But now he'd done that, now he'd shown that he *was* capable, he felt like he was falling at the first hurdle, and he had no idea which way to go next.

Come on, Tomek, he told himself. You either shut the fuck up and keep stumbling forward, no matter what's in the way, or you turn around now and head back to the starting line.

He decided the second one wasn't an option.

'We've got a window of seven hours where she could have gone missing. The two possibilities as I see it are, one: she left the house during that time and hasn't returned yet, or two: someone went to her house. It's as simple as that.' He turned his focus to the board again, created a circle in the middle of what was left of the white space, and fired two straight lines from it. One for leaving the house, the other for someone going to hers. 'Once we've ascertained which one of these it is, we can build the larger picture from there.' He pushed the lid on the pen with a satisfying and tangible *snap*, then returned to his seat. 'In the meantime, tell me everything you have on Angelica Whitaker. What do we know about her that can help us?'

Both detectives looked down at their notes, avoiding the question. Until Chey eventually summoned the courage to speak first.

'I've started to look through her Instagram, as it's the one she updates most regularly. She has two profiles. One's a personal account, which she uses much less, while the second is a travel blog/influencer type thing. She's got several thousand followers, but also has several thousand posts on each of them. It's going to take a fair amount of time to sift through it all. But from the brief research I've done and the first couple of posts I've looked at, she seems to post stuff about herself and about her life as well. What she's doing, where she is. But she doesn't say too much on the captions – sometimes it's just an emoji or two.'

'Could they mean anything to someone?'

'Possibly. I'd need to analyse who's liking and commenting.'

Tomek nodded. 'Rach?'

Detective Constable Rachel Hamilton cleared her throat before speaking. 'Xanthia Demetriou, one of Angelica's closest friends, was singing her praises. She didn't have a bad word to say about her. Life of the party, always bubbly, always outgoing and up for going out, she was happy to be around everyone and everyone was happy to be around her. Kind, caring, full of zest, always there for her. It was like she was in love with her.'

'They know each other from work, right?'

'Sort of,' Rachel explained. 'They *met* at work. But Xanthia now works at a chemist's. Not the career change she wanted, but the air steward market is tight at the moment. It was all she could find. Hopefully next year she'll be able to get something.'

'What did she have to say about last night?'

'Just that she had a good time. And she remembers clearly watching Angelica open the front door and close it behind her. So, according to her, she definitely got *in* the house.'

'And Zoë?'

'Backed up everything Xanthia said. She saw Angelica enter her home without issue.'

The question that still remained was how she'd got out of it.

CHAPTER FOURTEEN

The tinny sound from Kasia's cheap Dell laptop reached them on the sofa. She had locked herself in her bedroom after dinner, and was no doubt watching one of her benign, mind-numbing reality TV programmes or one of the chick flick series that seemed to be all over the various streaming sites. Whenever he logged into his Netflix or Amazon Prime, he was bombarded with teenage dramas and programmes that their algorithm fed Kasia to keep her engaged. It was enough to turn him off from watching anything. And potentially stop paying the bill altogether. But he knew that would be like cutting off her arm, or at least tying it behind her back while he forced her to catch the remote. So instead he would do the honourable thing and continue to clench his fist every time he saw the direct debits come out each month.

Tonight, however, he was very much in favour of the streaming services. Abigail was over, and he had allowed her to select a channel to choose from. He had no idea what she'd put on, but it enabled him to switch off and let his thoughts drift wherever they needed to go. While she was engrossed in her programme, his mind was getting lost in deep thoughts like, why are buildings called buildings when they'd already been built, and why do we say we're coming up for air when we're not even underwater? He'd been battling those particular conundrums for a good five minutes when Abigail placed her legs on his lap, demanding that he massage her feet.

'Haven't you been sitting at your desk all day?' he asked her.

'Yes. But in *heels*. You don't know what it's like.' She wiggled her toes in his face. '*Please*. They've been hurting so much today.'

Rolling his eyes, he said, 'You're more of a diva than I am. And I don't like it when I put gel in my hair and it's raining outside!'

'*Please,*' she begged, having listened to none of what he'd just said.

'Okay, if I get my feet massaged afterwards? I've got a lovely bunion that needs kneading out.'

Tomek had never seen her look so disgusted.

'That's fucking gross. I'm going nowhere near your feet.'

'But I've been standing on mine all day...'

His attempt at pulling the wool over her eyes with an adorable, innocent flutter of the eyelashes didn't work.

'Busy day?' she asked, relaxing her toes, as Tomek began to knead them with his thumb and knuckles like they were dough.

'Very.'

'What happened?'

'Woman in her late twenties was reported missing by her family. She went out last night with some friends, got dropped off at her flat, then disappeared. Her manager, who happens to be her sister-in-law, said she didn't turn up this morning for work.'

'And you can't find her?'

'Wouldn't be thinking about her if we had.'

'You're thinking about another woman?'

'Not in that way,' he said with a shake of the head. He stopped massaging her feet, and she wiggled her toes to remind him to continue.

'I was joking,' she said, then turned her attention back to the television for all of two seconds before returning it to him. 'Do you think she might be dead?'

Tomek could sense where the conversation was going.

'I dunno.'

'Do you think something happened to her?'

'Not sure.'

'Do you think you'll find her?'

He didn't answer.

'Did she get with anyone on her night out? Could it be them? What if it's one of her friends? Or maybe she went for a walk and someone abducted her...'

Tomek knew she was fishing for information, shooting a load of spaghetti at his face to see what stuck. But he wasn't going to rise to it, nor was he going to eat any of it.

'Listen,' he said, releasing his grip on her foot, 'when the time's right, we'll share the information with you.'

'Why haven't you already? If this is a missing person case, we can help you. Give us all the information you've got, show us what she looks like, and we can put the word out. What leads have you got?'

'None. Yet.'

'Why are you lying to me?'

'I'm not.'

'Yes, you are. I can tell when you're lying to me. I don't like that you're hiding something from me.'

All sensitivity and playfulness had gone from her tone. Now it had become irate, stern. Professional.

'I'm telling you the truth,' he insisted. 'We don't have any leads.'

'Why are you doing this to me? Why don't you want to help me? I've just started this new job. I could do with something like this. This would be really good for me to get the exclusive on this.'

'You're overreacting.'

'No, I'm not. You're the one lying to me, keeping stuff hidden from me. Who else have you told about this? Who's been flirting with you for the information?'

'You mean like you used to?'

She lashed out at him. A little kick on the thigh, like a hammer swinging down. It was only small, and didn't hurt him in the slightest, but there was intent behind it. And he was immediately reminded of why he didn't get into long-term relationships. His previous two had been similar. His first girlfriend, Kasia's mother, had verbally and emotionally abused him, constantly undermined him and made him feel small. His second official girlfriend, who had turned out to be a serial killer, had, aside from the killing aspect of her personality, been neurotic, jealous and a little psychotic. It was all he'd ever known. All he'd ever been used to. Perhaps he had a type – a type that made him feel tiny and useless.

'You're overreacting,' he repeated.

Another kick. Harder, this time.

'No, I'm not. We *need* this story, Tomek. Today, we ran a front page, a breaking news story about a group of kids from London who took a crab on the train all the way to Southend seafront so it could "live its best life".'

'And did it?'

Another kick. This time misfiring and narrowly missing his groin.

'That's the sort of shit we've been running recently. A fucking crab! Scraping the bottom of the fucking barrel.'

Tomek sniggered. 'Where'd they get the crab from?'

'Really? You think it's funny?'

'I can't believe you *don't*.'

'This is my fucking job we're talking about, and you're just laughing about it. I can't believe that's the first thing you think of. This is my career. If you can't take me seriously, then who the fuck will?'

Maybe the crab, Tomek thought, but kept it to himself. Instead, he went back to thinking about buildings and being underwater, and how, in that moment, he felt like he was struggling to come up for air.

CHAPTER FIFTEEN

Liam Dennis had never felt so alive, so full of adrenaline. He wanted to run through walls, jump off buildings, dive across the train track. His teenage body didn't know how to handle it, how to process it. But James and Ethan did. They had experience with this sort of thing, knew what they were doing. Were able to *control* themselves. They had suggested it to him that afternoon at school: slipping out in the middle of the night while his mum and dad were asleep, breaking in, putting his art skills to good use, then making it back home again before anyone woke up. Like nothing had happened. The risk Liam had was running into his dad. He always woke up super early for work, and Liam was paranoid he would come home at the wrong time, fully clothed, out of breath, his hands covered in spray paint. But Ethan had told him not to worry, that it added to the experience, heightened it somehow.

Liam wasn't entirely sure how, but he took Ethan's words at face value. He was in no position to do otherwise.

It was a little after two am. It was pitch dark outside, and everything was silent, save for the sound of the wind picking up leaves and dropping them a few inches away to a new resting place. It was the quietest he'd ever heard it. No traffic, no trains, not even the sound of the Thames Estuary reached them.

Ethan anticipated they would need no more than half an hour, and fully clothed, with their hoods pulled low over their heads, they started towards the location. They had agreed to meet on the other side of the train track that cut through the landscape towards Southend high street. It was more convenient for Ethan, and as the unofficial leader of the group, what he said went.

Their first obstacle was the train track, with seven hundred and fifty volts coursing through it. Liam had never crossed a train track before, never had the need to. But he'd read the horror stories. Of suicides, of kids jumping them in the middle of the night and getting seriously injured.

But not him, not tonight. He would make sure nothing happened.

Because it was his first night out with them, Ethan and James had decided he needed to go first. That it was only fair. An initiation, a chance for him to prove himself. And so, in the darkness, the only source of illumination the low sodium lights in the distance, Liam stepped onto the gravelled surface beside the live tracks. In the silence, he could hear the electricity raging through it, and he felt a buzz in the air, pressing against his legs like a force field. Carefully, he lifted his leg high into the air, like he'd been taught at karate, swivelled his hips, and then lowered it, dropping into a deep sumo squat. Then he repeated the process for the second portion of the track. High, swivel, drop, squat.

High, swivel, drop, squat.

High—

It wasn't until he was at the third track that he heard another sound. Just as he was about to swivel his hips, he saw Ethan and James sprinting across the gravel, hopping over each metal snake with ease, as though it was as easy as jumping over a stone on the ground. The two boys laughed at him when they reached the other side, cajoling him, the sound of their laughter absorbed by the surrounding trees and hedges.

'Fucking hell,' he said to himself, as he looked down at the metal pylon immediately in front of him. 'Come on. You can do this. Like jumping over a slide tackle.'

He lowered his leg, retreated a few steps, and steadied his breath, legs shoulder-width apart, arms by his sides, breathing deeply – his best Cristiano Ronaldo free kick impression. Then, when he felt confident enough, he sprinted towards his friends. One track. Two tracks. The sound of the canisters in his backpack rattled in his ears.

And he was there. Done. Easier than he'd thought.

He looked back at the sleeping snakes, at the distance he'd covered, his body swelling with pride. He felt invincible, the adrenaline reaching a new high.

'Come on, dickhead,' James said, slapping him on the back. 'Let's go!'

The boy grabbed his bag strap and pulled him up a slight incline, through a thick row of hedges. Liam winced and protected his face as thorns and stinging nettles lashed at him, cutting into his knuckles and forearms. A few painful moments later, they breached onto a residential street, filled with houses much too posh and expensive for his liking. He was used to the estate; here he got a sense that nobody talked to each other, nobody said anything. Not like at the estate, where everyone knew everyone – even if that wasn't such a good thing at times.

They paid little heed to the houses, however, because the treasure chest they were looking for was only a short distance away.

He had never heard of Park Road Methodist Church until lunchtime. He had no idea what it was used for, no idea how long it had been there, just that it had been empty and boarded up for years. Nobody ever went there, they'd told him, which was what made it the perfect place to go.

They kept their heads down as they traversed the quiet residential streets. Several of the driveways were filled with at least two cars, while the remaining vehicles spilled onto the street. There were no lights on in any of the houses, and the only source of light across the entire stretch of road was a single streetlamp that flickered intermittently.

A minute later, they arrived at the Methodist church. It was much more impressive than Liam had been expecting, but as he stared at it, he felt an overwhelming urge to run away; that it was tainted by evil spirits, haunted by the devil. He wasn't a religious or spiritual kid in the slightest, but an ominous premonition had suddenly crept over him and told him this was a bad place to be. That they should turn and leave, run away and never come back. But he couldn't say that. Not when James and Ethan were there. Not when they would tell the entire school and rip into him tomorrow. Maybe it was doubt, maybe it was fear calling him back. But he'd experienced those emotions before, and this was nothing like that.

'What you waiting for, mate?' Ethan asked.

Liam was surprised to see that both of them had made it to a side entrance, a wooden door with a flimsy padlock as a last line of defence.

'Ain't scared, are ya, bruv?'

Liam shook his head, trying to control the lump in his throat. 'Nah. I was just... I was just looking at it.'

He didn't want to be there.

He didn't want to be there.

Saying nothing else, he silently joined the two boys, huddling closer than he usually would. In his backpack, Ethan had brought a pair of bolt cutters. Where he'd got them from, Liam didn't know, but as he opened the handles to feed the bolt into the teeth, he paused.

'S'matter?' asked James.

'It's unlocked. It's already been cut.'

He didn't want to be there.

He didn't want to be there.

'Maybe someone's already done it,' James said.

'Maybe. But I was here the other night, and it weren't like that. You reckon it's Henry and them lot?'

'Could be,' James answered with a shrug.

Nobody said anything else on the matter. Then the two boys turned to Liam, looking at him expectantly.

'Go on, mate,' Ethan said.

'"Go on, mate" what?' Liam replied.

'You first. It's the rules. Your first time out with us, you get to go first.'

But he didn't want to go first. He didn't want to be there.

'It's cool. You can go. Show me how it's done,' he said, trying to mask the fear in his voice.

'The fucking door's already open. All you gotta do is push it.'

'Don't be a pussy,' James added.

'Yeah. Just fucking open it. It ain't that deep. Just push it. We'll be right behind you.'

Liam quickly realised he didn't have a choice in the matter. He'd come this far. He'd already jumped over four train tracks, bought and paid for the spray cans they were going to use. He'd invested time, money and energy – not to mention the absolute bollocking he was going to get from his parents if they ever found out – and so he couldn't back out now. What would they think of him?

'Mate, you coming or what? Think I can feel my hair starting to turn grey.'

Liam ignored James's jibe and brushed past him.

First time for jumping the tracks, he thought. First time for breaking into an abandoned church.

Slowly, he pushed the door. The hinge creaked loudly, the sound echoing throughout the hall. It felt heavy in his arms, and he had to use his whole weight to push it forward. Eventually, when the gap was big enough, he stepped in. The air inside was chilly, older, as though it had been sitting, waiting there for a long time.

That the spirits had been waiting there for a long time.

The light from outside barely filtered into the building, and so he pulled out his phone and switched on the torch feature. A wide cone of harsh white light illuminated the concrete floor. The door opened onto a small section of the church. He was half expecting to see an arrangement of benches and chairs facing an altar at some point, but there was nothing. The floor was completely empty.

Behind him, Ethan and James subtly entered, their movements cagey, tentative, just like his. It was comforting to know that he wasn't the only one whose arsehole was clenched.

He didn't want to be there.

They didn't want to be there.

Liam dropped his bag to the floor and pretended to stall going any deeper into the church by retrieving his spray cans. But Ethan and James had the same idea, and a moment later, leaving the bags on the floor, they headed towards the front of the church, their path illuminated by the torches on their phones. They only got as far as a few steps before they saw the body on the floor. Pale white beneath the already-white glow of their torches, lying there naked, staring into the ceiling.

The evil spirits.

The boys froze a moment, stunned and shocked.

Ethan was the first to react, proving that he was in fact the most scared of them all, by sprinting out of there, his scream shattering Liam's eardrums. He was immediately followed by James, who clattered into Liam on the way and brought him to his senses.

Then it was Liam's turn. He swivelled on the balls of his feet and raced out of there, tripping over the bags on the floor, and colliding with the door on his way out. Picking himself up from the ground, he joined the others a moment later, all panting, panicking, screaming their lungs out in the open before running away back towards the tracks, back towards home.

Tonight had been a night of firsts.

First time for jumping the tracks.

First time breaking into an abandoned church.

And now he could add the first time seeing a dead body to the list.

CHAPTER SIXTEEN

Tomek struggled to keep his eyes open. His second sleepless night in two days. The call, notifying him that a body had been found, had come in a little after three am, twenty minutes after he'd finally closed his eyes and felt himself doze off next to Abigail, whose earlier behaviour had been keeping him awake.

The responsibility of attending the crime scene typically fell to the deputy SIO, but because he hadn't appointed one, he'd nominated himself – and then called both Chey and Rachel on the way. He wanted them both there too, bleary-eyed and restless. The emergency call had been made by Vanessa Carmen, a neighbour who lived immediately opposite the Park Road Methodist Church. She had reported hearing screams from inside the church. At first she'd thought it was a ghost of some kind, a spirit returned to disrupt sleeping neighbours in the early hours of the morning. But when she'd seen three young boys, no older than teenagers, sprinting away from the building with their hoods pulled over their faces, effing and blinding, screaming for their mummies, she'd known something was awry. But she hadn't been brave enough to find out what it was.

'That place has always given me the creeps,' she said as she showed Tomek through to her living room. 'I almost didn't move in because of it. I dunno what it is. Just... something about it.'

Your imagination... Tomek thought, but kept it to himself. While he was waiting for the crime scene to be cleared, and for the pathologist to arrive, Tomek thought it worthwhile speaking with the key witness to glean as much information as he could from her, but it turned out that she'd already told the dispatch caller everything over the phone: that she'd been awoken by some loud screams, which she'd originally thought was a poltergeist of some kind, then she'd looked out of her bedroom window, only to find that it had been three teenage boys fleeing the church.

'And you didn't get a look at any of their faces?'

'I wish I had. But they were running in the other direction, towards the train line.'

Tomek didn't think it worth expending resources on trying to find the boys. Not yet. Not until he could confirm what was inside the church. After a brief moment of silence, Tomek thanked her for the witness statement and hospitality, then made his way towards the exit.

'I'm sorry I didn't go in to have a look,' she said on the doorstep.

'That's okay. That's our job.'

'Do you know what's in there?' She pointed to the church and lowered her voice, as though what they were discussing was supposed to be a closely held secret.

Tomek turned to face the church.

'I don't,' he said.

But I have a very good feeling I know who *is in there.*

'Guess I'm about to find out.'

❉

OVER FOUR HOURS LATER, Tomek was dressed in his white forensic suit, mentally preparing himself to enter the church. Entry into the Grade II listed building was now via the main entrance, at the front of the building, beneath its ominous and frightening spires. That way, there would be no risk of contaminating the side entrance that the boys had used. With him were Chey, Rachel, Lorna Dean the Home Office pathologist, and Rory Stevens, the crime scene manager. Through a narrow gap in the door, Tomek saw a small army of scenes of crime officers dressed in white, moving about the place, bathed in a forensic white light from the floodlights that had been set up in there.

Tomek was first in line to enter. Before he did, he took a moment to observe the building's structure: the architecture, the craftsmanship, the Kentish stone, the patio that had become overgrown with weeds and plants since its closure in the nineties, the soil that had been picked up by the wind and scattered across the edge of the building, the paint that had begun to flake and peel away, the stained-glass windows that had been boarded up and disregarded, a building forgotten about, left behind as the new age continued to progress and develop.

When Tomek finally received the go-ahead to enter, he inhaled deeply and stepped in.

It took a moment for his eyes to adjust to the harsh white light inside the church, but when they did, the tableau of Angelica Whitaker's pristine body lying naked on the cold concrete floor came into view. She lay posed on her back, legs straight, pressed together, toes pointed to the sky. Her arms were positioned at forty-five-degree angles from her body. Her head was resting perfectly, and her breasts dangled either side of her ribcage. None of that was shocking for Tomek. He'd seen naked bodies – dead, naked bodies – before. But what did disconcert him were the angel wings that had been painted behind her on the ground. Angel wings that had been painted with care, time, and attention. Angel wings that had been painted with blood.

Tomek felt a nudge in the back. He hadn't realised it, but he'd stopped moving, and the nudge in his back was Chey accidentally walking into him.

'Jesus Christ,' Chey muttered.

'Probably not the best place for blasphemy, Chey,' Tomek retorted as he moved around the body, keeping a wide berth around Angelica's limbs and the wings.

He and the rest of the team walked along the stepping plates that had been placed down by the forensics team. It was now that he examined her body in more detail. A face to a name. A naked body matching with what he'd seen from an Instagram post and a recent photograph from the family. In neither of those did Angelica Whitaker look as skinny and malnourished as she did right now before him. The digits of her rib cage were as prominent as the sun in the sky, her pelvis jutted out like the two church spires, and her cheeks looked as though she had either been born with astonishing genetics or had had a lot of Botox and work done to them. From the photos on her social media accounts, her body was supposed to look nothing like this. What was even more confusing was that there were hardly any indications of livor mortis. Tomek had no idea how long she'd been dead for, but judging by the pasty colour of her skin, and the smell that had started to form, it had been longer than a few hours, which indicated to him that she'd died on the night she'd gone missing. By that point, some twenty-four hours later, all of her blood should have started to sink, succumbing to the effects of gravity, and pooled at her lowest point. But along her back and the backs of her thighs, there was very little sign of that. Not as much as he would have expected.

Lorna Dean echoed his thoughts.

'I would expect to see a lot more,' she said, her fiery ginger hair burning through the fabric of her suit. 'Even for someone of *her* size.' There was a slight hint of jealousy in her tone as she said it. 'I also can't see any physical lacerations or wounds to the exterior, meaning there's no *obvious* cause of death.'

'Could she have overdosed?' Tomek asked, casting his mind back to the CCTV footage from the night she'd disappeared, and Adam Egglington's hand hovering over her drink on two occasions.

'Possibly.'

Tomek crouched down. The joints in his knees cracked and creaked as he rolled forward on the balls of his feet, wrestling against his inner balance. He ran his eyes along Angelica's body, this time hoping the new angle would give him a different perspective, a different inclination of the way she'd died. As Lorna had said, there were no physical marks on her body, no stab wounds, no puncture marks in the crooks of her elbow – nothing. Her skin, her muscles and everything about her exterior were perfect, emitting a soft glow underneath the white light. Which indicated the cause of death had been internal. That she'd possibly overdosed, or suffered a stroke or heart attack from whatever Adam Egglington had tried giving her – and quite possibly succeeded in. Though Tomek didn't think any of that was likely. Rather, this was the work of someone else. Someone who had inflicted death upon her in a different way. And he wanted to know how.

'Where's all this blood come from?' Chey asked as he reached out a finger to touch it.

'Don't!' Rory Stevens yelled, his deep baritone voice bouncing off the walls. 'Why would you want to touch it?'

'To see if it was still wet.'

'Or you could simply ask the fucking question. There's no need to be putting your hand into things. Did you do that a lot when you were a child? Putting your hand in the toaster when it was on, maybe? Playing with knives? Jesus fucking Christ, mate—'

'Watch it,' Tomek interrupted, pointing towards the altar. 'Matey's listening.'

Rory's brow furrowed beneath the top line of his hood. 'I think he's got bigger demons to chase, don't you?' Then he pointed to the angel on the floor. 'I can tell you that the blood's dried, so you don't need to touch it. Just use your eyes, please. We're all adults here. I'm confident we're all capable of that.' He moved his finger to the angel wings beside Angelica's body. 'We've taken several samples of the blood. Hopefully it's all from the same body, otherwise that might make things a little tricky. We've removed skin samples, discovered some hairs, dusted for prints, searched for fibres and trace evidence, and everything is photographed and documented. We'll send it all off for examination as soon as possible. We've also surveyed the entry points, and the bags of canisters that were left on the floor. It'll need a second opinion, but the bolt cutters we found on the floor look too small to have been the ones to break the lock over there.' This time he pointed to the wooden door at the other end of the church. 'Suggesting that the killer brought the body in through there, but couldn't close it.'

'Where are her clothes?'

Rory shrugged. 'We've searched high and low, but no sign of them.'

Tomek nodded thoughtfully. 'Any footprints or fingerprints by the door?'

'A couple. Some clearer than others. When they get back to the lab, we'll run them through IDENT1. Should have some news for you on that one by the end of the day.'

Tomek's version of the end of the day was different to other people's, and now that their missing person investigation had just been upgraded to murder, there would be no end of the day: the days would blur into one and roll into the next, without an end point in sight. Not until they could find their killer.

'Any fingerprints anywhere else?' Rachel asked as she manoeuvred around Chey and moved towards Angelica's head. 'Any on her body?'

Rory shook his head. 'None.'

'Nothing at all?'

'I can get the team to check again, but we used two different methods.'

Rachel crouched down beside Angelica's head. 'The killer must have used gloves of some description then. I'd imagine it's almost impossible to drag the body in here without so much as a fingerprint.'

Nobody said anything as she tilted forward, zooming in on Angelica's face.

'And they've put make-up on her,' she added.

'What do you mean?' Tomek asked.

'Different make-up.'

'How so?'

'Bloody hell,' she continued, talking to herself. 'It's better than anything I've ever been able to do. I know I don't wear a lot of it, but—'

'Rach,' Tomek interrupted sternly.

The constable noted the intonation in his voice and explained. 'I was looking at the photos her friends took from their night out, and in them, Angelica wasn't wearing any lipstick. But now she is. Her eyelashes weren't caked in mascara, but now they are. Her cheeks weren't tinted a hint of red, but now they are. And her eyebrows...' She zoomed in closer again. 'They look like they've been threaded, or shaped slightly.'

Tomek considered this. He made his way around her body, coming to a stop on the other side, opposite Rachel. He looked the detective in the eye.

'Could she have done this herself after she got home?'

'In twenty minutes? Not a chance. Maybe if she's a professional, but I don't think so. And I've seen flight attendants before – they like to take a long time to do their make-up, especially when they're working. Besides, it takes me a good hour to look like this every morning and this is only half decent.'

'Half decent? You? Never,' Tomek said.

'Shut it.'

He didn't need to be told twice.

'Whoever's done this has taken some serious time and care and effort to make her look this way. They would have had to spend a long time with the body. Either someone's infatuated with her, or they're a little fucked in the head.'

'Or both,' Tomek added.

CHAPTER SEVENTEEN

Rose Whitaker had closed her jewellery store early so that she could be with the family to hear the latest news. The four of them, with Tomek and DC Anna Kaczmarek, the team's family liaison officer, were gathered in Daphne and Roy's sprawling living room. They lived over thirty minutes away, in the quaint town of Witham, near Brentwood, a location made famous by the reality TV show, *The Only Way Is Essex*. Despite the appearance of wealth – with their Barbour coats, Joules bags, Ralph Lauren polos, and Nautica trousers – Roy and Daphne lived in a modest two-bedroom house. The property was built in the nineteen hundreds, and featured oak beams across the ceiling, tiled flooring from a local stonemason, and a brick fireplace. In the living room were two sofas, facing a small television in the corner of the room. Along the walls were several model aircraft perched on shelves, and photographs of Roy and Daphne throughout the years; photographs of them in different countries, with the year and location engraved in the picture frames. Tomek quickly counted fourteen. Fourteen countries that he'd only dreamt of going to. Mauritius. Bali. Thailand. Australia. New Zealand. And several more. And that was just in the living room; there had been dozens more in the hallway, stairs, and in the kitchen. Sitting alongside them, above the fireplace, were various artefacts and relics from each country that they'd brought back with them. Most interesting was a small wooden instrument in the shape of a maraca that had been painted with red, yellow, and white spots. Beneath it was a small plaque that read, *South Africa, 2003*.

Tomek was in the middle of staring at it when a tea was placed into his hands. He thanked Daphne, then took a quick, polite sip as Daphne returned to her seat and placed a hand on her husband's knee. From left to right were Rose, Roy, Daphne, and their son, Johnny, all wedged into the same four-seater sofa. On the end, Johnny sat tilted forward, elbows resting on his knees, hands clasped together, his left knee bouncing repeatedly, eyes fixed firmly on Tomek. It was clear to see from his pained expression, his narrow eyes and his pursed lips, that he was fighting back the tears. That he already knew what was coming. Seeing the family members sitting next to one another, Tomek wouldn't have said that they were related. There was no resemblance between Johnny and either of his parents. The man was physically much larger than his father, with broader shoulders, thicker tree trunks for legs, and more defined muscles. His nose was thinner, ears slightly pressed against his head, and his skull was an oval shape compared to Roy's and Daphne's circular skulls. Not to mention Johnny's balding hair that must have skipped Roy's generation. On the whole, Johnny Whitaker was blessed with the good looks that his father had never had. The same had applied to Angelica too.

'How was Dublin, Johnny?' Tomek asked, taking the man aback.

'Dublin?'

'Yes. Rose said you'd been away for work.'

'Ah, right.' He turned coy, nervous. 'It was... fine. Just a routine trip. Nothing too exciting.'

'Great.'

Now that little catch-up was over, Tomek cleared his throat and prepared himself to say the same thing he'd said hundreds of times over the years, the same words that never got any easier.

'I'm sorry to be the one to tell you this,' he started, his voice calm, neutral, 'but I thought it should come from me. This morning, a few hours ago, a body we believe to be your daughter was found in the middle of a church.'

The shrill cry left Roy Whitaker's mouth before Tomek could continue. He immediately began to sob and his head collapsed into his hands, his body shaking as the tears began to flow. Meanwhile, Johnny Whitaker leapt off the sofa and began pacing from side to side, hands clenched into fists, body tensed.

'No,' he said. 'No, no, no. She can't be dead. It ain't her. Can't be her.' Then he turned to Tomek and pointed an intimidating finger towards him. 'How d'you know it's 'er?'

'We don't definitively,' Tomek asked, his voice measured still.

'So maybe it ain't then?'

'Sir,' Anna said softly. 'We have reason to believe the victim in question is your sister. Now, her body's been taken away so we can conduct a post-mortem. And we are going to need someone to come down and identify the body for us. I understand this has come as a terrifying and painful shock to you all, but we will need to identify the body as quickly as possible so our investigation can continue.'

'Fuck no. I'm not going down there. I can't! Someone else'll have to do it!' Johnny yelled at the top of his lungs, as he crouched into a ball and began crying into his knees. Sensing her husband's obvious discomfort, Rose hurried towards him and consoled him with a hug. As she bent down to his side, he shoved her off and pushed her onto the stone floor. She quickly righted herself, and tentatively hovered beside her husband, failing to hide the embarrassed expression on her face. Next to her, on the sofa, Daphne had wrapped her arm around her husband and was rocking him back and forth like a baby.

'My angel girl,' Roy said between ragged breaths and behind the tears. 'How did... how did she look? Was she... was she... Did she suffer?'

'It's too early for us to say,' Tomek answered. 'The post-mortem will hopefully answer a lot of those questions.'

'How did she... how did she die?' Roy continued.

'Again, too early for us to say. The post-mortem will indicate that to us.'

'When is the post-mortem?' Daphne asked, her voice stronger, more held together.

'Tomorrow morning.'

Suddenly, Johnny stopped crying and stood, his back straight. 'Why've we gotta wait? Why so long?'

'It's just the time we've been given.'

'That's fucking bullshit! Why can't you do it straight away. I wanna know—'

Tomek rose from the sofa and stepped between Johnny and Anna. There wasn't much in it height wise, and they were both of a similar build, but Tomek had put his to more use, and was more than prepared to intervene if necessary.

'Listen,' he said, 'I understand that you're upset. But we're just trying to do our job. We want to find the person who did this to your sister as much as you do, okay?'

'I'll kill 'em! I'll fucking kill 'em!'

The movement was so sudden, so quick, there was no time for Tomek to react or even flinch. In a flash, Johnny had grabbed the nearest picture frame from the wall, yanked it from its hook, and launched it over Anna's head into the dining table. The glass smashed onto the surface, scattering across the floor. By the time Tomek had finally reacted, the man had picked up the South African musical instrument and had hurled it across the room in the same direction. Tomek grabbed the man's hands and held him back. Rose joined his side, and placed a hand on her husband's face, forcing him to look into her eyes. They held each other's stare for a fraction of a second – seemingly enough to communicate what needed to be said – and then she pulled him out of the living room and into the kitchen, slamming the door shut behind them.

'I'm sorry about him...' Daphne started, her voice softer than before. 'He's always... he's always had a temper.'

'It's fine. It's nothing we're not used to.'

'You're just trying to do your job.'

Tomek appreciated the sentiment with a soft smile and returned to his seat, reaching for his mug. For a long moment, he held it to his lips. The sound of arguing and sobbing and wailing filtered through from the kitchen, echoed by Roy's sobs right in front of them.

Meanwhile, Daphne's expression had become blank, vacant. She was lost in deep thought, staring at the place on the wall where the picture frame and instrument had just been. When she spoke, it took him by surprise.

'Where did you find her body, Detective?'

'Park Road Methodist Church,' Tomek answered.

Roy pulled himself out of Daphne's arms and they looked at one another.

'Park Road?'

'Do you know it?'

'It's... it's where the kids were christened,' Daphne explained. 'We were some of the last people to use it before they ran out of funding.'

Tomek made a mental note.

'Do you think the killer might have known that?' Daphne asked.

'Possibly,' Tomek said, though he decided not to add what he was really thinking: Either that, or the killer found an abandoned building by luck and used it as his art studio.

Daphne must have read the expression on his face, because she said, 'You haven't told us how you found her, Detective.'

Tomek swallowed deeply before responding.

'Are you sure you want to hear it?'

Daphne and Roy shared a glance before nodding simultaneously.

'She was naked,' he explained. 'Lying on her back, in the middle of the church. Around her body, wings had been painted in what we think was her blood. There were no obvious physical wounds or lacerations to her body, so we don't think she suffered. But what I can tell you is that we will do everything in our power to find who did this to your daughter, and Anna here will keep you updated with everything that comes in, when it comes in.'

Tomek gave Angelica's parents time to embrace one another, to be with one another in this moment where their lives had just become fractured, torn apart.

It was a while before anyone spoke. In the end, it was Roy who did. His face was flushed red, his eyes bloodshot, dribbles of snot hanging from his nose.

'I can't believe it,' he said. 'My darling angel baby girl. I can't believe she's gone.'

CHAPTER EIGHTEEN

Anna had buckled beneath the Whitakers' pressure and arranged for them to identify Angelica's body as soon as was practically possible. Almost four hours after their original meeting, and nearly ten hours in total since the body had first been found, Angelica had been moved from the church to the mortuary at Southend Hospital. Right now, Anna was down there with them, confirming Angelica's identity ahead of her post-mortem in the morning. Meanwhile, Tomek was in the major incident room with Chey, Rachel, and DC Oscar Perez, or Captain Actually, as he was more affectionately known. Since the investigation's upgrade to murder, Tomek had been allowed to draft in an extra member of the team, and so the number had increased from two to three. It was still a ridiculously low number for a murder investigation, but Tomek was confident he had the best people for the job.

They had locked themselves in the MIR for the past thirty minutes, leaving a note on the door saying that they weren't to be disturbed. A neighbour of Angelica's – someone who lived farther up the road – had sent in a handful of home security footage from their front door. It included footage from the night of her disappearance, but Chey had also requested the days prior to it, in case they noticed someone hovering around Angelica Whitaker's flat before she'd gone missing. First, they had started with the night of her disappearance, right at the time she'd left the house to go to the club. She had appeared on the camera screen at 10:30 pm, walking towards a taxi and climbing inside. Since then, all they'd watched was a handful of cars driving back and forth, and the odd outdoor cat strolling in front of the lens. Now they were up to 1:28 am, the time she was due back from the club.

She arrived a few seconds later. The image on the screen was black and white and heavily pixelated, which made it difficult to discern certain features – in particular the make and model of passing vehicles – but there was no confusing the cab that had dropped all the girls off, and there was no doubting that one of the passengers had been Angelica Whitaker. After sliding precariously out of the minicab, stumbling on her high heels and lowering her skirt to a more comfortable length, she kissed her girlfriends goodbye, shut the door, and then waved as the car had turned in the road and driven off. Then, once the car had disappeared out of shot, she stayed there, still waving, still watching, as if frozen.

For a moment, Tomek wondered whether she would either turn left or right – left towards her home or right towards her death. A second later, she turned left, sauntering drunkenly towards her house.

And then the footage went silent for a while. Nothing, save the odd leaf blowing or a fox trotting past. Tomek always found there was something eerie about looking at a still image on the CCTV. His brain knew there was nothing there, but because he knew it was a video, his mind played tricks on him and made him believe that something was going to jump out and attack him, like a scene from *Paranormal Activity*.

Tomek glanced at the timestamp on the screen. It said 01:51. One minute until her phone disconnected from the cell towers. Less than thirty seconds later, a car emerged from the main road, its LED headlights blinding the security camera and distorting their view of the vehicle. Tomek ordered Chey to pause the footage. He climbed out of his chair and moved closer to the monitor to inspect the vehicle. The lights were too bright, and it was shielded by other cars on the road. That, and the fact the footage's clarity was as grainy as something from the eighties meant it was impossible to identify the car.

Tomek told Chey to resume the playback.

Then, ten seconds later, with the car parked up on the side of the road, a figure emerged. Angelica. Dressed in what looked like the same outfit she'd been wearing only twenty minutes before. She skipped towards the car, climbed in, and then drove off, unknowingly heading towards her death.

CHAPTER NINETEEN

Tomek was certain Angelica Whitaker had climbed into the car because it was someone she had known. Someone she'd trusted.

Shortly after seeing the footage, he'd asked Chey and Martin to call round to the local taxi companies to see if they'd received any requests for a pickup at Angelica's house, but none of them had reported receiving any such calls. Then he'd asked them to put in a request with Uber for the same information. But he was doubtful. There was something about the way she'd skipped towards the car, with a spring in her step, and just climbed into the front seat without hesitation. There was none of that "Pick up for Angelica?" nonsense that came with getting into a taxi, that brief pause when you spoke with the driver to make sure he was in the right place. No, this was someone she'd known. Someone she was expecting.

And who else fit that brief better than an ex-boyfriend?

Tomek knocked on the door to Sammy Mercer's home and waited. A few moments later, the front door opened, and he was greeted by a woman in her late fifties, sporting a bobbed haircut with a pair of thick glasses pressed closely against her face. She looked at him, confused.

'Yes?' she asked, hesitation and caution lacing her tone.

Tomek took a step back to allay her incipient fear, then removed his warrant card from his pocket. 'I wonder if I'm in the right place. Does Sammy live here?'

'Sammy?'

'Yes. Sammy Mercer. I was wondering if I could speak with him.'

'Sammy? The *police*? What do you want with Sammy?'

'It's regarding Angelica Whitaker...'

The woman's face brightened at the mention of Angelica's name. 'Oh, Angie. I do miss her... and Sammy was never the same after they split up. But... but is she okay? Is everything all right?'

Tomek didn't have time for this.

'Is Sammy home? I really need to speak to him.'

'Oh. Yes. Right. Okay. Yes, he's in.'

As she called out her son's name, she pushed the door to, as though trying to stop Tomek from hearing. A moment later, a deep voice called from somewhere in the house.

'He's just on his way,' Sammy's mother said, but made no gesture to invite him into her home. They waited awkwardly, staring at each other, Tomek waiting to be let in.

When the invitation didn't come, he asked, 'Is it all right if I speak with Sammy inside? This is important.'

'All right, Mum, what's—'

Sammy jumped down from the bottom step and came into view. Attached to his head was a pair of gaming headphones connected to a PlayStation controller in his hand. Here was a man in his early thirties, wearing tracksuit bottoms and a T-shirt, who still lived with his parents and played video games. Tomek imagined the man had multicoloured LED lights flashing above his computer screen and behind his headboard, and a wall of Pokémon toys and cards taking pride of place on a bookshelf.

'Sammy, this is the police.'

'Hi.' Tomek smiled, giving a little wave.

He didn't wait for a response, nor did he wait for an invitation, he stepped into the cramped doorway and gestured towards another room inside the house. 'Shall we?'

'Mum, what's this about?'

'I don't know, darling. Why don't you do what the man says and we'll discuss it together.'

Tomek was reluctant to speak with Sammy with his mum present, but decided it would be the path of least resistance, and so he conceded. They moved into the kitchen, where Tomek rested against the counter beside the stove, and pulled out his notebook, crossing one leg over the other.

'Is it Sammy or Sam?'

'Sam's fine.'

The man lifted his chest, but there was no amount of puffing that meant Tomek would take him seriously, not while he still had the headphones on his head.

'I'll keep this short and sweet,' Tomek began. 'I'm here to ask you a few questions about your relationship with Angelica Whitaker.'

''Lica? Why? What's happened to her? She's not been saying stuff, has she?'

'What stuff would that be?'

'Just... stuff.'

'Care to elaborate?'

'Not until I know what you're asking about.'

'It's come to our attention that you were in a relationship together?'

'Yes...'

'How long for?'

'About six months.' The caution in Sammy's tone was abundant.

'Can you remember when it started? What month?'

Contemplation. 'March last year.'

'And six months would take you to September last year?'

'When she got back from the end of her season, yeah.'

'So she was with you throughout the season, when she was jetting around the world?'

'Yeah.'

'Did you see much of her during that period?'

'We tried. She came over once or twice. But in the end it was difficult.'

'I'm not surprised. Who ended it?'

'She did. Said that we were in different places, that I weren't *mature* enough.' He wagged the remote control in the air as he said it, making it difficult for Tomek to disagree with her.

'Of course,' he said, keeping some of the sarcasm in his tone. 'And how did you take it?'

'Not very well, did you, Sammy?' weighed in his mum, as she placed a hand on her son's back. 'Poor Sammy was stuck in his bedroom for ages. Didn't want to come out, did you?'

'*Mum*... he's come to see *me*, not you.'

'Right. Sorry, darling. You tell the detective, sweetheart.'

Sammy shot his overbearing mum an admonishing glare before turning back to Tomek. 'I... I really liked her. I thought she was the one, but I guess it wasn't to be. I'd talked to her about moving out and maybe moving in with her, picking up my life and moving closer to her. I was willing to do whatever it took to make it work, but she didn't want any of that.'

'She told you?'

'Well, no, not exactly...' Sammy set the controller down on the counter and removed his headphones. 'But I guess that's what she meant when she said we were in different places, we wanted different things.'

Tomek understood her reasons for breaking up with him, and part of him thought there was more to it than just a simple trajectory problem – a lot more. Perhaps it had been his immaturity, or the fact he had an overbearing mum who still hadn't pulled her hand from his back.

But what he was struggling to understand was how the two had got together in the first place.

'How did you first meet?' Tomek asked.

'On a night out. At a bar in Leigh. We got talking by accident, and then she eventually let me have her number. We spoke a couple of times after that and then I asked her out on a date. The rest just sort of went from there.'

Tomek nodded. Nothing out of the ordinary. A fairly standard, if not archaic, way of meeting people. Nowadays it all seemed to be online, with the likes of Tinder, Bumble, Plenty of Fish – and loads of other randomly named apps that were the benchmark for creating relationships in the twenty-first century.

'When was the last time you spoke to Angelica?' Tomek asked, taking a sudden change in direction.

So far, Sammy had been more than accommodating in answering his questions, despite his earlier protestations, but now he seized up, placing a hand on his controller again, as though it was his safety blanket. Either that or he was going to use the end to strike Tomek over the head. In which case, Tomek wanted to witness that. He could do with a laugh.

'A while ago,' he said, cagey.

'Could you be more specific?'

He turned his head to the side, keeping his eyes fixed on Tomek's. 'Why do you wanna know?'

'Because she was found dead this morning. We're conducting witness and character interviews as part of our routine enquiries. As her most recent boyfriend, we've come to hopefully exclude you from our investigation.'

Sammy dropped the controller onto the counter. His mum reached around him and embraced him, sobbing for some reason; sobbing over the woman she'd met a handful of times. Meanwhile, Sammy's face was blank, expressionless, looking like he'd just been asked to complete a sudoku for the first time.

'She's dead?' he repeated, his voice weak.

'Sadly, yes.'

'When? How?'

Tomek gave him the boilerplate answers. That they were still looking into it, that they couldn't say too much while the investigation was still ongoing.

'I can't believe it,' Sammy continued. 'I... it was only a couple of weeks ago when I last spoke to her.'

'You did? What did you talk about?'

'Well... maybe that was wrong of me to say. Let me rephrase. I messaged her, asking how she was and if she wanted to catch up or meet at all, but she didn't reply. She ghosted me.'

That was a new term Tomek was going to have to get used to. Good thing he'd heard it from someone else without having to embarrass both himself and Kasia by asking her.

'When was the last time you heard from Angelica?'

Sammy reached into his trouser pocket and pulled out his phone. He unlocked the device and scrolled through his messages with his ex-girlfriend.

'The last time she replied was December, just to say Merry Christmas.'

'Right. And how many times had you tried to make contact with her?'

Sammy made a quick count. 'Twenty,' he replied candidly, without any hint of embarrassment or shame in his voice. Twenty times in less than three months. Tomek didn't think he'd messaged Abigail that many times and they'd known each other for years. Now he understood what Elodie Locket had meant when she'd said that Sammy had taken the break up poorly.

'When was the last time you saw her in person?' Tomek asked.

'When we broke up. At least she had the dignity to do it to my face rather than over the phone. I don't think I could have handled that. Afterwards, I tried going to some of the places that I knew she went to, some of her usual haunts, but she was never there. I wanted to bump into her, maybe have a chat, see if we could get things off the ground again, but I think she'd started hanging out with new crowds because I never saw her anywhere.'

Probably because she was trying to avoid you, Tomek thought. Nor could he blame her. He would have done the same had someone like Sammy been in his life. The man should have concerned him, but he didn't. He didn't get the impression that the man was a killer. In a video game, yes. But in real life, with a woman he lusted over and wanted to make a relationship work with? Tomek wasn't so sure.

But it wasn't definitive. He'd been wrong in the past and was prepared to admit he could be wrong again. Until he asked the last question he had for Sammy.

'What were you doing two nights ago?'

'I was online, with some of my mates.'

'At two am?'

'Hmm. By that point, I was probably asleep.'

'You didn't drive to her house at all?'

'No.'

'She was seen leaving her house at just before two in the morning. It's the last time she was seen alive.'

He shrugged. 'Couldn't have been me.'

'No?'

'No, mate. I can't drive.'

CHAPTER TWENTY

Tomek pulled the car to a stop and switched off the ignition. Rain gently pattered against the windscreen. He let out a deep, heavy sigh. The hairs on the back of his neck were raised. Not from the soothing sound of the rain hitting the metal tin encompassing him, but because he was angry, frustrated. Something along the drive from the office, somewhere along the route he'd done so many times, had reminded him of the letter he'd received from Nathan Burrows.

Did Dawid ever tell you that he came to visit me once?

That his brother had visited Michał's killer and not said anything infuriated him.

It was many years ago now.

That he had kept it a secret all this time only compounded his disgust.

We talked, we discussed.

That Dawid potentially knew things Tomek didn't made him want to throttle his older brother. And not stop until someone forced him to.

Ever since Michał's death, the two of them had grown apart, distant. They had never truly been close beforehand, but their middle brother's murder had worsened the divide between them. It was no secret that everyone in Tomek's family harboured some sort of resentment towards him for the hurt and anguish he'd caused them over the years. Dawid's resentment had been muted, silent, but no less profound. His brother hadn't looked out for him on the playground, hadn't helped him with his homework, hadn't been there to support him like an older brother should growing up. Instead, he'd looked after number one, becoming the only shining light in their parents' eyes, and he'd lapped it up. Now he was a highly successful, highly paid insurance broker with a family – and secrets – of his own. Tomek couldn't remember the last time he'd spoken to Dawid. But something told him he was going to remember this conversation.

Looking down into his lap, he pulled out his phone from his pocket and found Dawid's number in his address book. As the phone trilled in his ear, he surveyed the street, his eyes gradually falling on the flat living room window. The lights were on, curtains still not yet drawn. Kasia had been home for hours, yet it was always the last thing she remembered to do.

'Hello, Mr Tumnus,' Dawid said suddenly in his ear. His accent was thicker than Tomek's, only because he was older and had found the transition from Polish to English much more difficult. 'This is a nice surprise. Is everything all right?'

'You tell me.'

A brief pause. Tomek heard the sound of a door shutting.

'What's happened?' Dawid asked. 'Is something wrong?'

'You tell me.'

'I would if I knew what you were fucking talking about, mate.'

'Nathan Burrows.'

Another brief pause. This time followed by the sound of footsteps. 'I'm familiar with the name. What's happened?'

'I bet you're fucking familiar,' Tomek said, feeling his body begin to swell with rage and aggression. 'I heard from him the other day. Found out that the two of you had had a little mothers' meeting a few years back, a little picnic where you spilled each other's secrets. How long were you going to keep that from me, huh? How long were you going to keep that a secret, eh?'

'Tomek, I can—'

'How come you didn't have the bollocks to say anything?'

'Tomek, I—'

'You know what you are? You're a coward. After everything that's—'

'Tomek!'

His brother's shout caused him to stop. It was so loud, Tomek removed the phone from the side of his face. He had never heard his brother raise his voice like that. He was usually calm, genteel. Not one to shout or get in your face.

'Would you just shut the fuck up for one moment?' Dawid hissed. 'I swear you sometimes love the sound of your own fucking voice, don't you? Jesus Christ, mate. Have you finished?'

Tomek said nothing.

'Good. Now, if you'll let me, I'd like to explain.'

Tomek opened his mouth to say something, but stopped himself.

'You're right, yes, I did go to see Nathan. But it was years ago. Four, maybe five. A long time ago. So long that I'd even forgotten about it. I don't know what possessed me to do it, and I don't know what made me keep it from everyone. I haven't even told Kristina, if it's any consolation.'

'It's not, but continue.'

Dawid sighed through the phone. 'What do you want to know?'

'What the two of you discussed.'

'I... I just had some questions.' A pause. 'I wanted to know *why*. The question had been burning a hole in the side of my head for decades, and I just had to know.'

'Did he tell you?'

'No.' Tomek could hear his brother shaking his head at the same time.

'What did he say?'

'Just that he was sorry. That he had been sorry for all these years. He said he wanted to make peace with us as a family, but I said that wouldn't be possible, not while Mum and Dad were still around.'

Something in the flat window flashed and distracted him. It was Kasia, finally shutting the curtains with a forceful swing.

'Did my name come up at all?' he asked.

'It did.'

'And?'

'He said he felt sorry for you.'

'Sorry for me? Why?'

'Because you were the one to see it. He had no idea that you were going to be there. He said he knows how much hurt and suffering he's caused you because he's been going through the same thing.'

Tomek didn't know what to say, didn't know how to respond. These were all things that Nathan had neglected to mention to him, things that he'd been too proud to say.

'Did you ask if there was anyone else with him when he killed Michał?' Tomek asked.

'Tomek...'

'Just answer the question.'

'He said he was alone. That nobody was there.'

Even though it was what Tomek had been expecting, it didn't stop it from hurting any less. And from the intonation in his brother's voice, Tomek got the impression that Dawid believed Nathan. It was just another battering ram into the defences that Tomek had built up for so long.

'I'm sorry, mate,' Dawid said, sincerity lacing his words.

Tomek caught the lump in his throat and cleared it. 'Why didn't you say anything?'

'Because I knew how you'd react.'

'Am I reacting the way you expected now?'

Dawid considered a beat. 'Well, I mean, at first you did – you wouldn't let me speak. But now... now, no, which makes me think a part of you's come to the same conclusion.'

Tomek didn't respond.

'I should have come clean,' Dawid continued. 'I should have said something sooner. But, look, nobody's perfect. I hold my hands up and admit that I fucked up. And for that, I'm sorry.'

'And so you should be.'

Tomek hung up the phone without waiting for a response, then headed towards the flat.

CHAPTER TWENTY-ONE

The water is warm against my body – our body. We're cocooned in the tub together, like two caterpillars entwined in one another. Angelica's resting on me, between my legs. Our bodies have become one. Her head rests heavily against my shoulders, the full weight of it dangling over me. I like the pressure it brings. It feels comforting, like she is the one protecting me. My darling angel.

On the side of the tub is a bar of cinnamon-infused Aleppo soap, one of the kindest soaps for the skin. Only the best for Angelica. The slab is big in my hands, but I don't expect there to be anything left at the end of tonight. I expect it all to be gone, rubbed gently yet thoroughly into her skin. First, I bring the shower head over her body and douse the top of her in a thin layer of water. Now, with her skin moistened, I begin massaging the soap into her. Starting with her shoulders, running it over the bone, gliding across her skin, all the way down to her arms, her hands, her fingers, where I scrub the suds and bubbles beneath her nails. Every part of her, every inch of her body needs to be cleaned. She must look angelic, perfect.

When I've finished with the arms, I move towards the breasts, my hands kneading them like dough, playing with them a little, running my fingers over her nipples, titillating myself in the process. I suppress the urge to climb atop her and suckle on them, chew on them with my teeth.

I can't. I've had my time for that. I mustn't be greedy. Mustn't spoil the cleaning process.

But it soon becomes difficult to complete it like this, with her atop me. I must get out of the bathtub and continue my work from outside, much as I don't want to.

Now I have a better view of her lying in the water, perfectly still, eyes closed, her body floating. This time there's no rise and fall of her chest, no pulsating of the veins in her neck, no movement beneath her eyelids. She is perfectly still. All mine. She has given herself fully to me, after all this time. Finally.

The next part of the cleaning process proves tricky. I have to keep one foot in the water while I do the rest of her body, massaging the contours of her limbs and muscles with the soap, rubbing it deep into her pores. When I get to her vagina, I reposition myself and her so that her legs are spread. It's awkward, but I make it work. For this part, I put a glove on and go in deep; the soap bubbling away inside her.

But the real fun is with her toes. Her little piggies. Her cute little piggies that slip and slide in my fingers like little sausages. I suckle on them, tasting them, licking them before cleaning them again. She has the most perfect feet, and I can't wait to paint them, to dress them up as perfectly as they deserve. She's going to look so beautiful for when they find her.

If they find her.

My darling angel Angelica.

CHAPTER TWENTY-TWO

Before nine o'clock the following morning, Lorna Dean, the Home Office pathologist, had completed Angelica Whitaker's post-mortem. But it wasn't until several hours later that Tomek and the team received the results.

'You didn't have to come all this way,' Tomek said as he took them from her.

'It's because I missed your face, obviously. I just can't get you out of my head.'

Tomek froze as he held the papers in his hand, staring into her eyes, his mind completely blank. A second later, Lorna burst into laughter, slapping him on the arm, unable to control herself.

'I don't think I've ever seen you so scared in my life,' she said. 'And I never had you down for someone so gullible, either.'

'Funny. There's a comedy show down at the Cliffs tonight. Are you performing? Think I saw your mugshot on the billboard down there.'

'Sadly, I'm fully booked,' she said.

Tomek unfolded the documents, and as he began to read, Lorna placed her hand over the notes.

'Part of the reason I came down is because I wanted to discuss my findings with you in person,' she explained.

'And the other reason?'

She didn't answer.

'I'll grab the team,' he said awkwardly, then left the room to save his blushes as much as her own. A few minutes later, the five of them were in the major incident room, looking up at Lorna expectantly. Tomek had no idea what was coming, but it had been all he could think about since finding the body. Wondering what the killer had done to it. How she'd died. Why she looked so malnourished and... empty. He was looking forward to hearing the answers.

Lorna was sitting at the other end of the table, like she was being interviewed. She cleared her throat before beginning. She spoke without the need for notes or commentary, as though she'd rehearsed it beforehand.

'Firstly, I want to cover the cause of death, as I know that's what you're all itching to understand, and then I'll cover some of the weirder, more peculiar points about this victim. Though, by the way, I must preface what I'm about to say with the following: you might want to keep some of the information about Angelica's death away from the family. As a mother myself, I don't think I'd want to know everything I now do about what happened to her.'

The atmosphere in the room cooled as everyone took a moment to heed her warning.

She continued: 'As I said, first, her cause of death. At first I thought it was alcohol or blood related. I thought she'd maybe drunk too much, been drugged, or had some sort of embolism, but there was nothing of the sort. It stumped me for a good hour, and it wasn't until I rolled her onto her front that I saw it.' Lorna wagged her hand in the air at Tomek to pass the manila folder she'd given him. He slid it across the surface and she caught it with the palm of her hand, her nails clicking on the table. She removed all the sheets and laid them out in front of her. Then she picked up one and handed it to the person nearest.

Oscar took it gently and inspected it. Then he passed it round until eventually it reached Tomek. At first he didn't know quite what he was looking at, and even after being told to rotate the page one-eighty, he still didn't know what it was an image of.

'Looks like a leg,' he said.

'That's because it *is* a leg,' Lorna responded. 'More precisely, it's the *back* of Angelica's right leg. What you're looking at there is the crease in her knee. Notice all the lines and indents where the joints meet?'

Tomek had no clue. And no matter how many times he tried looking at it from different angles, he still had no idea which way was up. It was like looking at a sonogram for the first time and confusing it with a Rorschach test.

'Ten points if you can see the wound.'

Tomek set the photograph on the table in the hope that the light above might miraculously cause the wound to appear like it was in invisible ink. But there was nothing. No puncture wound, no stab mark, no bullet hole. Nothing to suggest that there was a wound there at all.

'Are you having us on?' he asked, sliding the picture across the table in frustration.

'I wish. But no.' Lorna reached for it, then held it up to them and pointed to a small black dot on the back of Angelica's knee.

'That's a mole, isn't it?' Rachel asked.

'That's what I thought at first. That's why I didn't give it much of a second thought. But when I ran my finger over it, I noticed it was a hole.'

'A *hole?*' Rachel repeated.

'Yes, a hole, not a mole.'

'Like that TV show!' Chey said excitedly.

His excitement was met with muted, confused stares.

'You know the one. Is it cake or real food? Where people make cakes to mimic real-life objects.'

Tomek looked at him, deeply unimpressed. 'You watch that shit?'

'You don't?'

'I'd rather eat through a straw for the rest of my life.'

Before the conversation could descend further away from the point, Lorna knocked on the table, summoning their attention. 'Guys, we're getting distracted, all right. I get it, you're excited about this "is it a hole, is it a mole" thing, but on this particular occasion, I can tell you unequivocally that it's a hole. Now, can we move on?'

Tomek sighed. 'Yes.'

'Excellent. Would you like to know what the hole is for?'

'This isn't a trick question, is it, like we got asked in sex ed at school?'

'No. It's a real question. The hole was caused by a needle.'

'Right.'

'And then a tube.'

'A *tube?*'

'Correct. But not like the ones you find underground in London. This one was a plastic one. One you might get in hospital. A surgical tube.'

'Okay...' Tomek was lost. 'And what has that got to do with Angelica's cause of death?'

To answer his question, Lorna pulled out another photograph. This time it was of the angel wings that had been painted on the floor of the church. Everyone else immediately made the leap, the connection, but Tomek was still a few seconds behind.

'The killer drained the blood from her body and used it to paint her angel wings,' Lorna said, giving him a helping hand. 'By my estimations, they must have drained over three litres of blood. Maybe four. That's what killed her.'

That explained why she'd looked so emaciated, so... skinny.

'How?' Tomek asked.

'Gravity and a heartbeat, I assume. My guess is that she was still alive when it happened, though she would have been unconscious, and so her heart continued to pump blood through her body and out of the tube, and then when the blood levels became too low, she passed away. All the killer had to do was wait.'

'How long might something like that take?'

Lorna shrugged. 'No idea. But judging by the size of the hole, and the vodka Red Bulls pumping blood around her body, I'd say it would have taken about forty minutes, maybe an hour.'

Tomek turned to the portion of the whiteboard he'd written on the other day. He looked at the timeline so far.

01:28 – *Angelica arrives home*
    01:52 – *Angelica leaves, gets in car*
    09:00 – *Angelica supposed to start work*

NOW HE MENTALLY ADDED ANOTHER hour-long break in that timeline.

'So the killer must have driven her some place, knocked her unconscious or put her under somehow, and then spent an hour draining the blood from her body.'

'That's about right,' Lorna answered. 'But they would have needed an even longer time to complete the rest of what they did to Angelica's body.'

'*The rest?*'

Tomek wasn't sure he was prepared to hear the answer. When he'd first seen the body, he hadn't thought anything malicious or untoward had happened to Angelica. Then again, he hadn't thought that the killer had drained her body of its blood either, so what did he know?

'Post-mortem, Angelica's body was cleaned and shaved,' Lorna continued.

'Cleaned?' Tomek asked.

'Yes. Using Aleppo soap. Cinnamon-scented Aleppo soap.'

'How do you know?'

'I recognised the smell. It was still on her skin even after all that time.'

'And she was shaved too?'

'Yes. When I tell you this woman's skin was like a baby's bottom, I mean it. There was nothing left on her, not even the fine white hairs you get on your forearms and cheeks. It looked like she'd never grown a single hair in her life. It was like she'd just come out of the womb.'

In his mind, he conjured images of the killer bathing Angelica's body in water, rubbing a bar of soap into her skin, and then shaving her armpits, legs and pubic region, before taking the blade across the rest of her skin. The time, patience, and care required was what unsettled him.

'What else did they do to her?' Rachel asked, looking slightly uneasy in her chair.

'The killer also painted her finger- and toenails and applied a full face of make-up.'

'To make her look like an angel,' Tomek added.

'I said that, didn't I?' Rachel commented. 'I said to you it was probably some of the best make-up I've ever seen.'

'So the killer must have known how to do professional-looking make-up?' Tomek said.

'So it could be a woman?' Chey asked.

'Statistically, yes. There aren't many men I know that could do make-up that good,' Tomek answered.

'But there's one more thing you haven't heard yet,' Lorna interrupted, knocking on the table again with her knuckles.

'Which is?'

'That she was raped. Not aggressively or anything like that. But there were signs, just some slight bruising. And whoever it was was... well *endowed*, shall we say. Some of the bruising went deep. But what's more is that there was no evidence of it. No DNA. No ejaculate. My theory's that they used a condom and when they cleaned her body, they cleaned the inside of her as well. They left nothing.'

'Jesus,' Chey said softly, staring at the surface of the table. 'He drained her, raped her, cleaned her, shaved her, painted angel wings behind her... who the fuck is this guy?'

'Either someone totally infatuated with her or a sadistic fuck,' Rachel said, the venom from her tone leaking into the room.

'Quite...' Lorna added tentatively.

'That's not everything, is it?' Tomek asked. He could sense in Lorna's tone that there was more, and her expression confirmed his suspicions.

'This is the last of it, I promise.'
'Go on...'
'After I cut her open, I found something I wasn't expecting.'
'Right. What is it?'
'Well, she was pregnant. Had been for about three months. She was just one of the lucky ones who doesn't look it.'

CHAPTER TWENTY-THREE

Tomek wanted to be the one to tell the Whitaker family about what had happened to their daughter. Well, not *all* of it. There were some details, some pieces of information he thought best to keep from them, to save them the horror and grief of hearing it all. Instead he would keep it light.

Joining him was Anna. In the short time that Anna had been acquainted with the family, she'd reported that none of them had taken the news well: Johnny had claimed more priceless treasures from his parents' travels as his playthings; Roy had shut off completely and wasn't eating or drinking anything; and Daphne had spent the morning staring at old photographs of Angelica and Johnny playing in the garden.

'It's like watching a play,' Anna whispered as she opened the front door for him. 'And not a good one. Honestly.'

Tomek admired her Eastern European brashness. There was no colour to her speech. She said what she thought, dealing with black and white only.

He found the three family members in the living room, sitting on the sofa in the same order they had the day before. The only omission was Rose, who had her jewellery store to tend to. Had it not been for the change of outfits, Tomek would've thought that none of the Whitaker family had showered. Their faces were stressed, cheeks and eyes reddened from crying, their hair unkempt and messy. But what was more interesting was the dynamic between them. At first, Tomek had thought that Daphne was the one keeping the men of the family together, but now it was clear to see that had fallen apart completely; they were all sitting apart from one another, not a single inch of their bodies touching, as though they repulsed each other. In the past, he'd seen families behave in the exact opposite manner; holding hands, arms around one other, embracing each other, brave, warm, consoling. Except now the Whitaker family was cold, as though they were sitting in the middle of a therapy session rather than a meeting with a detective to hear the results of their dead daughter's post-mortem.

'Thank you for having me back in your home,' Tomek muttered. As he lowered himself onto the sofa, he noticed Johnny Whitaker's piercing stare, the dark brown eyes, burning holes into him.

'You don't need to say any of that,' the man retorted. 'Just... just get on with it.' He rocked himself backwards and forwards, massaging his knuckles, looking like he was ready for a fight.

Tomek turned to Anna, who gave him the nod of approval. There was nothing she wanted to add before he spoke.

'This morning the pathologist conducted the post-mortem on Angelica, and—'

'Yes, yes, yes. We know all that. Just... just tell us what you found out, for fuck's sake.'

'Johnny!' Daphne smacked him on the arm.

'Sorry... *Please*,' the son added defiantly, like a spoilt brat. 'Tell us what you found, *please*.'

After outburst from the petulant fuckwit, Tomek didn't want to. But that wasn't fair to Roy and Daphne who were sitting patiently. Their arsehole son shouldn't be the one to stop them from hearing the news.

'This morning, the pathologist sent me their report. I've been through it, and I've come to tell you that your daughter was killed by loss of blood. There was alcohol found in her blood, and we've sent samples away to see if there was anything else in there, though I'm fairly confident that she may have been spiked by someone in the club. Her blood was drained from her body, and we think it was used to paint the angel wings behind her. Now, there were some other anomalies that they found. For whatever reason, the killer bathed your daughter, cleaned her, shaved her, and applied a full face of make-up.'

'Shaved her?' Roy asked.

'Yes. Her arms, legs, armpits – everywhere.'

'She was always so self-conscious of her forearms,' Daphne added absent-mindedly, staring into the middle space, lost in her own thoughts.

Tomek opened his mouth to respond, but Roy beat him to it.

'Did you say they applied make-up to her as well?'

'Yes.'

'Why would they want to do that?'

'Maybe they wanted to make her look pretty, Dad,' Johnny snapped.

Tomek ignored the comment and continued. 'It seems whoever did this put a lot of time and care into "looking after" your daughter. We don't know why yet, but we hope to find out soon.'

Tomek looked at each family member, taking his time to observe them.

'I understand this is a lot for you to take in, but there's also something else you should know.'

'What?' Johnny hissed. In the last few moments, since Tomek had been watching him, Johnny had started to rub his hands more aggressively, massage his knuckles more violently. Tomek half expected the man to leap across the room and throttle him.

'Angelica was pregnant.'

At this point, the entire family's reaction changed. It was as though they could tolerate the news that she'd been cleaned, well looked after, but they drew the line at her pregnancy.

'She was *pregnant*?' Daphne asked.

'Are you sure?' Johnny asked.

'Yes. We're sure.'

'How far along was she?'

Just as Tomek opened his mouth, Roy blurted out the answer. 'About three months.'

Then the temperature plummeted in the room as Daphne and Johnny simultaneously sucked all the air out of it.

'Three months? What the fuck do you mean, three months?' said Johnny as he leapt off the sofa and brandished a finger at his dad.

'Roy, what're you talking about? Are you telling me you've known our daughter was pregnant, that she had been given the gift of life, and you didn't tell me, that you did nothing about it?'

Roy struggled off the sofa and placed a hand on his son's chest to keep him at bay.

'You're wrong. I *did* do something about it. I told her she wasn't keeping it. I said she needed to get rid of it.'

'Why would you do that?' Daphne asked, rising to his level by standing on the sofa, looking down at him with her arms placed on her hips.

'Because she's not ready for a kid. I didn't want her having it. No, not when it was out of wedlock.'

'So you forced her to get rid of it?'

'I just told her where I stood. We argued, then she ran away. I thought she was going to do the right thing, but evidently she didn't. I didn't give her the coat hanger, did I?'

'I bet you fucking had one in your hand though, didn't you, Dad? Not the first time, is it?' Johnny remarked.

Daphne turned to her son, then her husband.

'What's he talking about, Roy?'

'Nothing.'

'*Roy?*'

'Nothing.'

And then she slapped him hard across the cheek. She jumped down from the sofa and pointed her finger at him, holding it a few inches from his face. For someone so small and petite, she seemed to swell.

'What did you do?'

'Nothing. I...' He collapsed onto the sofa, dropping his head into his hands.

'He's done it before,' Johnny began. 'When Ange was eighteen she got pregnant, he found out, saw the pregnancy test in her room, and he took her to the doctor, made her get rid of it.'

The temperature dropped a few degrees further as Daphne inhaled deeply again. This time she raised her hand and brought it down on her husband, much harder, striking him across the face. The sound reverberated around the room. Tomek and Anna were first to react. They jumped off the sofa, Anna pulling Daphne away.

'I think everybody needs to calm down,' Tomek said. 'There are clearly some things you need to work through and discuss amongst yourselves, but one thing I think you all need to remember is that Angelica's dead. No matter what happened in the past, you need to have her at the forefront of your thoughts now. We need to find her killer, and we need your help to do so, but that won't be possible if you're slapping and hurting each other. Now, if we have to put you in separate corners like a bunch of fucking children, then we will. I didn't want to have to talk to you like that, but, well, you've made me.'

In an instant, the three family members' behaviour changed. They lowered their heads and dropped their voices, apologising softly as they returned to their positions on the sofa, Roy massaging his cheek, moving his jaw to make sure it was still attached.

'Thank you,' Tomek said with a heavy sigh.

'How is it that we can help you, Detective?' Daphne asked.

Tomek perched himself on the edge of the sofa, lest they kick off again.

'For starters, I wondered if you knew the names of any former romantic partners Angelica might have had.'

CHAPTER TWENTY-FOUR

The first name that had come out of Angelica's family's mouths was Cole Thompson, who Angelica had been in an on-off-off-on relationship with for six months almost two years ago. There had been no mention of Sammy Mercer, no mention of the thirty-year-old gamer who still lived at home with his mum. Perhaps she had been too embarrassed to introduce him to them, hadn't wanted to show him off. Or perhaps she had simply used him for another purpose, like learning how to be good at *Call of Duty* or *Grand Theft Auto*. Tomek didn't know, but he thought it very telling. According to Daphne and Roy, Cole was the perfect suitor for her, and Daphne had always hoped that they might stay together, that he might one day become their son-in-law, and raise the family's status just as Rose had when she'd joined. They said he was kind, considerate, caring, and very, very, very funny – "do you remember that one time" Daphne had started before losing herself in a story about them all going out for a family meal at a classy restaurant. Tomek had let Daphne and Roy reminisce while he'd asked Johnny for his thoughts on the man. They had been condensed down to one word: legend. Tomek thought it was a bit much, considering he'd only known the man for a short while, but he hadn't wanted to impose. He had, however, enquired the reason they'd broken up.

'I don't know, actually,' Daphne had said. 'She didn't tell us much more than that they weren't going to see each other anymore. She didn't want to talk about it. And it's such a shame because he was so sweet, so nice. He was like a member of the family already.'

Echoes of Sammy Mercer's mum talking about her son rang in his ears as he pulled up outside Cole Thompson's house. The twenty-nine-year-old lived in a two-bedroom bungalow in Rayleigh, and as Tomek knocked on the door, he was greeted by a small, bald man carrying a rucksack over his shoulder.

'Mr Thompson?'

The man stopped just as his short leg made the long journey from the doorstep to the ground. He stood with one foot on the concrete and one still inside the building, his knee coming up to his chest.

'I'm *a* Mr Thompson, yes. The other one's at work.'

'Cole?'

'That's my son. The one at work. What's this about?'

Tomek showed his warrant card and explained he wanted to speak with the man's son.

'He's not done anything, has he?'

'Hopefully not. We've just got some questions we need to ask him regarding his relationship with Angelica Whitaker. Does that name mean anything to you?'

The man finally stepped out of the house and brought his other leg down. It was surprising how much shorter he was than Tomek. He repositioned his backpack on his shoulder in an attempt to make himself seem larger. 'Ange? Yeah, I remember her. Right stunner, she is. Dunno how he ever managed that one, but what's he got to do with her.'

Tomek ignored the question. 'Can you remember the last time you saw her?'

It didn't take long for the man to answer. 'The other week. Cole said she was coming round while his mum and I went out for dinner. We saw her when we got home.'

'The other week?'

The man nodded.

That was much more recent than the two years since the rest of the family had seen him.

'Might I get his work address, so I can speak with him?'

❄

COLE THOMPSON WORKED as a senior accountant for a small, chartered accountants on Rayleigh high street a short drive from his parents' bungalow. The office was above a Superdrug, and when Tomek found him, the man was at his desk. He was dressed in a loose-fitting shirt, undone at the collar, and a pair of smart trousers. In the room the air was cool, blasted by an air conditioning unit to one side, presumably to mask the smell of the five sweaty men in there.

Cole Thompson was a physically attractive man, with all the right characteristics for him to feature on a magazine front cover somewhere: perfectly manicured hair without a single strand out of place, a fantastic jawline that was sharp enough to cut cheese with, broad shoulders that filled his shirt and then some, and a pair of thick-rimmed glasses that seemed to accentuate his almost symmetrical face. Not to mention the smell of aftershave that wafted up Tomek's nose the moment he came across to him, helped along, of course, by the air conditioning. In many ways, he reminded Tomek of the estate agent who'd sold him his flat; the only difference was that Cole didn't have any Turkey Teeth on him – garish, fluorescent white teeth that had been done on the cheap by a so-called professional overseas.

'Cole?' Tomek said.

Cole approached with his hand outstretched. 'That's me. How you doing?'

'Good.'

'Great. How can we help? I don't recognise your face. Have you ever worked with us before?'

Tomek decided to indulge him. 'No, but I'm looking to. Do you have a private room we could sit in? I have business that I'd like to speak to you about.'

Face beaming, flashing a set of naturally straight teeth, Cole grabbed his laptop from his desk, led him into a small, equally chilly room, and pulled out a seat for Tomek.

'You won't be needing that,' Tomek said, pointing to the computer.

'No?'

Tomek tapped on the table patronisingly. 'Why don't you take a seat and let me tell you about the business I wanted to discuss with you. My name is Tomek Bowen, and I'm a detective sergeant from Essex Police. I didn't want to say too much out there in case your colleagues got curious.' Cole opened his mouth to speak, but Tomek shut him down. 'Don't worry, you're not in trouble, yet, but there's something you need to know. Yesterday, Angelica Whitaker's body was found in a church in Westcliff. It's come to our attention that you were once in a relationship with her for roughly six months. Though when I just spoke to your dad, he said that she'd come round the other week. Would you mind telling me about your relationship with Angelica?'

Cole's mouth remained open, strings of saliva dangling from the top of his mouth to the bottom. For a long while, he didn't say anything, just stared at Tomek, taking it all in, processing it.

'Take your time,' Tomek said. 'I imagine this is a shock.'

The man nodded, but his expression was vacant, thousands of miles away, hidden behind a barrier in his mind.

'She's... she's...'

Tomek said nothing. Waited for him to get the words out of his mouth properly.

'She's... she's dead. Angelica? And you're... you're sure it's her?'

Tomek nodded.

'And... you want to speak with me... but you've already spoken to my dad. And you want to speak with me...'

'We already are talking,' Tomek replied then added, 'Sort of.'

'Right. Yes... yes, we are. But, what... what...?'

Tomek sensed the man was going to have trouble with the final question, so decided to help him out. 'What do I want to speak to you about? Easy. I want to know everything about your relationship. When was the last time you saw her? How frequently you saw her. Where you were Friday night. That sort of thing.'

Cole's face remained expressionless, his mouth still open. However, the strand of saliva had now snapped and disappeared back into his mouth.

'Could I have a drink, please?' the man asked.

'A drink?'

'Water. I need water.'

Tomek swivelled in the chair and looked through the windows in the room, searching for a water fountain. When he couldn't see one, he climbed out of the chair, exited the room and asked the nearest colleague.

'Water?' the man asked, confused, as though he'd never heard of it before.

'Yeah. The liquid. We need some in there.'

The man tilted forward in his seat to look at Cole. 'I thought he would get it for you.'

Tomek turned to look at the man still sitting there, staring into nothing. 'He's just doing some really *deep* thinking in there at the moment. I offered to help while he processed some things.'

A moment later, he had two cups of water in hand and returned to the room. He set one down in front of Cole and returned to his seat. The man picked it up and slowly held it to his lips.

'You good?'

'Yeah,' Cole whispered. The intonation in his voice belied his choice of words.

'Excellent. Let's start with your relationship with Angelica, shall we? When did the two of you start dating?'

'Two years ago, roughly.'

'And how long were you going out for?'

'About six months.'

'Who ended it?'

'I did.'

'Why?'

'It... I, I, I wasn't interested in anything long term.'

'And she was all right with that?'

Finally, Cole closed his mouth and swallowed. As he spoke, he was unable to meet Tomek's gaze, and he continued to stare into the wall behind him, as though he were a sleeper agent who'd just been activated by a key phrase.

'She felt the same way,' he explained.

'So what happened after that? Why was she round yours the other week? Have the two of you tried to rekindle your relationship?'

'Sex.'

Cole said it so abruptly that Tomek thought the man was propositioning him.

'Sorry?'

'Sex. It's...' He trailed off, closed his eyes and shook his head. When he opened them again, he met Tomek's gaze for the first time. 'It was just sex. Has been for the past four or five months or so. She... she DM'd me at the end of summer, when she got back from her season, October time, and we've been sleeping together ever since, friends with benefits type of thing.'

Tomek was familiar with the term, just as he was familiar with the term Netflix and Chill, which involved neither Netflix nor the act of chilling.

'When was the last time you saw her? When your mum and dad went out, or more recently?'

Cole paused a beat. 'That was the last time, yeah. We were supposed to meet up the other night, but she cancelled 'cause she said she was going to a party.'

'Do you know which one and where?'

Cole shook his head, his pristine hair holding firm against the movement.

'And what were you doing three nights ago?'

'What night was that? Friday? I... I was out with this lot.' He pointed to the team outside the window. 'We were at the pub.'

'Which one?'

'Paul Pry. We went for a few after work. Bit of a tradition on a Friday. We usually stay till late, then regret it the next day.'

Tomek made a mental note.

'Speaking of regrets,' he said, 'it's also come to our attention that Angelica was pregnant. You didn't by any chance happen to know anything about that, did you?'

Cole scratched the back of his neck. 'She'd told me, yes. I knew. But... she didn't know whose it was. She didn't know if it was mine or someone else's.'

'Do you know who else it could have been?'

He shrugged. 'She didn't elaborate, and I was too stunned to ask. I just assumed it was mine. She would have got pregnant around Christmas, New Year time, and at that point she'd come over about four times. She was lonely. Got that seasonal depression thing, plus I think she'd just found out that they weren't keeping her on for this summer.'

'They weren't keeping her on?' Tomek repeated.

'Yeah. She got really upset about it. Devastated, I think she was. She said she just needed someone to keep her company.'

'Did you use protection?'

Cole nodded fervently, as though it was a given. 'Every time. Never go anywhere without one. Always got one in my wallet, just in case.'

Just in case. Tomek scoffed internally. Then took a sip of water. 'How did you take the news? What was your reaction?'

'I... At first I panicked. I didn't want her to keep it. I didn't want anything to do with it. I wasn't ready for that type of thing. But then, after a couple of days, I eventually came round and told her that I'd be there to support her. We didn't have to stay together or anything, but I just wanted to be a part of the kid's life. Now... now I guess I won't be able to.'

Very admirable, Tomek thought. It reminded him of his situation, where Kasia had been thrust upon his doorstep after her mother had been arrested for drug dealing. He hadn't had a choice, but Cole had, and he'd done the respectable thing by committing to the baby's future, even if it wasn't his. It was just a shame it had ended the way it had.

Tomek reached out a hand. Cole eyed it suspiciously, then shook it. They held each other's gaze, saying nothing, both men understanding the silent expressions on their faces.

'Thank you for your time,' he said, as he made to leave.

Tomek's hand was on the door handle when Cole told him to wait.

'Have you spoken to Shawn?'

Tomek released his grip.

'Shawn?'

'Yeah. Shawn Wilkins. Some guy who's been infatuated with Angelica since I can remember. Stalking her, commenting on her posts, sending her things. Sometimes took it too far. Think she had to get a restraining order against him at some point.'

'Shawn Wilkins – is that his name?'

'Yeah. Don't know much more about him though. But if you're looking for her killer, then he might be a good place to start.'

CHAPTER TWENTY-FIVE

Tomek would have liked to look into Shawn Wilkins, but on the drive back to the incident room, he'd received a phone call from Victoria, summoning him to her office. On the phone she had been blunt and to the point – no different to normal – but there had been a certain sense of urgency in her voice that he'd never heard before. And as soon as Tomek entered her small room on the second floor, he found out why. Waiting for him, standing by her side, was Nick Cleaves. The chief inspector was leaning against the wall, arms folded, head down, like he was in a 1950s gang or a character out of *West Side Story* ready to break into song and dance.

Neither looked excited to see him.

'Take a seat please, Tomek,' Victoria said, pointing to the chair as if he couldn't see it in front of him.

As he lowered himself into the seat, he was transported thirty years into the past. Two months had gone since his brother's death, and he'd been summoned to the head teacher's office for skipping science, his least favourite subject of all. One of the teachers had found him wandering through the corridors, running his fingers along the wall, scuffing the floors with his shoes. He'd been sentenced to a week in isolation where, with the help of some of his colleagues in there who were brave enough to create a diversion, he'd later escaped – an act that put him at risk of getting further isolation, or even expelled. Tomek had been a naughty kid following Michał's death. He'd struggled to stay focused and found he'd lost all interest in his education. But what had surprised him most was that he hadn't left the grounds. If he wanted to truant, to skip classes and embrace the freedom of running around Leigh-on-Sea while everyone else was at school, he could have done. But instead, he'd stayed on the school grounds, running through the corridors. *Hoping* to get caught. Crying out for attention, screaming for help. And when he'd sat in that headmaster's chair, he'd felt a sense of relief. It had worked. The punishment was all part of it. But now, as he sat there, holding Nick's imposing stare, he felt the complete opposite, filled with worry, a deep knot forming in his stomach.

'Welcome to your first meeting as SIO,' Nick said as he pushed himself from the wall. 'This is where the fun begins.'

Something told Tomek that wasn't true. The knot tightened.

'The usual format for this is that I ask Victoria the questions, and she has all the answers. Sometimes she knows the meeting's happening, sometimes she doesn't, but I expect her to know the answers all the same. Do you see what I'm saying?'

This was a completely different Nick to the one Tomek had known and dealt with for the past thirteen years. Sure, he'd been in confrontational meetings with the chief inspector in the past, but nothing like this. This was on a different level to anything he'd ever been used to. And now he was beginning to get a flavour of what it had been like for Victoria since she'd come in; his respect for her grew a few fractions.

'I see what you're saying, yes,' Tomek answered.

'Great, because if you do eventually become an inspector, then this is the sort of standard we will hold you to. Do you understand?'

Tomek swallowed deeply and dipped his head.

'Excellent. Victoria, he's all yours.'

Nick returned to the wall and folded his arms again. Clearing her throat, Victoria switched off the computer and looked down at some notes in front of her.

'What's the latest with Operation Butterfly?'

Tomek told them, starting with the discussions he'd had with Angelica's family, through to the post-mortem, all the way up to his meeting with Cole Thompson less than an hour before. They gave nothing away in their expressions, nodding gently as he spoke.

So far, so good. He hoped.

Then Victoria's intonation dropped a few levels. 'Where are you with your budget estimates?' she asked.

'Budget estimates?'

'Yes. How much of the money allocated to this investigation have you apportioned to the respective expenses?'

Tomek's face had never fallen faster. He opened his mouth, but it fell shut again.

'How much do you expect forensic analysis to cost? Do you anticipate you will be over budget or under?'

More opening and closing.

'Do you expect there to be a lot of overtime? I noticed the team were working till late last night, including yourself. Has that been agreed with the staff?'

Tomek opened and closed his eyes, hoping that the answers might materialise in front of him. But they didn't. Instead he was looking at two deeply unimpressed seniors, their disappointment growing with each unanswered question.

For a few moments, he didn't say anything. In fact, he wasn't even sure he was breathing. Time seemed to slow, and the world came to a gradual, steady halt. The sound of brakes screeching reverberated in his skull. A heavy weight descended on his chest, and he felt his pulse quicken.

'I... I don't know,' he said, his voice broken, coming out as a whisper.

'What don't you know?'

'Any... any of it,' he said. 'Neither Chey nor Rachel have come to me about overtime requests.'

'So they're working for free?'

'I...' He tried to think back to the last time Nick had discussed overtime with him and how the conversation had gone. He drew a blank. 'No. I'll... I'll make sure they're paid, but...'

'But what? How much is that going to cost us?'

Tomek said nothing, continuing to stare blankly at Victoria. Now he understood how Cole Thompson had felt: lost, empty, devoid of any comprehensive thought.

'I don't know.'

'And what about the cost for forensics? What tests have you done so far?'

'The... the...'

Come on, you know this!

'We did... we did...'

Fucking think!

'Angelica's body,' he said, stuttering. 'We sent some blood away for analysis. We... we want to see what's in her blood. And... and we're looking at fingerprints on the church door, and...' There was something else, something important, but it had slipped his mind entirely.

'What else are you going to need to analyse?'

'What else?'

'Yes. What else, based on your recent investigations, do you think you're going to need to send off?'

Tomek just shook his head. Instinctive, muscle memory. The best thing he could think to do.

Victoria sighed and looked at the piece of paper in front of her, the list of things she had left to grill him on.

'Moving on – your team's work ethic. How would you say it is so far? Any bottlenecks? Any causes for concern?'

Tomek had none, but was unable to articulate that in a cohesive response.

'Because I've noticed that Chey hasn't been pulling his weight,' she continued. 'While you were out this morning, I caught him several times on his phone. And looking at the action report on HOLMES, it's clear that he's got a lot of tasks still outstanding. What do you have to say to that? Are you giving him free rein or is it poor management on your behalf?'

Suddenly, something came over Tomek. He wasn't so bothered about the attack on *his* character; it was the one on Chey's that finally knocked some sense into him.

'That's not true. He's been doing loads of work for me.'

'Like what?'

'You can say all you want about me, but don't say anything about my team. If they're not working up to your standards, then that's on me. Nothing to do with him, Rachel, or anyone else. That's my responsibility as a leader, as SIO.'

Victoria pursed her lips, tilted her head to the side in a brief display of appreciation. 'Very well, but remember that shit rolls downhill, Tomek, and sometimes there's no way to stop it.'

Tomek didn't agree, though he chose not to say anything.

'Do you have anything you'd like to add?' Nick asked from the back of the room.

He shook his head.

'Excellent.' Nick pushed himself off the wall again. 'It's come to our attention that we've been receiving lots of requests from Abigail at the *Southend Echo*. There's been a lot of noise on social media about what's been happening with Operation Butterfly, and yet we've not released any statements. Have you discussed a media strategy with Anna yet?'

You couldn't fucking wait, could you, Abi?

'I... No, no, we haven't discussed anything yet. I will... I will have a word with Abigail about it.'

'You need to speak with Anna first,' Victoria said. 'You can't be the one to bridge the gap between Anna's job and Abigail's. That's not how it works.'

'I know, but—'

'Put the personal relationships aside and focus on what's good for the family and what's good for the investigation.'

The pressure on Tomek's chest increased. He was having his arse handed to him on a plate. He knew he wasn't coming out of this meeting with a gold star or anything. It was straight to isolation for him. And this time, he didn't feel any of the relief he'd felt all those years ago. There was no cry for help that had been answered. No hunger for attention that needed sating. In fact, it was the opposite. He wanted out; he wanted away from it all, away from the spotlight. To wander along Leigh-on-Sea seafront while the rest of his colleagues were tucked up in class.

'Lastly,' Nick continued, 'before we let you go for the evening: what's your current hypothesis?'

Straight to the point.

The vacant expression returned to Tomek's face. His mind turned blank.

'What direction are you leading the investigation, and why do you think that?' Nick persisted.

His mouth fell open, but still nothing came out.

Nick continued: 'Was Angelica Whitaker murdered by someone she knew, or was this a random killing?'

CHAPTER TWENTY-SIX

Tomek hadn't been prepared to answer the question in Victoria's office. Not yet. Despite the odds being fifty-fifty at face value, and the decision almost certain in his mind, it was the trajectory of the wrong decision that concerned him. If he made the incorrect choice, and it wasn't until they were a week, two, three down the line before they noticed, then there would inevitably be a shitstorm and a monumental amount of work to backtrack, reprocess, and reconduct themselves. They would almost have to start again, regroup, reconvene. And he wasn't prepared to fuck up that much on his first case. He wasn't willing to stake his claim just yet. Not on a case like this. As such, the decision weighed heavily on his shoulders, and he felt the pressure of it. While he was leaning towards one of the two options – that Angelica had known her killer – he wanted to keep as open a mind as possible.

Several hours later, after what had quickly become an afternoon heavily laden with budgets, forecasting, and pretending to read the team's daily reports, Tomek slotted the key into the lock and twisted. It was a little after six pm, one of the earlier nights he'd had in a while, and he found Kasia in the kitchen, unloading a baking tray from the oven.

'What's on the menu tonight?' he asked.

'Chicken nuggets and chips.'

Of course it was.

'Sounds delicious.'

'Yeah.'

Tomek hung his backpack on the back of the front door, dropped his keys in a small box inside a chest of drawers, and made his way to the dining table. In the kitchen, Kasia tipped the baking tray to one side and began decanting her food onto her plate. Just as he was about to make a comment, he noticed something on the table. Another envelope, the HMP Wakefield logo stamped on the top right. Tomek's name scribbled in barely legible handwriting.

Another letter from Nathan.

'Hey, I was thinking of going to see Yasmin at the weekend, but—' Kasia started, but Tomek ignored her.

He grunted something, not entirely sure what, then headed to his bedroom. He closed the door gently behind him, unable to take his eyes off the document. He weighed it in his hands, wondering whether it was heavier or lighter than the last. Heavier. Definitely heavier. He raised it to his nose, sniffing, waiting for his senses to find anything untoward rubbed into the envelope. Nothing.

The first time he'd received a letter, he'd been gripped with fear and dread, a pang of nausea tearing through his body as he'd read it. The second letter had been a similar sort of affair. But now, for this one, strangely, he felt a scintilla of excitement, a lust to know what was inside. Like he was twelve again, receiving his first letter from his pen pal in Africa.

Perching himself on the end of the bed, he shut out all noise (he could hear Kasia's knife and fork clinking on the plate) and turned the envelope over. This time, the back had been sealed with tape. Perhaps that was why it felt heavier. Or there was something inside... something Nathan had included that he wanted Tomek to see.

Wedging his thumb in the fold, Tomek ripped through the envelope and dropped it to the floor. The letter was the same as usual – a single piece of A4 paper that had been folded into thirds. Except stapled to the back of it were two squares of paper, torn, messy at the edges. Curiosity getting the better of him, he looked at those first: on them were two different mobile numbers, one on each page. After a quick check on the letter he'd read the other night, one of them was the same mobile number that Nathan had provided. Tomek ignored the numbers and, feeling like a teenager reading a love letter for the first time, he opened the page.

Dearest Tomek,

i haven't had a singel response from you at all reesently and I'm starting to get a bit wurried about the letters going missin. i really do hope you are reeseeving them. That is why i have decided to right them more freekwently so that you have a higha chance of reeseeving them. Belt and braces, one of the guards called it the other day.

Anyway, i wanted to let you know that I've been doing some thinking and I wanted to let you know that I never apologized for what I did to your brother. I am sorry, to the bottom of the heart and I do hope you can foregive me. There was a lot of things going on in my life when I did that to him. Wood you like to hear them?

My mum and dad used to hit me. It might not be much of a surprise to you, but those bastards beat the living shit out of me every day for ten years, from when I was five to when I was fifteen. It didn't matter what I did, it was always something wrong. And they speshally didn't like it when I answered back. My mum was the worst. The drink and drugs made her lash out, and dad was too weak to defend him and me, so he started going along with it too. The things I did to your brother was a retaliashun, I didn't know what came over me and I had all this anger and frustration that came out on your brother. That's why I did what I did to him. He didn't deserve it, but neither did I deserve it when my mum broke my arm in the door, when she shoved me into the fridge, when she slapped me and made me undress and put my hands in the air and beat me and smacked my dick and said nasty things to me. Neither of us deserved what happened to us, and as for my mum and dad, fuck knows where they are. I HOPE THEY'RE FUCKING DEAD.

I never told no one that before, so I hope you can keep it a secret please, Tomek. I trust you, mate. It can be our little thing between us.

I've nearly run out of room now, and I don't like turning over the page because it looks messy and gets confusing, so I'm going to have to write you another one some other time. I've stapled two mobile numbers to this sheet so you can call me. I wasn't sure if the other one got lost, and if the guards take it away then I have a spare one. Does that make sense?

I can't wait to hear your voice.
Send my love to the family,
Nathan

TOMEK STARED at the words on the page, at the harsh scribbles where Nathan had made a mistake and corrected himself (though it made no difference to the subsequent spelling as he made the same mistakes again). He admired the man for trying, for writing as much as he had. It couldn't have been easy for him, growing up like that, abandoned, abused, emotionally and physically neglected. It made sense now that he hadn't had the resources or care and attention needed to develop his reading and writing skills. Other than simply surviving in that household, there would have been nothing else on his mind.

As Tomek sat there, turning over the sentences in his mind, he felt a pang of guilt and remorse overwhelm the excitement and curiosity he'd felt before reading the letter. He didn't know why, but he suddenly felt an affinity to the man who'd killed his brother. Perhaps it was because he'd known what it was like to be outcast from his family – it wasn't anywhere near the same level that Nathan had experienced, but following his brother's death, his parents had neglected him, stopped loving him, they had left him to process and deal with the trauma of his brother's death alone.

In that way, he and Nathan Burrows were very much alike.

Tomek turned over the page and tore the stapled squares off. He looked at the numbers, contemplated adding them to his address book. In the end, he put them with the folded letter in the back of his wardrobe with the rest of them. If he wanted to call Nathan – a real possibility he was now considering – then he would know where to find it.

Just as Tomek closed the wardrobe shut, the doorbell to the flat rang. Abigail. She was staying over. The fourth night in a row. He wondered whether they would need to have the chat about staying over for good soon.

As he opened his bedroom door, he caught Kasia hovering outside, frozen, feet planted on the floor, caught in the moment between running towards either the front door or her bedroom.

'What do you think you're doing?'

'Nothing.'

'You been eavesdropping?'

'No.'

'What are you doing outside my room then?'

'I came to ask a question.'

Lie.

'What?'

'Erm...' Kasia couldn't answer.

The doorbell sounded again. Longer this time. Tomek's frustration began to bubble.

'Pardon? What were you going to ask me?'

'Erm... I... I wondered...'

'Yes?'

Another ring.

'Can I meet up with Yas at the weekend?'

'Yas?'

'Yeah. She wants to go Lakeside. And I need some... some new underwear, and...'

Another ring.

'For fuck's sake! I'm coming!'

Ignoring Kasia, Tomek spun on the spot and raced to the front door. He slammed his hand on the handle and yanked it open. There, on the other side, was Abigail, wearing an impatient and aggrieved look on her face. Her hair was messy and in her hand she carried a laptop bag filled with documents.

'You couldn't have fucking waited?' he snapped.

'Good evening to you, too. Shall we try that again?'

Tomek shook himself to. 'Sorry. I didn't mean to. I just... stressful day.'

'Tell me about it. Is it safe to come in or do you need me to knock again?'

Tomek stepped aside and let her through. As he closed the front door, Kasia slammed her bedroom door, the sound reverberating throughout the flat. She shut it so hard he thought he could hear the wood splintering.

'Everything all right?' Abigail asked, caution in her voice. 'What have I come home to?'

Tomek didn't like that.

Come home.

As though it was her home as well now. As though she'd just imposed herself on it without consulting him or asking how he felt about it. He didn't like that at all.

'I didn't realise this was your home,' he said, cold.

'Okay... I'm sensing there's something a little more behind that comment than the obvious. I didn't mean it like that. Sorry if I—'

Tomek turned his back on her and moved towards the kitchen. There, he started preparing dinner. Spaghetti Bolognese. Simple, staple. And one of his favourites to cook. He spent the next twenty minutes chopping the onion, stirring the meat, cooking the pasta as Abigail told him about her day. About how there was nothing going on. How there had been nothing to report for days. And with each comment, she had made a jab at him, poking at him, questioning him on why he and the team hadn't given them any information about the body that had been found at the church.

'I mean, throw me a bone here, Tomek,' she said. 'We've been feeding off scraps and we're starting to run out.'

'I know.'

He wasn't in the mood to deal with her right now. In fact, he wasn't in the mood to deal with anyone or anything. Not after the afternoon he'd had. Not after the letter, which had completely fucked with his circuitry.

'Did you hear what I just said?'

Tomek continued to stir the meat, staring into the sauce.

'Tomek!'

'Yeah.'

'You're not listening to me.'

'I am.'

'What did I just say?'

'About being hungry.'

'For a fucking story, yes. But that's not what I meant. I really need your team to give me something here. We've sent over so many fucking emails and questions about the girl inside the church, but nobody's replying.'

'Could you just stop?'

Tomek took the wooden spoon out of the pot and slapped it onto the counter. Sauce splattered onto the tiled wall and nearby toaster and kettle.

'Could you just stop for one fucking second?'

The outburst was sudden and startled even himself. It was the first time he'd ever reacted or behaved that way, and he didn't like the man he'd just become.

'Where... where did *that* come from?' Abigail's voice was a combination of pissed off and hurt. Though he sensed he was about to receive as good as he'd given. 'Don't talk to me like that. All I asked was a fucking question. You're the one not listening to me, so don't get on your fucking high horse and give me all that, okay? You're supposed to be an adult, and you're supposed to be the SIO of a murder investigation. How fucking hard—'

'Supposed to be the SIO?' he retorted. '*Supposed* to be? What's that *supposed* to mean?'

'You're the one in charge of this investigation. You get to decide what happens and what doesn't. Why is it taking you guys so long to give us the information?' Abigail's eyes widened and her lips parted as realisation dawned on her. 'Have you told them not to, is that what it is? Have you been withholding information from us? Why would you do that? You know how much this means to me. I can't believe you'd do something like that. We're supposed to be a partnership, a team. This is my dream and you're fucking ruining it. I've been waiting for this moment for ages, and you've fucked it all up for me. Today we reported on a massive hole in the beach at Southend seafront, which a local space photographer and enthusiast thought was a meteorite that had landed from space. Turns out it was just some fucking guys with a massive shovel and a lot of time on their hands. You see! I can't be going back to that shit all day. I'm better than that. I've got aspirations.'

She raised her hand in the air, then climbed an imaginary ladder. But Tomek wasn't paying attention to that. All he could think about was that hole.

'How...' he started, slowly turning towards her. 'How... how big was it?'

Abigail's cheeks turned red. The lines on her forehead multiplied and her crow's feet deepened. Her pupils narrowed and her nostrils flared. All that was left was the vehemence that came out of her mouth.

'Fuck you,' she spat. 'Fuck you, and fuck this place. I'm out of here. Goodbye!'

CHAPTER TWENTY-SEVEN

The world's turned a shade of red. A deep, dark red that makes it feel like there's blood all over my eyes. My blood. Michał's blood. Angelica's blood.

As I run, I see the kids hanging around outside the off-licence. One of them's leaning on the handlebars while one of them's holding something in the air. I think it's a fucking spade, but I can't be sure. It's got a handle and everything, and it's fucking shining under the shop lights, so it almost certainly looks like a spade. But before I can give it any more thought, I come across the Magnet kitchen shop. And this time I see Abigail in the car park, standing next to the man I've seen so many times before, so many times, but never fully paid attention to. Except it's not Abigail. At least I don't think it is.

She's wearing Abigail's clothes, yes, but her face is blurred, and it's white, the colour of a bedsheet. And behind her is a red car. But when I look again, I realise it's not a red car. It's a pair of wings. Angel wings. Bloody angel wings.

And then it cuts.

I'm in the field. The wind's picked up, and it's starting to spit a little, gently raining blood. Even the darkness of the park has turned red, tinged with death.

I duck beneath the railing and sprint through the mud. There, standing over Michał is Nathan Burrows. He's wearing a pair of grey jogging bottoms and a stained grey sweatshirt. He's unshaven, and his hair is long and slightly ragged. His teeth are sloped to one side and his eyebrows have met in the middle. I see a monster in front of me, standing alone, shoulders rolled forward, legs shoulder-width apart, arms down by his sides, staring at me, almost taunting, waiting for me to make the first move.

And I do. I'm the first one to blink. Literally.

But when I open my eyes again, Nathan's turned into a fifteen-year-old boy. Wearing the same blue Lonsdale tracksuit and black trainers he'd worn when he'd killed Michał. Except now there are two people standing behind him. A man and a woman, on either side. His mum and dad. They're dressed in casual clothes. His mum's hair is tied in a ponytail that seems to list to one side, as if it's been pulled by someone else in an argument. On the other side, Nathan's dad stands the same as him, with the shoulders, with the arms. The only difference between them is the receding hairline and the chubbier stomach. Aside from that, they're almost spitting images.

The three of them, staring at me.

And then Nathan waves his hand at me, almost as though he's calling me over, beckoning me.

And then it cuts.

I'm driving in the car, the police car, with Dad by my side. The sound of the windscreen wipers thrashing from side to side is the only noise in the car. That and the sound of the rain. We're driving, driving, driving. I have no idea where we are; I just know we're going to the station. When we get there, the police officer opens the door for me and leads me into the building. The lights are so bright I can't see anything. All I know is that the man is guiding me, that I need to follow him. Eventually, after a few minutes of speaking to people, hearing voices and names I don't recognise, I'm ushered into a small room. It's well lit, there's a nice sofa, and a television playing some mundane programme that I'm not paying attention to. It's designed to calm me down, but I can't focus on it. All I can see is Michał's blood on my hands, mixed with the dirt beneath my fingernails. It's on the walls. It's in the fabric of the furniture. It's everywhere. I ask to go to the toilet, to clean my hands, but nothing happens, nobody answers. I begin to panic, my chest rising, falling, rising, falling, until my head is light and dizzy. I move back towards the sofa to sit, reach for the bottle of water on there, and just as I unscrew the lid, the door opens. Standing there, dressed in police uniform, is my mum. Her sparkling pink nails cling to the door handle.

'We're ready for you now, Tomek,' she says, before changing my life forever.

CHAPTER TWENTY-EIGHT

The atmosphere inside the car was awkward and frosty. Neither of them had said a word to each other that morning except for the essentials: "Good morning", "Ready to leave by eight?" and "Your lunch is in your bag".

Tomek had loads he wanted to say, namely a massive apology, but he didn't know how to say it. It wasn't something he'd ever had to do before. He wasn't used to apologising. In the past, whenever he'd broken up with a girl or told them that the morning after the night before was where their relationship ended, he'd always brushed it off with a shrug and a roll of the eyes, heedless of the other person's feelings. They were in his life for one night, maybe two, and one night only. Except with Kasia, she was in his life for the rest of his, and she wasn't a one-night stand. She was his daughter. And that was a completely separate ball game.

So far, on the drive to school, Kasia had been plugged into her headphones and had ignored him entirely. He'd attempted to steal a few glances her way now and then, but she was so engrossed in her phone and music that she didn't notice him – or, if she did, she didn't let on in the slightest. He didn't know where she'd got her poker face from, but he didn't appreciate it.

After twenty minutes, he eventually pulled up outside her school. Well, not quite outside the school; she liked him to park farther down the road so none of her friends saw her getting dropped off, presumably because she might have been seen as some sort of social pariah. For a brief moment, Kasia didn't move. A part of him thought she might be preparing herself to say something, but when it didn't come, when she reached into the footwell for her bag, hugged it tightly against her chest and opened the car door, Tomek pulled her back in by the arm.

'Can we talk about last night?'

Slowly, Kasia unplugged the headphones from her ears. She kept her gaze fixed on him. It was clear to see from her expression that she was eagerly awaiting his apology, that she was hurting.

'I'm sorry,' he said, blunt, to the point. 'I'm sorry for lashing out at you and ignoring you. I... It's not an excuse, but I had a busy day yesterday, and I shouldn't have brought it home with me. I should have left it at the door, and I'm sorry for that. I...' He inhaled deeply and turned to look at the dashboard. 'I got another letter last night, yes, and thank you for not opening it. I just needed to read it in my room, alone, as they're... they're a lot for me to process.' He sniffed hard as he thought of what to say next. 'I don't have a problem with you seeing your mate at the weekend. I should have said that right then, but I had a lot going on in my head. Again, not an excuse, I know. I'm owning up to it, and I'm sorry. If you need a lift or need me to come pick you up from Lakeside, then just let me know and I'll be there, okay?'

Kasia's expression remained unchanged. She unplugged the headphones from her phone and began wrapping the cable around her hand. 'I'm sorry, too,' she said, her voice weak.

'What for? You have nothing to apologise for.'

'For snooping outside your room.'

'Oh, right. That...'

'I shouldn't have done it either. I was being nosy. That's... that's no excuse, as well. I know.'

Then she did something that completely took him aback. She clenched her fist, placed it in the centre of her chest, and rubbed the fist in a circle a few times.

'What was that?'

'"Sorry" in sign. A girl in my class is deaf, and she uses it whenever she doesn't understand the question.'

Tomek placed his fist on his chest and made the same movement.

'Sorry,' he said.

'Sorry,' Kasia repeated. Then she hovered in her seat, something still on her mind. 'Have you apologised to Abigail yet?'

'No.'

'Are you going to?'

'I don't know.'

'I heard what happened last night. It sounded bad...'

'Yeah.'

'Are you going to talk to her about it?'

At some point, he'd have to. That was the adult thing to do. There would be no hiding from it now, not when they were so far gone in the relationship that he couldn't get cold feet and back out. No, he'd be required to stick at it for some time before any of that could happen.

'I'm sure you'll work it out,' Kasia said, though he could tell from her voice that she didn't mean it.

'Her birthday's in a couple of weeks,' he said.

'What... what's that got to do with anything?'

He shrugged, staring out of the window. 'I don't know.' Then his eyes fell on the dashboard. It was 8:35. 'You'd better go. Don't want another late note from Miss Holloway.'

Her eyes flashed with fear.

'You saw that?'

'It's fine,' he told her. 'I saw it on your report card the other day – snooping through your bag, sorry – but didn't say anything. So on this one you get a free pass. Just make sure it doesn't happen again.'

Kasia responded by rubbing a circle onto her chest. Tomek replied in the same way.

A second later, she was out of the car, walking up the street, wearing a backpack that was two sizes too big for her, and texting on her phone. Tomek turned to look at the rest of the kids doing the same. Clones, carbon copies of one another: heads down, earphones in, their entire world encapsulated in a black mirror rather than the world around them. Even those in groups were listening to music with one earphone in while pretending to communicate in the real world.

Tomek was so focused on the kids from Kasia's school that he almost missed his phone vibrating. He fished inside his pocket and pulled out the device. It was his dad, Perry.

'Everything all right, Dad?' he asked as he placed the call on loudspeaker and pulled away from the side of the road.

'Everything's fine.'

'You sure? Unlike you to be calling this early. Aren't you usually still struggling to get out of bed at this time?'

'You mock, but this arthritis malarkey's gonna catch up with *you* one day, son. So don't get too cocky. Besides, I've already made breakfast, cleaned the kitchen, hoovered the downstairs, fixed the tap in the bathroom, and put a load of washing in the machine. And now your mother's got me in the garage because the lamp on her bedside table's broken and it needs immediate fixing otherwise she won't be able to read her books in bed tonight.'

'Ouch.'

'Don't get married. It's never-ending.'

Tomek chuckled as he focused on turning at a junction.

'How's everyone?' Perry continued. 'Kasia? Work?'

Tomek gave him the SparkNotes version of the night before, keeping the details about the letter from Nathan, and the discussion with his brother, away from his dad.

'Ouch,' Perry replied.

'Yeah.'

'Want to talk about it?'

'No. It's okay.'

'Okay. All right, well...'

That was all that needed to be said on the matter. They'd handled it like men, without actually saying anything at all, and now it was time to move on. Fortunately, there was something else on Perry's mind.

'While I've got you,' he said, lowering his voice so that it was little more than a whisper. 'There's something I've been meaning to ask.'

The sound of tools and metal clanging rattled in the background as he spoke, presumably to stop his mum from overhearing.

'Right...' Tomek answered.

'It's about Nathan.'

Tomek hesitated. Had Dawid spoken to him?

'Okay...'

'When you went to see him the other month, you said that he told you he'd acted alone.'

'Yeah. That's right.'

As Perry struggled to get the words out, the sound of tools moving gradually increased.

'And I wondered... I wondered if, you know, if you believed him?'

'If I believed him?'

'Yeah. Do you think there's still this second person out there or do you... do you think he really acted alone?'

Tomek wondered where his dad was going with this, and what had made him bring it up after several weeks. Tomek had told his family about his visit to Nathan Burrows at HMP Wakefield a few weeks before, and his dad hadn't raised any concerns then. In fact, he'd sided with Tomek's mother and finally, as a family, they'd agreed to let it go. After thirty years of constantly seeking closure, they'd decided that Nathan Burrows had acted alone, that nobody else had been with him, and that Tomek had imagined it. All that pressure, all the burdens had been lifted from their lives and they'd become closer. But now Perry had finally voiced his concerns, away from his mother's listening ears.

'What's brought all this on, Dad?' Tomek asked.

'I was doing some thinking,' he said. 'That's all. Just wondered whether you've changed your mind.'

'I...' Tomek hesitated. He didn't know what to say. He didn't know what Perry was expecting him to say. He inhaled deeply, held it there, then let the air out of his lips slowly. 'I don't believe him,' he said, unsure of himself. 'I think... I think Charlie's still out there, yes.'

'And all that stuff the other week at dinner? That was for your mother's benefit?'

Tomek mumbled, unable to answer.

'Good. Keep it that way. She's been much better since you came out and said what you said. She's happier, she's different. I haven't seen her like this in nearly thirty years. She's a completely different woman.'

'She's still got you cleaning and fixing things for her, though.'

'She's still got me cleaning and fixing things for her, yes. But, trust me, it's the happiest she's ever been. And I don't want anything to change that right now. So... so keep it from your mother, okay? Don't say anything to her, and neither will I. Our little secret.'

There was nothing *little* about this. Not when it came to Michał. Not when it involved Nathan Burrows.

'I knew you were hiding something from us that night,' Perry continued. The sound of movement and metal clanging into metal returned. 'I could see it in your face that you still believed it. And I just want you to know that I believe you too. I knew it wasn't in your nature to let this thing go so easily. You've been fighting it for the last thirty years, and I know you'll keep hunting the bastard down for the next thirty, right to the end. I know you'll do what's right for our family, son. I know you'll find him, because he's out there somewhere. I can feel it. I know it, you know it. And I know you've got it in you to find him. Keep fighting, kiddo.'

A lump swelled in Tomek's throat. A pat on the back, vindication, a nod well done. The first time his father had told him he was proud, that he believed in him. Thirty years too late, but it was there, nonetheless. And as

Tomek pondered it for a moment, he realised what that little speech was: his father, begging for help, begging for Tomek to find Michał's second killer, because he too had carried the same burden all these years, just in a different way, hidden from the rest of the family. And now he was making it abundantly clear to Tomek what needed to be done, and that he would be by his side every step of the way.

CHAPTER TWENTY-NINE

Finding Shawn Wilkins, the man who'd been convicted of stalking Angelica Whitaker, should have been a quick search, a quick look on the register. But it had been anything but. His registered address had been at his parents' house, but when Oscar and Rachel had turned up to bring him in for questioning, they'd learnt that he'd moved out. The only problem was his parents were talkers, and had kept them both occupied for two hours before eventually giving them the information they needed.

While he was waiting, Chey had spent the last twenty minutes listing all the evidence they had against Wilkins to him. Several counts of standing outside Angelica Whitaker's house in the middle of the night, sometimes sitting in his car, watching her through the window with the lights on, following her in the middle of the street at night and in broad daylight, turning up at Whitaker's, the jewellery store unannounced, pretending to buy something (and even doing so on one occasion, then giving it to her as a gift), messaging her repeatedly on social media and via text message, frequently using fake accounts and new mobile numbers to reach out to her, and constantly commenting on every one of her social media posts with the phrases, 'My gorgeous angel' and 'My angel's got her wings back', as though they were boyfriend and girlfriend. The only problem was, Tomek wasn't listening to any of it. His thoughts were hundreds of miles away in Wakefield, loitering outside the prison, looking up at the iron bars outside the grey and murky windows of the building. Then his thoughts cut to the field of the playground where his brother had died – the playground that was still there, except it looked completely different thirty years on. This time he pictured the bench with Michał's name on it. He hadn't sat on that bench, let alone seen it, in years. And now there it was, crystal clear in his mind's eye.

'Sarge?'

The voice went in one ear and out the other.

'Sarge, you there?'

Tomek was standing with his back to Chey, staring out of the window that looked over the car park. He was only vaguely aware of the man's reflection in the glass. But as Chey moved behind him, it wasn't the reflection that distracted him, it was the car that had just pulled into an empty space near the building's entrance. Rachel. Parked up at a jaunty angle as she'd swung it into the space. A second later, he watched her get out of the car and move to the back, from where Shawn Wilkins emerged. The man was a small giant from up there at the second-floor window. He was almost twice the size of Rachel, with great, stooping shoulders that never seemed to end, and a gait that made him look like a gentle giant. He waited patiently for Rachel to retrieve something from the back of her car and then followed a few paces behind.

It wasn't until they were a few metres away from the building that Tomek spotted a figure leap out of a car nearby and sprint across the car park. By the time he noticed what was happening, it was too late, and like a mother deer watching its foal get knocked down by a car in the middle of the street, Tomek felt helpless. The figure, wearing a black hoodie, covered the distance with ease, and a moment later, was on them. He swung a right hook at Shawn Wilkins and connected with him cleanly, sending the small giant to the floor. But that wasn't enough for the assailant. Pushing Rachel to one side, he grabbed Shawn by the collar and began punching him in the face repeatedly, kicking him in the stomach and legs while the man was incapacitated.

Tomek didn't need to see anything else. He charged out of the room and headed towards the stairs, leaping down them two at a time, holding onto the wall for support. When he came to the bottom, he tore through a set of double doors and out into the open. By the time he made it outside, the situation had already been contained by a handful of uniformed officers who had been nearby. It had taken three of them to subdue the attacker, with one on the man's neck, while the other two straddled him and began placing a set of cuffs around his wrists.

'Get off!' the attacker screamed.

Meanwhile, Rachel was tending to Shawn Wilkins. The man was sitting on the ground, legs astride, head lowered between his knees as a river of blood streamed from his nose.

First, Tomek checked on Rachel.

'You all good?'

She looked up at him, flustered. 'What the fuck was that all about? He came out of nowhere!'

'Not from up there, he didn't.' Tomek pointed to the window. 'Do you know who it is?'

And then Tomek saw for himself.

The man was dragged to his feet with the help of a fourth uniformed officer. Arms behind his back. Dirt and pieces of gravel attached to his face.

Staring back at him was Johnny Whitaker, Angelica's brother and staunch defender.

CHAPTER THIRTY

It had taken over an hour to stop the blood from streaming out of Shawn Wilkins' nose, at least to a point where he didn't need to replace the tissue that was lodged up his nostrils every two seconds. The medically trained professionals in the building had tended to him, fixed him up, and sent him into the interview room in the same outfit he'd been attacked in, stained and covered in blood. Sadly there were no replacements, and even if there were, Tomek doubted any of them would fit. Joining him in the interview room was Rachel. It was a voluntary interview, so Shawn was allowed to leave at any time, though Tomek suspected the man would want to look at pressing charges against Johnny Whitaker, and Tomek was keen to force the man to stay for as long as was necessary by keeping that part till the end.

'Shawn Wilkins...' Tomek began.

'Yes?'

'Is that you?'

'Yes.'

'And you live at Crescent Drive, yes?'

'My parents do.'

'But you don't?'

'You know where I live. You picked me up from there.' Shawn pointed to Rachel, but Tomek ignored it.

'How long have you lived there?'

Shawn shrugged. 'Two, maybe three years.'

'So why haven't you updated our records?'

'What records?'

'The restraining order against you from a Miss Angelica Whitaker.'

Shawn placed his giant hands flat on the table and slowly dragged them back as he reclined in his seat. It was a simple, innocuous move, and yet Tomek sensed an air of threat behind it. The man was giving him Ed Kemper vibes. 'That what this is about? You've brought me in here because my details are out of date?'

It was Rachel's turn to speak. 'No, we've brought you in because we had some questions about it.'

Shawn's face contorted into a frown. 'Surely everything's on the file? The short of it is that I can't go within a few metres of her.'

'How many, precisely?'

'A hundred.'

'That's a lot more than a *few* metres,' Tomek said. 'What did you do to warrant that?'

Tomek knew the answer to the question – Chey's words were vague and quiet in his mind – but he wanted Shawn to spell it out for them.

'It's all there in my file,' the man replied defiantly.

'Why don't you tell us what it says?'

'I'd rather not go over old ground. It's difficult.'

'But not nearly as difficult as you made life for Angelica Whitaker, right?'

The man didn't like the tone in Tomek's voice. Tomek could see him backing into the corner, his hairs on end, claws at the ready.

'What is this about?' he asked. 'Why have you brought me here? And why the fuck is someone assaulting me outside? I want to press charges.'

Rachel raised a hand to placate him. 'We can discuss that later,' she began. 'But first, I'd like to know when you first met Angelica? How did the two of you come to know each other? It was on a flight, right?'

There was something about her tone, the sensitivity behind it, the calmness, that made even Tomek receptive to her questions. She had a different way of dealing with people, and more often than not, it worked. Especially when she was trying to clear up Tomek's mess.

'I was flying back from Madrid,' Shawn began, keeping his eyes focused on Rachel. 'I was with a couple of mates. We'd gone on a lads' holiday. Sedate, quiet, nothing too brash. It must've been about three years ago now. And we was flying back in the middle of the morning. We was all knackered and the rest of my mates was asleep, but I couldn't. I was just looking at the most beautiful woman I've ever seen, mate. She was stunning. You shoulda seen her. Figure like a model's, the most gorgeous eyes, hair all done up nicely, make-up on point. There was just something about her. So I started talking to her at the back of the plane while everyone was asleep or had their headphones in, and we really hit it off. I was throwing out some one-liners, she was flirting back. But then that was it. The end of the flight came and she was gone.'

As Shawn Wilkins spoke, his eyes and face illuminated with fervent desire and animalistic hunger. The look on the man's face disconcerted Tomek. If he was enjoying *thinking* about Angelica this much, how had he behaved when he'd been near her?

'How did you track Angelica afterwards?' Rachel asked.

'Insta,' the man replied quickly. 'Found her account on Insta. Didn't take too long really, I already had a first name, and managed to put together the rest. Then I messaged her. She didn't have her account on private or anything, so I just reached out to her. I shooted my shot, and she replied. Surprisingly, she remembered me. I must've made an impact on her, and then things sort of went on from there.' He finished the sentence with a nonchalant shrug, as if Tomek and Rachel should be in awe of his prowess.

'How?' Rachel asked, her tone flat, measured. Meanwhile, thoughts of Kasia had started to enter Tomek's head: how she would be at risk of this type of thing in the years to come; of how some men couldn't control themselves and took it one step too far; how she would have to be careful every day for the rest of her life if nothing changed.

Another shrug, another show of defiance. 'You know, I just messaged her a couple of times. We talked about loads of stuff. Her work, how she was looking forward to the end of the season because she needed a break, but wasn't looking forward to it because it meant she wasn't fulfilling her passion anymore. Then she told me what she liked to do, where she liked to go, what she did in the evenings. So accidentally on purpose one night, I bumped into her at Memo. She was surprised to see me, so I took that as a good thing, and then I followed her back to hers in a different cab.'

'Did she ask you to?'

'Well, not *exactly*. But I could tell she was up for it, you know. She'd definitely been giving me the signs.'

Out of the corner of his eye, Tomek noticed Rachel bristle with discomfort at that comment.

'And when she turned you away, what did you say?' Rachel continued, her voice breaking slightly.

'Turned me away? She didn't turn me away. We had sex that night.'

Tomek could feel Rachel's lungs deflate. Disappointment seeped from both of them, that Angelica had been so quick to get into bed with someone she barely knew, and someone who had followed her home without seeing the risk that he'd posed.

'But I didn't rape her or anything. That's all on record. She admitted that it was consensual.'

But that was when the infatuation progressed, Tomek thought. Moved up to another level, and another level after that. The more she ignored him after coming to her senses, the more she pushed him away, the more it made him hungrier, the more he became desperate for her attention, for *her*. And what concerned Tomek the most was that there was no remorse, no acknowledgement that what he'd done and the way he'd behaved was wrong, immoral, fundamentally wicked. He looked proud of his behaviour, and delighted at the fact they were talking about Angelica.

Before the meeting, Chey had printed out the list of evidence Angelica had supplied when applying for the restraining order. Tomek consulted it. By now, the constable's rendition of the facts had been completely drowned out by the information Shawn Wilkins was giving him.

'Says here you sometimes turned up at her house unannounced, and her place of work on several occasions?'

The man's eyes lit up. 'You have no idea how many times I took random flights to random countries from Southend Airport just in the hope that she might be on one of them. The number of times I must have gone all the way and then come all the way back, it was insane.' He let out a little chortle, enthused by his own fond memories of the experience. 'And then when I found out she worked with her sister-in-law, I saved myself an absolute *fortune*.'

Tomek pictured it now; Angelica working contentedly in the jeweller's, dealing with a customer, showing them the perfect ring or necklace that would make them the happiest people on the planet, then her attention being distracted by the man who'd just entered, grinning at her, his beady eyes watching her every move, waiting for her to finish so he could pounce, leaving her no route of escape.

'I'm sure you did.' Tomek was disgusted. 'Do you mind if I ask you a few questions?'

Shawn granted Tomek permission with his enormous hands.

'What do you do for work?'

'I work in the library in Hadleigh.'

'How long have you been there?'

'Ten years.'

'What's your favourite genre of book?'

'Fantasy. *Game of Thrones*. That type of thing.'

'Have you ever been to any of those comic cons?'

'Couple of times. Why?'

'Have you ever fantasised about Angelica being a character from *Game of Thrones*?'

'Maybe...'

'Have you ever called Angelica an angel?'

'Yes.'

'Have you ever referred to her as having wings?'

'Only because I was pleased to hear she'd been rehired for the next season. It was my little celebration for her.'

'Have you ever broken into her home?'

'What? No!'

'Have you ever thought about hurting Angelica?'

Hesitation.

'No...'

'Ever thought about hurting *anyone*?'

'No.'

'Have you ever killed anyone before?'

'What?'

And that was the end of it. Tomek had hoped his quick-fire round of questions would garner more fruit, but not on this occasion.

'Where are you going with this?'

'Nowhere,' Tomek lied. Time for a change in direction. 'Where were you on Friday night?'

'At home.'

'Your home?'

'Yes.'

'Alone?'

'Yes. Why? What happened Friday night?'

'Nothing.'

'Then what are you asking me all these questions for?'

Tomek shrugged. 'Curiosity.'

'Has something happened to her?'

'Who?' Tomek asked, being deliberately obtuse.

'Angelica! Has something happened to my angel?'

Tomek let his brain absorb the sentence before responding, 'I'm not sure what you mean.'

The excitement on Shawn's face quickly turned to rage, his expression filling with venom. He turned to Rachel, and pointing to Tomek, asked her, 'What's fucking going on here?'

'I'm not sure what you mean, sir.'

Shawn slammed his palm on the table.

'Are you fucking kidding me? What fucking bullshit is this? I don't have to fucking sit here and take this.' He started out of his chair, waited for either Tomek or Rachel to stop him, and when neither of them did, he slammed the chair into the table and stormed towards the door.

'Didn't you want to look at pressing charges?' Tomek called.

Shawn paused, frozen, with his hand wrapped around the handle. The rise and fall of his chest was visible from the table, the sound of his breath louder than the air conditioning unit.

'Fuck it,' he said. 'It's you two I should be pressing charges against.'

And then he stormed out, slamming the door shut behind him.

With the noise of his heavy footsteps receding, Tomek turned to Rachel, and said, 'My, my, what a temper.'

CHAPTER THIRTY-ONE

Tomek bumped into Rose Whitaker on his way out. The jewellery shop owner was flustered, disgruntled. She clutched her bag, tucked beneath her arm, tightly against her chest, and swivelled her head like a dog on high alert. She was in the reception area, anxiously waiting for someone to approach her.

'I presume you're here to speak to your husband?' Tomek asked light-heartedly.

'I almost didn't come,' she snapped.

'No?'

'It's the last thing that fucking piece of shit deserves.'

Tomek sensed there was something else going on, something other than the inconvenience of having to close her jeweller's early to pick up her husband who'd stupidly got himself arrested for assaulting someone outside a police station. If there was, she didn't choose to elaborate.

'I'm glad you're here, actually,' Tomek continued, then pointed down a corridor. 'I was wondering if I could grab you for a few minutes to ask you some questions about your husband and Angelica?'

Rose rolled her eyes. 'No problem. The fucking idiot can wait as long as I tell him to.'

That said, she followed him into one of the vulnerable witness rooms that were designed to be comfortable and homely for those that needed it most – children and victims of rape and trauma. Tomek gestured for Rose to sit on the sofa while he perched himself on the edge of an uncomfortable wooden chair that bruised his coccyx as soon as he sat on it.

'Drink?' he asked.

She declined with the shake of her head and then set her handbag on the sofa, finally relinquishing control of it in an environment she clearly felt safe in.

'First time in a police station?' he asked.

'Yeah.' She scanned the room with equal amazement and concern, like she was viewing it through augmented reality. 'Sorry, it's just... weird, you know. Gives me the creeps.'

Tomek chuckled. 'It's fine. We get that a lot. It's an unfamiliar and uncomfortable environment for ninety-nine per cent of the population. I think you'd be weird if you *didn't* get weirded out by being here.'

An awkward laugh. 'You're probably right.'

Tomek moved the conversation on. For this he didn't need a notebook or the notes app on his phone. He wanted to use the best app available: the one between his ears. He just hoped the lack of sleep over the past few days hadn't messed with its circuitry.

'Forgive me if this is an imposition,' he started, 'but I'm sensing some hostility between you and your husband.'

She scoffed. 'You can say that again. Can you believe that bastard lied to me, lied to all of us?'

Tomek said nothing. Waited for her to continue.

'That little rat wasn't in Dublin the night Angelica went missing,' she said.

His ears perked up.

'No, that little shitbag was sleeping with another fucking woman. Some Irish bitch he met at a conference one night a few months back. They've been having an affair ever since. So every time he says he's going to Dublin for work, he's just been shagging this woman instead. Except this time, they decided to change things up. Do you know how? That poor excuse of a human being booked an Airbnb along Southend seafront. Fucking *one* mile away from our house! Not only was he shagging her behind my back, but he was also doing it right under my fucking nose. He might as well have done it in our own one!'

'"Our own one" what?' Tomek asked, confused.

'Above the shop,' she explained, 'there's a flat that we recently bought. We plan on turning it into an Airbnb, a cute little place for people to stay on the Broadway. It's handy because I'm right beneath it, so anytime guests arrive I can check them in and check them out without any of the faff. We're renovating it at the moment. Well, I say *we*, it's me doing all the work, mind. It's my name on the agreement, my name on the mortgage. I wake up, go to the shop, spend all day working in there, then in the evenings I go upstairs and do some of the cleaning, the plastering, the drilling, the sawing, the lot. Meanwhile, he's shagging Miss Potato Head over there.'

Tomek had heard all he needed to on that. He didn't want to upset her any more, and he didn't want to pry more into what was clearly a raw and open wound for her (even though the gossip in him was intrigued), so he turned the focus of the conversation onto Angelica and her brother. As soon as the focus switched to her sister-in-law, Rose's shoulders relaxed, her body decompressed, and the veins in her arms and temples quickly disappeared.

'Tell me about them as siblings,' Tomek said. 'I'm keen to know what they're like. Do they get on? Do they argue?'

'Why?' she asked.

'Because I got the impression he was a protective older brother, that he liked to look out for her.'

'Yeah. I guess you could say that. He always liked to keep an eye on her in a big brother kind of way. But don't get me wrong, they also argued and bickered a lot, usually about nonsense – just like siblings do, I guess – but there were a couple of times that he flew off the handle with her.'

'Like when?'

'When he found out that she'd been sleeping with her ex, and that she'd been inviting guys over to her house all the time. He told her to have some respect for herself, to behave better.' She pushed a strand of loose hair behind her ear and brushed the underside of her nose with her hand. 'Personally, I didn't have a problem with it. It's her body. She can do what she wants with it, so long as she's being careful.'

'But she wasn't, though, was she?'

Tomek was referring to her pregnancy, and he wondered if Rose knew about it.

'Well, no... No, I guess she wasn't.'

So she did know.

'When did Angelica tell you?'

'She didn't have to. The warning signs were there. I mean, Johnny and I have never tried for children – thank fuck, not after what he's just done – but I know what to look out for. She tried to hide the morning sickness as much as she could, but I eventually cottoned on to the fact something was wrong. I mean, I've worked with her every day for the past six or seven months, so there was no hiding it. She tried to fight it, bless her, to deny it, but in the end, I convinced her to go for her scans. I was more than happy to go along with her. But she begged me not to say anything to anyone.'

'Johnny wasn't the only one keeping secrets in the marriage then.'

The words had slipped out of his mouth before he realised. Yet Rose's reaction wasn't what he'd expected.

'They're hardly the same,' she said calmly. 'He was sleeping with someone behind my back while I was looking out for his sister. They're completely different.'

Tomek nodded. 'You did what you had to do. Did you know that she'd told Roy as well?'

Rose nodded. 'She's always been much closer to her dad than her mum. That's just the way it seems to work, isn't it? I mean, me, I was never close to mine, but they were *really* close. And I've often thought of Roy as a father figure. He's kind, considerate. But he has a temper on him as well. He lost the plot when she told him. And I mean *lost* it. You thought Johnny was bad the other day? You should have seen him.' She turned to face the green carpet, lost in a sudden thought. 'I wonder what he told Daphne happened to the vase in the end.'

Tomek thought of the former airline pilot for a moment. On the two occasions Tomek had seen him, the man had come across as even tempered and well mannered, not the aggressive individual Rose had just described.

'Has he ever hit Daphne at all, or have you ever heard of any abuse in their relationship?'

Rose pursed her lips and shook her head. 'Johnny's never mentioned it.'

'Have you ever seen him lose his temper in any other instance?'

Rose lowered her gaze to her lap and began picking at her hot pink nails. A few moments passed before she spoke. Tomek allowed her the time and space to feel comfortable.

'I guess you could say he's been aggressive towards me,' she said. 'Not *at* me. *Towards* me. Indirectly. Shouting and arguing with Johnny about me. At the start of the relationship, Johnny told them I wasn't very devout, but neither are Johnny and Angelica, which is a truth they're not willing to hear, and Roy didn't like that, said Johnny needed to be with someone of the same faith, someone who had the same values and believed the same things as they did. It caused a lot of arguments between them, and I thought there was a time where we might have to break up, it got that serious. But throughout it all, I had Angelica.' A tear began to form as Rose thought of her sister-in-law. 'She was there for me when I was new to the family. She helped me come to terms with my new life, with my new mother- and father-in-law. She was my rock. Every time we went to a family function where I didn't know anyone, she was always by my side, doing the job my husband should have been doing – introducing me. Instead, he was off getting pissed with his cousins and flirting with his second cousins once removed or whoever the fuck they were.' She caught a tear with her finger, but it was useless against the heavy stream of them coming down her face. Tomek reached for the box of tissues on the table and passed it to her. 'In those moments, I really felt alone, and when I needed my husband most, he was elsewhere. But I had Angelica by my side. That was the type of person she was. Compassionate, loving, heartfelt, without a bad bone in her body. It's just... it's just such a shame she went through what she went through.'

Tomek's interest was piqued once again. He was learning more from this woman than her entire family combined.

'Why do I get the feeling you're talking about something other than her murder?'

Rose began fiddling with the tissue between her fingers. 'You mean you don't know yet?'

'You're going to have to enlighten me.'

'She was depressed,' she said, then paused a beat. 'Now, I know that word gets thrown around a lot, but hers was seasonal. It was really bad during the winters – every winter. Whenever summer and her dream job as a flight attendant was over for the year, she get really down. Like some days, it was a struggle to get her to come in. Some weeks she'd go out drinking all the time, sometimes going to the club on her own, sleeping with a lot of guys. I don't know what it was or what kick-started it, but she was crying out for help massively, and nobody seemed to do anything about it. None of us were equipped to deal with it, myself included. I hated seeing her do that to herself. The alcohol, the drugs—'

'Drugs?'

'Cocaine, weed. Never anything else. But nobody else knew. For some reason, she always told me what she'd taken.' She shrugged. 'I don't know, I guess she always saw me as an older sister that she could look up to and trust. I just wish I'd done something to protect her.'

'You shouldn't blame yourself.'

'I guess.'

Tomek leant forward, placing his elbows on his knees and smiling warmly at her. 'How long has this been going on?'

'A few years,' Rose answered. 'Four, maybe five. But Daphne and Roy don't want to know anything about it. They're living in denial. It's got progressively worse as the years have gone by, but this winter, surprisingly, it got much better. She was coming in on time. She was happier. She was her usual self, you know?'

'Any idea why?'

Rose took a moment before replying. 'I've been thinking about this a lot since she died, and I remember this one time she told me about a guy she'd met on a flight once. Eccentric millionaire-type character who invited her to a special, adult-themed club on the flight. I... I think she went along to it once, but I don't know if she ever went back. Either way, ever since then it was like she was back to her old ways.'

Tomek felt his pulse quicken.

'I'm going to need you to tell me everything you can about this man and this adult-themed club.'

CHAPTER THIRTY-TWO

By now, my darling angel's been unconscious for half an hour. The chemicals that must have been given to her by someone else have taken hold of her. Her pulse has quietened, the blood slowing across her body. She looks calm, restful, peaceful. Angelic.

And now it's time to begin the next phase of the evening.

I'm no surgeon, but I like to think I've got a steady hand – steady enough to cause as little damage as possible, anyway. On the floor lies the plastic tube, coiled in circles like a snake. At one end is the needle, sticking out of one end of the tube like a tongue. At the other is a large plastic pouch. I reach for the needle, then roll Angelica's body over to one side. The movements must be careful, tender, delicate. She is delicate, a statue carved out of marble by God, by the best sculptor in the world. Her body and soul must be treated that way. Nothing can go wrong.

When she is in position, I hold her leg firmly in place, and inject the needle into the back of her knee. The needle enters the skin with ease. A little blood spills, but I catch it with a wipe. And after a few seconds of squeezing the pouch attached to the cable, creating a vacuum, blood begins to flow through it, smooth, steady, graceful. Within an hour, the bag will be filled and her body will have nothing left to survive. I place a hand on her wrist, feeling for the pulse. It's smooth, steady, like the flow of blood from her leg. She is none the wiser, completely oblivious. I could not imagine doing this if she was awake, or if she had died beforehand. That would not have been right. Instead, it is better for her to pass like this.

I sit beside her, crouched by her stomach, holding onto her hand. I give the bag a few more squeezes now and then to speed the process up, but I'm happy *for this to take as long as it takes. I want to be by her side. I need to be by her side, watching over her, protecting her, cleansing the body, taking it in for the final time.*

Gradually, as the blood slowly leaves her body, her pulse begins to weaken, the bones on her hips and ribs becoming more prominent. The life is literally being sucked out of her, like the air escaping from an inflatable mattress, and as the last of it is pulled from her, I watch her intently, finger stuck to her wrist, feeling her pulse.

Weaker. Weaker still.

The gap between each beat of her heart grows greater and greater.

Until the rise and fall of her chest becomes flat, almost invisible, but the moment she dies, I can tell. The pulse suddenly stops, the breathing falters, her chest freezes, and then a moment later her body deflates as her soul leaves her body and journeys to the next life.

At last, she is dead.

CHAPTER THIRTY-THREE

Rose Whitaker knew little about the adult club Angelica had told her of. Her sister-in-law had been shy on the details, both before the event and after, and all Rose knew for certain was that it was an invite-only affair, a prestige place for people to gather, presumably for social drinks with perhaps a darker, sordid side to it. Tomek hoped it wasn't the Southend Seven, a local gentlemen's club in the heart of Southend, formerly operated and run by the city's political elite. Now abandoned and closed down, it had once been the home of a small sex-trafficking ring. Tomek's immediate thoughts had jumped to that conclusion, that Angelica had been swept up in it somehow, but he quickly dismissed it as soon as Rose had confirmed it was somewhere outside Southend, somewhere in the Essex countryside.

In the meantime, following the meeting with Rose, Tomek had sent Oscar and a team of scenes of crime officers and uniformed constables to search for the invite inside Angelica's flat. It was a printed document, Rose had said, no larger than A5, with Angelica's name on it in a cursive, handwritten font, the date of the event and the organiser's contact details on the reverse. Now they had a brief description of what they were looking for, it was hoped that they might find something that had previously been overlooked in the original search of Angelica's flat. Despite the detailed description, however, and despite the number of people looking for it, Oscar and the team had been unsuccessful, and after a six-hour search which had taken them close to the early hours of the morning, they had called it a day. It was nowhere to be found.

Tomek had lain awake throughout the night, turning thoughts over in his mind. Thoughts of the case, and of the argument with Abigail. It had been more than twenty-four hours since their bust-up and he hadn't heard from her. Not a text, not a phone call. She hadn't even sent him a funny meme or video on WhatsApp, which in today's world was sacrilegious for some. He had run through the argument several times in his head, playing it through in different scenarios, imagining how it might have gone differently if he'd shouted louder or responded with certain comebacks (hindsight was a wonderful thing in those situations), and by the end of it, he'd decided he had nothing to apologise for. Sure, he'd overreacted, shouted in her face, had a go at her. But she'd pushed him over the edge, overstepped the mark and crossed the boundary. Not to mention she'd insulted his integrity and called into question his capabilities in his role. His first time managing an investigation, and she'd belittled him. Added to the earlier grilling he'd received from Victoria and Nick, for a brief moment, he'd questioned whether he was capable of the task, whether he had what was required.

He continued to wrestle with his thoughts, his crippling, debilitating sense of doubt, the same that Angelica had felt at the end of each season ("Why won't they keep me on?", "Am I good enough to stay the whole year?", "Will they accept me back?") the following morning as he entered Whitaker's Jewellers. Rose had called him before nine o'clock, just as he was on his way to work, notifying him that she'd found the invitation in one of Angelica's jackets that she'd left in the staff room. Tomek had been more than happy to turn round and pop over to inspect.

The front of the shop was entirely floor-to-ceiling windows, showcasing rows of delicate and ornate diamond and gemstone jewels sitting neatly on soft velvet displays. Rings, necklaces, earrings. Some of the prettiest and most intricate designs Tomek had ever seen. And if he thought the exterior was spectacular, he was in for a shock when he entered. As soon as he stepped through the door, he got a sense that this was a safe space, a welcoming place for people – confused boyfriends and husbands who were well out of their depth – to come looking for engagement rings or generous gifts without the threat of some commission-hungry zombie pressuring them into a purchase. This was Rose's lifeblood, and he sensed she would know when to toe the line and when to step just over it.

The middle of the shop was dominated by a large glass display case. In it, dozens of earrings of varying shapes, sizes and carats dangled from stylish branches, surrounded by a bed of leaves and twigs. To his right, running along the wall, was a similar display case, except it had been littered with sand and various seashells and stones picked up from along the beach. To his left was a large wooden scale-model sailing yacht called *The Rose* that sat in the centre of the display. Necklaces and bracelets, including their charms and price tickets, hung from the masts and other parts of the boat. At the back of the shop, sitting behind a cash desk, was Rose. She climbed out of her seat and rounded the desk.

'Each display's a representation of Leigh-on-Sea and beyond,' she said, making her way towards the display on Tomek's right. 'Our lovely little fishing history,' she continued. 'An homage to the fish and oysters that are farmed there. The diamonds and gems in this one are yellow to represent the sand.' She joined him in the centre of the room, moving slowly, elegantly, almost seductively. 'This one represents Belfairs, one of my favourite woods. Sometimes Johnny and I would go for walks round there in the summer.' She pointed to the emeralds, and after her moment of reflection was over, she moved to the sailing yacht. 'Johnny bought me this when I first opened the shop. Said it was a good luck charm. Shame it wasn't a real one. That would've been nice. Still, next best thing, I guess.'

'It's the gesture that counts,' Tomek replied. 'Though I think you're missing one...'

'One what?'

'A display.'

'Oh?'

'Where's the mud? You can't have a display dedicated to Leigh and not have one that contains a shit load of mud.'

The corners of her lips rose. 'You read my mind,' she said, as she pointed to a corner of the wall to Tomek's right. He hadn't noticed it, but hidden behind a concrete pillar was another display case, smaller, with brown paint on the base and wooden poles protruding from it.

'Is that supposed to be the pier?'

'I know it's cheating. Southend... not quite Leigh-on-Sea. But that one's for the tourists.'

'Do you get many?'

'More than you'd think.'

'None from Dublin, I hope.' The words left his mouth before he was able to catch them. His hand flew to his mouth, then he lowered it. 'I'm so sorry, I—'

'She'd better hope she doesn't end up in here by mistake,' Rose replied, taking Tomek by surprise. 'I've got sharp tools in the back. And machines. Might run her fingers under one of my grinders, then poke her eye out with the fucking stud from one of these earrings.' She picked one up from the nearest display and, gritting her teeth, stabbed her invisible opponent repeatedly with the tiny pin.

Tomek chuckled, relieved that she saw the funny side of it.

'I'd say that's the least she deserves,' he said, though without realising why. He didn't know why, but he felt an attraction to Rose. One that he shouldn't, one that felt wrong. But perhaps that was why he felt that way in the first place; because he knew he couldn't, because he knew he shouldn't, that it was taboo. She was attractive, intelligent, and had her own business. She was respectable, successful, driven, hard-working, and he admired that about her. But as he thought about her in that way, what she would be like to kiss, an image of Abigail entered his head, and he quickly turned his attention to the woodland display in the middle of the room. Green, Abigail's favourite colour.

'You still need something for your girlfriend?' Rose asked.

Tomek did a double-take, suddenly shy. 'Oh, that? No... no, I don't think so.'

'Oh?'

'Yeah.'

'Trouble in paradise?'

'Kinda. Though it's not quite the same as your situation. I guess people would call it a rough patch.'

'I was going to say, if you need to borrow any stabbing pins, you know where to find me.'

Tomek *did* know where to find her. And from the flirtatious grin on her face, she was more than happy for him to come round again, and again, and maybe a fourth time.

An awkward silence came between them. Tomek briefly forgot what he was there for and it wasn't until a customer came through the doors that they both sprang to life. Rose told the customer that she'd be with them shortly, then gestured for Tomek to follow her to the back office. The room was no larger than a small bathroom. Most of the space was taken up by several coats hanging from a peg and a couple of pairs of shoes stacked atop one another on the floor. Rose reached into a light green jacket on one of the pegs and removed a small white card. As she handed it to him, she said, 'You'll have to let me know what it's like if you end up going. Ever since she told me about it, it's piqued my curiosity.'

Tomek nodded. He thanked her, then left her to the customer. As she wandered off, addressing the man who'd just entered, Tomek surveyed the document. It was smaller than A5, made from thick, expensive card. In the middle, handwritten in black calligraphy, was Angelica's name. Beneath it were the words, "...is cordially invited to a night of dalliance and debauchery with other devilish debutantes." At the top of the card was an image of a masquerade ball mask with a small emblem emblazoned in one eye. At the bottom was the address.

Melback Manor, Burnham-on-Crouch.

With the owner's name and contact number on the reverse.

CHAPTER THIRTY-FOUR

The man they were looking for was called Micky Tatton. The woman behind the reception desk at the sprawling countryside estate had told them he would be on his way down in a few minutes. In that time, Tomek and Rachel asked her a few questions about the place, pretending to be a couple that were looking to have their wedding ceremony there. Melback Manor, she said, was first built over five hundred years ago by the Tudors, and had been in the Tatton family for nearly two centuries. Opening to the public in the early two thousands, the mansion and adjoining cottage had become a favourite for soon-to-be newlyweds, with over a thousand weddings conducted in twenty years. They were open forty weeks of the year, with the remaining twelve shut for maintenance and refurbishment.

As a prospective customer, that little detail stuck out to Tomek, so he asked more about the estate and what needed repairing.

'The cottage on the south side is the newest part of the property, but it's the one that needs the most work, sadly,' she explained. 'We have a lot of guests who stay with us, as I'm sure you can imagine, and all that movement in and out of the rooms means there are always things that suffer from wear and tear. But fortunately, our teams are always on hand to fix or replace anything should you need it. We have several packages, each one unique to you, depending on your price range and requirements. I can get one of our staff to take you through them if you'd like?'

Mercifully, before Tomek could answer and get himself deeper into the rabbit warren of lies, a man appeared in a wooden framed doorway.

'Mr Tatton!' she said, as she rounded the desk and placed a hand on his arm.

The man came to an abrupt stop and, despite the obvious grievance at the interruption, he wore a pleasant, welcoming, if somewhat forced, smile. He was in his mid-fifties and was dressed in a light blue suit and matching tie. His hair was thick, wavy, and combed backwards stylishly. His jawline was rough and handsome, and he had a messy beard that hugged his face. He looked like he'd come from somewhere in Mayfair or Westminster, with a silver rod shoved so far up his arse that it was visible in his mouth every time he spoke – but what else did you expect from someone who'd inherited his family's two-hundred-year-old fortune?

'Good afternoon,' he said in a deep baritone voice, polite and formal. 'How may I assist you? Are you guests or looking to take out one of our packages?'

'Neither,' Tomek answered.

'Yet,' added Rachel, with a little side glance to Tomek.

Micky chuckled nervously. 'Well, whatever it is, I'm sure we can accommodate you.'

'Fantastic, just what we wanted to hear.' Tomek reached into his pocket and produced the invitation, covering Angelica's name with his finger.

As soon as the man recognised what it was, his mouth fell open, and he began to babble. He stood there, surveying Tomek and Rachel intently. Tomek could see confusion on the man's face as he tried to work out whether he recognised them.

'I understand,' he said quickly. 'Why don't you follow me? My office is occupied at the moment, a business meeting, boring stuff really, but I'm sure we can find a room somewhere to discuss things further. Why don't we walk and talk?'

Tomek and Rachel obliged. He took them through a large open doorway into a small seating area, through another door, into a larger space, this one filled with enough sofas and chairs for them to get comfortable. In the corner was a grand piano, sitting with its lid down, closed, unloved. The room, and to an extent the entire building, smelled of old, hundred-year-old furniture that was well past its restoration date, wooden beams that had soaked up so much moisture over the centuries that they were beginning to rot, and thick layers of dust that had formed in the nooks and crannies of the walls and ceilings. Some might have called it rustic, original, part of the identity of the place. Tomek called it stale and in need of a clean. Which, given the fact the place was closed for twelve weeks of the year for restoration purposes, begged the question of what they spent all that time cleaning?

'We currently have a wedding going on,' Micky Tatton explained, 'so I won't be able to take you through the gardens. But, depending if we get lucky, you might get to see the cottage.' Micky came to a stop, raised a finger for them to wait, then checked the nearby corridors. When the coast was clear, he closed the door and returned. 'Forgive me, I don't recognise your faces, but then again I wouldn't, would I?'

Tomek didn't know to what he was referring, but decided to indulge him.

'No. No, you wouldn't.'

Micky leant in, keeping his voice low. 'I don't... I don't usually discuss The Nights in public, especially in such an open space, but... I guess I can make an exception. Did you... did you meet at one of The Nights of Eden?'

Tomek and Rachel glanced at one another. How far were they willing to take the deceit? In the end, Micky beat them to it.

'Well, I never thought I'd see the day,' he continued, jumping to his own conclusion. 'Two of my companions meeting and falling in love, come to ask about wedding venues – *here* of all places!'

Rachel linked her arm under Tomek's, but he shooed her off.

'We're not here about wedding venues,' he said bluntly. 'We're not even together.'

'But the...?'

'The invitation, yes. It belongs to Angelica Whitaker.' He showed it to Micky again, this time revealing the name.

Micky inspected it, fear creeping into the whites of his eyes. He took a small step back. 'Who are you?'

'We're the police,' Tomek said with a flash of his warrant card and a cheeky-chappie smile. 'We wanted to ask you a few questions about—'

'No. No police. I've never broken a law and I don't plan on it. Everything's legal, above board and consensual. I make everyone sign an NDA, so there's no chance of this sort of thing happening.'

'What sort of thing?' Rachel pressed.

He couldn't answer.

'You don't know why we're here because you haven't let us explain,' she continued. 'If you'd let my colleague finish, you might have understood why we've come.'

Micky looked up at Tomek expectantly. 'Well?' There was urgency in his voice now. He was keen to get this over with as quickly as possible.

'Tell us more about the place first,' Tomek replied.

'Like what?'

'Like how many rooms you've got. How many guests you can hold. About *you*. Your history.'

'How is that relevant?'

Tomek shrugged. It wasn't. He just wanted to make the man sweat a little longer, prolong the paranoia. After a few minutes of explaining about the Tudor features of the building, Micky had echoed everything that the receptionist had told them, almost verbatim. Then he went on to explain he'd inherited the land after his father's death and in a bid to break free from the aristocratic mould that his parents had destined for him, he'd taken the entrepreneurial decision to open the mansion up to the public as a wedding venue and operate it as a successful and prominent business on the Essex coast.

'Now will you tell me what this is about?' Micky asked as soon as he'd finished.

'It's about Angelica Whitaker. Do you recognise that name?'

The man dropped his head a fraction. 'Yes.'

'How do you know her?'

At that point, a group of four wedding guests, drunker than a teen on their eighteenth birthday, entered the room and interrupted them. Micky explained that they were having a private meeting and asked the guests to find somewhere else to have their catch-up. It took a few moments for the words to register in their drink-addled minds, but when they eventually did, the guests left disgruntled, mumbling under their breath.

'I don't know Angelica well,' Micky explained as he shut the door behind them. 'I only know her name and what she does for a living.'

'How?'

'Because I first met her on a flight, and the name badge on her uniform gave it away.'

Tomek didn't appreciate the sarcasm.

'Explain how you came to give her this then.' He waved the invitation in the air.

Micky moved to a small chair and perched himself on the edge of the seat, while Rachel and Tomek remained standing.

'I was on a flight,' he started. 'France to Southend, I think it was. I was meeting one of our wine suppliers. We buy direct from the vineyards. And I just remember seeing her and thinking, that's the most stunning woman I've ever met. And so I started chatting to her. She was funny, lively, energetic, the rest of it. It was towards the end of summer, so I asked her what she was doing after that, and she said she didn't know.

Said that she had some job lined up in a jeweller's which she wasn't too keen about. So I thought I'd invite her to one of The Nights of Eden. To be honest, she looked like she needed some excitement in her life, something to keep her going, something to remind her what it's like to be alive.'

'Is that what these "Nights of Eden" are then? Reminders of what it's like to be alive?' Tomek made no attempt to hide the cynicism in his voice.

'I think so, yes. And so do a lot of our members.'

Tomek finally took the plunge and joined Micky on a chair next to him. It was beautifully designed, looked handmade, and was perfectly sculpted, but it was a bastard to sit on. The cushion was rock solid, and the wooden spine of the chair dug into the small of his back. What made it worse was the fact it probably cost a fortune; he couldn't imagine spending so much on something so uncomfortable just to enhance the aesthetics of a room. He'd rather sit on the floor.

'How do your "Nights of Eden" work?' Tomek asked once he'd got himself as comfortable as he could. 'What happens at these things?'

'You know you don't have to put them in quotation marks all the time,' Micky snapped. 'They're real events that real people come along to.'

'So, you should be able to tell us what happens at them,' Rachel noted forcefully.

Micky shook his head profusely. 'No. That's strictly confidential.'

Tomek had hoped he would say that. 'Are they still confidential when one of your attendees was found murdered the other day and your name and this place has come up in our investigations?'

The man had nothing to say to that. Just looked at them blankly.

'Didn't think so. So why don't you cut the confidentiality crap and just tell us what we need to know? It would save us all a lot of time and stress. Otherwise my colleague here can arrest you on suspicion of murder and we can have this discussion down at the station? It's no skin off our nose either way.'

Eventually, the realisation that he didn't have a choice dawned on Micky. Before continuing, he checked the corridors again and locked one of the doors on the other side of the room to ensure they could speak without fear of being interrupted again.

'What... what do you want to know?' he asked, his voice faltering.

'All of it. From the top.'

Micky took a deep breath in, began tapping his foot nervously on the floor, and slowly exhaled, whistling through his mouth. It was clear to see this went against everything he believed in, that it pained him just thinking about letting all his dark little secrets out. But he had no choice. Ahead of his speech, Rachel prepared her pen and notebook.

'Listen,' he started, already setting the tone of what he was about to say. 'You have to understand that this is a world with which you're probably not familiar, that you may never understand. There's nothing wrong with what we do, nothing immoral or corrupt or illegal about it. It's just... different.'

'Okay... You've got your caveat out of the way, now you can tell us everything.'

Micky swallowed hard. 'On the first weekend of every month, Friday through Saturday, I host a party night. The Nights of Eden. It's invite only. The rest of the property is closed, so no weddings, no guests, and everyone attending must come in fancy dress.'

'Fancy dress?'

'Let me finish!'

Tomek raised his hands in mock surrender. He didn't need to be told again.

'Fancy dress can be anything,' Micky continued, letting out a heavy sigh, 'but it's like a masquerade ball, like the type you used to get in the old days. So face masks, like the Venetian ones you see on TV, are required to protect your identity, or at least some elements of your identity. Some people come with devil masks, others the generic masquerade masks. Others wear anything that covers their entire face. Angelica, I remember, usually comes in the same outfit: an angel, complete with skimpy little white dress, feathered wings attached to her back, white eye mask and a golden halo above her head. To the best of my recollection, she's been to every meeting since I first invited her back in September. She hasn't missed an event yet – most people don't once they get a taste of it.

'There are certain rules that everyone must follow if they wish to attend. First, you must kiss the hand of the person who arrived before you, and then you must wait for the next person to arrive to kiss your hand. It creates a chain, and the aim is to arrive as early as possible so you're not the last one in. That person is usually left standing outside in the cold for the entire evening. Once guests are inside, they must then offer a sacrifice. Don't worry, it's not anything morbid or bloody, it's an offering to me, as their host. They have to give me something of theirs: an item of clothing, food, drink, any possession they might have that they're willing to sacrifice. Then, after that, they must kiss Paddy the Pig. Again, don't worry, it's nothing sordid. It's not like you have to kiss a real one. Paddy's a taxidermy of a pig we once had in the family many generations ago. He was said to have brought our family good fortune in the past, and so I hope he gives all my guests good fortune, too. It doesn't matter where you kiss him, or for how long, so long as your lips touch a part of his body, I don't mind.'

This was getting weirder by the second. Normally, Tomek would have called bullshit on everything the man was saying, but for some reason he unequivocally believed every word that came out of Micky Tatton's mouth. He was stunned at the sort of bizarre rituals Micky had his guests follow, and wondered what type of person would be willing to agree to them. It was the sort of thing you'd see in films and TV dramas – the high-society secret parties, the political and social elite committing nefarious acts on animals in a bid to win a higher social standing – but he never thought he'd come across it in real life.

'Inside The Nights of Eden,' Micky continued, 'we have different rooms for different things. There's music provided by a DJ playing in one of them, bars where you can buy drinks. People go in there just for a dance, a little bump and grind. Then we have other rooms where people enjoy themselves a little more freely, and with fewer clothes on, if you know what I mean.'

Tomek knew exactly what he meant, but he couldn't forgive the man for saying "bump and grind". Nobody of his age should be saying that type of thing. It made him cringe.

'What happens in these rooms?' Rachel asked, more to point up Micky's awkwardness rather than her own naïvety.

'You want me to spell it out?'

She prodded her pen on her notebook. 'If you could. I've got to write it down, and I could use a hand with the spelling as well.'

A long, heavy sigh left Micky's nose. 'In a couple of the rooms there's... there's... it's an orgy, okay? Beds, sofas, cushions, apparatus – all over the place. Music in the background. A lot of fragrance in the air. And people just... doing what they want to do to one another.'

'Got that, Rach?' Tomek asked.

'*Doing what they want to do to one another*,' she repeated, then looked up from her notebook. 'Have you ever had an instance where someone did something the other person didn't want them to do?'

'You mean rape?'

'Or sexual assault. It comes in many forms.'

Micky shook his head so hard that his cheeks caught up with the rest of his face a fraction of a second later. 'Never. No. Absolutely not. I have never had any such instance. Like I said, everything is consensual.'

'But if something did, would you tell us?'

'Yes.'

'That wouldn't interfere with your NDAs at all?'

'I... I don't sign one, so I'm not bound by anything.'

'Just your own moral compass,' Tomek retorted.

If Micky Tatton took offence at the comment, he didn't show it.

'What else goes on?' Rachel asked.

'More sex,' Micky replied bluntly. 'Couples, trios, as many people as they like, can go into some of the private rooms and sleep together. There are toys, straps, whips, anything they want. It's all supplied to them.'

'Protection?'

'We have condoms, yes...' Micky hesitated, his mouth open.

'Why do I sense a "but"?'

'But half of them have been pierced. It's one of the rules we have. There's a pot of them in the corridor, you reach your hand in, take one, and...'

'And hope for the best?' Tomek finished.

Now he was beginning to wonder about who the father of Angelica's unborn baby might be.

'Anything else?' Rachel asked.

Micky shook his head.

'Did Angelica ever use any of these rooms?' Tomek asked.

The man picked at his fingernail. 'Yes. She explored all of them. More so the private rooms than the public one.'

'Do you know who with?'

Micky thought on that for a beat. 'No. No, I don't know who he is.'

'Why not?'

'Because he wears a donkey mask.'

Tomek sniggered. 'A donkey mask?'

'Yes, a donkey mask.'

'And you can't see his face?'

'No. That's part of the point. At The Nights of Eden you can be whoever you want. You have no limits, only the ones you place upon yourself. You have complete and utter freedom and control to do what you want and be who you want. You can really let yourself go. The masks hide the individual, so there's no chance of being caught or noticed out in the real world. Her particular lover chose to wear a donkey mask, just the same as she chose to wear an angel mask.'

So she'd been sleeping with an ass.

'We need to speak with him,' Tomek told Micky. 'You need to contact him and put him in touch with us.'

Micky Tatton didn't like the sound of that.

'I don't have his number. The only way you could find out who he is would be if you came to one of The Nights of Eden yourselves.'

Now it was Tomek's turn to dislike something. But as he turned to face Rachel, he realised she didn't share the same sentiment. Her eyes beamed at the prospect of attending one of these events, of seeing the decadence and debauchery in the flesh. She looked as though it was something that bizarrely excited her, that it may have been on her bucket list.

'There's one this weekend,' Micky added, as if to sweeten the deal.

'Great,' Rachel replied. 'Give us a time and we'll see you there.'

'Just remember to make sure you're on time, if not a little early. We wouldn't want you hanging around outside, missing out on all the fun.'

'No, we definitely wouldn't,' Tomek retorted.

'Oh,' Micky added, 'and don't forget your costumes.'

CHAPTER THIRTY-FIVE

The last two days of the week passed in a blur. The team had been so full on that Tomek had barely had time to stop and think about Friday night's activity. He was starting work at seven, leaving Kasia to make her own way to school, and in the evenings he wasn't getting home till eight or nine, arriving home to a ready meal in the microwave and a daughter who'd locked herself in her room, leaving the television and sofa for himself. He hadn't watched anything; he spent his evenings working on the case, going over the team's notes for the day, handling all the administration headaches and pain-in-arse parts of the inspector's role he'd been handed. All of this had meant there was no time for Abigail to come over. Not in the afternoons, not in the evenings. He couldn't remember the last time they'd messaged one another. And when they had, it had only been brief, small talk, almost platonic. Tomek knew what that meant in today's instantly connected society: that their days as a couple were numbered. That their relationship was coming to a gradual close. And, to think it had happened only a few weeks after he'd introduced her to his mother. That his mother had approved and spoke highly of her, and yet he hadn't been able to see it through. Was there something fundamentally wrong with him? Or was he just incapable of love? He had battled that question alone in bed at night. In the end, he'd decided that he wasn't worthy of love, that he was an idiot, an immature, childish idiot who always threw away a good thing. A childish idiot who always got scared at the first sign of trouble, because, in the past few days, thoughts of Rose Whitaker had frequently entered his mind. Her smile, her dress sense, her mannerisms. The way she controlled herself. On several occasions, he had fought the urge to pop into the jeweller's just to make unnecessary conversation, just to see her face. He only hadn't because, as far as he was aware, he and Abigail were still boyfriend and girlfriend, and it would be the worst type of betrayal. It wasn't what she deserved. He'd made that mistake in the past, and he wasn't prepared to do it again.

But right now, all Tomek could think about were the numbers, the budgets, the facts and figures that he'd memorised ahead of this meeting. It had been in the calendar all week. The last thing on a Friday. And so he'd had plenty of time to prepare. Which meant the expectation placed upon him would be even greater.

Tomek waited outside Nick's office, listening for the call. When it came, he placed a nervous hand on the handle and stepped in. Wearing one of the fakest smiles he'd ever pulled off, he nodded to Nick and Victoria and seated himself opposite them.

'Thanks for coming,' Nick started. He cast a quick side glance at the time on his computer monitor, and added, 'And with a couple of minutes to spare, too. The old Tomek would have got that the other way round. I'm impressed.'

'God bless modern technology and alarm systems,' Tomek replied. 'I imagine back in your day you had to wait for the suns and the moons to cross paths before you knew what time it was, right?'

'Almost,' Nick answered. 'It was the sun, moon, and Ur-an-anus – sorry, I mean, you're an arsehole.'

Tomek fired a finger gun at the man, accompanying it with a little wink. 'Touché.'

Before they could continue their slightly immature banter, Victoria interrupted by clearing her throat. She gave them each a scolding look, like a disapproving mother, and said, 'Have you prepared everything we asked?'

'Only one way to find out.'

'Good. So give us the latest.'

Straight in for the jugular. No hanging about.

Time to sink or swim now, mate.

'This week myself and Rachel spoke with a man called Micky Tatton, the owner of Melback Manor, and the organiser of The Nights of—'

'Ah, yes. I heard about this from Chey,' Nick interrupted. 'The place that has the little sex parties.'

'*Big* sex parties, if what we were told is true.'

'I also hear you've bagged yourself an invite.'

'For work purposes—'

'I wouldn't say that qualifies for overtime, would you, Victoria?'

The inspector gave a leering grin. 'Absolutely not.'

'Exactly my thinking. Sounds like there's going to be more fun than fact-finding.'

'Sir...'

Nick raised a hand to stop him. 'Just remember to behave yourself, Tomek. You're representing the police when you go along to this... orgy.'

Tomek opened his mouth to fight the decision, but quickly realised defeat.

'As I was saying, we're going to one of The Nights of Eden tonight. Our aim is to speak with someone we've dubbed "The Donkey Man". We don't know what he looks like, or anything else about him, other than the fact he goes to these things wearing a donkey mask. Hopefully, he's not hung like one. We're hoping to see what he can tell us about his sexual encounters with Angelica.'

'Perv,' Nick said flippantly. Then, more seriously, he added, 'And you think this person might have had something to do with Angelica's murder?'

Tomek hesitated. 'We're keeping our options open. As far as we've been able to discern, Angelica Whitaker was no stranger to sex, which muddies the waters a little when it comes to her pregnancy. But from our discussions with Cole Thompson, one of her current sexual partners, she always ensured he wore a condom. We can only assume that this rule extended to the random people she picked up on nights out. The only instance where that isn't the case is at The Nights of Eden. According to the owner, half of the condoms are pierced, half aren't, so it's very possible that The Donkey Man is the father of Angelica's unborn child, and there's every possibility that she told him on the night she died and he killed her.'

Nick nodded thoughtfully. Tomek thought he saw an ounce of pride in the chief inspector's expression. 'Understood. Continue.'

Tomek did as he was told. 'Also this week, the team has been interviewing the rest of Angelica's friends and colleagues. They've taken over thirty witness statements and checked various alibis with the aim of doing more over the weekend and early next week. The teenagers who discovered the body have come forward and given us detailed accounts of what they did and what they saw. The poor bastards got the fright of their lives. Hopefully, they'll think twice about breaking and entering again. The analysis on the padlock that was broken to get into the church has come back, and until we can find the cutters that were used to do it, there's not much we can follow from there. The blood analysis also came back: they found Rohypnol in her bloodstream, and so we think that Adam Egglington, the guy she was dancing with at the club on the night she died, was successful in slipping something in her drink. As for Angelica's clothes and phone, they're still nowhere to be found. Every opportunity we get, we're searching for them in suspects' homes with the necessary warrants. We've done several rounds of forensic analysis on some of the hairs and trace fibres found at the crime scene, but so far nothing's come back with any degree of success. The hairs that were discovered were found to have come from the paintbrush used to paint the angel wings. I'm still pushing for more forensic analysis on the bits that were picked up at the scene.'

'Why?' Victoria snapped.

'Because I think there must be something there. The killer must have left a trace.'

'And what about the budget? You don't have that much left to play with, and continuous rounds of forensic examination are going to blow a pretty large hole in a fairly small budget.'

Tomek shrugged, then continued with his explanation. 'Also, Chey, meanwhile, has been looking into the CCTV footage from around Park Road Methodist Church. We've had several neighbours come forward with home security footage of the night Angelica was murdered, but so far nothing concrete has come up. We anticipate that she was killed between two and four in the morning, and was then dropped off at the church a short while later. We think the killer might have been cutting it fine with painting the wings before it started to get light and people started to wake up for the day job, but regardless, they were able to get in and slip out undetected. In addition to all of that, Chey has been looking at footage in the surrounding area and along the main roads at that time. Fortunately, it was the early hours of the morning, so we're hoping that we can find one or two cars that might have been on the same roads that followed the journey from Angelica's house to her crime scene. But so far nothing's come of it.'

Victoria opened her mouth to speak, but Tomek cut her off.

'Also, Chey has been diving deep into Angelica's social media accounts, making a note of all the names of those who used to comment on her posts, and anyone who messaged her online, across all her accounts. We also found a Tinder and Hinge account, which we've started to scour. She spoke to a lot of men in the past few months, but so far, none of them are screaming out at us. But if anything changes, Chey will be the first to know.'

'Chey's been busy,' Victoria remarked bluntly. After her last comments about the constable, Tomek had taken it personally and decided to defend his team member as much as possible. Now she had no leg to stand on if she chose to launch another attack on the young detective.

'No busier than usual.'

Tomek noticed the chortle escape Nick's lips. He caught it escaping any further by asking, 'Have you got any suspects?'

'A few.'

'Who?'

Tomek rattled them off: Shawn Wilkins, the stalker who had overstepped the mark on several occasions; Cole Thompson, the friend with benefits and possible father to her child whose alibi ran out after one in the morning; Micky Tatton, and The Donkey Man. Tomek had other suspects floating about in his mind, but decided to keep those quiet for now. They were based solely on intuition and a feeling deep in his stomach. He pointed out that, if they were able to find any DNA at the scene, he would be able to answer her question more definitively.

'And in the case you don't find any DNA, what then?' Victoria said. 'You need to have a backup. Run me through what you think happened to her. What's your hypothesis?'

Tomek shuffled in his seat. He'd prepared for this, rehearsed it. 'Angelica Whitaker went out with her friends. Four of them in total. They were at Memo in Southend, where she was dancing with Adam Egglington. At one fifteen am, her and her friends went home. She was dropped off first at one twenty-eight, then, a little under twenty-five minutes later, she was picked up in a car. At around the same time, her phone was switched off. We do not know why. It was either done manually or it had run out of battery. We've reached out to her provider for the call logs or last messages she sent, but they don't have any information for us about who she was contacting. We believe she may have been using WhatsApp because there's no record of any messages being sent on her social media accounts. And to complicate matters, she doesn't have a laptop, just an iPad without the app on it, so there's no way of us logging into her WhatsApp account without access to her phone. Anyway, shortly after she was picked up, she was taken somewhere, killed, raped, shaved, cleaned, drained, and then she was transported to the church, where her blood was used to paint angel wings behind her.'

Nick and Victoria nodded politely, making notes in their books as he spoke.

'What sort of person did this? Do you have an answer for that yet? Do you think it was random or someone she knew?'

That particular question had stuck with him the most since their first meeting. Of them all, he'd torn that one apart from all angles imaginable, and he was now prepared to lay his claim on one choice with a fairly high degree of certainty.

'I think this is someone who knew Angelica. Someone who knew her very well, intimately. Someone who *adored* her. They took so much time cleaning and preparing her body that this was carefully thought out. They would have needed a place to do it quietly and without threat of interruption, and crucially, they would have needed to know that she was baptised there. I don't think that's a detail we should overlook. But rest assured we're looking into all possibilities, and we're working round the clock to find out who did this.'

'Excellent. Thanks for that,' Victoria replied, flat. Tomek was taken aback by how blunt she was. Perhaps he'd been naïve to think she might stroke his ego and give him a pat on the back for a job well done so far.

'How are we looking on budgets?' she asked, going back to her earlier question.

He told her.

'Very good,' she said. 'I think that's all from me. Nick, any questions?'

The chief inspector shook his head, so Tomek dragged himself out of the chair and headed out of the room. As he shut the door behind him, he caught Chey leaving the kitchen, a mug of tea in his hand. As soon as he locked eyes with Tomek, a childish grin exploded onto his face.

'What is it?' Tomek asked, suddenly feeling deflated and defeated.

'You looking forward to your sex party tonight?'

'I'm not going there to have sex, Chey.'

'Not tonight, you won't. But that doesn't mean to say you might not go there next month on a *personal* basis.'

Tomek hadn't considered that. Maybe he would.

'Just make sure you've got the same costume, so people recognise you.'

'What did you say?'

'Your costume. Make sure you wear the same one so people know who you are.' Chey stared into Tomek's eyes, and after a few moments, said, 'You *do* have a costume for tonight, don't you?'

He shook his head.

'Fuck! I completely forgot. Could you get me one?'

'Absolutely not. No way.'

Tomek reached into his pocket and produced his wallet. He pulled out a handful of notes. 'Here's fifty quid,' he said.

'How old are you? Who has cash these days? It's all on your phone or on contactless.'

Tomek ignored the comment. 'Take it to the nearest fancy dress shop and get me one. Please. I don't have time to go out before the meet.'

Chey surveyed the money in Tomek's hands. At first he was dubious, hesitant, but then excitement quickly kicked in. He snatched the money from Tomek and said, 'I get to keep the change?'

'Fine.'

'Awesome! Leave it with me. I'm going to get you the best outfit ever.'

And with that, the young man grabbed his coat and car keys and hurried out of the room. It wasn't until the slow door to the incident room finally closed shut that Tomek realised he'd just given fifty quid and the instruction of finding a fancy dress costume to the worst person possible: an immature twenty-five-year-old. It was like giving a firearm to a baby.

Not a good idea.

Before he could dwell on it for too long, his phone began vibrating in his pocket. He pulled it out and saw who was calling: Abigail.

The first time in nearly a week.

Big of her, he thought, to make the first move. He admired and respected it.

'Hey,' he answered.

'Hey.' Her voice was awkward, cold.

'You all right?' he asked.

'Yeah. You?'

'Not bad. Busy.'

'Same.'

'Yeah.'

'So...' she started. 'Do you... I was thinking, what're you doing tonight? I thought maybe I could come round to yours, we could cook a chilli or some fajitas, watch something on the television and maybe talk about what happened...'

The hesitation and fear in her voice were tangible, like she was clinging onto his every word, and for every second that passed, every second that he didn't answer, her grip gradually weakened and weakened.

'Abs...' he began. 'I would love to, but...'

'It's fine. I understand.'

'I've got a work thing. Otherwise I would...'

'Yeah. No, I get it. I...' She sniffed back the catch in her throat. 'Maybe some other time.'

'Yeah. Maybe some other time.'

CHAPTER THIRTY-SIX

Tomek had never wanted to hurt anyone in his life more than he wanted to hurt Chey for what he'd done. The team, of which there had only been a few left at the time – mercifully – had burst into fits of laughter as soon as they'd seen the outfit the young constable had chosen for Tomek. The little prick had left it right to the last minute before giving it to him as well, leaving Tomek with no choice but to wear it. He'd done a lot of stupid things in his life, the majority of them when he'd been in his early twenties, when he'd been young, naïve and fearless, and hadn't cared what anybody thought about him. But now, at over forty years old, he had never felt more self-conscious than he did as he pulled the car into Melback Manor's sprawling estate. The sound of gravel crunching under the tyres was the second loudest sound in the car – second to Rachel's unbearable sniggering.

'You can either shut up or I'm turning this thing around and going back home,' he told her.

'Yes, sir, sorry, sir,' Rachel replied before breaking into another fit of laughter.

But before Tomek could retort, or even think about turning the vehicle around, a man wearing a tailored suit and Volto mask approached them, his hands behind his back. He waited patiently for Tomek to lower the window.

'Your keys, sir,' the man said, his voice feigning a faint Italian accent.

'There's a fucking valet?'

'Yes, sir. You can collect your keys at the end of the night.'

Tomek sighed. 'Let me guess, I have to find them in the bottom of a fishbowl, do I?'

'Yes, sir.'

'Brilliant.'

The man opened the car door for Tomek and took a step back, keeping his arms politely behind his back. Tomek was left with no choice. He didn't like the idea of leaving his car in the middle of a country estate with no immediate access to his keys, but he quickly realised he was going to have to fully immerse himself in the experience whether he liked it or not. Reluctantly, he climbed out of the car, handed the keys across, and watched as the man drove off into the darkness round the corner of the estate.

'You'll get it back,' Rachel said as she joined his side. 'Right after he's taken it for a joyride.'

'Funny.'

'Hope you've got some cash for a tip.'

Tomek looked down at himself, gesturing to his outfit. 'Where the fuck am I going to keep spare change?'

'No place I want to know about.'

Rachel brushed past him and made her way towards the entrance. By the front door, two metal flame heaters were positioned to keep guests warm as they came in; large, perfectly manicured shrubs were placed by the stone pillars, and a chair had been provided on the stone patio. A woman was already sitting there, perched on the edge, leaning forward eagerly. She was dressed in a black funeral outfit, with a wide-brimmed sinamay hat base and fascinator on her head, her face covered by a black lace veil that carefully distorted her features. The woman's excitement grew as they approached.

It was a little after seven pm. The Nights of Eden had begun at six thirty, and already the sound of chatter, conversation, laughter and music – along with some other sounds Tomek tried hard to ignore – permeated the air.

'How long you been waiting for?' Rachel asked the woman.

'That's an unfamiliar voice,' she replied seductively. 'I don't recognise it. First time?'

Tomek didn't like the way she eyed him up in his costume.

'Is it that obvious?' Rachel asked.

'It's not a bad thing. We like a bit of fresh meat. Especially you...' The woman nodded at Tomek's groin, at the bulge in his pants that had been caused by the crotch of his outfit, squishing and lifting things into an unbelievably uncomfortable position and making it look like he'd shoved a couple of socks down there. When Tomek didn't say anything, the woman added, 'Well, aren't you going to kiss my hand?'

Tomek looked at Rachel. Rachel looked back at him. The time had come. The first part of the ritual. They had a decision to make. Who would be first?

'I'm not doing it,' Tomek said to Rachel.

'Would you rather kiss my hand?'

'That could be weird. But either way, one of us is going to have to kiss the other's—'

'How about I make it easy for both of you?' The woman sauntered towards Tomek and held out her hand, wiggling her fingers in front of his face. For a long moment, Tomek observed her nails. They were flame red, with small sparkles at the tips and immaculate, as though they'd just been done a few hours before.

Closing his eyes, Tomek took the woman's icy hand, held it in his, and then kissed it.

'There,' she said, lowering it gently, 'that wasn't so hard now, was it? There's plenty more where that came from inside.'

'Fuck my life,' he whispered as the woman winked at him, turned her back on them and headed inside, her long black dress chasing after her down the corridor.

Tomek and Rachel looked at one another in disbelief. Everything that Micky had told them about – the kissing ritual, the waiting ritual, the dress code – had all been true. A part of Tomek, a massive part, had hoped that it was all a con, some elaborate laugh that Micky Tatton would be having at their expense, but it wasn't. This was very real for a bunch of people, people that walked around him, along the street, in the supermarket, people who looked innocent on the outside but had a secret, decadent, salacious life behind closed doors.

'What's the matter?' Rachel asked. 'You look upset.'

'Of course I'm upset, Rach. I'm wearing a fucking American policeman's outfit that's at least two sizes too small. The assless chaps are riding up my arse *and* up my groin, both of which are almost on full display if it weren't for the shorts I put on underneath. The top is so tight I can barely breath, and I'm fairly sure the buttons are designed to come off with a single pull, which makes me believe this is the sort of thing a male stripper might wear. I'm wearing a fucking policeman's hat but a robber's face mask, which confuses the message entirely. I can barely see through the fucking slits, I've got a pair of plastic handcuffs digging into my fucking hip, and to top it off, I have to carry around *this*.'

Tomek brandished the oversized police truncheon that had come as part of the outfit. It was at least two feet long, and almost two inches thick at its widest point. Not only was it a pain in the arse to carry, but it was also seriously heavy, and written down the side, embossed in gold, were the words, "You've been naughty".

'I'm gonna fucking kill him tomorrow when I see him,' Tomek hissed. 'I'm gonna fucking kill him.'

'He saw an opportunity, and he took it. You can't blame him. You'd have done the same.'

Tomek would, of course he would. In fact, he would probably have done something worse, much worse. But Rachel didn't need to know that. It was all right for her. She had been in charge of her own outfit and looked respectable dressed in a black and pink jockey costume, complete with leather knee-high boots, a whip, flat cap, and goggles over her eyes. She wore it well, and it suited her.

'Now I have to kiss *your* hand,' she said.

'No, you don't, I reckon we can—'

Tomek was going to say that they could get away with it, that nobody would be watching. But Rachel didn't give him a chance to finish. Instead, she lunged for him, grabbed his hand, and kissed the back of it. Her lips were moist, sticky with lip gloss that glistened beneath the firelight.

As Tomek pulled his hand away, he said, 'Well, that was weird.' Then he began rubbing the area of skin she'd just kissed.

'I'm not diseased, Tomek.'

'I know. It's just... You're absolutely loving this, aren't you?'

She shrugged. 'I've been in need of some excitement in my life recently.'

'Save it for next month's visit. You can come on your own. Tonight we've got a job to do.'

'Yes, sir, sorry, sir. Have I been naughty, sir?' she joked playfully.

'Fuck off,' he told her, then turned slowly towards the entrance, towards the music, towards the sex.

'You scared?'

'No,' he said. 'I just have absolutely no fucking idea what to expect when I go through that door.'

She slapped him on the back. 'Keep an open mind. Remember, there's a lot of stuff like this that goes on in the world. More than we probably know. By the end of it, you'll have broadened your mind. And, hey, maybe you'll have learnt a thing or two.'

Tomek turned to face her. 'You're sick, you know that?'

She shoved him in the back. 'Go on, get in there and scout the place out. I'm waiting for my lady knight in shining armour to come and kiss me on the hand.'

'I hope it's a wrinkly old man with no teeth,' he told her.

With that, he turned his back on her, and before crossing the threshold into the unknown, inhaled deeply. He held the breath for a long time, until he could no more, then let it slowly out of his nostrils. The tension in his shoulders and upper back reduced gradually.

Then, with a long stride, he went through the front door.

The entrance to the building that he had walked through only a few days before seemed to take on a new life in the darkness. Candles adorned the surfaces, flickering in the gentle March breeze, emitting an abundance of scents filling the air with a soft, subtle fragrance. The walls and furniture shook with the vibrations of heavy bass playing deep in the building. Tomek reached a hand out to the wall and felt it ripple through his skin, up his arm and into his chest.

Dumf. Dumf. Dumf.

Either that, or it was his pounding heartbeat breaking through his ribcage.

A few strides in, he came to the next ritual. It was hidden behind a purple velvet curtain, a large glass dish containing an assortment of items. So far, the guests had already sacrificed a packet of ham, a tape measure, a lightbulb, some underwear, a single sock, a mini-USB, a pencil, and a protein powder scoop amongst many more random household items. Tomek was surprised to realise how many people were already inside. He reached inside the small chest pocket of his outfit and retrieved his sacrifice: a bottle opener. A broken one that he'd found in the kitchen in the office. He placed it in the bowl, then brushed his hands on his top before moving through another curtain. There, sitting on a small bar table, was the taxidermy pig.

'Fuck a duck,' he said as he stared at the poor animal. Images of a few weeks before flashed in his mind. He'd been trapped in the middle of a pigs' pen at a farm, surrounded by seven giant beasts as they'd feasted on a human body. Tomek had tried to save him, but almost come close to death himself. He hadn't thought of bacon or red meat since then, and now a reminder of that night was staring him in the face. To make it worse, now he had to kiss it.

Before doing so, he surveyed the small section of the room. That was when he noticed the security camera in the corner of the ceiling, trained on him, a red light flashing in the black dome. The sick pervert, Tomek thought, watching us while we do this shit. Reluctantly, realising he still had no choice in the matter, Tomek bent over and kissed the animal on the back. Its skin and fur were rough against his skin, and he was certain a hair became stuck between his lips.

He took a moment to compose himself and prepare for what lay beyond the next curtain. By now, the soothing, comforting smell of the candles had disappeared and been replaced with the smell of decadence, sweat, and perfume.

'Fuck it. Here goes nothing.'

Tentatively, he pushed the velvet curtain aside with one hand and stepped through. Once on the other side, the sound of music increased tenfold. It was like stepping into another building, pounding, pulsating. He entered in the middle of a corridor. A small signpost immediately in front of him offered two options: "The Room" to the left, and "The Rooms" to the right. Tomek didn't need to know any more to understand which one was which. But before he could make a decision, a large painting hanging from the wall above the signage caught his attention.

'It's called *The Garden of Earthly Delights*.'

The voice took him by surprise. He turned to see Rachel behind him, emerging from the curtain.

'The fuck did you get through so quickly?'

'Someone saved me.'

'No lady in shining armour?'

She shook her head, disappointed. 'Just some bloke wearing a traffic cone costume.'

Tomek stifled the snigger, then turned to the painting on the wall. 'You're a fan of art?'

'No. I just *know* about it, that's all. The same way *you* might know about fixing toilets, *I* know about art.'

'Sexist. You could have assumed I might know about gardening, or doing make-up.'

'Now who's sexist?'

Tomek nudged her in the shoulder, then pointed to the painting. 'Go on then. *The Garden of Earthly Delights*...'

'By a bloke named Hieronymus Bosch in the fifteen hundreds. It's called a triptych, which means it's split into three sections. For this one, each section depicts a different move closer to hell. On the left is the Garden of Eden, where everything's pure and clean. Then you have *The Garden of Earthly Delights*, where everyone's naked and appears to be fucking each other surrounded by a load of fruit, and on the right you've got his depiction of hell, where things just get a bit weird.'

'It's all a bit weird.'

'There's been much scholarly debate whether the central panel is a moral warning or a depiction of paradise lost.' The voice was a deep baritone. Familiar. Then a figure emerged, wearing a mayoral outfit, complete with chains and a cloak draped over his shoulders. On his head, he wore an Italian Renaissance hat with an Arlecchino face mask over his eyes. Tomek recognised him immediately. 'Personally, I think it's the latter, a reflection of paradise, of enjoyment, free spirit, the ability to do things without retribution. It was the inspiration behind The Nights of Eden, and I'm very proud to have this painting here. It always catches our newcomers' eyes. Angelica was standing in the same position as you two are now, staring up at it in awe, asking the same questions.'

'And what did she have to say?'

'She found it delightful as well.' Micky Tatton moved in front of them, blocking Tomek's view of the bizarre yet equally enrapturing painting. 'Have you found what you were looking for?'

'We've only just arrived,' Rachel answered with too much excitement in her voice for Tomek's liking.

'Excellent, then you have all evening to get yourselves acquainted with our activities. Please, feel free to let yourself loose here. There is no judgement, and all our staff are required to sign an NDA as well. Nobody other than the people you see tonight will know about what takes place.'

'Do you not need us to sign one?'

Micky shook his head. 'Given your roles, I don't think that will be necessary.' As he started off, he stopped and made a half turn. 'Oh, and love the outfit, by the way. I can tell you're going to be a fan with many of our guests.'

Tomek felt a knot tighten in his stomach, and a rush of blood to his penis. It was all very confusing.

A moment later, Micky Tatton was gone. Now that was out of the way, they could begin. The only problem was choosing a room. Left or right. In the end, after a brief argument, they settled on The Room. Left. Tomek had already envisaged what was in store for them, but it was nothing close to the reality. Tomek had never seen so much bare flesh and genitalia – and more concerningly, *ham* – in his life. The room they'd just entered was the wedding hall where newlyweds were supposed to enjoy the happiest days of their lives. But instead of two couples standing hand-in-hand at the head of the room, it was filled with two dozen individuals currently fornicating and penetrating each other. There were half a dozen soft velvet sofas, three water beds, and a couple of beanbags and armchairs. The lights were dimmed, and there wasn't a single candle in sight – presumably for safety reasons. Before them, bodies were entwined in one another, couples, threesomes, foursomes having sex, perched on the beds, over the armchairs, against the wall. There wasn't a single free space left. It was like looking at a scene from *Game of Thrones*. Tomek didn't know where to look, and for a long moment, he stood perfectly still, unable to tear his gaze from a man in his mid-fifties standing behind another man, bent over the arm of a sofa. Meanwhile, on the outskirts of the room, men stood with erections, masturbating at the scenes. The faces of everyone inside the room were covered. Face masks ranged from a Zorro mask to a ski mask, all the way to a paper bag that had been cut open at the eyes and mouth. But no matter where he looked, when he was finally able to tear his gaze from the homosexual act happening right in front of him, he couldn't see anyone wearing a donkey mask.

'Jesus Christ...' he whispered.

'Hey, handsome,' a voice said beside him. The figure – a woman, definitely a woman, naked, wearing a medical face mask and wartime nurse's hat with a big Red Cross on it – began touching him on the shoulder, making her way down his arm. A second later, she arrived at his truncheon and inspected it. 'Been a naughty girl, have I? Maybe you should punish me in one of the smaller rooms. Would you like that?'

'Ah, fuck.'

Tomek very quickly felt out of his depth. He had an extremely attractive woman right in front of him, and all he could think about were the men masturbating, touching themselves as they watched.

'Rachel... Help...'

At once, Rachel stepped in front of him and kissed the woman, hard and full on the lips. 'He's taken for the moment, sweetheart,' she said as she pulled away, 'but maybe when I'm finished with him, how about you and I have some fun together?'

The woman looked visibly disheartened to hear that Tomek was taken off the market, but elated at the prospect of spending some time with Rachel afterwards, even though it wasn't going to happen. Quietly, the woman slipped away, and Tomek thanked Rachel for coming to his rescue.

To their left was a small walkway that led to a bar. They cut through the entrance and ordered themselves a soft drink each: Coca Cola for Tomek, lemonade for Rachel. Beside them, on a nearby sofa, were two men doing lines of cocaine off each other's stomachs, like it was a shot of vodka and they were on some party island in the middle of the Mediterranean. One of them snorted hard and looked up at Tomek, his nose and mouth covered in white powder. 'Care to join us?'

Tomek baulked at the man's remark and watched him rub his nose for a few seconds before replying. 'Not for us, thanks. Where'd you get it from?'

'BYOD. Bring your own drugs,' the man replied, then went back to his cocaine, this time doing a line from the other man's arse cheeks.

'Guess that doesn't make it illegal,' Rachel whispered in his ears.

'Even if it was, we probably couldn't arrest 'em. Imagine the amount of naked flesh that would come running out of here if we did. We'd have to sanitise everything at the station, and even then I don't think we'd ever get it clean.'

'So long as no one does a dirty protest,' Rachel added.

Once they'd received their drinks, they returned to the orgy. Within seconds of their return, a man approached them, completely naked, wearing a pilot's hat and a pair of tinted ski goggles over his eyes. He was overweight, with incredibly hairy arms and the chest of a bear.

'All right there, darling?' he said to Rachel. 'Don't recognise you.'

As soon as Tomek realised he wasn't the target, he took a step back, quietly sipping his drink.

'Tomek...' Rachel said, holding out a hand for him. 'Tomek...'

'Don't know who you're talking to.'

'This your first time here, darling?' the man insisted.

'I'm with him,' Rachel said, grabbing Tomek and pulling him over.

'No, we're not.'

'*Yes*, we are.'

'That's all right,' the man said. 'You can ride me like a horse as much as you want, I still won't bite.'

'No, thanks,' Rachel insisted. Then added politely: 'Maybe some other time.'

Reluctantly, the man shuffled away, shoulders slumped, clearly upset at the rejection. Once he was out of earshot, Rachel pulled Tomek down to her eyeline.

'What the fuck was that about? I came to your rescue when *you* needed it.'

Tomek shook his head. 'I'm not kissing no man on the lips.'

'Coward,' she hissed.

But before he could respond, something caught Tomek's eye. A figure. Naked from the neck down, wearing nothing but a silicone donkey mask over his face. Bewildered, Tomek slapped Rachel on the arm repeatedly until he caught her attention.

'You go,' he said.

'Why me?'

'Because you're a girl, and last time I checked, he'd been sleeping with Angelica, who was also a girl.'

'Thanks for the biology lesson,' she said in a huff, before setting her plastic cup (also presumably for safety reasons) on the arm of the sofa and making her way towards The Donkey Man. Meanwhile, Tomek followed slowly behind, hanging back and watching from afar, cautious not to get too close.

'Hey,' Rachel said.

The man looked down at her. 'Hey, how you doing?' he replied in a soft French accent.

'Fancy going to a private room?'

'Sure.'

It was that easy. Ask and you shall receive. No foreplay, no introductions, just, "Do you want to fuck?" "Yes!" "Excellent, come this way."

'Mind if my friend joins?' she asked, pointing to Tomek.

'Erm...'

'Great.'

Without waiting for a response, Rachel grabbed Tomek by the arm, and dragged him out of the room and into the corridor. As they neared the individual rooms on the other side of the manor, the sound of sex grew louder and louder. Women and men screaming at the top of their lungs, bedheads and other items banging into the walls. Fortunately, they found an empty room at the end of the corridor, and Tomek shut the door behind him. Inside, the room was quiet, still. In the middle was a four-poster bed with a handful of sex toys – dildos, whips, stirrups, chains – laid out on the surface. Tomek didn't want to know whether they'd been used or not, didn't want to go anywhere near them. This was a simple hotel bedroom that had been turned into a sex dungeon, and he never wanted to stay in a hotel again.

Then The Donkey Man clapped his hands, bringing Tomek out of his reverie.

'All righty then. Shall we?'

Rachel's voice turned authoritative. 'Actually, no. We'd rather not, thank you. We wondered if we could ask you a few questions about your recent relationship with Angelica Whitaker instead.'

'What? What're you talking about?'

'Angelica Whitaker.'

'Who are you?'

Rachel reached into her bra and produced her warrant card.

The man inspected it, then looked at Tomek in disbelief.

'This isn't just a costume, mate,' Tomek said, waving vigorously.

Then The Donkey Man became suddenly aware that he was naked and covered himself with his hands. Though it was already too late. The damage had been done, the image – along with many others – was etched into Tomek's mind. 'What's this about? Can I... can I put some clothes on?'

'No need,' Rachel said. 'I'm not interested in any of that, nor is he. What's your name?'

Still protecting his dignity with his hands, the man perched himself on the edge of the bed. 'Florian. Florian Meunier. I...'

'What can you tell us about Angelica Whitaker, Florian?'

The man reached for the nearest pillow and placed it on his lap. 'I don't know who that is.'

'Yes, you do, but you probably know her more by her outfit than her name. A woman who used to come here always dressed as an angel. Ring any bells?'

A look of recognition flashed across Florian's face. 'Yes, but I... I did not know her name was Angelica.'

'Well, now you do. And we've also come to tell you that she's dead.'

'Dead?'

'Her body was found the other day. She was pregnant. We understand that you have slept with her on multiple occasions. Is that correct?'

Florian's gaze fell to the shagpile carpet on the floor as he became lost in deep thought. 'Yes. Yes, we slept together.'

'Can you tell us how many times?'

'Four. Maybe five.'

'And you used the condoms outside? Some pierced, some not.'

'Yes... Yes, but I never thought *this* would happen.'

'Which bit? Her being killed or her getting pregnant?' Rachel asked.

'*Killed*? You never said she was killed. You don't think... you don't think I had something to do with it, do you?'

Tomek took that as his cue to step in. 'That remains to be seen,' he said. 'So Angelica never told you that she was pregnant, or that it could have been yours?'

The man looked shell-shocked. 'No. Nothing.'

'Did you ever spend the night with anyone else? Did you ever see her go into a room with someone else?'

Florian shook his head. 'Only ever me. But...' He hesitated. 'We also had a threesome once, but that... that was with another woman.'

Tomek's eyes fell to the strap-on dildo at the head of the bed.

'Have you ever spoken to Angelica outside of this environment?' he asked.

'No.'

'Never messaged her online or on social media?'

Another shake of the head.

'Would you be willing to come down to the station so we can discuss this in more detail?'

'Of... of course.'

'Tomorrow?'

After a few seconds of processing, Florian finally answered yes, then proceeded to give Rachel his contact details. Just before they left him to his thoughts, alone in the room, she placed a hand on his shoulder, thanked him for his time, then followed Tomek out of the room. Together they headed towards the exit. Outside, Tomek found the valet, searched through the bowl for his car keys, then waited for the man to bring it round.

The valet arrived a moment later. Tomek thanked him, then climbed into the front seat. As he shut the door behind him, he turned to Rachel and said, 'We must never speak a word of this to anyone. Agreed?'

'Agreed.'

CHAPTER THIRTY-SEVEN

Tomek wanted nothing more the following morning than to knock the smug little smile from Chey's face. The twenty-five-year-old had looked as though he'd just won the lottery. And to make things worse, Tomek and Rachel had arrived at the same time, making it appear as though they'd spent the night together and were doing a police version of the walk of shame.

'So...' he said, leaning back in his chair, chewing on the end of his pen, his unbearable grin still visible. 'How was it?'

'Don't fucking start,' Tomek called as he dropped his bag beside his desk. 'You've got some fucking grovelling to do.'

'Why?'

'*That* costume.'

Chey burst into laughter, his voice breaking midway, flooding through the office. They were the only three in there, first thing on a Saturday morning. Soon the place would begin to fill up.

'Did you get any photos?' the constable asked.

'Perv,' Rachel retorted, seriously at first, then her face cracked and the two of them collapsed with laughter at Tomek's expense. 'It was possibly one of the funniest things I've ever seen.'

Tomek gave them both the finger. 'Do you know what's funnier? When I put the two of you on performance reviews. Who'll be laughing then?'

'Nothing will be funnier than the memories I have from last night,' Rachel remarked.

Sensing they were about to disclose on all the gossip, Chey climbed out of his chair and hurried over.

'You can knock that smirk off your face,' Tomek told him. 'We're not telling you anything.'

'Come on! Wouldn't you be a little bit fascinated if you were in my position?'

Yes. Yes, he would.

'No,' Tomek said, 'because I have some respect for the investigation. If I need to know something, then I'll wait to be told.'

It was a cold, stone-faced lie, and they all knew it. As Tomek turned to switch on his computer screen, out of the corner of his eye, he saw Rachel lean over to Chey and heard her whisper, 'It's all right, mate. I'll tell you everything later.'

'Like fuck you will,' Tomek snapped, spinning so fast he made himself dizzy. 'What do you want to know? We got there, all dressed up, had to kiss each other's hand, kissed a pig, got some drinks, saw a lot of sex, saw a lot of knobs and vaginas, and then spoke with a suspect.'

'You found a suspect?'

'Course we fucking did. We didn't just go there to see what all the fuss was about.'

Rachel scoffed playfully. 'Speak for yourself, Sarge.'

Tomek did a double-take on her, then turned to face Chey. 'Right. Well, *I* went there for investigative purposes. If I'd known Rachel was going there for something else, I might've taken you instead.'

The young man's face lit up.

'Sarge, come on, think about that for a second,' Rachel implored. 'Him... twenty-five years old... going *there*. That would be like letting a fox loose in a chicken farm. It'd be a fucking massacre.'

The fervent nod and smile on Chey's face confirmed Rachel's analogy.

'In that case, if I have to go again, I'll go alone,' he said.

Chey and Rachel looked at one another, giving each other the eye. 'Yeah, all right, Sarge. Course you will. We see how it is.'

Tomek sighed and rolled his eyes. 'Behave. Don't be so childish.' He was keen to move the conversation away from himself, Rachel and The Nights of Eden, so asked, 'Anyway, what did you spend your Friday night doing, young Chey? Crying yourself to sleep because you missed out?'

'No, actually. While you two were fulfilling your fantasies at your little sex party last night, I was having a little party of my own scrolling through Angelica's Instagram.'

Tomek looked at him, concerned. 'That's equally weird, mate.'

Chey's expression dropped. 'I know. I heard how it sounded. But hear me out, I found something I think might be interesting.'

Tomek waited for the man to elaborate.

'I found a blog!' he exclaimed. Now the excitable, puppy-like expression had returned to his face, but for very different reasons. 'It's called "My Little Corner Of The Internet" – which is actually the URL for it as well. It's one of those Blogspot things from the early two thousands, where it's literally just text and a couple of images. There's nothing fancy going on.'

'How did you find it?' Tomek asked, eager to start at the beginning before Chey got lost in his own excitement.

'It was at the bottom of her travel Instagram account,' he answered. 'I finally reached the bottom of her feed after days of going through each post. Her first ever one. It was a little selfie with a caption about people going to her blog where she would post more in-depth information about her travels.'

'And that was the only time she posted the link?'

Chey shrugged. 'Guess she thought that people would see it and remember it. It was a few years ago, before they fucked about with all the algorithms and organic reach was much better than it is nowadays.'

Algorithms. Organic reach. Words he'd been forced to learn very recently, but still had no clue what the fuck they all meant.

'Did you read any of the blog posts?'

'Started, yeah. But there's a lot. The thing goes back as far as 2016, the same as her Insta, but there're over two thousand posts on there. One for each day, sometimes more. I think she originally used it for her travel diaries, but then as she realised nobody was finding it, I think she started to use it as her journal.'

Tomek's ears perked up.

'When was the last post?'

'Day she died.'

Tomek wagged his finger in the direction of Chey's computer monitor.

'Do you have it on your screen?'

'You can get it on yours, Grandad. It's on the Internet. Anyone can view it.'

Bastard, Tomek thought. That was the sort of thing he would have said to Nick. In fact, he probably had said that exact thing to the chief inspector at some point. And now he had passed the mantle down to Chey. He was impressed.

'Go on then, smart arse. Show me.'

Within a second, the constable had loaded up Tomek's portal, opened a web browser and found Angelica's Little Corner of the Internet. The homepage was simple. The logo of her website was at the top of the screen and looked like she'd typed it into WordArt and turned it into an image. On the right was a photo of Angelica in a bikini, with sunglasses the size of a snorkelling mask covering her face, a beach and palm trees behind her. Beneath it was a chronological list of all the blog posts over the years, from 2016 to present. On the left side of the page was the latest post, dated the day of her death. The timestamp said it had been posted a few hours before she'd met up with her friends.

Tomek leant closer and squinted at the screen. He'd noticed recently that as he got older his eyes had started to falter, blur a little more than they used to, but had done nothing about. He wasn't going blind yet, so what was the worry?

Eyes almost shut, he began reading:

HELLO LOVELY,

Another day of work done. Feeling better about myself today. Got a big night out with the girls tonight which I absolutely can't wait for. I need to get ready in a couple of hours so I'm going to keep this one nice and quick. Should be a fun evening. Feels like we haven't been out together forever. A proper girlies night. And to think it's going to be the last one before the season starts again, which I'm buzzing about. Can't wait to see all the girls' Instas looking lush and lit in the coming weeks. It's going to be a great send off, and I've got a feeling we're going to go out with a bang!

Anyway, that's all I've got time for, lovely. Until next time.

'WHO'S *LOVELY*?' Tomek asked.

'Why you are, Sarge,' Rachel mocked.

Tomek shot her an unimpressed glance. 'You know that's not what I meant. Who do we think she's talking to?'

'Herself, maybe? As a reference in case she reads it later on?'

Tomek considered, turned to Chey, and asked, 'Can you print them all out?'

'Print them?'

'Yes. You know, black and white ink on paper.'

'But why? That's going to make so much waste.'

'The reasons are twofold, young Chey.' Tomek raised two fingers up at the constable, and not the nice way round either. 'One, so we can share them amongst the team and read them to expedite the process. Two, to prepare ourselves in case anything happens with the domain and we lose all the evidence.'

A stunned look crept across Chey's face.

'That's right,' Tomek replied smugly. 'I know about domains. And that reminds me of the third reason.' Tomek flashed his middle finger at Chey. 'Because I told you to. Now Rachel and I have to go. We have a meeting with someone from last night to prepare for.'

'They're coming back for round two?'

Tomek reached into his backpack, removed the costume Chey had bought him, and launched it into the man's lap.

'You owe me fifty quid for that. I want my money back.'

'I don't think they accept things that have been worn, Sarge,' Chey said, looking at the outfit with his beady eyes.

'Who said anything about returning it?'

CHAPTER THIRTY-EIGHT

Tomek was having difficulty looking at the man properly. Despite the fact Florian was nicely dressed in a smart white shirt with thin cotton jumper and a pair of navy chinos (the French just knew how to look good, didn't they?), the only image Tomek had of the man was his slightly tanned naked body, large penis dangling between his legs, and a latex donkey mask placed over his head.

'What time did you finish last night?' Tomek asked, desperate to fill the silence.

Florian was of slender build, with little in the way of muscle and fat on him. He looked as though he'd been athletic in a former life, but had perhaps given that up in his pursuit of more decadent thrills. His shoulders were hunched and his frame seemed to shrink behind the table.

'I left shortly after you both did. That is unusually early for me, as sometimes I stay the night in one of the rooms in the hotel, but I decided to head home. I was unable to think about anything else other than what you told me.'

The man was visibly shaken up and disturbed by the news of Angelica's death. Tomek wondered how much of it was genuine, and how much an act.

'What time do these things usually finish?' Rachel asked.

'Three in the morning. Sometimes four, if there are a lot of people. Basically, until people start to feel tired and go to sleep in the rooms.'

Rachel opened her notebook to a new page. 'When did you first meet Angelica Whitaker? Can you remember the date?'

The man shook his head. 'I think it was the first time that she attended The Nights of Eden.'

Tomek hated that name. It sounded like some sort of cult.

'I think it was back in September,' he added.

'And how did you two meet?'

'She was waiting outside when I got there, but before I kissed her hand, I spoke with her a little bit. I didn't recognise her, you see, so I wanted to get to know her a little better, put her at ease. I liked the look of her. Her body was nice, make-up, hair. She looked very pretty. But she would not tell me her name. In the end, I called her my angel. Then I found her inside the room. At first she didn't know what to do or who to speak with, but...' He licked his lips. 'But because she had already spoken with me, I guess you could say she felt more comfortable.'

'You two took a room together?'

Tomek remembered how easy it had been for Rachel to secure a night with Florian.

'Yes. I... I...' He began scratching the back of his head, withdrawing more and more into himself. 'I, you could say, I took her virginity. It was her first time there, and it was her first time with—'

'We get it,' Tomek interrupted, raising a hand for the man to stop. 'What happened after you'd "been" together?'

'She went one way, I went another.'

Rachel scribbled away intensely, her writing gradually becoming less and less neat and legible as she struggled to catch up.

'When did you see her next?' she asked.

'At the next meeting, a month later.'

Rachel waited until she'd finished writing everything down before continuing. They were on her time now. 'And you two spent the night together again?'

'Yes. We spent many nights together. Each time we used protection, of course.'

'Of course.'

'But... after what you said last night, I... I want to know if the baby is mine. Is it possible to take a DNA test, to find that out?'

Rachel opened her mouth to speak, but Tomek beat her to it. 'What's the point? The baby's dead. Nothing would be gained from that.'

Florian prodded the side of his head. 'For my own sanity.'

Tomek told the man that it wouldn't be possible. 'It was less than three months old, from what I understand. We may never know the father. I'm sorry.'

The man dropped his head, looking deeply into his lap. They both gave him a moment to compose himself and his thoughts.

'She was one of the most beautiful women I have ever seen,' Florian explained, talking to his knees. 'She was like a portrait from the Renaissance. She was like the Mona Lisa.'

'Are you an art fan, or just have a casual interest?'

'I'm an artist.' At that, Florian lifted his head with a morsel of pride that was lost amongst the grief and despair.

'What do you paint?'

'Anything and everything. My surroundings. Landscapes. People.'

'Did you ever do one of Angelica?'

The man nodded slowly. Then, without saying anything, he reached into his pocket, unlocked his phone and scrolled through his camera roll. A few seconds later, he found the photo he was looking for and slid the phone across the table. Tomek reached for the device and held it between them. On the screen was a close-up of an angel, perched on the edge of a bed, half naked. The woman in the painting was unmistakably Angelica, with the long black hair, the dark eyes, the slim figure, the jawline, cheeks, nose. It was eerily accurate.

'How did you do that?' he asked.

'From memory. After our first night together, I was unable to get her out of my head. I had such a clear picture of her that I needed to get her down on the canvas. It was the only way I could get her off my mind.'

It was clear to see that Florian had been, and was quite possibly still, infatuated with Angelica. Infatuated with her the same way that all the men in her life seemed to be. From Micky Tatton striking up conversation with her on board a European flight, to Shawn Wilkins liking and monitoring every waking (and sleeping) moment of her life, to Sammy Mercer, who still believed there was a scintilla of hope they might get back together again. She was adored, loved, admired, and in some cases lusted after. And in the end, it had led to her death.

'Did you ever get a chance to show it to her?' Rachel asked.

Florian shook his head. 'I tried. I sent it to her mobile number, but I think she must have given me a wrong one, because she never replied. And I couldn't show her in person because there are no phones allowed, so she never got to see it.'

And now she never would.

CHAPTER THIRTY-NINE

Tomek had been staring at the picture on his computer screen for almost half an hour. With each scroll of the mouse and prod of the arrows on the keyboard, he saw something new, a new detail, a new layer of meaning. He had never been massively into art – he thought it was all bollocks and that the artists just painted whatever they wanted to paint, and that there was no hidden meaning behind the artist's choice to use one particular stroke or colour over another – but there was something about this particular image that had piqued an interest within him, an interest he didn't know he had. The naked bodies, the enlarged fruit, the curious and unusual animals, the descent into depravity and hell. It fascinated him, and admittedly, despite himself, he was feeling a little inspired. That perhaps he could try something like that, something unique and representative of sin and lust. But then he remembered that he could barely draw a stick man, so an accomplished tapestry of art like *The Garden of Earthly Delights* was well beyond his capabilities. Still, it was nice to dream to think he had it in him.

As he scrolled across to the right side of the triptych, the dark and demonic depiction of hell, Tomek's phone began vibrating on the table. The sudden sound and movement made him jump. Fortunately there was no one nearby to see it. He reached for the device and glanced at the caller ID. At once, all the inspiration, wonder and creativity that had been garnered from the painting, leached out of him.

It was Abigail. Possibly calling to ask him about coming round, or to argue with him about the night before. Or possibly, and much less likely, she was calling about work and what information he might have for her.

Only one way to find out. Pushing himself away from the table, he bit the bullet, darted into a small office, and answered the call.

'You all right?' he asked tentatively.

'Yeah. You?'

'Yeah. Not bad.'

'Good.'

Tomek waited for her to speak. Neither of them wanted to be first. Neither knew what to say. Just as Tomek opened his mouth, Abigail interrupted.

'Come down,' she said.

'Pardon?'

'Come down. I want to speak to you.'

Tomek looked around the room, panicked, as though his girlfriend might suddenly appear from behind a wall like a ghost.

'What are you talking about?'

'I'm outside. In the car park. Come down.'

Tomek scurried round the table, his knees bumping into the chair and table legs, as he rushed towards the window. There she was, her bright red SEAT parked in the corner of the car park. He inhaled deeply, observing her. He had no choice.

'I'll be down in a minute.'

❄

THE TEMPERATURE inside the car was colder than the air outside. The engine was switched off, which meant she wasn't planning on going anywhere fast, and to really drill that point home to Tomek as he climbed in, he noticed the car keys were on her lap. An extra step required before she could drive away in a state of anger or frustration.

He expected the worst.

Abigail's hair was pulled from her face with the help of a hairband. She was dressed in a blazer and smart trousers, with a plain white shirt. Pinewood and ochre oozed from her body and quickly filled his nostrils. Her make-up had been delicately done, yet it was unable to hide the deeply unimpressed and aggravated expression in her face and eyes.

Tomek said nothing as he shut the door, filling the space with silence.

It didn't last long.

'How was last night?' she asked.

He sensed the accusation in her tone immediately.

'Last night?'

'Yeah. With your girlfriend.'

Rachel. The Nights of Eden. Fuck. But how could she have possibly known?

'How do—?' Tomek started, but she cut him off.

'I saw you two going out together.'

'What do you mean, you saw us?' Tomek took a moment to think. He'd driven to Rachel's flat, already dressed in his costume, waited for her, and then driven them both to Melback Manor. Which meant: 'You followed me?'

'I saw it all,' Abigail replied, venom lacing her words. 'You picking your new girlfriend up, taking her to that country house. The two of you looking fucking stupid. What were you two doing there, going to a fancy dress party together, eh? How long's it been going on?'

Tomek didn't know whether to laugh or shout. He was in a state of both disbelief and fury. Disbelief that she thought he and Rachel were together, and fury that she'd followed him – *stalked* him, no less. He didn't know where to start. In the end, he said nothing, staring blankly at her.

Which did nothing to calm the situation.

'How long have you two been seeing each other? Bet you're all cute, aren't you, going to a little fancy dress thing together? Bet you panicked when I asked to see you last night. How many times have you blown me off for her? Were you seeing her that Wednesday when I wanted to come over, but you said you had to get Kasia some emergency bits from the shop? Or what about the weekend where I said you could come over, but you said you had rugby and then were going to the pub with Sean and Warren? Were you fucking her instead?'

Tomek was lost. He couldn't even recall those two instances. They had been so long ago. But that wasn't a problem for Abigail. She had the memory of a Mensa member.

'Have you got all this saved in a diary or something?' Tomek asked.

'Answer the question,' she snapped.

'No.'

'So it's true then?'

'No.'

'Then why won't you answer me.'

'Because you're being fucking stupid.'

'What were you doing at that hotel last night?'

'Work.'

'Yeah, right. Is that what you call it? Is that some little nickname the two of you have got for it?'

Tomek turned away from her, his gaze falling on the dashboard. For a moment, he switched off as she continued ranting at him, screaming in his ear, the words gradually becoming dull and muted. It wasn't until she slapped him on the arm that he came to.

'Are you even listening to me?' she yelled. 'I'm trying to have a conversation with you here.'

'No, you're not. You're shouting at me, and now you're hitting me. You're also accusing me of shit I haven't done, of something you've got into your head that isn't even real. There's nothing going on between Rachel and me, and there never will be. We were doing a work thing last night, and that's all you need to know.'

Tomek placed a hand on the door handle. She held him back with a strong, vicelike grip.

'Where do you think you're going?'

He could almost see the steam coming out of her ears.

'Back to work. And I think you should do the same.' He opened the door, then turned back to her. 'I also think we need some time apart, a break, or something, I guess. I'll speak to you later. I've got a murder investigation to go back to.'

CHAPTER FORTY

It took Tomek over an hour to calm down, to clear his mind. Not only had Abigail broken and destroyed his trust, but she'd also shown her true colours. She had resorted to following him, tracking his movements like he was a lost pet. He didn't know whether he could tolerate someone like that in his life, constantly having to explain where he was and who he was with. Life soon got pretty depressing that way, and he had more important things to worry about. Shortly after returning to the incident room, Tomek had bumped into Sean, one of his closest friends in the force, by accident. Recently they'd drifted apart, but that hadn't stopped them from being friends, not deep beneath the surface. And it certainly hadn't stopped Sean from noticing the disconcerted and pained look on Tomek's face. And so the two of them had found a small office, where Tomek had let it all out, like they used to, like they'd done so many times before, sharing their lives with one another, leaning on each other for advice and guidance. Then Sean had told him how it was, reminded him of the advice he'd given Tomek at the beginning of his relationship with Abigail: that their relationship had been transactional, built on the two of them scratching each other's backs to get ahead, until eventually they'd fallen into the relationship. In a way they'd both got what they wanted: a new job each. But it wasn't working for their relationship. And Tomek admitted that Sean had been right. That he had used Abigail for information in the past and vice versa, and that now it wasn't healthy, sustainable. A part of him had known it at the time, but an even bigger part hadn't been arsed to do anything about it. And now here he was, here they were, facing the end of the relationship. Tomek should have felt bereft, upset about it, but he didn't feel anything. Perhaps it was the stoicism within him, the fact that he hadn't felt anything in the thirty years since his brother's death, the emotional suffering and turmoil he'd gone through still playing with him even years later. Perhaps he would feel *something* at some point. Maybe. But right now, he had a meeting to attend, and he wasn't going to miss it on account of someone he'd known intimately for only a couple of months.

He found Chey, Rachel, and Oscar sitting in the incident room, quietly discussing amongst themselves. Tomek shut the door behind him and moved to the head of the table, where he grabbed a whiteboard marker. He removed the cap and found a clean space on the nearest whiteboard.

'All right, you bunch of reprobates,' he started. 'Let's wrap our heads round this shit. Combine our minds and let them canoodle and contort into one.'

'Are you feeling all right, Sarge?' Chey asked.

Tomek ignored the question.

'Our brains need to get down and dirty, and we need to come to terms with what we know and what we don't. Oscar!' Tomek bellowed the man's name, filling the small room. He pointed the pen at the constable, then said, 'What do you have to tell me?'

Oscar looked to his colleagues for guidance and assistance, but none of them had any idea, so they shrugged and left him to it.

'About what, Sarge?'

Tomek shook his head in frustration, then began scribbling on the whiteboard. If they weren't going to help him, then he was going to have to do it himself. He started by writing Angelica's name in the middle of the whiteboard, then around it he created a spider's web of words: *make-up, rape, cleaning, Church, angel wings, car*. As soon as he'd finished, he slammed the lid shut, retreated a few steps and stared at the board, saying nothing, losing himself in his thoughts. Thirty seconds passed, a minute. But in truth he wasn't taking anything in. At least, not entirely, not consciously. His mind was elsewhere, thinking about Abigail, about their time together, even though he knew he shouldn't, even though he'd just convinced himself he didn't care about her.

Tomek could hear the team whispering to one another.

'Sir...?' It was Chey who was the bravest to speak. 'Sir, are you all right? You... you haven't said anything for about a minute.'

'Actually, it's been two,' added Oscar.

'There's The Captain!' Tomek exclaimed. 'It's been a while. I've missed hearing your little voice pop up. "Actually!", "Actually!", "Actually!"'

With each rendition of Oscar's catchphrase, Tomek became more and more farcical and childish with his hand gestures. Before he could do another, Rachel leapt out of her seat and stepped in front of him.

'What're you doing?' she whispered loudly.

'What?'

'You're being a bit of a dick. Why you laying into Oscar like that?'

And then he came to. He blinked hard, shook his head, turned to Oscar. The man, who usually sat bolt upright with perfect posture, was now sitting slumped in his seat, head tilted forward.

Guilt suddenly washed over Tomek like waves in a storm, battering him in the stomach repeatedly. He was hurting, even if he wouldn't admit it to himself, and he had taken it out on Oscar. That wasn't fair to Oscar, nor was it fair to the others in the room.

'Sorry,' he whispered to Rachel.

'It's not me you should be apologising to.'

As Rachel returned to her seat, Tomek apologised to The Captain sincerely.

'It's all right, Sarge. I know how I can be sometimes.'

Now the guilt was ripping his stomach open.

'Don't stop,' Tomek said. 'I love it when you correct people. Less so when it's me. But I think it's what makes you you. Don't stop that on my account.'

'Wasn't planning on it, actually,' the man replied with a warm smile.

Tomek shot Oscar a finger gun. 'That's my captain, oh my captain.'

'Actually, it's "O Captain! My— "'

'Don't push your luck,' Tomek said firmly, giving the man a wink before returning his focus to the whiteboard. Before beginning again, he inhaled deeply. 'Angelica Whitaker,' he said. 'Her killer. Her killer's profile. I want us to spend some time working out *who* could be behind this. But first, any word on DNA analysis?'

He looked out at a bunch of blank faces.

'Nothing concrete yet, Sarge,' Oscar replied.

'Okay. Keep pressing the button on it. There must be something there.' Tomek then turned his attention to the whiteboard again. He prodded at the words on the board. It wasn't until he looked at them that he realised how illegible they were. Ignoring the fact, he pointed to the word *rape*.

'This helps us narrow it down,' he said. 'We're looking for a man.'

'Right,' Chey responded, slightly hesitant.

'And what men did Angelica have in her life?'

Chey reeled off the names. From her brother and father to Shawn

Wilkins, her stalker, and Cole Thompson. From Sammy Mercer to Florian Meunier.

'Lovely. Next. The cleaning.' Tomek repeatedly tapped the pen against his chin. 'The killer spent a *long* time with her body, cleaning it, shaving it, doing whatever else he did to it. That's someone who's composed and measured, someone who is in love with Angelica so much that they wanted to iron out all the slight blemishes, the little imperfections.' He turned to the room. 'Who fits the bill on that?'

Brief pause.

Rachel chose to speak. 'Shawn Wilkins is the obvious choice.'

'Good. And why's that?'

'Because he hasn't left the woman alone since he first met her.'

'Okay. And not Florian?'

Rachel tilted her head to the side, as if she was confused. But then the cogs in her brain began to turn, and she reconsidered. 'I mean, he's slight and small, and a little timid – very timid, in fact. But I don't think... He doesn't look like he had it in him.'

'It's always the ones you least expect,' Tomek told her, adding, 'Just something to think about. Plus, our friend the donkey also likes to paint. I had a look at some of his work on his website, and they're very good, very realistic. Not to mention he's got experience painting angel wings.'

Tomek moved towards the whiteboard and circled the words "cleaning" and "angel wings", then drew two lines towards Florian's name. The other line he drew connected "cleaning" to Shawn Wilkins.

'Does anyone else know how to paint?' Tomek asked.

'I mean, I drew a forest one time when I was in school,' Chey answered. 'Got a C for it at GCSE, but that's about as far as my skills go.'

'Brilliant, congratulations. I'm sure your parents were proud. But that's not what I meant. Let me rephrase that: do any of our *suspects* know how to paint?'

'It's not something we've asked them,' Oscar replied.

'Then make a note to follow up with them on that. And loop Micky Tatton into those questions as well; he's a fan of art, so might know a thing or two about painting too.'

Next on the list was the church.

'Angelica's mum said that Angelica was christened in Park Road Church. I think that's more than a coincidence,' Tomek explained, then added Johnny and Roy Whitaker's names to the board. 'For obvious reasons, they're the only people who could know that.'

'Shawn Wilkins might, Sarge,' Rachel added.

'Possibly. But how?'

She shrugged.

'The only way would be if she's posted the information online somewhere, or discussed it with one of her exes. Chey? Anything on social?'

The young constable shook his head.

'What about the blog? How are you getting on with the printing?'

'It's going to take me all week, but we're getting there.'

Tomek nodded thoughtfully. He cast his gaze around the room seeing the expressions on his colleagues' faces. There was a mixture of confusion and excitement there. The sense that they were close. That one of the people on the board was responsible for killing Angelica Whitaker. Tomek had been in the same situation many times before, looking at the evidence, looking at the witness statements and the list of potential suspects, and relying on his intuition, that little knot in his stomach, to guide him in the right direction. Before he could do anything else, the door opened, and in stepped DC Anna Kaczmarek. Her body froze as she realised she'd just interrupted. Tomek invited her in, and she took a seat.

'Sorry...' she said as she placed two thick folders on the table. 'But I have an update.'

Tomek's eyes widened. 'Go on.'

'It's about Johnny Whitaker.'

Tomek pursed his lips and folded his arms.

'Speak of the devil. You've got us all on tenterhooks now, Anna.'

'I've just found out from his parents that he wasn't in Dublin like he said he was,' the family liaison officer explained.

'Yeah, that's right, he was with the woman he's been having an affair with,' Tomek elaborated, unable to hide the disappointment in his voice.

'Wrong.'

'Wrong?'

'For the past eighteen months, Johnny Whitaker has been performing at the Cool Cats and Kittens drag club in Southend. He goes by the name of Johnny Bra-vo, and performs there every month, complete in drag costume, make-up, and high-heeled boots – the lot. Rose found his costume and make-up in his wardrobe the other day. When I went round to see her, she told me he hadn't denied it when she'd confronted him about it. He lied to us, and he lied to his family about the woman from Dublin, though I should probably add that he performs in an Irish accent. Why, I'm not so sure. I didn't ask. But there was no other woman, because *he is* the other woman.'

Tomek paused a beat to consider. He didn't know much about that world, but what he did know, from stealing a couple of glances from the television screen while Kasia had been watching *RuPaul's Drag Race*, was that drag acts were exceptionally good at make-up, and certainly in his daughter's opinion, better than most women.

Tomek's eyes fell to the last word on the board.

Make-up.

The killer was someone who knew how to professionally apply the chemicals that had confused and bewildered so many men across the world better than a woman could. Which narrowed their suspect list down drastically.

'What was he doing at the time of the murder?' he asked.

'I've spoken with the venue, and they've confirmed Johnny finished his act at one in the morning,' Anna answered.

Plenty of time for him to come back and pick up his little sister.

Plenty of time to kill her and clean her body.

After all, if he'd lied to the police twice, then what else could he have been lying about?

CHAPTER FORTY-ONE

The first thing Tomek noticed was the mantelpiece. The former priceless ornament that had been unfortunately broken in Johnny Whitaker's fit of rage, had since been replaced with another priceless ornament, like Roy and Daphne had a plastic dump bin full of them out in the garage. One out, one in. No expense spared. The current replacement was a human skull that had been carved from stone. The markings and indentations in the forehead and eyes, deep and prominent, implied that it had been transported from somewhere in South America. Tomek picked it up. Heavy, weighty, certainly enough to do some serious damage.

'We got that from Peru in the summer of eighty-nine,' Daphne said as she came to a stop by his side. In her hands, she held a mug of tea for him. 'We'd not long been together, and it was our first holiday. We wanted somewhere neither of us had been before. It was beautiful. I'll never forget it.' She took the stone head from Tomek and held it up to the light. 'This is from a temple in the middle of Peru. It is said to have belonged to the Chavin, a long-lost civilisation from around a thousand BC. It was the first major culture in the country, but very little is known about them. I found this little thing just sitting on the floor.'

'Just sitting on the floor?' Tomek was dubious.

'Yeah.'

That this piece of history had lain dormant, untouched for millennia, and the first person who'd stumbled across it was a flight attendant for British Airways on a holiday with her boyfriend was somewhat unbelievable.

'So it was just lying there, and you decided to take it?'

'Well...'

'You didn't find it in a gift shop then?'

'Well, no...'

'Right.'

And there Tomek was, thinking it had been a replica from China, not a stolen artefact. Was that how they'd acquired the rest of the possessions in their home? Looting and stealing them like a pair of private colonisers? He didn't know. But he was sorely tempted to call the Peruvian National History Museum, if there was such a thing, and report a crime. Before Daphne could justify her actions any further, her husband entered the room. He was flustered, his hands flapping in the air, and was dressed in dark navy trousers and a thin jumper. A pair of glasses were positioned on his head, and he was covered in flecks of paint.

'Sorry,' he said, breathless. 'I was just working on my plane.'

Tomek shook his hand.

'Hope that's not a euphemism.'

'Sorry? Oh. *That*. Good one. No, I was putting the finishing touches to my model airport. I'm working on a Boeing 787-8 at the moment.'

'It keeps him quiet,' Daphne commented with a hint of disdain in her voice. 'Sometimes he's locked up in there for hours.'

'Right,' Tomek responded.

'I've got terminals and everything. All the luggage carriers, fire engines, safety trucks, the tugs, even the little figures on the ground waving the indicators. It keeps me busy.'

'How does it work?' Tomek asked. 'Do you just buy them as is or do you have to paint them, like in Warhammer?'

'Personal preference. But I prefer to paint them myself. First you have to dip them in solution so the stickers just slide off. Then wait for it to dry and *voila*! Your canvas is ready to begin.'

'Nice,' Tomek said, though he had no interest in anything like that. Not because he thought it was stupid or childish, but because he didn't have the time to be interested in it, whereas for Roy it had been a lifelong passion, a hobby that had turned into a lucrative career, and now in his retirement he'd found a different outlet for his love of aviation. 'How long have you been doing that for?'

'Twenty years. The airport's changed gradually in that time – buildings have come and gone, the layout's changed, the people have melted in the sun – but the passion's remained.'

Tomek offered the man a thin smile, gestured for him to sit in his own home, then joined Anna on the sofa. She had been waiting patiently, silently, listening to their conversation from the comfort of the chair.

'It's good to see you again, Anna,' Daphne noted, as the sides of her mouth flickered into a warm grin.

'Surprised you're not sick of me,' the constable replied.

'Never.'

Tomek believed her. Anna was one of the best, exceptional at her job. And while she wasn't always there to deliver good news, she was able to help ease the pain, the hurt, the suffering of a loved one's death in a caring and compassionate manner. She was their safety blanket, their support system. And when that was taken away, Tomek wondered how the couple might cope afterwards.

'We're sorry to disturb your afternoon,' Tomek began, 'but we were wondering if we could speak to your son.'

Daphne and Roy glanced at one another. 'We... we think he's at the pub,' Daphne answered. 'To be frank, we don't actually know where he is.'

Tomek's eyes narrowed.

'After all the mess that's come out with him and Rose, we invited him to stay here, but...'

'But he hasn't actually stayed here at all,' Roy finished. 'He said he was going to the pub, that was on the first night with us, and he hasn't been home since.'

'Have you spoken to him?' Tomek asked.

'Oh, yes. Daphne's been on the phone to him nonstop to make sure he's still alive.'

'And?'

'He's alive,' the woman answered softly. 'Just very, very drunk.'

'Has he ever had an issue with alcohol before?'

The husband and wife looked at one another again. Tomek saw straight through it. 'He used to binge a lot when he was younger,' Daphne answered. 'In his early twenties, you know. Blackout drunk. To the point where he was vomiting in his sleep. But we managed to get him out of that period of his life with God's help, didn't we, sweetheart?'

'Yes,' Roy replied. 'He was a different man back then. He wasn't our son. We hardly recognised him, so we took him into the church and made him go cold turkey.'

Clearly, the turkey wasn't cold enough.

'What's the name of the pub he said he was at?' Tomek asked.

'The Prince Albert,' Roy answered.

'Unfortunate name for a pub, but I guess it makes sense, given everything.'

'What's that supposed to mean?' Roy asked, accusation heavy in his tone.

Tomek hesitated, catching himself before he opened his mouth. Then he looked at Anna, who shook her head surreptitiously.

'Forgive me. You don't know, do you?'

'Know what?'

'About your son.'

'What about him?'

Tomek leant back on the sofa, leaving Anna to explain. The news would be better coming from her. She was much more tactful when it came to this sort of thing.

'Does the name Johnny Bra-vo mean anything to you?'

'You mean the kids' cartoon?'

'Not quite. It's the name of a drag act.'

'A *drag* act...?' Daphne repeated, realisation quickly dawning on her.

It took her husband a few seconds to catch up, and when he did, he leapt out of his seat.

'Drag? Are you saying my son's gay?'

'Not necessarily,' Tomek interrupted. 'Perhaps he just enjoys dressing up as a woman.'

'Yeah, but that means he's fucking gay. My son, Johnny, gay!'

Just as Tomek was about to respond, Roy began pacing, shaking his head. Then he made a sudden move towards the patio doors and looked out onto the garden beyond, arms behind his back. Tomek's first impression was that he was more upset about his son dressing up as a woman than he'd been about his daughter's death.

'I don't fucking believe this,' he said. 'How long's this been going on?'

'I think that's a discussion you need to have with your son. Right after we've finished with him, that is.'

Without warning, Roy punched the glass. Once, twice, three times, pounding his fist on the window. Then he turned round, grabbed the Chavin stone head, and launched it into the glass. The head bounced off the double glazing, cracking it slightly, then fell to the floor, landing in a mess of pieces.

'What is it with this fucking family and fucking secrets?' Roy yelled.

Yes indeed, Tomek thought as he rushed to calm the man. What is it with your family and secrets?

CHAPTER FORTY-TWO

All it had taken for Roy Whitaker to calm down was a single slap on the cheek from his wife. As if she'd knocked the devil and anger out of him. Shortly after, he'd returned to normal again. Realising that they had nothing more to add or to learn, Tomek and Anna left them to process the latest information about their son. But first they had a stop to make: a quick pit-stop at The Prince Albert. The pub had been first built in the early nineteen hundreds and resembled the Shakespeare Globe, with its white walls, wooden beams and thatched roof. Inside, the pub was equally archaic. The furniture was made from wood and looked as though it was handing out splinters at the same rate the bar was serving beers. The ceiling was too low and the wooden beams offered Tomek a chance to attempt an assault course he'd never tried before. A thick, cloying musty smell lingered in the air, and it was all thanks to one person: the man sitting in the corner, slouched in a chair, head forward, tucked into his chest, spittle dangling from his mouth, a half-empty glass of lager perched on the edge of a coaster. If it weren't for the steady rise and fall of his chest, Tomek would have assumed the man was dead.

'Don't worry,' the bartender, a twenty-something bloke with the first showings of a mullet, called from across the bar. 'I give him a nudge every hour just to make sure he ain't croaked or nothing.'

Tomek looked at the beer glass. 'How many's he had?'

Shrugging, the bartender replied, 'Since I've been here today, I'd say maybe about three-ish.'

'And in total?'

Another shrug. 'Ain't been here as long as he has.'

'Brilliant. Do you think maybe you should stop serving him?'

The young man raised his arms in mock surrender, admonishing himself of all blame and responsibilities. 'I just do what I'm told. And if he wants a beer, then I pour him a beer. So long as he can pay, it ain't a problem to us.'

'His liver might have something to say about that.'

Tomek handed the glass to Anna and told her to take it to the bar. While she was there, she leant across to the bartender and quietly whispered in his ear. A word of warning, no doubt. Tomek pulled a seat from beneath the table, and as he sat, prodded Johnny Whitaker's arm. The man's body rippled and shook from the assault, but he didn't move. Next, Tomek slapped him twice on the cheeks. Still nothing. Comatose, unconscious. It wasn't until Tomek asked for a glass of water from the bar and threw it over him that he finally came to.

'Wahblugarf,' Johnny mumbled.

'Johnny, can you hear me?'

'Fugoff.'

'I think he's trying to tell you to fuck off,' Anna said as she joined him.

'Now that's a language I can speak.'

Tomek leant across and continued to slap him lightly on the cheeks, alternating each time Johnny rolled his head to the other side. Nearly a minute later, Johnny's eyelids opened, revealing a set of eyes the colour of his sister's angel wings. The man looked as though he'd been on a five-day bender and wasn't even through the worst of it yet. His hair was dishevelled and greasy, and his skin was equally oily and clammy, alcohol and guilt seeping through his pores. His breath was so strong it forced Tomek to hold his own while he waited for the man to become cogent, and a thin river of snot had run down his nose and into his mouth. The man was in a state, and in desperate need of sobering up.

Anna handed Tomek a glass of water. Tomek took it from her and held it to Johnny's lips. But it was pointless. His face was so slack it was impossible to part his lips wide enough for the rim of the glass to fit, and Tomek wasn't keen on becoming his carer. At least, not without the aid of a glove.

'It's like feeding a child,' Anna commented.

'A fat and ugly one.'

'They're all fat and ugly at some point.'

This was ridiculous. Right now, Johnny Whitaker was just existing. He had no faculties about him, no sense of where he was; he was in no fit state to do anything, let alone answer questions about the lies and secrets that had torn his marriage and family apart. He needed to get to a hospital.

Tomek pulled out his phone and called an ambulance. It arrived over twenty minutes later, after struggling to navigate the narrow country lanes and small, almost unusable pub car park. A few minutes after its arrival, Johnny Whitaker was in the back of the van, and on the way to Broomfield Hospital in Chelmsford. Tomek and Anna stayed with him every step of the way, like they were his loved ones, concerned and worried for his welfare, even though Tomek had no sympathy for the man at all; the pain and suffering he was currently enduring had all been self-inflicted.

After nearly two hours of sitting in a hospital bed, hooked up to a drip, having wasted the NHS's time and resources, Johnny Whitaker was finally ready to answer some questions.

As soon as Tomek was given the all-clear, he wasted no time in getting the man's attention.

'Johnny, my good man!' he yelled on purpose. The man winced and recoiled in the bed at the sudden burst to the eardrums. 'How are you feeling? Better?'

'Why... why are you shouting?' the man said as he fought against the still slightly slurred speech.

'Just making sure you can hear me, mate. You were pretty fucking out of it back at the pub.'

'The... the pub?'

'You don't even remember being at the pub?'

The man shook his head so slowly it was almost like he was a sloth.

'Oh dear, you have been drinking a while, haven't you? What can you remember from the last few days?'

Johnny's gaze gradually moved from Tomek to the blanket, slowly, almost robotically, as though his buttons had been switched off. Either that or he was malfunctioning.

'I just... Rose... I remember—'

'Fighting with Rose? Tell us about that.'

'You... you know already?'

Tomek patted the man's thigh patronisingly. 'I do, yes. But I want to hear your version of events. What do you have to say for yourself?'

Somewhere, somewhere deep inside Johnny's brain, the switches turned back on and the cogs began working again, because he slowly lifted his gaze back up to Tomek, his eyes a little clearer, more focused this time.

'She's a cunt,' he spat.

Tomek placed a hand on his breast pocket. 'You want that on the record or...?'

'She's a cunt.'

'And why's that, Johnny?'

'Because... because she is. I swear to God, the next time I see her...'

'The next time you see her, what?'

'Nothing. She's a cunt.'

Tomek could tell this was going to be an even longer process than he'd anticipated.

'And why would that be, Johnny? How did she find out that you've been secretly performing as a drag act in Southend for the past eighteen months? How do you think she felt? Because it seems to me like *you* were the one lying to her. Not the other way round. So doesn't that make *you* the cunt, Johnny?'

The man muttered something unintelligible.

'How did you react when she confronted you with it, Johnny? Did you hit Rose, Johnny?'

The man shook his head.

'What would have happened if it was the other way round? What would have happened if you'd found out she was having an affair, or that she was dressing up as a man? Would you have hit her then, Johnny?'

Another shake.

'Who else knew about this, Johnny? Who else knew you'd been lying to your entire family, lying to yourself? Angelica? Did she know?'

Tomek noticed a flicker of the eyes, a movement of the muscles in his face. It was only minor, but noticeable to Tomek's highly trained eye.

'She did know, didn't she? She found out, didn't she? How?'

'Her... her friend,' the man started. 'They invited... I was performing...'

'So she saw you. She saw you and suddenly your secret was out. What did you do when she confronted you with it?'

The man turned unresponsive again, his body sloping to one side like a stroke patient.

'Did you get angry towards her, Johnny? Did you kill her because she threatened to tell Rose about your big secret? Is that what happened?'

The man raised an arm and started to swing it towards Tomek, but the movement was so slow Tomek would've had enough time to leave the room, fill a small cup of water and return to his seat before it hit him. As the man realised his mistake, attempting to punch a police officer wasn't the smartest idea at even the best of times, his eyes widened and he lowered his fist before any contact was made.

'Did you just try to assault me?'

'No.'

'Yes, you did. I fucking saw you do it. I have a witness.' Tomek pointed to Anna, who was sitting on the other side of the bed, quietly making notes. 'You tried to punch me. That's a very serious thing to do, especially to a police officer. Would you like me to arrest you?'

Johnny shook his head.

'I should. I *really* should. I mean, you've already proven how violent you are. Punching Shawn Wilkins in the face repeatedly. Who's to say you've never punched your wife or never hurt your sister? Maybe even killed her.'

Johnny's brow furrowed as his expression tightened. 'I... never... killed... her...'

'So you say, but I'm having difficulty believing anything you tell me right now. So far, everything you've said has proven to be a lie. First you were away for work, then you were having an affair, and now you're secretly a drag queen.' Tomek shuffled forward on his chair, and leant forward, placing his elbows on his knees. 'Why don't you be honest with me, Johnny? Why don't we start with an easy one: what did you do after you finished your act at Cool Cats and Kittens on the night Angelica was murdered?'

CHAPTER FORTY-THREE

Kasia was waiting for him as soon as he opened the door, a look of concern across her face.

'I watched you walk up from the window,' she told him.

'Okay...'

'I wanted to give you this.'

In her hand, she held an envelope.

Nathan.

'Why?' he asked. 'I thought we agreed to leave it on the table, just in case...'

'I know, but this is the third one in, like, less than a week.' She shrugged. 'I dunno. I just wanted to make sure you got it.'

Tomek took the envelope from her carefully and observed it, turning it over in his hands. The edges of the seal were torn slightly. 'Have you tried opening it?' he asked.

Kasia shook her head.

'Why do you look so worried?' he asked.

'I don't like how many we're getting,' she said. 'It... it makes me feel uncomfortable. I... I read one of the other ones you got.'

Tomek chose not to react immediately.

Kasia continued: And... and I wish I hadn't. But, it was so difficult not to open it. I'm sorry, Dad. I know I shouldn't have done gone through your stuff. I know it was an invasion of your privacy, but... I was just curious.'

Before Tomek opened his mouth to respond, he wanted to think about it first. He was furious, livid with her for going through his personal property – his letters from his brother's killer, no less. He expected that from Abigail, but not Kasia. Kasia wasn't supposed to care about those letters. She was supposed to treat them with as much flippant disregard as she did a council tax bill or a letter from the estate agents. But she hadn't. She'd searched through his things and betrayed his trust. For a second time.

On the other hand, the more rational portion of his brain came into play now; she was curious. She was only thirteen. Innocent, young, naïve. Perhaps she'd done it because she'd felt she couldn't ask him about them, or she didn't know how, and this had been the only way for her to find out the answers for herself. The problem was now she had the full truth, with all its jagged edges and cuts, and not the softened, smooth version Tomek would have given her.

'Kash...' he started, but she cut him off.

'How does he know my name?'

Fuck.

'Did you tell him?'

'No,' Tomek answered. 'Absolutely not.' He placed both hands on her shoulders, immediately calming her down. 'I don't know how he knows your name. I've been trying to think about it, go over the time I saw him, question whether I said anything to him about you, but I'm certain I didn't. I don't know how he knows your and Abigail's names. It's been something I'm looking into.' Then he wrapped his arms around her and pulled her into his chest. There wasn't much physical connection between them as father and daughter, but Tomek felt it appropriate. Right now she needed reassurance, to feel safe. In the past, she had been the victim of a personal attack that had almost killed her. It was something she lived with every day, and Tomek wanted to ensure there was no anxiety or concern for her to face.

'You're safe,' Tomek told her. 'He's in prison. He can't hurt us. He can't do anything to me, to you, to anyone. Okay?'

Kasia looked up at him, fear and paranoia, with a glint of belief, swimming in her big brown eyes.

As they broke away from the hug, she asked, 'Are you angry?'

Tomek ruffled her hair. 'No, of course not. I should have told you. I should have been more open with you. That's on me. You have nothing to be sorry for, okay?'

'Okay,' she said, not looking convinced. 'I'm sorry, Dad.'

Tomek pulled her in for another hug, squeezed her tightly, then let her go. 'If you ever have any questions about what happened to Michał and all the rest of it, then you just ask, all right? And...' He inhaled deeply, composing himself for the next part. 'If you ever see anything suspicious or something you think I should know about, you let me know. Deal?'

'Deal.'

With that, Tomek opened the letter and began reading.

> Dearest Tomek,
>
> I hope you will see that my spelling has significantly improoved since last time. Some of the people hear try to help me with my spelling but I tell them I would like to learn on my own. I have all the time in the world and I would like to do something for myself at least once in my life. Sometimes I think about the things I've done and what I might be doing if I didn't kill your brother. Do you ever do that? Have you ever thought about what you might do if you stopped being a police officer? I think I'd like to be a painter or decorator, do something with my hands. We have a lot of woodwork and craft classes hear to keep us entertayned. They are some of my favorit. The other day I built a small birdhouse. The man who taught me how to do it said he was really impressed and was going to put it in a garden centre and see if anyone wants to buy it. If they do, then the man said I can get some of the money for it. I told him to make sure that it goes into a garden centre near you in Essex, but I don't know if he will. I really like my hobbies. Do you have any? The warden has to make sure there are loads of guards around becos sometimes we have hammers and other tools. Some of the other inmates in here have tried to start fights with them, but I stay away. It's all very silly.
>
> Tomorrow... But it might have already gone by the time you get this, I don't think the post here is very fast, and

maybe it isn't very reliaball either. But anyway tomorrow they are coming again and this time they are teeching me how to build something out of iron. I dunno what it's called, but if you're interested, I can send it to your home address. The guards round hear don't normally let things that size go out, but I think they'll make an acception for me.

Anyway, thinking of you.
Nathan

PS - I still haven't heard from you yet on either of my mobile numbers. I've written them again for you on the back just in case. Please do not lose it.

PPS - I have written Michał's names on the bottom of the bird house I made, in case you wanted to go into a garden centre and look for it.

PPPS - I only learnt about this PS stuff the other day. It's cool isn't it!

'WHAT DOES IT SAY?'

The voice sounded distant, like it was coming from outside, and pulled him away from his thoughts.

'Dad, what does the letter say?'

'Nonsense,' he said absent-mindedly.

'What?'

'Nonsense. He's... he's just talking about a birdhouse he made.'

A birdhouse with his brother's name on it.

Tomek didn't know why, but all he could think about was that wooden birdhouse. It was probably four pieces of wood glued together with a large circle cut out on one of the walls. It was probably made from a kit: all the pieces coming together in a box and all Nathan had to do was stick them together with some PVA glue. There was no craftsmanship involved, no real skill required. And yet Tomek wanted it.

I have written Michał's name on the bottom.

Tomek handed her the letter. She took it from him carefully and began reading. He watched her eyes move from side to side as she started a new line, her brow furrowing, face contorting.

'He's given you his mobile number again?' she said.

'He's keen for me to have it.'

'Have you messaged him?'

Tomek told her he hadn't.

'Are you going to?'

To that, he didn't have an answer. The thought had crossed his mind several times. But he hadn't acted on it.

Yet.

After she'd apologised to him again for going through his belongings, Tomek made them dinner. Oven pizzas. Pepperoni for himself. Ham and pineapple for her. While the food was cooking, Tomek snuck away to his bedroom. Under the guise of getting changed out of his work clothes and into something more comfortable, he perched on the end of the bed, holding the letter in one hand and his phone in the other.

He prodded the screen with his thumb and it awoke, revealing his wallpaper: a stock image of Earth. The Face ID setting did its job and unlocked the device. All he needed to do now was swipe up, which he did. Then, cautiously, he moved towards the Contacts app on his phone and hovered his finger above the small plus in the top corner of the screen. Held it there. Thinking, contemplating, deliberating.

And then he did it.

He pressed the button and added both the mobile numbers Nathan had given him to his address book. Before he could do anything with them, the buzzer from the oven sounded, signalling the pizzas were ready.

CHAPTER FORTY-FOUR

The birds are all I can hear. Dozens, hundreds, if not thousands, of them singing their chorus, communicating to one another up in the sky. I can hear them over the sounds of the cars, of the wind, of the kids on the opposite side of the street. I'm too scared to look up, but I imagine they're all flying above me, watching me run towards the park. Maybe they're trying to communicate with me. Screaming at me to stop. Screaming at me to hurry. Trying to tell me that Michał's already dead, that there's nothing I can do.

Maybe they're the voices of the dead that he's about to join.

When I finally enter the park, the noises disappear, silence everywhere, save for the sound of a single bird flying into a nearby tree. I glance at it, but in the darkness it is invisible, vanished. And then I look down a few degrees and see Nathan Burrows standing there. He's forty years old again, dressed in jeans and a thin burgundy sweatshirt. He looks normal, as though he was just about to go out for a meal with friends, and not like he was serving a life sentence for murder.

My initial reaction is that he's been released, that he's been watching my every move somehow, but that's not possible. I know it can't be.

He's standing there at the back of the field with his arms behind his back. I move towards him, slowly removing my backpack as I go. I drop it to the ground, onto the mud and grass. Until I come to a stop a few metres away from him, my dead brother lying in the middle between us, his body perfectly still.

Before anything happens, I look down at my hands. They're big, muscular, veiny, covered in hair. These aren't the hands of a ten-year-old boy; they're the hands of a forty-year-old man. My hands. Two adults, two fully grown *men revisiting a thirty-year-old crime scene. It's the first time the two of us have met like this before. I should want to leap across Michał and wrap my hands around Nathan's throat. I should want to leap across my dead brother's heavily mutilated body and punch the fucking shit out of him, beat him to death. But I can't. I can't move. In fact, I don't want to move. Something's stopping me, something's holding me back.*

Fear, perhaps.

Maybe grief, guilt.

Or maybe it's sympathy.

I don't know, but whatever it is, it's keeping me perfectly still.

A few moments like this pass. Of silence, of nothing but the wind rustling through the trees.

There are no cars, no birds now.

Just Nathan and me.

And then he says to me, 'I'm sorry for killing your brother, Tomek. I regret it every day of my life.'

'It's fine,' I respond, 'I understand.'

CHAPTER FORTY-FIVE

The letter, just like all the others, continued to play on his mind. The following day, Tomek arranged an early Sunday morning run with an old school friend, Warren Thomas. The two didn't say much to one another as they jogged along the Southend seafront, battling headfirst into the winds, skipping past the early-morning families and dog walkers. There wasn't much to say. Instead, Tomek used the time to clear his head, process his thoughts, process the dream.

It's fine... I understand.

What the fuck was that all about?

What was wrong with him? Why wasn't he admonishing his brother's killer? Why was he basically forgiving him and excusing everything he'd done to Michał and everything he'd done to his family ever since? It didn't make sense, and in truth, it disconcerted him a little. He either needed to make contact or he needed to cut ties immediately. The former was his preferred choice, but his concern was that the more he stuck with it and the more he entertained Nathan, the more the man would stick in his head and continue to haunt his dreams. If he let it fall to the wayside and he blocked the man out of his life (how exactly, he wasn't sure yet), then he would never get the answers to his questions, never get the closure he needed.

It was Catch-22, and he didn't know what to do.

Like with most things (case in point, Abigail) he pushed it to the back of his mind and let it stay there until the time was right. It was Sunday. The day of rest. It could wait for another day.

After he'd said goodbye to Warren, he'd driven back through Leigh Broadway and spotted an empty parking space along the high street – a rarity on any day of the week, no less a Sunday – and quickly pulled into it. Shutting off the engine, he climbed out of the car and made his way to Whitaker's.

The shop was empty, a slow day, by any standard, and Rose was sitting at the back of the building, crocheting on her lap.

'Not interrupting, am I?' he said sarcastically. 'You look busy. I can come back at a quieter time.'

As soon as she realised it was him, the incipient expression of anger caused by his comments, immediately fell.

'And you look like you've just been for a swim in the sea,' she retorted. 'I hope you're not bringing any sand onto my floor.'

Tomek pointed to the large display cabinet that contained the model yacht her husband had bought for her. 'Just add it to your beach scenery,' he replied.

'Do you want it?' she asked, taking him by surprise.

'Pardon?'

'The boat. Do you want it?'

'Why would I?'

And then he realised.

'I reckon you could get a decent amount for it,' he said.

'I don't want a decent amount. I don't care if it burns or if a seagull shits all over it. I want it gone.'

'Just the one seagull or a flock of them? Because that's a lot of shit just for one seagull.'

'I don't think there's any shortage of them,' she said. 'All I've got to do is leave it outside for an hour or two and it'll either get nicked or shat on by the wildlife out there.'

Tomek shook his head as he made his way over. 'You don't wanna use those seagulls, they're way too sensitive. I know a guy.'

'You know a guy?'

'Yeah.'

'A seagull guy?'

'Yeah. I got a seagull connect.'

Rose dropped her crochet into her lap and burst into a fit of laughter until the point where Tomek thought he saw tears forming in her eyes.

'Who the fuck has a "seagull connect"?'

'Definitely not me.' Tomek shot her a finger gun. 'But I bet that's the first time you've laughed in what felt like a long time, am I right?'

'Maybe,' she said, suddenly turning coy.

'Good. Then my deed here is done.'

'You can save another damsel in distress now.'

Tomek chuckled. He was enjoying the causal flirtation. And to his surprise, this time he wasn't feeling guilty about any of it.

'I was hoping I could speak to you about something, actually,' he said.

'It'll cost ya.'

'That's what I'm worried about.' He spun on the spot and moved to the display in the centre of the shop. By the window, he pointed to a silver bracelet with two green charms on it: a four-leaf clover and a small kitten hugging a ball of yarn to its chest. 'I'm after this,' he said.

'Things back on track with the girlfriend now then?'

Tomek shot her a look that said, "Don't be silly".

'I was thinking more about my daughter. She's thirteen, been with me for a couple of months, and I feel like she needs it. She's been through a lot, and I don't know why, but I feel like this could be a nice thing to do for her.'

'It's a *lovely* thing to do for her. She'll be thrilled.'

Rose donned a pair of gloves, inserted a key into the top of the cabinet, and fished inside for the bracelet. Then she placed it on a small plush cushion.

'Now, before we go any further, do I get mates' rates, or a blue light discount at the very least?'

Rose's cheeks warmed. 'You can get one better than that. Because you cheered me up, I'll give you family discount and knock fifty per cent off.'

Tomek was taken aback. 'I couldn't possibly... That's too generous.'

She touched him on the arm playfully, though there was a sense of intent behind it. 'Nonsense. Either you take it or I won't sell it to you at all, and then your daughter will be left upset and disappointed.'

'Guilt tripping... You're quite the salesperson.'

'It's how I've learnt to get what I want.' Rose moved towards the cash desk and began bagging the bracelet up. First came the small navy felt pouch, complete with Whitaker's branding in silver foiling. Next was a "With Thanks" business card placed on top. Then she transported the two items onto a bed of straw paper and wrapped it twice, before eventually putting it into a branded paper bag. Tomek watched as she moved deftly and elegantly between each stage in the process.

'You've done that before.'

'This is only my second time. Business has been lean.'

Tomek smirked, then readied his debit card.

A few seconds later, she rang up the total, and he paid. Then she placed the receipt in the bag and left her hand there, waiting for him to reach out and touch it.

'This wasn't the only reason you came here, was it?' she asked.

Tomek stuttered.

'It's about my husband, isn't it?'

'Have you spoken to him?' Tomek reached out for the gift. Eventually she relented and let him have it.

'Not since I kicked him out, no.'

'Would you like to know where he is?'

'Not particularly. So long as he's still alive to sign the divorce papers, I don't care where he is, what he's doing, or how he's doing. He's been lying to me about all those things for long enough anyway, he should be able to handle it. By now, he's a fucking expert.'

Tomek looked down at the floor. 'He's in hospital. We found him at The Prince Albert, near Roy and Daphne's. Severely drunk. Almost thought we might have to pump his stomach. He didn't have many nice things to say about you, mind, but I guess you don't have any nice things to say about him either. Regardless, he's in Broomfield if you fancied the journey.'

'Fuck no. He can stay there for all I care because he certainly ain't coming anywhere near here, the house, or the flat upstairs. Can you believe he tried to stay there after I kicked him out?'

'I can,' Tomek replied without meaning to sound condescending and sarcastic.

If she was offended by it, she didn't show it. 'I told him he could fuck off. My name's on all the agreements. I have all the risk. They're *my* properties. He's allowed nowhere near them.'

Tomek was reminded of his conversation with Johnny Whitaker.

'Has he ever been violent towards you?'

Rose shook her head.

'Has he ever emotionally abused you?'

Another shake.

'What about his dad, Roy? You ever seen any aggression out of that man?'

This time, Rose took longer to answer the question. She pondered on it, let the thoughts ruminate around her skull as she searched through the hard drive.

'I mean, he's never been physically violent towards me, a bit weird and aggressive sometimes, but I've only heard of one instance with him and Daphne. Johnny told me there was a time when they were on holiday and he hit her across the face while the kids were in the swimming pool. Johnny wasn't sure if he'd seen it or not. All he saw was his mum holding her face. But he never said anything at the time. I think he was, like, ten, eleven, so probably didn't know any better.'

Tomek shifted his weight from one foot to the other.

'And that was the only time?'

She shrugged. 'That he told me about. Doesn't mean to say it didn't happen when they weren't there.'

Tomek cast his mind back to his visits to the Whitaker family home; whether he'd seen anything untoward. The dynamic between Roy and Daphne had switched multiple times. Sometimes Daphne was the one in charge, looking after Roy, and the next it was the other way round. There was no obvious power dynamic or threatening overtone that he'd been able to pick up on. Regardless, he made a mental note to follow up with Anna on it. She'd spent more time with the family; she may have seen or noticed something.

Just as Tomek was about to leave, Rose added, 'He's never been physical with me, but...'

Tomek gave her as much time as she needed to continue. This wasn't the sort of thing that could be rushed.

'He... he came on to me one time, which I thought was a bit weird.' She inhaled deeply, as if preparing herself to relive the memory. 'We were at a family wedding – some distant, second cousin-six-times-removed thing. I didn't know anyone, and neither did Johnny, but he said he wanted to go because he loves weddings and they're always a good excuse to have a good time and get as pissed as you want. This was back when he was going through the worst of his drinking problem.'

'Daphne and Roy told me about that,' Tomek interrupted. 'Said that they'd sat him in front of God and got him off the drink cold turkey.'

Rose scoffed. 'That's what they wanted to believe, but it didn't last long. Don't get me wrong, Johnny was still drinking, but he wasn't drinking as much. And whenever we went round his parents' for a meal or event, he was just very good at hiding it and making sure he didn't get caught – along with everything else, it would appear.' Rose rolled her eyes and continued with her story. 'Anyway, about two hours into this wedding, Johnny was already on the dance floor, dancing, talking to anyone and anything that would give him the time of day; I think I saw him talking to a plant at one point. But while Johnny was dancing, Roy came over to me, sat right beside me and put his arm round my back. At first I thought, all right, he's come over to say something, but when he didn't move it, I started to get a bit worried. Then he began stroking my arm, squeezing my shoulder. I felt super uncomfortable, and like I couldn't call out for help. No one else was nearby to come and rescue me: Angelica and Daphne were on the dance floor as well, swinging around with each other. And then he leant into my ear and grunted.'

'Grunted?'

'Yeah. Like a sexual grunt type of thing.'

'Did he say anything?'

She nodded.

'Yeah. He called me an angel for looking after Johnny the way I had been, and then left. I mean, he was pretty drunk as well, but... I dunno, it just felt weird, you know?'

'Yeah,' Tomek said. 'I know.'

CHAPTER FORTY-SIX

He had no idea what was on the television. Some crap that he'd let Kasia put on because she had a load of homework to do on her laptop, she'd told him, and apparently she couldn't focus unless she had something on in the background. Her teenage mind didn't like the silence, and her attention span had become so poor from the constant barrage of dopamine coming from her phone that she couldn't focus on any one thing for longer than a few minutes, which meant Tomek was forced to endure it as well.

He had tried to keep himself busy with errands and tasks, but his mind and body were knackered. His legs ached from the run and his head hurt from the information Rose had given him. As he sat there, staring at the television screen, he'd tossed around thoughts of Johnny and Rose Whitaker in his mind. Of the pool, of the wedding ceremony. Of Roy Whitaker, the esteemed and highly decorated pilot, assaulting one woman and crossing the line with another.

'Dad, can I have a glass of Coke, please?'

Kasia was sitting cross-legged on the sofa, her laptop resting on her knees. Dangling from her wrist was the new bracelet she'd thanked Tomek for a hundred times. It jangled every time she moved her wrist, clattering into the side of the laptop, making Tomek immediately regret buying it.

'You know where the fridge is,' he told her.

She glared at him. 'I'm busy.'

'So am I.'

'I've got maths homework to do!'

'And so do I. Like counting how much your bracelet's gonna cost me to insure in case you ever lose it.'

Her expression dropped. 'Funny. Now, can I have a Coke, please? You can get yourself one as well, if you want.'

'Fucking make the drink myself, while I'm at it, shall I?' he said as he lifted himself off the sofa.

'Swearing!' she called.

Tomek groaned and reached into his pocket, found some loose change and dropped it into a jar. In the past couple of weeks, the two of them had introduced a swear jar. It was mostly for Tomek, who had little control over his mouth at times, but there had been a few occasions where Kasia had been forced to dip into her pockets (which were really *his* pockets) and contribute some money (which was really *his* money) to the fund. By the end of it, when it was full, they would no doubt spend it on a takeaway pizza or Chinese, which was more a reward than a punishment, and seemed to negate the point of the swear jar in the first place. But neither of them was complaining.

As Tomek opened the fridge and reached inside for the can of fizzy drink, he felt his phone vibrate. He checked the caller ID before answering.

'To what do I owe the pleasure?' he said.

'You can have all the pleasure in this one, mate,' Nick replied loudly.

'Oh.'

'Because I'm going to get no pleasure from what I'm about to tell you, kid.'

Tomek glanced over at Kasia, who was looking back at him expectantly. He retrieved a can of Coke from the fridge and passed it to her before moving back into the kitchen, where it was quieter and more private.

'Go on,' he told Nick.

'I wanted to give you a heads-up,' the chief inspector continued. 'So you can hear from someone you know before it becomes common knowledge. As of tomorrow, Victoria will be taking over as SIO of Operation Butterfly. You will still have a deputy SIO role, but she will be bringing in the rest of the team to assist with the investigation. She's raised her concerns about how long things are taking and how much of the budget's been blown unnecessarily on overtime and forensics. She's worried that it's all been wasted and managed ineffectively, and on this occasion, I've agreed with her. Sorry, it's a shit thing to tell you on a Sunday, but these things happen, mate. It's nothing personal. We're just doing what's best for the investigation.'

Which he'd been leading. Which he'd been running from the start. It was impossible not to take it personally. He felt betrayed, stabbed in the back. The rug had been pulled from beneath his feet, and he had landed so hard on his arse that he hadn't heard Nick finish the call. It wasn't until he heard the tone in his ear that he eventually came to.

'Everything all right?' Kasia asked tentatively from the living room.

Tomek's eyes fell on the swear jar.

'Yeah,' he lied. 'Everything... everything's fine. Now, come on, get back to your homework. But please don't expect me to help with any of it because algebra was one of my least favourite subjects.'

CHAPTER FORTY-SEVEN

The first thing Tomek noticed as soon as he entered the office the following morning was everyone's eyes boring into him. For some reason, he was one of the last in, and so he had the luxury of dealing with the team's judgemental and awkward stares pointed in his direction as he made his way to his desk. He could sense their thoughts too, pulverising his skull. Pity, a large dose of pity filled with an extra helping of guilt.

Tomek didn't need it. He wasn't in the mood for it. And he certainly wasn't in the mood for a conversation with Victoria.

The conversation with Victoria.

But he had no choice; a minute later, she emerged from her office and called him over. Feeling like a child who'd just been pulled out of class by the headteacher, Tomek made his way towards her office, except this time there were no jeers from his classmates.

'Morning, Tomek,' Victoria said, holding the door open for him.

Tomek grunted a hello.

'Please, take a seat.'

He did as he was told.

'I know it's first thing on a Monday, but there's something I need to tell—'

'I know,' he replied. 'Nick told me.'

'I see,' she said calmly. If she was disappointed and upset with the betrayal, she didn't let on. In fact, there was a resignation in her voice that indicated she'd known Nick would be the one to break the news first. 'And did Nick explain why?'

Tomek pursed his lips, promised himself he wouldn't say anything, then nodded.

'I see. And... did he mention the part about Abigail?'

Tomek tilted his head to the side. 'Abigail?'

Sighing, Victoria rolled her eyes and muttered, 'Of course he didn't, the coward.'

'What's Abigail got to do with any of this?'

'She called up the other day,' Victoria explained, 'and spoke to Martin. She asked him for details on the case and, in what can only be described as a state of mild fucking panic, he gave her some information.'

'Martin did?'

Victoria raised a hand to placate him. 'Don't worry. It's being dealt with. I'm handling it.'

He clenched his fist on his knee, digging his nails into his thigh. 'What did he tell her?'

'The information about the angel wings and the location of where Angelica Whitaker's body was found. Also that she was taken a few minutes after being dropped off at home.'

'That much?'

'I'm afraid so. And...' She inhaled sharply. 'He may have also let slip that she's... how shall I say? That she's had a lot of sexual partners in the past.'

'Brilliant.'

'A few of the comments on the *Southend Echo*'s social media posts have been disappointing, to say the least.'

'Middle-aged rape sympathisers saying that she deserved it somehow?'

She lowered her gaze. 'I'm afraid so.'

Tomek let out a long, deep breath. 'When did this happen?'

'Saturday,' she answered.

After The Nights of Eden. After the argument.

'And Martin?'

She huffed, shaking her head. 'Like I said, I'm dealing with it.'

And that was that on the matter. There was nothing more that he could do. Nothing more to add. Abigail, the spiteful bitch, had circumvented him, gone behind his back, and preyed on a clearly inept and inexperienced DC who had nothing to do with the investigation and had told her everything he'd overheard and everything she wanted to know. *That calculated, conniving...*

Victoria clapped her hands, pulling him from his reverie. 'As Nick explained, I'll be overseeing everything from now on, so you'll be reporting to me. Much the same as you have been since I joined, it's just, now—'

'I'm back to my former job title.'

'Pretty much.'

Tomek left the room in a huff and headed straight towards the small kitchen area at the back of the office. There, he made for the coffee machine. As the machine whirred into life, he rested against the countertop, staring into the plughole of the sink nearby. A second later, his phone began vibrating.

A part of him hoped it would be Abigail so he could launch a verbal assault on her and officially end their relationship for having reduced his involvement in Operation Butterfly. A part of him wanted to fly off the handle at her and let her have it. But, disappointingly, it wasn't her. It was a number he didn't recognise.

Tentatively, he answered the call and held the phone to his ear. 'DS Tomek Bowen speaking.'

'Detective, it is you!'

The French accent gave him away immediately.

'Good morning, Florian. Is everything all right?'

'As fine as can be. I haven't been able to stop thinking about everything all weekend.'

'Sometimes it can take a while to process.'

'As I said, I was doing some thinking,' the man continued, as though he wasn't listening to Tomek at all.

'Oh, yeah?'

'And I remembered what you said about calling if I think anything might be important.'

'Okay...'

'And I was thinking about this all weekend, and I do hope you'll forgive me for not mentioning it earlier. I did not think it was important, but now I do...'

'Any time now, Florian,' Tomek said, checking his watch.

'Right. Of course. Forgive me. I haven't been nervous like this in years.'

Tomek imagined the artist pacing around his studio, surrounded by a dozen more paintings of Angelica on the walls.

'It's about Angelica...' the man continued.

'Yes, I gathered.'

'On more than one occasion, her and I... we... we spent the evening with another woman. The three of us, in one of the rooms. And... and I'm fairly confident that she slept with the same woman alone. I don't know if it's important, but... I just thought I would let you know.'

CHAPTER FORTY-EIGHT

Tomek did think it was important. He thought it was very important indeed. His mind, after he'd eventually hung up the phone with Florian, immediately went to Angelica's crime scene, to her body lying face up on the floor. The make-up, the shaving, the care and attention – the almost *womanly* care and attention – that had gone into cleaning and preserving her body in death. And then his mind had transported him to one of the rooms. With Florian, with Rachel, with the four-poster bed in the middle of the room and the sex toys lying on it.

The dildo.

All this time, they'd concluded that she had been raped by a man. A man who'd worn a condom and cleaned up after himself. But what if there had been no penis at all? What if it had been a twelve-inch rubber dildo like the one he'd seen on the bed instead?

It wasn't impossible.

After his call with Florian, Tomek had sent Rachel and Chey out to speak with Angelica's closest friends, Xanthia, Elodie, and Zoë. If Angelica's bisexuality went beyond the exploration and experimentation of the rooms at Melback Manor, Tomek wanted to know about it. If she had other female sexual partners that they, and her family, didn't know about, they would need to track them down and question them because Tomek was adamant there was a lead there. A faint, almost intangible one, but a lead all the same (and after his previous spiel to Victoria about having overturned all the stones and followed up on the leads, he didn't want this one to come and bite him in the arse). In order to give himself a head start, meanwhile, Tomek was on the way to the manor. Accompanying him was

Oscar, the only other officer right now that he trusted fully, and one of the last remaining members of his original team. So far, neither of them had said anything, neither wanting to be the one to tackle the elephant in the cabin, but Tomek didn't mind. Sometimes he enjoyed the silence, the vacuum of a long drive. It helped reset his thoughts. And as he pulled up to Melback Manor, thirty minutes later, he had only one thought on his mind: Micky Tatton.

After rolling the car to a slow stop in the car park on the other side of the building, Tomek was transported to that Friday night. How different the place looked in the daytime, now that it had been tinged with depravity and salacious behaviour in his mind. He couldn't look at the building the same way, at the staff that had seen things they'd been sworn to secrecy over. They were all carrying with them a secret, and he wondered how many more they might have.

And in particular, how many more Micky Tatton might have.

Tomek and Oscar found the owner outside in the manor grounds. He was standing inside a timber gazebo that was situated in the middle of a small lake to the south of the property, deep in conversation with a member of staff. The gazebo was painted moon white, with six wooden struts supporting it in the water. Small lanterns adorned the walkway, and vines of synthetic flowers were wrapped around the gazebo's pillars. In the water, lily pads and fallen leaves floated on the surface, gently moving in the breeze. Surrounding the waterline was an arboretum of oak, elm and birch trees, their leaves sprouting as the seeds of spring began to grow. To the right, a large water feature sent plumes of water vapour into the air. Tomek found the noise soothing. It reminded him of a water fountain they'd had growing up; lying in the garden in the summer as a teenager, letting the sun scorch his body, hearing the gentle rushing of water from the fountain beside his head like he was in the middle of an Indonesian rainforest.

As they approached, Micky Tatton, the hotel owner, caught sight of them, whispered to the member of staff, and then sent them on their way. The female staff member avoided their gaze as she sidled past on the narrow walkway.

'Sergeant,' Micky said. 'What a pleasant surprise.'

He held out his hand for Tomek. Tomek took it, then stepped aside for Oscar.

'Who do we have here?' Micky asked.

'DC Perez.'

'Pleasure,' Tatton replied.

'No weddings today?' Tomek asked.

'Not on a Monday. No one wants to get married on a Monday, even if it is considerably cheaper.'

'I imagine you've got a lot of cleaning to be getting on with still.'

Micky's face scrunched in discomfort. 'Always plenty of cleaning to do. Even the most well-behaved guests make more mess than they realise.'

'I can only imagine how much mess the worst behaved guests make,' Tomek replied. Out of the corner of his eye, he noticed Oscar's face contorting in polite confusion.

Before replying, Micky turned to the water and gestured at the trees. 'Gorgeous, isn't it? This is my favourite part of the entire property. Sure, some of the original features are still here from its inception – like the chimneys, the doors, and some of the windows – and you've got the tunnels and some of the master bedrooms. But out here... out here you feel isolated from it all. This is where we create memories for people, and by standing here, I feel like I'm a part of that somehow.'

So not only was he a part of people's sexual deviance, but he was also trying to wedge himself into the happiest memories of his customers' lives. The man was a control freak.

He continued: 'Sometimes I come out here for some quiet reflection. And also for some ghost hunting!'

'Ghost hunting?' Tomek asked, unable to hide the cynicism in his voice.

'If you believe in that sort of thing, of course. I do, but not many agree. Besides, it's fun for the kids, keeps them entertained.'

'What ghost?' Tomek asked, deciding to indulge the man.

'It's said that my great-great-great-great-great-grandfather's wife committed suicide here a few hundred years ago. According to legend, she wasn't so happy about the marriage, and at that time saw no way out, so she killed herself. But the story goes she liked the grounds so much she decided to stay, and I think she might have wanted to get some revenge as well since, her ghost's been spotted several times. I've seen her once, but I know she's been around more than that. Sometimes I can feel her presence in the room.'

'Was she around at the weekend?' Tomek asked. 'Can't imagine she would have been too happy with what she saw.'

Oscar's face contorted even more.

'We may never know. It's not like I have security cameras installed in each of the rooms...' Micky cleared his throat. 'Anyway, gentlemen, I digress. I presume you've come here to ask me some more questions about Angelica?'

'Yes,' Oscar said. 'It's come to our attention that she spent the night with a woman while she was here. Can you remember who?'

Micky leant to one side, peering round Tomek to see if anyone was nearby. Once satisfied there was no one within earshot, Micky answered, 'It's not uncommon. Our guests spend the night with whomever they desire.'

'Yes, but there was a particular female guest Angelica spent the night alone with, and on more than one occasion.'

Micky folded his arms across his chest. 'Florian told you that, did he?'

'Florian?' Tomek repeated, alarm bells ringing. 'I thought you didn't know his name?'

The man stuttered. 'I...'

'How much more do you know about him? Can I see your phone?'

The man's hand involuntarily flew to his breast pocket. 'No. Absolutely not.'

'Why not? What have you got to hide?'

'You can't ask to see my phone.'

'Yes, I can. I'm not taking it by force. I'm allowing you to volunteer your phone to me. If you give me permission, there's nothing wrong with that. However, the fact you don't want me to have it is only going to make me think that you're hiding something. Which, given the fact that you lied to us about not knowing The Donkey Man's name—'

'Donkey Man?' Oscar interrupted, curiosity getting the better of him.

'I'll explain later,' Tomek told him, then quickly returned to Micky. 'The fact that you lied to me about not knowing who Florian is makes me think that you do have something more to hide. Now, I'm going to ask again, and this time I'll make it easier for you: do you know the woman Florian's referring to?'

The man hesitated, a struggle playing out on his face. It was clear to see that he knew the answer, but didn't want to give it up.

'Might I just add that failure to give us this information, if it later comes to light that you knew what we were after, means you're interfering with an investigation and could lead to jail time,' Oscar added.

That always worked.

'Fine,' the man said in a huff, then reached into his pocket and handed Tomek his phone. 'Her name's Emilia Solveig. She owns her own hair and beauty salon in Southend. She's been coming to The Nights of Eden for about a year now. I first invited her to join after bumping into her at her salon. It was late, and I needed a haircut. She was the only place open.'

'And you just ended up talking about deranged sex parties and orgies with a complete stranger?' Tomek said loudly on purpose. His voice travelled across the water, but it was quickly drowned out by the gushing water fountain.

'Quiet! Don't say it so loudly. Not everyone knows what goes on here.' Micky sighed heavily. 'She... she was in a difficult place, all right. I'm sure she'll tell you all about it when you see her.'

CHAPTER FORTY-NINE

Emilia Solveig was thirty-two years old, with long blonde hair that had been curled into tight, perfect ringlets. Her face was covered with make-up, but it had been expertly applied, as though she spent the better part of two hours on it every morning, and several years of her life training to do it professionally. She was in the middle of cutting a customer's hair when Tomek and Oscar entered her salon. The inside of the salon was a cacophony of noise: heavy bass playing in the background, hair dryers blasting warm air, water cascading from a shower head, and loud chatter, combined with the sound of scissors cutting, and tinfoil tearing. Tomek had no idea what was going on, he was used to a simple short back and sides with a little trim on top, but this was industrial on another level. There were four customers in total, each being tended to by a member of staff, all in various stages of the haircutting process.

Emilia, at the other end of the row of chairs, noticed them in the mirror and turned to face Tomek.

'All right, gents?' she asked. 'Appointments only, lads. We don't do walk-ins.'

'But you did for Micky Tatton,' Tomek said.

At that, Emilia paused, set her scissors down on the counter, and made her way cautiously towards Tomek. As she approached, Tomek studied her face, trying to work out if he'd seen her on Friday night, whether he recognised her out of costume.

'Why you sayin' that name round here?' she asked, keeping her voice low. ''Oo are you?'

'The police,' Tomek whispered. He kept his warrant card in his pocket, lest any of her customers or colleagues see. 'We were wondering if we could ask you a few questions about a friend of yours.'

'A friend? Who?'

'Angelica.'

Emilia's face glazed over. Her lips parted and her expression fell behind a wall of deep thought.

'Angelica? She... what's happened?'

'Could we go somewhere more private?'

Emilia turned behind her. 'There ain't nowhere. I...'

Tomek gave her the opportunity to finish up with her customer. In the meantime, he and Oscar were happy to take seats. Tomek watched the process in amazement. The cutting, the washing, the shampooing, the tinfoil, the dyeing. All of it to make their hair look nicer. Tomek never gave much thought to his own. Just keep it short, apply a bit of gel now and then, let nature and the wind take care of the rest. He realised he had it much easier. Not to mention cheaper. He had baulked at the price of a full haircut for Kasia when she'd asked him. Over two hundred quid for a full cut, dye, and the rest, whatever that entailed. For that price, he joked, he would need to take out a mortgage for it. In the end, he had resorted to buying some box dye from the supermarket for a fraction of the price and supervising her while she did it herself. Beyond that, it was all lost on him.

Twenty minutes later, Emilia Solveig was ready. She grabbed her coat from the wall behind the counter and held the door open for them.

'I'm in desperate need of a coffee,' she said as they exited the salon. 'Though for this, I fear I might need something stronger.'

Tomek didn't tell her otherwise. Fortunately, the coffee shop she took them to was right next door, and after a few minutes of waiting, they found a small bench in a nearby park.

'Firstly,' Tomek began, 'thank you for taking the time to speak with us. We appreciate this is all a bit out of the blue, and you probably have a lot of questions. Hopefully we can answer some of them for you, but we're hoping you can answer all of ours.'

'Of course,' she replied, her voice weak.

'Last week, Angelica Whitaker, a woman we believe you know intimately, was murdered.'

'Murdered?'

'Murdered, yes. How do you know Angelica?'

'She...' Emilia sipped on her drink slowly, taking her time to soak it all in. 'We met at the manor, at one of The Nights.'

'Can you remember when?'

'I think it was her first time. Some time back in September, maybe. I... we bumped into one another at the bar. She seemed nervous, a bit shocked by it all. I tried talking to her, but she wasn't very receptive. I think she was a bit out of her depth.'

'But the two of you grew closer in following meetings?'

Emilia dipped her head. 'The second time, I bumped into her again – she always wore the same outfit, so I knew it was her – and then we spent the night together with a man dressed as a donkey.'

Florian.

So far everything checked out; before they'd come to speak with her, Micky Tatton had explained the bare bones of everything he'd seen, picked up, or overheard about Emilia and Angelica's developing relationship. It was now up to Emilia to apply the meat to the skeleton.

'The three of us spent the night together. I think... I think it was her first time with a woman, I'm not sure. But she enjoyed it. We were gentle with her. Careful.'

Just as Tomek opened his mouth to ask a question, a teenager on a bike rushed past them, blasting music from a speaker hitched to the back of his bike.

'Did the two of you ever spend the night together alone?' he asked.

'Twice,' she said. 'It was... How much detail do you want?'

'As much as you're willing to share,' Tomek answered, then braced himself.

'It was magical,' she answered. 'Some of the best sex I've ever had with a woman. I don't know what it was, but there was something different about Angelica. More experienced, more accomplished, more... experimental. She was completely different from the first time I met her, and all in the space of a few visits. I don't know if that meant she was experimenting with someone else or what, but...' She took another sip of coffee as she trailed off. 'Afterwards, we would sit and talk, you know? Get to know each other on a deeper, personal level. She was... she was special, you know? I know it sounds silly to say, given the context of how we met and everything, but...'

'You started to develop feelings for her?' Tomek said, already sensing where this was headed.

'Yeah. She was just... so charismatic, you know? She just got me, understood me on a deeper level. Like I say, I don't know if it was the alcohol or the drugs, but things just got deeper for me.' A long, heavy sigh left her lips, and her gaze fell to her feet. 'But it didn't for her,' she continued. 'I got her number and tried to meet up a couple of times outside The Nights, but it just... it just didn't work. She was always too busy, and I was running this place. She ghosted me a couple of times. But I always looked forward to seeing her again, spending the night with her at the manor, you know?' She hesitated, took another sip. 'And then I saw her with another woman, some woman dressed in black overalls and a welder's mask. I don't know her name or what she looked like underneath her costume, but her and Angelica became inseparable. I didn't spend another night with her after that. She was gone, had moved on to the next thing.'

Tomek didn't know what to say. It wasn't really the sort of thing you consoled someone over. And even if it were, he didn't have the first idea how to respond. And judging by the bemused and lost look on Oscar's face, nor did he.

'How did that make you feel?' Tomek asked in the end, as the cogs in his brain began to turn. 'Angry? Upset?'

'Betrayed,' Emilia answered.

'Did you love her?'

'I... I think so. Even though it sounds silly to say it.'

'Not if that's how you felt,' Tomek remarked. He decided to change course. 'How long have you been doing hair and make-up for?'

'All my life. It was all I was ever good at at school, so I got my qualifications and I've been running my place for about five years now. Before that I was doing hair and make-up for a couple of the television shows on BBC and ITV.'

'Nice,' Tomek said. 'You must have a lot of patience for that. I hear sometimes it can take hours to do hair and make-up.'

She shrugged, nodding. 'It can. But once you know what you're doing, you can shorten that time substantially.'

Now it was Tomek's turn to nod and take a sip from his drink. For a moment, nobody said anything. Tomek watched a group of mums wheel their prams across the field. One of them let a dog off the lead, and with the help of a catapult, launched a ball fifty yards across the grass. The dog bounded across the field for it, eventually catching it in its mouth before racing back to its owner.

'We have to ask,' Oscar started, breaking the silence. 'But what were you doing last Friday night? Not the one just gone; the one before.'

Emilia began playing with the cup in her hands, composing herself. Thirty seconds later, she answered the question.

'I was out with my friends. We were at Memo bar in Southend. I saw Angelica at the bar, dancing with some guys, but I don't think she recognised me. I was going to go over to speak with her, but to be honest, by that point, I was done with her. I didn't want anything more to do with her.'

Interesting, Tomek thought. Perhaps Emilia was so done with her, so upset and betrayed by Angelica's actions, that she'd reacted and killed her.

CHAPTER FIFTY

There were few times in Tomek's life when he felt genuinely concerned. Like the time he'd come face to face with his brother's killer, or the time he'd been dangled over a bridge across a train track. But none of them came close to the concern he felt when he saw DC Chey Carter's face as he returned to the office. The smirk on the constable's face was wide, leering, creepy. And to make it worse, there was a demonic look in his eyes, as though he'd been possessed by something and Tomek was his next victim.

'Oh God,' Tomek said. 'What have you done? You've either fucked up badly or you're about to give me the best news ever.'

Chey said nothing. Instead, he gestured for Tomek to follow him into a small room. In his arms, the constable carried his laptop. As he shut the door behind them, Tomek said, 'You're not handing in your notice, are you?'

'What, and lose any chance of becoming your best friend? I don't think so, Sarge. You can't get rid of me that easily.'

'Nor can I get rid of that fucking smile,' Tomek replied. 'Stop it. It's scaring me.'

The constable's face fell on command.

'Better?'

'Better. Much, much, much better. Don't ever smile like that again. You'll get yourself arrested.'

'I'd be more than happy for you to arrest me, Sarge. And after the stories I'm hearing from the weekend, you might be happy to do it.'

Tomek held his breath. 'The fuck is that supposed to mean? What stories have you heard? What's Rachel been telling you?'

He knew it was a bad idea putting the two of them together. They couldn't be trusted. Rachel – she was the problem. She had enjoyed Friday night far too much. He knew she'd want to tell everyone on the team what they'd seen, and he'd been foolish to think they could keep it a secret, despite their agreement.

'Nothing juicy, sir. Just that you attracted quite a lot of attention,' Chey answered.

Tomek puffed his chest out and tried to hide his embarrassment. 'I did all right, thanks.'

'So did Rach. Though not the type of attention she was looking for, if her account's anything to go by.'

'We were there strictly on police business, Chey. Nothing happened.'

The constable set his laptop on the table in the middle of the room and lifted the lid. 'Do you reckon you could get me an invite to one of these things, maybe?'

Tomek didn't answer.

'On a strictly professional basis as well.'

'You whore,' he replied, sniggering. 'The organiser wasn't too keen on having us there in the first place. I can't imagine he's going to be too thrilled when we start multiplying and different people turn up every month.'

Chey rolled his eyes. 'Killjoy.' Then the young man turned his focus to his laptop, and as he logged in, he explained, 'We spoke with Angelica's friends again, as requested. And one of them, Xanthia, her name is, well, she gave us a little more than we were hoping for.'

'Right.'

Chey finished what he was doing on the computer and looked up at Tomek. 'Turns out that Xanthia and Angelica had had a little thing going on,' he explained. 'A drunken one-night-stand type of thing.'

'Yeah, I got that.'

'But it was more like a two-, three-night-stand thing. They'd spent a couple of nights together after they'd gone out for drinks as a group. It was always after a night out, and they never mentioned it to anyone else.'

'It was their little secret,' Tomek said, his mind whirring. Could this have been the other individual that Emilia Solveig had been referring to? The welder?

'It was more than a secret,' Chey continued. 'For Angelica, I'm told, it didn't happen. She always denied it whenever Xanthia tried to bring it up, but then when they later got drunk together, things would happen. And then the next day Angelica wouldn't remember a thing.'

The cogs began to turn faster now.

'Could Xanthia have drugged Angelica so she'd forget?'

Chey considered that for a moment. 'I... I hadn't thought of that. But we can look into it. I mean, she works in a pharmacy, so she might know how to access that type of thing.' Realisation flashed across Chey's face, and Tomek could see the young man making a mental note, a frame of reference for his learning later down the line. At last, Tomek had imparted some wisdom to the constable.

'Was that everything? Is that what the smile on your face was about, or was there something else?'

The smile returned. Tomek was unable to look the man in the eye.

'Something else,' Chey answered.

Pointing to the laptop, Tomek said, 'Go on, show me. Your face is reminding me of some of the blokes from Friday night, standing on the edge of the room touching themselves.'

That seemed to get rid of it; Chey prodded the Enter button on his keyboard, and after the screen had illuminated, spun the machine round to him. On the screen was Angelica Whitaker's blog. "My Little Corner of the Internet" was emblazoned at the top of the page, with a small image of a beach to the right. Beneath it was an article dated two weeks before, titled, "Where would I be without you?"

Tomek took control of the laptop and scrolled down the page, his eyes scanning the length of the post.

'You got the SparkNotes version, or you want me to read it all?'

'Neither, Sarge,' Chey said, taking the laptop back. 'I want you to listen.'

Surprised, and a little offended, Tomek leant back in his chair, folded one leg over his other knee, and waited patiently for the explanation.

'You asked me to print out all the blog posts, yes?'

'Yes.'

'Which I did. And I gave them out to each member of the team, so they could start reading them, right?'

'Right.'

'But when I got back from my meeting with Xanthia, I realised there was a slight issue with the printing. Actually, it was a major fucking issue—'

'What was the issue?'

'...but I fixed it, and—'

'What was the issue, Chey?' Tomek insisted.

The man sighed, turned to the screen, and scrolled to the bottom of the webpage. As he swung the device round, Tomek noticed the mistake. At the bottom of the blog post was a section for comments. A place for random strangers, or close friends and family members, to comment their thoughts on whatever they'd read from Angelica's Little Corner of the Internet.

'This was missed out on the blog posts when they printed.'

'So our lot have been reading through a bunch of shit, basically?'

Chey shrugged. 'Not entirely. There's some important stuff in there, but the real juicy part is this here.' The constable prodded the screen so hard the machine almost toppled backwards. He was pointing to the comment at the bottom of the webpage.

'So proud of everything you have overcome, my angel. You've got your wings back. Always thinking of you.'

Chey's eyes widened with delight.

'My angel...' Tomek continued, his thoughts shooting off on a tangent. 'My angel...'

'And there are loads more like that as well, all saying similar things. Sometimes Angelica replies, sometimes she doesn't.'

Tomek finally came to. 'She's communicating with the person?'

Chey nodded.

'Does that mean she knows who it is?'

A shrug. 'Possibly. There's no way to tell. We can't exactly ask her.'

Tomek pondered this for a moment, letting his thoughts percolate around his head. Then he pointed to the last word on the comment.

'Can we work out where the messages are coming from?'

The smile returned to Chey's face. 'I was hoping you'd ask that. I looked through the last couple of months' worth of posts, and saw about fifteen different comments, each saying the same thing, so I sent it down to digital, and they were able to trace the IP address.'

Tomek felt himself leaning forward involuntarily.

'And?'

Just as Chey was about to respond, the door opened. In stepped Rachel. She hovered in the doorframe.

Chey continued, regardless. 'The posts have been coming from a public computer in Hadleigh library.'

Tomek struggled to stifle his excitement. Now it was his turn to wear a creepy smile. 'Good work, mate. You remind me more and more of a young Tomek Bowen every day.'

'Fucking hell,' Rachel said, still standing in the doorframe. 'That's the last thing the world needs.'

CHAPTER FIFTY-ONE

In the time that it took uniformed officers to find Shawn Wilkins at Hadleigh library and bring him in, Tomek and the team had only been able to scour and analyse the last eight months of blog posts from Angelica's Little Corner of the Internet. In total, they found over a hundred comments from their mysterious commenter, all saying the same thing: "My angel's got her wings back.". The exact words that Shawn Wilkins had posted under her Instagram posts. Chey had even been able to plug the comments into an online software that turned them into a word cloud: a visual representation of the frequency with which each word appeared. The larger the word, the more times it had been used. Unsurprisingly, "my" and "angel" were at the top of the list, dominating most of the space in the word cloud. Tomek had never seen the software before, and had been dubious about its purpose at the start, but after seeing the results, he'd decided to print them off and take them with him down to the interview room.

Since Tomek had last seen him, Shawn Wilkins' hair had become messy and unkempt, as though he hadn't washed it the whole week. Inside the interview room, he was slouched in the chair, leaning against the wall, with his temple resting against the surface . His eyes were bloodshot, a thin line of stubble had started to form on his jaw, and the evidence from his meeting with Johnny Whitaker the other day was still visible on his nose.

'Good afternoon,' Tomek said as he entered and dropped a folder on the table.

The man grunted in response, avoiding eye contact.

Tomek pulled the chair out from beneath the table and crossed one leg over the other. Confidence bubbled beneath his surface, and he was unable to stifle the smirk on his face.

'How are you doing today, Shawn?' he asked, excitement lacing his tone.

'Why am I here?'

'We just have some more questions for you.'

'Why'd you have to come down and bring me in here?' he asked, sounding like a petulant teenager. 'Now everyone at work's gonna know I'm being questioned about this shit.'

That sounded like a Shawn problem, nothing to do with him.

'I hope you didn't cause a scene,' Tomek said. 'Otherwise that would only add to the speculation.'

Shawn turned his nose up at Tomek, pulling a face. 'You still ain't told me why I'm here.'

'All in good time,' Tomek replied as he prodded the folder on the table. 'All in good time.' Tomek dragged the folder slowly towards him and opened it on his knee, keeping it out of Shawn's eyeline. Then he looked at the first page. There, in front of him, was the homepage of Angelica's blog. Tomek removed it from the folder and slid it across the table. 'Do you recognise this, Shawn?'

Shawn gave the sheet a second's glance. 'Yeah.'

'What is it, please?'

'Angelica's blog.'

'And how do you know about it?'

'Because I've seen it before.'

'How many times would you say you've seen it?'

A shrug. Nonchalant, dismissive, like he'd just been asked if he wanted to get the next round – only if he had to.

'If you had to put a number on it,' Tomek insisted. 'How many times? A dozen? Fifty? A hundred?'

'I dunno.'

'So it's safe to assume you've seen it a lot then?'

'Maybe.'

'And how did you come by this little corner of the Internet, Shawn? Did Angelica send you the link directly, or did you find it via other means?'

Shawn sighed deeply, heavily. So deeply that Tomek felt the air brush against his knuckles.

'I saw it in one of her Instagram posts,' the stalker admitted. 'There isn't anything wrong with that. If she wanted to make it private, she could have. If she didn't want people to find it, then she shouldn't have posted it online. She's the one who put it out there. It's not like I went looking for it.'

'And that's absolutely right,' Tomek said.

'Eh?' Shawn muttered, taken aback.

'I agree. It's a website, websites are there to be found. Just like social media pages. I don't have a problem with you looking at it, but what I do have a problem with, and what I want a little more clarity on, is if you've ever posted anything in the comments? From what I gather, this website didn't get much traffic, so was this another one of your ways of reaching out to Angelica, letting her know you were watching her, keeping tabs on her life?'

'No!' The man's voice filled the small room.

Tomek wasn't listening. Instead, he removed the next sheet from the folder and set it on the table. 'This is one of the comments we've seen: "Wishing I was inside you right now, my angel." Posted at one thirty-two pm on the twenty-third of January. Pretty grotesque stuff for a lunchtime, wouldn't you agree?' He pulled out another sheet, read it, then laid it on top of the first. 'This one's a little tamer: "You are the most precious thing in the world to me, my angel." Also posted at a similar time. And then there's this one. And this one. And this one.'

And on it went, each time Tomek placing a printout on top of the last, until he came to the last page – the word cloud.

'You used to call Angelica an angel, didn't you? It's quite a common phrase here,' he said, gesturing to the word cloud. 'I've seen you post the same thing on her Instagram posts and in her direct messages. That was a particular phrase of yours, no?'

'A lot of people called her that.'

'How do you know?'

Shawn didn't answer.

'Do you recognise any of these comments?' Tomek asked as he fanned the sheets across the table.

'No,' the man replied bluntly.

'You sure?'

'Yes.' He tilted forward in his seat. 'I've never seen those before in my life.'

'You sure? Don't you find it interesting that all the comments are posted at a similar sort of time? What time do you usually have lunch when you're working?'

'One-ish.'

'Interesting. And how long did you say you've worked at the library?'

'A couple of years.'

'Even more interesting.'

Tomek said nothing for thirty seconds. He was waiting for Shawn to nibble on his last comment, but when it didn't come, he added, 'Would you like to know why?'

'No.'

'Well, I'm going to tell you, anyway. You see, we've traced the IP address for these comments, and guess where they're being posted from.'

Shawn said nothing. Either he was incredibly dense and didn't know the answer, or he did, in fact, know the answer and was too afraid to admit it.

Tomek pulled out another sheet. On it was a printout of Google Maps street view. He slid the document from the folder and set it down delicately, before prodding his fingernail into the centre of the page.

'Right there,' he said. 'Look familiar?'

Shawn didn't need to see the document to know where Tomek was referring to.

'Anything to say to that?' Tomek asked.

'I didn't post those comments. They weren't from me.'

'You work at the library. You're the only one with a connection to Angelica. You're the only one who's stalked her on every platform imaginable, and when she blocked you on the rest and got a restraining order against you, you thought you'd harass her on her blog, her little corner of the Internet. Sound about right?'

Shawn slammed his fist against the wall. 'I didn't fucking post those comments!'

'How can you prove it?'

The man's face contorted in anger.

'Got CCTV in the library we might be able to take a look at?'

'Of course not. It's a fucking library. Barely enough money to keep us going as it is. Besides, no one wants to steal fucking books.'

'So no CCTV then?'

'No, all right? No, we don't have any fucking CCTV.' Another slap on the wall. 'But I didn't post those comments, and I didn't have anything to do with Angelica's murder. Because if I did, you'd of found my DNA on her, but you haven't, have you? You haven't got a single strand of concrete evidence that points to me. Now, if that's all you got, then I'd like to get back to my job please, and don't ever come back to my place of work again. You hear me?'

'Or what?' Tomek asked as Shawn threw the chair behind him and towered over him. 'You'll kill me, too?'

CHAPTER FIFTY-TWO

The interview with Shawn Wilkins had gone nowhere. Tomek hadn't got the result he'd been hoping for – a confession of some kind – and by the end of it, Shawn had threatened to lodge a formal complaint with the Independent Office for Police Conduct following Tomek's behaviour and what Shawn had branded as "harassment". After being convinced otherwise by Rachel, who'd stroked his ego (and his arm) a tad, Shawn had stormed out of the station and headed back to the library.

When he returned to his desk, Tomek found Oscar sitting in his seat. The constable was deep in conversation with Anna, discussing the stalker's behaviour. As he arrived, Oscar explained that the uniformed officers who had been sent to the library to conduct a sweep of the place had confirmed that no CCTV was kept on the premises for longer than forty-eight hours, and that there was no way of discovering who'd accessed the computer and what they'd viewed. It seemed then that there was no tangible, physical evidence that could be used to charge Shawn Wilkins. It had been that way from the start. Nothing concrete. The killer had done such an exemplary job of killing Angelica and cleaning the crime scene without leaving a trace that it had left Tomek and the team fumbling about in the dark.

Tomek still carried the burden of the investigation on his shoulders. Even though it had officially been moved across to Victoria, he still saw it as his own. He'd started it, and now he wanted to finish it. The only problem was the toll it was taking on his body. He hadn't been eating properly. He'd skipped a handful of dinners and lunches, as he'd wanted to work through without breaks. He hadn't been sleeping properly either, his mind showing him images of Angelica's angel wings every time he closed his eyes, and as he looked at himself in the bathroom mirror before leaving that day, he realised for the first time the effect it had been taking on his hair and beard. What was once an immaculate, almost pitch-black head of thick hair, and a dark, striking beard, had now become soiled with a few greys. Disaster.

On the way home, he stopped off at the supermarket and purchased some hair and beard dye. That was his evening sorted – after Kasia had gone to bed, of course. He wouldn't be able to handle the ridicule and abuse he would no doubt receive if she saw him. Him, a forty-year-old man, dyeing his beard and hair? What was the world coming to? She would tell her friends, and then they'd tell their other friends, and eventually his secret would be out to all the parents and the teachers.

But his plans for the evening were threatened by the figure standing outside his house, wearing a long, thin coat, and holding a cigarette in her hand.

'When did *that* start?' Tomek asked, pointing to the stick of tobacco.

Abigail blew a large plume of smoke into the air. 'About the time I found out I was going to be the editor. Promotions aren't all they're cracked up to be.'

You can say that again.

'What are you doing here, Abigail?'

'Full name, eh? It's like that, is it?'

'Answer the question.'

She took another long drag of the cigarette and let it fall from her mouth as she spoke. 'I wanted to see you. I was hoping we could have a chat.'

'Not in there,' he said, gesturing towards the living room window on the first floor. 'Not after last time.'

'Fairs. Where then?'

Tomek raised his hand, rattled his car keys, and unlocked the car. Behind him, the orange lights flashed and a small *beep* sounded. Seconds later, they were inside.

'I tried calling you,' she said, shutting the door behind her.

'Have you?'

He knew she had. He'd seen the countless phone calls and had ignored them – some, at least. The others had arrived while he'd been in interviews or out in the field.

'I've been busy,' he said.

'Is that how it's going to be?' she asked, accusation in her tone. 'I call and you ghost me? I call and you pretend I don't exist?'

'I said I was busy, not that I've wiped you from my memory.'

'That's the way it feels,' she said, gradually becoming more and more incensed. Meanwhile, Tomek kept his voice cool, measured. They were in a confined space, and while nobody would be able to hear them, he wanted enough room to defend himself if things became... physical.

'I seem to remember I was the one who wanted space, Abi. What does space look like and mean to you?' He pulled out his phone and loaded the call log. 'Because right now I'm seeing fifteen phone calls in the last three days and you standing right outside my front door. That doesn't seem like giving me space.'

To that, Abigail had nothing to say. The smell of smoke leached off her clothes, breath and skin, and Tomek could sense it seeping into the fabric of his seats, staining the inside of his car. He wanted to wrap this up.

'Plus,' he continued, 'what's this I hear about you going behind my back and asking Martin for information – information he wasn't primed to give – about *my* case?'

'You... you asked for space. And... and that was me giving you space. I didn't want to hassle you with it.'

'No, you went one step further and undermined me with Victoria and Nick. Now they've brought Victoria back in and reduced me to deputy SIO. That's interfering with my life on a whole different level.'

'But it's my career,' she said, sounding almost defeated.

'And it's mine, too.'

She looked at her lap and began digging her thumb in her palm. 'Where do we go from here?'

'I don't know.'

'I mean, about work. I'm still going to need to come to you for information, and you're still going to need to come to me for support.'

Tomek inhaled deeply, composing himself. He couldn't believe he was hearing this. There she was, sitting there, playing with her thumbs, acting all innocent and coy, concerned about how this would affect their working relationship, how it would affect *her* career.

'Let me make this easy for you then, Abigail. Nice and easy. You and me – done. We're over. No more coming round for sleepovers, no more dinners, no more sex. We're through. And as for our professional relationship, nothing changes. Though I think for the foreseeable future, we should avoid working with each other as much as possible. And if you ever come round my house unannounced again, I will make life very difficult for you.' Tomek leant across the car, reaching over her lap, and opened the door for her. 'Goodnight Abigail,' he continued. 'Enjoy your evening.'

CHAPTER FIFTY-THREE

Tomek had stayed in the car for another twenty minutes, breathing, thinking, controlling his temper, until the rumble in his stomach became so loud and so aggressive, and the stomach pains so agitated, that he had been forced to go upstairs in search of food. Fortunately, he found Kasia in the middle of making beans on toast, and when asked if he'd like some, he told her he could murder some. There was something so delightfully simple about beans on toast that excited him and his stomach. Perhaps it reminded him of his childhood. Or perhaps it was the crunch of the lightly toasted bread, the sweetness of the unhealthy dose of tomato sauce, and the saltiness of the melted cheddar sprinkled on top. Either way, it was one of the best meals he'd had in a long time, far surpassing the meal they'd had to celebrate Abigail's promotion.

Tomek was still thinking about it as he entered the office the following morning. In fact, he'd even thought about having the same for breakfast. The only problem was, now that his favourite café, Morgana's, had recently closed following a human trafficking investigation, Tomek was in search of a new establishment to indulge in the delectable delights of greasy bacon and double heart attack specials. Instead, as he entered the office, he was greeted with a depressing sachet of Quaker Oats in his desk drawer, a relic of a historic dieting phase he'd gone through several years before. No matter how many times he tried to eat healthily, it never worked. The only thing stopping him from putting on serious weight was his daily run along the seafront and recreational sports activities on the weekend – though most of those had fallen to the wayside in recent months.

'That's a sad-looking bowl of porridge,' Chey said as Tomek returned to his desk, reluctantly, with the bowl of food burning his hands. 'Looks like a dog just threw up.'

Tomek looked down at the bowl, then at Chey, then back at the bowl again. 'Fuck's sake. Why'd you have to say that? Now I just wanna throw it all over you.'

Tomek feinted the bowl towards Chey, and the young constable flinched out of the way. As he stumbled, his foot caught on the side of a desk chair and he staggered backwards, falling to the floor. The office erupted into a chorus of laughter.

'That'll teach you to take the piss out of my food,' Tomek said as he made his way to the kitchen and began pouring it into the bin.

A moment later, Oscar entered behind him, standing in the doorway to prohibit anyone else from entering.

'Morning, Sarge,' he said, caution lacing his tone.

'Morning, Captain.'

'Have you heard the latest?'

'That stepping on three cracks will break my mother's back? Yes.'

'No. About the DNA.'

Tomek stopped what he was doing and set the bowl on the kitchen counter.

'DNA? What DNA?'

Tomek held his breath.

'The DNA that was found at Angelica's crime scene.'

Tomek's eyes widened. He held his breath. 'We've got the results?'

'Seven o'clock this morning.'

Tomek shuffled closer to the constable.

'And?'

'We've got a match.'

Finally. After all his persistence.

Fuck you, Nick. And fuck you, Victoria.

'And?' he said. 'Whose is it? Shawn's?'

Oscar shook his head. A smirk crept onto his face.

'The DNA found belongs to Johnny, Sarge. Johnny Whitaker.'

CHAPTER FIFTY-FOUR

Tomek pulled the car into Daphne and Roy Whitaker's driveway. He leapt out before it had stopped rolling in park mode and, slamming the door shut behind him, he sprinted across the forecourt towards the Whitakers' front door. He pounded his fists. Three, four times. No answer.

He tried again, this time leaning to the side and pressing his face against the living room windows. No movement.

First the hospital, and now this.

Tomek did not know where Johnny Whitaker was, and neither did the hospital. According to the district nurse, Johnny had been discharged several hours before, with no forwarding address or communication made to his next of kin, who happened to be his parents. Tomek had assembled a team and instructed them to visit The Prince Albert, in case Angelica's brother had returned to his watering hole, but they'd found nothing, and were currently on their way to meet him now.

Tomek turned to the front door and pounded his fists on it again. Still nothing.

Just as he crouched down and opened the letterbox to scream through, the door flew open. Tomek stepped through without approval, and without waiting for his presence to register.

'What the fuck?' Daphne screamed as she was forced back by Tomek's sudden and forceful intrusion.

'Johnny,' he said, almost breathless. 'Where is he?'

'Who?'

'Your son.'

For a moment, a long, painful moment, Daphne said nothing, simply stared at him as though he'd asked her for the square root of a million.

'Where is your son?' Tomek repeated. 'We need to speak to him.'

Still nothing. Perhaps it was the shock of his sudden presence. Or perhaps it was the steady realisation of what Tomek was asking: that the only reason Tomek could be asking for her son – *again* – was because they'd found something, something that connected him to his sister's death.

'Hospital...' she muttered, her mind a hundred miles away.

'Discharged. As of three hours ago. Now we don't know where to find him. Have you seen him?'

Slowly, staring into the black space behind him, Daphne shook her head.

'Where's your husband?'

'Outside. In the garden.'

Almost as if on cue, Roy Whitaker appeared in the hallway, wearing a pair of gardening gloves and a light green fleece vest.

'Sergeant...' he started. 'What're you—?'

'He wants to know where Johnny is,' answered Daphne.

'Johnny? Again? Why?'

'Because we have some more questions to ask him.'

'About what?'

Tomek didn't want to get into that right now, but he quickly realised it would be the only way to expedite the process.

'Evidence,' he said coherently, his breathing returned to normal. 'We've found his DNA at Angelica's crime scene. We just want to know how it got there.'

Daphne's hands immediately flew to her mouth. Roy's look of consternation and concern changed to dread and disbelief.

'Johnny... Angelica... No... Surely not...'

'Surely,' Tomek said.

And don't call me Shirley.

'But how? When? Why?'

'I don't know, but I'm hoping your son can answer those questions for me. When was the last time you saw him?'

Roy removed his gloves and set them on a nearby surface. 'Not since he left the other day. Like I told you. Did you find him at the pub?'

Tomek nodded and explained that they'd subsequently taken him to the hospital.

'Have you tried there?' Roy asked.

Fucking hell, they were going round in circles.

Tomek confirmed they had, then asked, 'Do you have any idea where he might be? Any idea at all?'

Johnny's parents looked at one another, eyes wide, mouths open.

Then they both shook their heads and said no, they had no idea where their son could be.

But Tomek did. At that moment, he knew exactly where to find him.

CHAPTER FIFTY-FIVE

'So this one, this one is one of my favourites,' she explained. 'It's cut from my favourite stone, sapphire.'

'Handmade?'

She nodded politely. 'Yes. Everything you see here is handmade by me. I have a little workshop out the back where I craft my little creations.'

The woman placed the ring on her finger and held it up to the light, admiring it for a moment. 'You're very talented.'

'Thanks.'

Rose had heard enough. This woman was a time waster. Plain and simple. Interested in one thing and one thing only: wasting Rose's time. Over the years, she had developed a knack, a canny ability to sniff out the shit from the "I'll pay anything for this shit!" and she could usually see them a mile off. This woman, however, had given her cause for the benefit of the doubt. There had been something about her that had made Rose second-guess her instincts. Perhaps it had been the designer fashion, or the freshly bleached blonde hair, or the husband who was clearly punching above his weight, drooling behind her every step, but as soon as she had bared her teeth at the price tag attached to the ring and started asking her fucking inane questions, Rose had decided the woman's time was up. Time to get out and come back when they could afford her jewellery. She took the ring back from her and started to treat them with contempt, to ensure they knew that she'd sussed them out. After a few more interactions, they finally got the hint and started to leave. Rose showed them the way out.

'If you need anything else, you know where to find me,' Rose said behind a forced grin. The couple quickly receded onto the busy high street, melting into the backdrop of other pedestrians. As she shut the door behind her, she whispered to herself, 'Fucking idiots,' and made her way back to her crocheting.

She'd finished the angel doll that she'd made in memory of Angelica, and was now moving on to her next creation: a small police officer, complete with blue hat and blue uniform, even if the image she was using looked more like Postman Pat than Mr Plod.

She was in the middle of getting her equipment out when the shop door opened. Before greeting the customer, she inhaled deeply, switched on the pleasant, customer-facing smile that was growing increasingly hard to do, then turned to face the newcomer.

She froze.

There, standing in the doorframe, was her husband. The man she felt she barely knew, his shoulders hunched, towering, domineering.

Rose's immediate thought was not for her safety, but for the safety of her creations. The man was a walking ape, and from the pale, haggard, slightly yellow cheeks in his face – not to mention the stench of alcohol seeping from his pores – he was still drunk.

'*You*,' he said.

She didn't think it was possible to slur a one-syllable word, but somehow he found a way.

'What the fuck are you doing here?' she retorted. 'Get the fuck out of my shop. You're not welcome here.'

But he didn't heed the warning. Instead, he shut the door behind him, slammed the door bolt into place, then locked the deadbolt. The sounds echoed throughout the shop like gunshots, ricocheting in her ears.

And then it stopped.

The two of them were separated by only a few feet. Him, outweighing her three to one. Her, without a phone beside her or the reactions to move faster than him.

Johnny made the first move. Despite his inebriated state, he covered the shop floor in almost a single stride, clattering into the display cases on the way, and was on her in an instant. Without hesitation, he grabbed her shirt by the collar, yanked her away from her chair, and dragged her out of the back of the shop by her hair. Rose screamed as searing pain flared on her scalp. There was nothing she could do, nothing she could think to do other than hold Johnny's hand to lessen the fiery pain.

After fiddling with door handles at the back of the shop, they entered a small hallway. The door to their right led to the flat upstairs, where Rose had spent almost every night for the past few months. And yet she had very little to show for it. There was no carpet yet. The floor was messy and covered in tools and sawdust. The walls needed sanding, skirting boards applying, and plaster scraping over the surfaces. The lights, radiators and kitchen appliances all needed an electrician to visit, as did the wall sockets and extractor fan. The only thing that did work, however, was the water. She had plenty of running water, and the most advanced room in the flat was the bathroom.

But Johnny didn't seem to care about that. He didn't seem to care about anything other than hurting Rose.

As soon as the front door to the flat slammed into the adjacent wall, he threw her down on the floor and straddled her. His immense weight pressed her down and kept her there. He was far too strong for her.

And then he wrapped his hands around her throat. Immediately, she felt air expel from her throat and lungs. Then she felt her breathing tighten, her throat crush, her lungs collapse.

'You fucking bitch!' Johnny yelled. 'You had to fucking find out, didn't you? You had to fucking ruin my life! I will never forgive you!'

There was a demonic look in his eyes. The same one she had seen once before. When they'd first got together and Johnny had protected her from some creep on the train after a day out in London. The anger and fury had been directed at someone else that time, but it had been there all the same. At the time, she'd foolishly mistaken it for safety, a form of protection. Now she realised that same level of protection was killing her, rapidly suffocating the life out of her. And there was nothing she could do about it.

CHAPTER FIFTY-SIX

If there was one thing Tomek hated most about his hometown of Leigh-on-Sea, it was the parking. He was absolutely, unequivocally, a hundred per cent certain that he had lost over a day of his life trying to find a bastard parking space, particularly along Leigh Broadway. And now, today of all days, there was nothing. He had driven round, up and down, in and out, for five minutes, trying to find somewhere suitable. Until eventually, he had pulled rank and mounted the pavement outside the shop. He was out of the car in an instant and hurrying towards the front door of the jewellery shop.

It was locked.

On the two occasions he'd been there, it had never been locked. He checked the time – 13:37.

The middle of the afternoon. Whitaker's should have been open. The displays were still complete in the windows, so where was Rose?

Tomek banged and banged, but he knew it was futile. That he was too late. That Johnny was in there somewhere. He cupped his face to the glass but saw nothing, just an empty shop.

And then he remembered the flat above. Tomek craned his neck skyward, in the hope that he'd see the two of them chatting amicably through the glass, but he knew that wasn't a possibility.

Johnny was angry, livid even. He'd killed before, and he could very well kill again.

Behind Tomek was a group of uniformed constables who'd followed his movements. Two of them had just parked beside him and were in the middle of disembarking their vehicle when he ordered them to try the back of the shop. In the meantime, another pair of officers had arrived on foot.

One of them was carrying an enforcer, a large battering ram designed to destroy even the strongest of doors. The constable raised it high into the air, and with the helping hand of practice and a good set of muscles, let gravity do the rest. The door only required one hit before it buckled and gave way.

At once, Tomek and the rest of the constables flooded into the shop, squeezing past one another, fighting for first entry. The inside was empty, desolate. At the back of the room, Tomek noticed an open doorway. He headed straight towards it and came into a small hallway that reminded him of his own flat – cramped, old, and smelling of damp. The door to his immediate right was open, and there, in the hallway, he heard sounds of discomfort and struggling.

'This way!' he yelled to the constables.

Tomek was the first to go. First to take the plunge and race up the steps. He jumped them two at a time until he came to the top and burst through the door at the top of the stairs.

There he was, Johnny Whitaker straddling his wife, pinning her down, crushing the life out of her.

Tomek didn't hesitate. He approached the man from behind, wrapped one arm around Johnny Whitaker's neck, then locked it in place with his other arm and began squeezing. Hard. Giving him a taste of his own medicine. Surprisingly, the man lasted longer than Tomek expected – ten seconds instead of five – before he eventually released his grip on Rose's throat and fell to the floor. Tomek held onto him until the man blacked out and the muscles in his upper body relaxed.

CHAPTER FIFTY-SEVEN

Four hours later, and Johnny Whitaker was finally ready to be interviewed. A quick test of his blood levels and a look at some CCTV footage had shown that since his discharge from the hospital, the drag star had ventured into The Broadway, a pub that was situated immediately opposite Rose's jewellery shop. From there, he had found a table beside the window, ordered himself five pints, and sipped them patiently, biding his time, keeping a watchful gaze on the shop entrance. When Rose had got rid of her last customer, and Johnny had summoned enough disdain and frustration towards his wife, he had staggered across the road, stumbled into the shop, and locked them both in.

Tomek knew the rest.

With him in the interview room was Rachel, Johnny, who looked worse than he had the last time Tomek had seen him, and his solicitor, sitting on a single chair at the back of the room. In the corners of the room, video cameras recorded the meeting, and a digital recorder sat on the table against the wall. Rachel pressed the On button and began recording. After she'd completed the formalities, it was Tomek's turn to question Johnny.

'What were you doing at Whitaker's jewellery shop this afternoon?' Tomek said, struggling to stifle a yawn that had come from nowhere. It had been a long day, and he needed a drink at the end of all this.

'No comment.'

'What happened inside your wife's shop, Johnny?'

'No comment.'

'Why did you lock the door?'

'No comment.'

'How did you gain access to the flat above the shop?'
'No comment.'
'What happened in the flat above the shop?'
'No comment.'

Johnny's face was one of resolve, screwed into a tight ball of indignation and contempt. His arms were folded across his chest and his shoulders hunched upwards, almost into his neck. The man had changed significantly since Tomek had first met him. He had become a shell, broken. He looked as though he hadn't eaten in weeks, and had relied solely on alcohol as a source of sustenance.

'Why did you strangle your wife, Johnny?'

The man didn't flinch.

'No comment.'

Tomek sighed internally. This was going to be a long evening.

'We have evidence to prove you did it. Several police officers' witness statements. I saw it with my own eyes. Why don't you answer the question? Why did you try to kill your wife?'

Johnny poked his neck out and hissed, 'No comment,' then recoiled backwards.

'Is it because she outed you, found out your secret?'

'No comment.'

Tomek looked down at his notes, found the conversation he'd had with Johnny in the hospital bed.

'You said to me the other day, and I quote, "I swear to God, the next time I see her..." What did you mean by that, Johnny? The next time you saw her, you were going to kill her? Did you want to kill her because you think she ruined your life?'

Nothing. The man's expression was blank.

'Because from where I'm sitting, it seems like you did all that yourself.' Tomek eased himself into the seat, mirroring Johnny's posture. 'You're the one who lied to her all these years. You're the one who lied to your parents... your sister.' Tomek let the last comment hang in the air before continuing. 'Tell me about the time she found out you were a drag queen.'

Before responding, Johnny slowly turned to his solicitor, gave the man a look, then turned his attention back to Tomek. 'She went to one of my shows,' he said. 'It was a complete fluke, a total coincidence. She didn't know I was going to be there, and I had absolutely no sense she would be there either. It was... it was a shock.'

'Who saw who first?'
'Why's that relevant?'

Tomek shrugged. 'Curious.'

'She saw me,' Johnny replied with a sigh. He began rubbing his knuckles with his thumb. 'Came to find me out back once I'd finished. Fortunately, she saved me the embarrassment of coming backstage with her friends.'

'What did she say?'

More rubbing. More aggressively this time, as he relived the events in his head.

'I expected more from her, you know. She was the younger one, the freer one. The one who'd managed to get away from all of Mum and Dad's bullshit, despite them virtually hating her for it. She didn't have the same religious shackles that they'd tried to place on me. She didn't have to attend church every Sunday like I did. She didn't have to deal with any of that, and I thought, out of everyone, she'd be more understanding. But she was disgusted with me. Said what I was doing was immoral and unethical. That she was going to tell Mum and Dad. That she was going to tell Rose.'

There was a steeliness in his voice, as if he was choking back the tears.

'And did she?'

Johnny shook his head.

'Because you made sure she couldn't, didn't you?'

'No! Absolutely not.' The man slammed his hand on the table. Tomek had seen enough cretins to know when a move like that was imminent, so didn't flinch. 'I know where you're going with this, but I had nothing to do with what happened to Angelica. I convinced her not to say anything to anyone – money, it was always money with her, and lots of it – but she always held it against me. Like siblings do. She promised she wouldn't say anything, and I believed her. I had no reason to kill her.'

Tomek pulled out a sheet of paper and slid it across the table. Curious, Johnny leant in and inspected the document. Tomek prodded the sheet with his forefinger.

'That says otherwise,' he explained.

'What is it?'

'That there is evidence linking your DNA to the DNA sample that was found at your sister's crime scene.'

'*What?*'

'Which bit do you need clarifying? How long your sentence might be, because—'

'That's not my fucking DNA!' Johnny screamed. 'That isn't mine. I've been set up. I've—'

'So you weren't at Park Road on the night of her murder?'

'No!'

'But this says you were...'

'No! I wasn't!'

'So if you weren't there, tell me what you were doing?'

Johnny said nothing.

'You still can't tell me, can you? According to my notes, you finished at the club about one o'clock in the morning. At that point, Angelica was still in Memo. She didn't get dropped off until half past, and she didn't leave until approximately ten to two, which would have left plenty of time for you to leave Cool Cats and Kittens, and drive towards her house to pick her up.'

'I... I... I told you I've been set up! That wasn't me. I wasn't there, I promise. I was...'

Tomek waited, nodded slowly. 'Go on.'

Johnny let out a long, steady breath. 'I was with someone. A guy. A customer from the club. He... we got talking after I'd finished and we went back to his place. He... he has a place along the seafront in Westcliff. We... we spent the night together. His name... his name's James Fry. I can give you all his details. But... I swear to you, that wasn't me.'

CHAPTER FIFTY-EIGHT

The Fork and Spoon stank of sweaty men and stale lager. The owner, Jim, an old friend of Tomek's, had let standards slide since he'd last visited. The furniture was dirty and haggard, the carpet stained and unkempt, and the beer selection poorly stocked. The only sign of renovation and innovation, was the vending machine in the corner that was emitting a light as bright and harmful to the skin as the sun. The machine was supposed to be an extra revenue stream for the owner, but Tomek was sure he'd seen that same packet of Salt and Vinegar Walkers in the same position, dangling a fraction off the edge, since the time it had first been put in. At the bar were Sean, Rachel, Oscar, and Chey. Tomek had been in desperate need of a drink, and so everyone else in the team had come along with him. There was no cause to celebrate, not yet, at least; Johnny's alibi still needed checking out, but it was looking good. They had DNA that connected him to the crime scene. There was no escaping that. Besides, he fit the bill: he knew everything about Angelica; he knew the significance of the church; he knew that her nickname was Angel; he knew how to apply make-up; he was in possession of a penis, so would have been able to rape her with ease. The only concern Tomek had, and it had grown rapidly ever since Johnny had come forward with his new alibi, was that his anger problem didn't match the killer's profile. Johnny had already proven he was aggressive and violent, as the bruises around his wife's throat confirmed, but there had been no physical evidence on Angelica's body. Nothing. No bruises, no blunt force trauma. Nothing to suggest that he had acted wildly. Tomek was admittedly having a hard time imagining the same man he'd seen straddling his wife with his hands wrapped around her throat, draining the blood of his sister, then gently cleaning her body.

It disconcerted him.

Before he could think on it any further, the team arrived from the bar. Sean set Tomek's drink in front of him and shimmied in beside him on a wobbly chair.

'Cheers for the hand there, mate. Really appreciate you carrying the drinks for us,' Sean joked.

'I carried this team during the investigation for long enough. About time you did the same.'

'Carried us?' responded Anna as she took a sip of her gin and tonic. 'You weren't the one spending all your time with Roy and Daphne. Never before have I seen a couple so distant and separate from one another. And my parents are divorced.'

Tomek lowered his glass to the table. 'That stark, was it?'

'Like you wouldn't believe. A couple of times I got there and Daphne had no idea where Roy was. Said that he'd just gone out without saying anything.'

The cogs began whirring.

'Does he do that often?'

'Yeah. Couple of times a week for the past thirty years, apparently. All manner of times.'

'Does she know what he does or where he goes?'

Anna shrugged. 'Goes for walks, mostly.'

'Walks?'

'Yeah, where you put one foot in front of the other,' Chey interrupted to chuckles of laughter.

Tomek flipped him the finger, then returned to his conversation with Anna.

'He just goes out for long walks?'

'Yeah,' she said. 'It was all in my reports. Did you... did you not...?'

He hadn't, no. He hadn't found time to read through the team's daily summaries, thanks to the mental distraction Abigail had caused over the past few days. That, and the feeling he'd had of being completely out of his depth. Making the step up to inspector, he now realised, had been a culture shock he wasn't expecting. The spotlight that was thrust upon him, the laborious admin, the sensation of dread that tightened in his stomach exponentially as each day passed without success. And to top it all off, there was the time it had taken away from being at home and with Kasia.

His daughter had become a new responsibility in his life, and he wasn't sure if he was ready for another one.

'Are we sure this guy's not a stalker or serial killer?' Rachel asked sincerely.

It was a second before Tomek came to. He shook his head.

'No. No, we aren't.'

Just as Rachel opened her mouth to respond, Martin interrupted.

'Enough about work,' he said. 'We do that all day, every day.' He took a first sip of his beer, set it down, then turned to Tomek. 'I saw your young lady friend the other day.'

'Which one was that?' Sean responded. 'There have been quite a few over the years.'

'The one who writes for the *Echo*.'

'She's not my young lady friend anymore.'

The team suddenly turned to him, shock across their faces.

'Since when?' Rachel asked.

'The other day. Things got a bit too... transactional, shall we say.'

Rachel placed a hand on his shoulder. 'Say no more.'

'I wanted to apologise for it though,' Martin continued, though nobody was giving him any attention. 'She asked me for information, and...'

'I know,' Tomek replied.

'You know? How?'

'Because it's one of the reasons that Victoria stepped back in as inspector.'

'Fuck.' The man's expression turned vacant, and he stared into middle space. 'My bad.'

'It's fine. I'm all right with it, in all honesty. A moment of epiphany, if you will.' He took another quick sip of his drink, surprised to see how little he had left already. 'But I'd stay away from Abigail, if I were you. She wants you for one thing and one thing only.'

'His annoyingly beautiful long hair that's better than any woman's I've ever seen?' Rachel joked. 'No offence, Anna.'

'None taken. I'd shave it all off and give it to myself if I could.'

'Funny you should say that,' Martin began, clearing his throat. 'Because the girl I've been seeing wants me to shave it.'

'What!?' came the resounding echo from the entire table.

'Why does she want to do that?' Chey asked.

But before Martin could reply, Rachel stepped in and said, 'Whoa, hold up, hold up. There are a couple of points we need to discuss. Firstly: *girlfriend*? Since when?'

'No. Not girlfriend. Girl I'm seeing.'

'Cut the shit. It's the same thing. How long's this been going on, and why haven't you told us?'

'Because... I guess I just haven't thought to.'

Tomek thought he knew why. Martin was one of the newest additions to the team, having joined at the same time as Victoria, and a part of him had felt left out, slightly ostracised by the team as he'd struggled to wriggle himself through a crack in an already close-knit team. It was only natural that he hadn't felt comfortable enough to share intimate details of his personal life with them yet.

'You have to tell us,' Rachel continued. 'We have a right to know. We're a work family.'

For the first time in a long time, Tomek saw a smile on the man's face.

'Tell us everything,' Anna insisted.

'Her name's Lauren. She works in digital marketing, lives in Leigh-on-Sea, and we met... we met online.'

'Lovely,' Rachel said as she leant across the table and stroked his arm lovingly. 'I'm pleased for you. Do you like her?'

Martin turned shy, like a schoolboy. 'I think so.'

'Have you met the family?'

'Yeah.'

A chorus of "*oohs*", highly emphasised and over the top came from the entire table.

'Must be serious,' Chey said.

'Yeah, but her dad's an arsehole.'

'That's because dads *are* arseholes,' Tomek said. 'I'm the same with Kasia. Overprotective. And it's my job to embarrass her and everyone else that comes into her life.'

Thoughts of Roy Whitaker flashed into his mind.

'Thanks for the advice,' Martin said.

'Speaking of advice,' Rachel started, 'what's this with the hair thing? Why does she want you to cut it?'

Martin looked at the table and began drawing a circle with his finger on a beer mat, his ponytail serendipitously falling over his left shoulder. 'She just doesn't like it. Says it's too long. Was only fashionable in the seventies. Thinks I should shave it all and send it to charity.'

The deflation in Rachel's shoulders was visible. She placed both hands on Martin's and looked him in the eye.

'Do you know what I say to that?'

'What?'

'It pains me to say it, but I think you should know. That's what families do. They tell us when things are going well and when things are going bad. But fuck that bitch. Nobody should make you feel less about yourself. If she doesn't like it, then she can find the door. You need someone who wants you for you. And not just someone who's going to mould you in their own image. Nuh uh.'

'Fuck that bitch,' Martin replied. He said it so quietly, so calmly, that Tomek almost didn't hear him. 'Yeah. Do you know what? You're right. Fuck. That. Bitch.' Then he downed the rest of his pint, slammed the glass on the table, and said, 'Right. Who wants another? Next round's on me. And I'm in the mood for doubles.'

CHAPTER FIFTY-NINE

Tomek felt embarrassed by how much his head was pounding the following day. Now he knew how Johnny Whitaker had felt for the past week, drowning his sorrows at the end of a row of bottomless drinks. Tomek had told himself that he would only stay for one – Martin's round – but one had turned into two, two into three, and then by the fifth he'd been forced to walk home. Kasia, to her credit, hadn't given him any sympathy as he'd stumbled through the door at the still respectable hour of nine o'clock, nor as he'd emerged from his bedroom, having overslept, the following morning. He wasn't twenty-one anymore, and he was fooling nobody if he thought he could keep up with Chey and Rachel, who were considerably younger than him. The walk to the pub car park that morning had felt like the walk of shame, each step reminding him of the hangxiety, anguish, and regret. Stepping through the office, however, his emotions brightened slightly as he realised everyone else was also just as worse for wear. Rachel's hair was loose and untidy, her make-up even more so. Chey was slumped in his chair with a large two-litre bottle of water resting under his chin, waiting to be consumed at any moment. Martin was wearing a pair of sunglasses, and Sean had a packet of paracetamol beside his mouse, which, from the looks of it, had been emptied by the rest of the staff.

'Morning, team!' Tomek bellowed loudly on purpose, to a chorus of groans.

He suddenly felt a lot better. And on the balance of things, he was probably the least hungover out of everyone. Maybe he could pretend to be twenty-one again after all.

'Trust we all had a good night's sleep, but we can't let ourselves get complacent. We—'

'Tomek,' Sean interrupted weakly. 'I love you and everything, but shut the fuck up.'

Before Tomek could respond, the landlines in the office rang. Out of the corner of his eye, he saw Rachel and Chey cup their ears and turn away from the phones. After a few moments, nobody had answered, and nobody looked willing either.

'I'll get that then, shall I?'

Tomek reached for the nearest phone and answered it.

'Hello?'

'Hi,' the voice said. 'It's Sharon. Is one of you able to come down? There's a woman here who'd like to speak to someone about the Angelica Whitaker case.'

'Did she say what it was about?'

Tomek could sense Sharon shaking her head. 'No, sorry.'

'No problem. I'm on my way down now. Tell her I'll be two minutes.'

※

TOMEK'S immediate thought was that the woman who'd stolen Angelica's heart from Xanthia and Emilia Solveig had come through the doors – they had so far been unable to find the mysterious welder from The Nights of Eden parties – but it wasn't that at all. The woman who had entered the police station that morning was in her sixties. Sylvie. Small, petite, with professionally- styled, bleached blonde hair. She wore light make-up on her face and was dressed smartly. She looked as though she had been attractive when she was younger, and after years of continuing to look after herself, she still looked attractive now.

'I hope I wasn't interrupting you from anything,' she said.

'Not at all,' Tomek replied. 'We're always happy to help. What was it you came in for?'

Tomek had prepared a box of tissues on the table in case whatever she wanted to discuss was raw and painful and would bring a multitude of emotions to the surface. She ripped a tissue from the box and began playing with it, more as a form of comfort than for the removal of any tears.

'I understand a young woman named Angelica Whitaker was murdered the other week,' she said softly.

'That's right.'

'Have you made any arrests yet?'

'We have,' Tomek answered after a short pause.

'I was wondering if you might be able to tell me who it is you've arrested?'

Tomek took another moment. This time to stop himself from accidentally leaking Johnny Whitaker's name to a complete stranger.

'I can't share that with you, no. It's a private and confidential matter.'

'Ah. I see. Well...' She made a small tear in the tissue. 'If I say his name, will you make a note of it?'

Tomek confirmed he didn't have a problem with that.

'Does the name Roy Whitaker mean anything to you?'

Tomek began writing the name as she said it, then caught himself again.

'That wasn't part of the agreement. That wasn't very fair.'

'I know,' she said. 'Please, forgive me.'

Tomek set his pen on the table. 'Why do you say that name?'

'Because...' Now the tears started. Slow, steady, nothing but a single tear at first. She gently hovered the tissue beneath her eye in anticipation. 'Because, about thirty-five years ago, we used to work together. He was a pilot for British Airways and I was a flight attendant on several of his flights.'

That explained her good looks.

'We did a lot of long-haul flights together. Bali, Indonesia, the Caribbean. And so we often had to spend a couple of nights in the hotels to get over the jet lag before we flew back. One night, we got drinking in the hotel bar in Barbados and, well, he took advantage of me.'

Tomek nodded slowly, letting her know that he was listening to her.

'Took advantage of you, how?'

'He... Rape. He raped me. In the hotel room. I don't remember it fully, but I know it happened. I'd had a few, but not enough to forget what had happened the night before.'

'Did you confront him about it?'

She shook her head.

'Did you tell anyone?'

'Only some former work colleagues, many, many years later.'

'Had any of those people worked with Roy? Any of them experience something similar to you?'

Sylvie nodded weakly.

'Six of them said he'd raped them too. I'm not alone. I don't know what happened to that poor woman, and I feel so sorry for her family, but not that man. That man is evil and dangerous. And you must look into him because I fear he has done something so much worse than anything he's ever done before.'

CHAPTER SIXTY

Roy Whitaker had come in without a fuss. He hadn't argued. He hadn't kicked off or tried to escape. He had behaved himself, all the way from his front door to the interview room where he was now.

'I will keep this short,' Tomek began. But he had no intention of keeping it short at all. He wanted the man to sit and grow increasingly agitated the longer he was kept there. 'Does the name Sylvie Weiss mean anything to you?'

'Sylvie...? Weiss?'

'You may know her by her maiden name: Greene.'

'Sylvie Greene? Yeah. It rings a bell...' The reticence in his voice was tangible.

'Can you tell me where you know her from?'

Roy hesitated, brushed his hair backwards, then patted it repeatedly, so it sat firmly in place. 'We used to work together. She was one of the air stewards. We did a lot of long-haul flights together, to the other side of the world.'

'Did the two of you ever stay in hotels when you were on the other side of the world?'

'We all did. It was a stipulation from the airline. We'd just flown ten, eleven, twelve hours. They weren't going to make us fly straight back. We needed a rest, so we stayed a couple of nights, then returned.'

'Do you remember much about the time you first met Sylvie?'

'Why?'

Roy's tone rose steadily, as did the level of concern in his voice.

Tomek ignored the counter question and continued. 'Had you met Daphne by this point, or did Sylvie come before you met your wife?'

'I don't see what this has got to do with anything.'

'Do you remember staying in the Hilton in Barbados?'

'What?'

'The summer of eighty-eight.'

Roy shook his head in disbelief, as if trying to piece together his thoughts.

'I don't have a fucking clue what you're talking about!'

'So you don't remember being at the bar with Sylvie at the Hilton in Barbados during the summer of eighty-eight?'

A long, empty breath left Roy's lips. 'I thought you'd brought me here to discuss Angelica.'

'That's correct, but first I want to discover what happened between you and Sylvie on the night of the fifteenth of July 1988.'

And then the act stopped. The confused and disbelieving expression fell from his face and was replaced with a sinister glare.

'She been to see you then, has she?' he asked.

'That's not relevant. Answer the question: what happened between the two of you on the night of the fifteenth of July?'

Roy chortled and folded his arms across his chest. 'I bet she has, hasn't she? She's probably got some things to say, I imagine. Probably told you them already, otherwise why else would you be asking me about this?' He shook his head, chuckling slightly. 'I never did anything she's accusing me of. I don't know what it is she thinks I've done, but I didn't do it.'

'What about what six other women are saying you've done?'

'What's that?'

Tomek moved the conversation along.

'I understand you like to disappear and leave the house at random for a couple of hours on end, is that right?'

'You been talking to my wife as well?'

Tomek pulled a face. 'There's no problem with that, is there? Unless you're worried there's something she might tell us.'

The walls of Roy's defences went back up again.

'No comment,' he said.

'Where do you go when you leave the house alone?'

'No comment.'

'What do you do?'

'No comment.'

'Who do you meet up with?'

'No comment.'

'How long have you been doing it for?'

'No comment.'

'Did it start after your night with Sylvie? Prowling the streets at night—'

'I don't *prowl the streets*. I'm not a fucking serial killer, if that's what you're trying to insinuate.' The sixty-one-year-old's defences went crashing back down. And Tomek had a job trying to find the balance to keep him where he wanted him.

'What are you doing, then?'

'Walking. Clearing my thoughts. Sometimes I look up at the sky and watch the planes go over.'

Plane watching? That was what he was doing in the middle of the night and during the day, for hours at a time? Tomek was dubious.

'What about on the night of Angelica's murder?' he asked.

'Seriously?' Roy hissed, shocked. 'You want to go down that route? I've already told your team I was home, asleep with my wife at that point. I had nothing to do with her murder. I can't believe you would accuse me of having anything to do with what happened to her. It's bad enough that Johnny's been thrown into all of this.'

'You're right, you did say that you were sleeping. But given what we now know about your random and sometimes inexplicable disappearances, I thought I'd ask again for your whereabouts on the night of your daughter's death. Is there anything else you want to tell me?'

The man collapsed back into his chair and folded his arms again. 'Absolutely not. I had absolutely nothing to do with my darling angel's death. I find the insinuation abhorrent. Firstly, I was asleep when it happened. Secondly, I live half an hour away, so you would have seen my car travelling through the traffic lights and speed cameras. Have a look. You can check.'

Tomek said nothing. Waited.

'Secondly, and this should have been the first point, in all honesty: *why*? Why would I do that to my daughter? I loved her more than anything. I adored the earth she walked on. Why would I kill her?'

'Because you, a heavily devout Methodist, didn't agree with several of her habits. You couldn't stand the fact that she'd got pregnant again, that she was having relationships with both men and women, that she was taking drugs and abusing alcohol. You couldn't stand that she was in a dark place and she was doing all the things you despised.'

Tomek couldn't believe he'd just said that. But he could sense the direction the conversation was going – downhill – and so he'd wanted to get it all out in the open.

'She was sleeping with women? Taking drugs? My Angelica?'

'Are you pretending you didn't know?'

'I'm *telling* you, I didn't know.'

Tomek swallowed deeply. The decline was gradually becoming steeper and steeper.

'But even so...' Roy continued. 'I... That wouldn't have bothered me. Not in the slightest. I don't have any issues with any of those things.'

From his tone, it was clear to see he didn't believe a word of what he'd just said.

'Nor do you have a problem with rape either, by the sounds of it,' Tomek said. The words left his mouth before he could stop them, and he immediately regretted it.

'Excuse me? Is that what this is about? Is that what Sylvie's been saying about me? Absolutely not. And you fucking believe her? You have no evidence against me for her claims. And you have no evidence against me for what happened to Angelica.'

'Is that an admission?'

Roy caught himself before responding. 'Absolutely not. I didn't kill my daughter. Not only do I not have sufficient reason to, but I was also asleep while it happened, and I can't do half the things you said happened to her.'

'What do you mean?' Tomek asked.

Roy sighed, rolled up his sleeves. 'I don't know how to do make-up. Not in the slightest.'

'You've worked with gorgeous women all your life who constantly wore make-up. Your wife and daughter did the same. It's possible that you picked it up by osmosis.'

'By *osmosis*? Are you insane?'

'You can paint,' Tomek said, rapidly coming to the realisation that he was losing this, that the decline had now become almost vertical and there was no way to stop himself.

'I can paint? What the fuck's that got to do with anything? Oh, you mean the *wings*? Please. I paint miniature aircraft, that's not the same.'

'It requires a steady hand and patience, all qualities which the killer possessed.'

'Are you hearing yourself right now? Are you hearing the words coming out of your mouth? You genuinely think I killed my daughter, and the only reason you're pinning it on me is because I can use a fucking paintbrush? Are you inept?'

Tomek said nothing. Felt himself going into free fall.

Roy continued: 'Furthermore, I have never shaved my body; my armpits, my arms, legs, thighs. Only ever my face, and even then I've never been able to grow much. I have never used the date rape drug or whatever it was you found in her system. And I have *never* raped anyone in my life. How dare you try to pin this on me even though you know full well that you've not got any evidence to substantiate any of these bullshit and outlandish claims.'

CHAPTER SIXTY-ONE

Tomek had let the man leave, though he hadn't gone without a fight. As Tomek had escorted him out of the interview room and out of the building, Roy Whitaker had whispered empty threats and insults into his ear: that he was a terrible detective, that he was going to end up in a ditch somewhere someday for pissing off the wrong person, that he didn't deserve to be a detective, and that he was going straight to his lawyer. Tomek took the insults on the chin; he'd heard them all before, and then some. But that didn't stop them cutting deep down, far below the surface. He could feel them, slicing away at his identity, his ego, his belief in himself. But the pain was so stunted, so muted after all these years that he'd learnt to ignore it, disregard it until it was no longer a problem. Until, perhaps one day, it might just come up to the surface like a dead body floating on the water.

Closing the door behind him, Tomek breathed a heavy sigh, releasing the tension and pressure in his shoulders, back, and neck. The past few hours, hearing Sylvie's accusations, investigating them with the team, and speaking with Roy Whitaker, had taken it out of him, mentally, emotionally, and physically. And the pounding headache hadn't helped, either.

He counted down from ten before heading back upstairs to the incident room, back to the madness. The journey was slow and laboured as he meandered through the corridors, taking his time, thinking about what he could have done differently, what he could have done better. But, in the end, he decided there was nothing. His hunch about Roy Whitaker having had some involvement in Angelica's death was wrong. The evidence against his son, Johnny, was irrefutable – the DNA found at the crime scene, and the last-minute alibi that had turned out to be a lie – and Tomek had tried to convince himself otherwise.

When he finally made it back to the incident room, some two minutes later, he called Oscar over and asked him to retrieve Johnny Whitaker from the holding cell. They still had a few hours left on the custody clock, but Tomek saw no reason to keep him there any longer. While Oscar hurried downstairs, Tomek knocked on Victoria's door and entered without waiting for a reply. He found her in the middle of a phone call. She apologised to the person on the phone, then hung up.

'This'd better be important,' she said. 'Any luck with Roy?'

Tomek shook his head.

'And the clothes?'

'Still nothing.' After the DNA discovery and Johnny's arrest, Tomek had ordered the team to inspect the Whitaker home, searching for Angelica's missing clothes and mobile. The search had been unsuccessful. 'My guess is that he disposed of them somewhere.'

'Okay. What did you come here for?'

'To tell you, I'd like to charge Johnny Whitaker with Angelica's murder.'

Victoria considered for a moment. 'You've completed all the paperwork?'

Tomek nodded.

'And called the CPS?'

'I'm about to.'

'All right. And the evidence?'

'Watertight. Unless he has any more imaginary one-night stands.'

'Then he's all yours.'

❆

TOMEK FELT BEREFT. There was no enjoyment in him, no enthusiasm. It seemed to have been drained out of him the same way Johnny Whitaker had drained the life out of his sister's body. They had their man. They had their killer. So why was he feeling like this? Was it because he'd messed up so badly with Roy that he was still feeling guilty, or was this the mother of all hangovers giving him a monumental case of hangxiety, filling him with an unending sense of dread and doubt? He didn't know. But at least he wasn't feeling as bad as Johnny Whitaker. After explaining to the man that he was being charged with his sister's murder, and that he would be sent on remand somewhere, the man had broken down in an uncontrollable fit of tears, begging, pleading for Tomek to reconsider. There was no chance, Tomek had told him. It was too late, the damage done. There was no hiding from it; he would have to live with his actions for the rest of his life. At first, Tomek had expected the man to break into a fit of rage, to lunge at him, to assault him and convince him to change his mind with the end of his fist, but Johnny Whitaker's reaction had been different. One of remorse. At that moment, his opinion of the man changed.

'Is there anyone you'd like to call?' Tomek asked him at the custody desk. 'Last chance.'

Johnny Whitaker stood in the police-issued tracksuit, red-eyed and broken. He stared blankly at the wall, his mind completely devoid of thought.

'Would you like to call your parents?'

Nothing.

'Rose?'

Johnny slowly turned his head to Tomek. 'Absolutely fucking not.'

CHAPTER SIXTY-TWO

Tomek didn't blame the man. He wouldn't have been in a very chatty mood either. But he'd charged enough people to know they'd later come to regret it, that they would do anything to have the opportunity to make one last phone call as a free person again.

Shortly after Johnny had been booked in, Tomek had left to give Rose the news. First, he'd tried Rose and Johnny's house, but nobody had been home. And then he'd remembered that she would be in the flat, conducting more gruelling and never-ending renovation work. Following the incident involving Rose and her husband, the place had been examined for evidence, but it had been quickly cleared. The numerous police witness statements had negated the need for them to hang around any longer than was required. Tomek hadn't spoken to her since that night, but he wanted to be the one to tell her in person what was happening with her husband.

Mercifully, as though the gods were looking down on him kindly, he found a parking space along the Broadway, directly outside Whitaker's Jewellers, on the first attempt. He hopped onto the kerb and made his way to the rear of the shop, entering through the back door, which to his surprise, was unlocked, and he came to a stop in the hallway. Immediately in front of him was the entrance to the back of the jeweller's. Tomek remembered it from the other night. Through the gap, he saw the small office space and the cloakroom. Angelica Whitaker's coats and belongings were still in there, hanging from a couple of pegs on the wall. Tomek poked his head through tentatively, in case he set off any motion detectors or alarms like something from a *Mission: Impossible* movie. The inside of the jeweller's was empty, still. Eerily still, like walking into a museum in the dead of night. And then he heard it: the soft rumbles of music playing through a speaker, drowned out by the sound of banging and drilling.

Tomek turned on the spot and headed up the stairs.

'Rose?' he called out from the bottom step, announcing his presence. 'Rose?'

No answer.

※

CHEY WANTED nothing more than to go home. He hadn't felt this hungover since the weekend in Zante with his schoolmates. There, he'd had the sun, copious amounts of greasy food, sugary drinks to hydrate him, and the glorious beach to make him forget about the hangover. Instead, here, he was surrounded by people he considered much older than him, a stuffy office that circulated stale dirty air, and a coffee machine that, despite all the plaudits the rest of the team gave it, spouted out weak coffee. All he wanted was to go home and have a long, overdue sleep. But Castle Point County Council had put paid to that. They had just sent through several reams of CCTV footage from Hadleigh library's car park. It had taken an age for some poor civil servant to find the footage, and even then, they'd only been able to go as far back as two weeks, right around the time of the last comment on Angelica's Little Corner of the Internet. Yes, he wanted to go home, but he also wanted to get this done, off his list so that he had one less thing to worry about the following morning as there was bound to be something new by the time he arrived. Or two, or three.

With what he told himself was his last cup of coffee of the day, Chey returned to his seat and unlocked the machine. On the screen was a still image of Hadleigh library car park. Behind it was the busy London Road, and beyond was Morrisons supermarket. The time on the screen was 13:18, approximately five minutes before the comment had been posted from within the library.

Chey pressed play and watched as dozens, hundreds of cars, sped along the road, racing to make the nearest set of lights. Until a car that looked remarkably similar to the grainy footage from outside Angelica Whitaker's house pulled in off the road and swung into an empty space.

'Fuck me,' he muttered as he saw the driver climbing out of the vehicle. 'Tomek!?'

Chey peered round his monitor, searching for Tomek, but the sergeant wasn't there.

'Anyone know where Bowen is?' he called to the half-empty office, standing out of his seat.

'He's gone out, I think,' Rachel replied.

'Think he's gone to give Rose Whitaker the news about her husband,' Martin added.

'Shitting Nora.'

❄

TOMEK HELD his breath as he reached the final step. Cautiously, he poked his head through the open door and knocked loudly, but it was drowned out by the sound of banging. Rose, dressed in white overalls covered in paint, had her back to him, and was in the middle of demolishing a bookshelf unit with a hammer.

'Rose!' Tomek called.

Still no answer.

He didn't want to approach her. Not while she was wielding a hammer. He could only imagine the damage she might do to him if she thought he was an attacker. Or, worse, her husband coming back for round two.

Instead, he grabbed a piece of broken plywood and launched it gently in her direction. It collided with her left leg, and she spun on the spot, brandishing the hammer in both hands, ready and willing to use it. As soon as she recognised Tomek, the tension in her body released and she lowered the object to her side. Before saying anything, she rushed over to the speaker and switched off the music.

'Tomek,' she said, sauntering towards him, brushing the hair out of her eyes. 'What are you doing here?'

'Sorry to interrupt,' he said. 'I didn't want to come anywhere near you, not while you've got that in your hand.'

Rose looked down at the hammer, then set it on a toolbox.

'Have you come to help?'

'Not really,' he said. 'This type of thing's never been for me. My dad used to build houses for a living, had his own construction company, so this is right up his street.'

'Should invite him over. Maybe he could give me a hand.'

'I'll see if he's about.' Tomek placed his hands on his hips and surveyed the room. In the day since he'd last been there, Rose had managed to gut the kitchen entirely, and tear down a wall that connected it with the living room, leaving a nice, open-plan space. 'You've been busy.'

'I've been through a lot,' she answered. 'Turns out destroying stuff is good for the soul and the immune system.'

Tomek chuckled.

'Are you here to compliment my work?'

'No.'

'If you haven't come here to help,' she started, 'and if you haven't come here to compliment my work, then what have you come here for?'

'It's about Johnny.'

At the mention of her husband's name, the joy in her face fled.

'Oh.'

'We've charged him with Angelica's murder and attempted murder on yourself this afternoon. He's being sent to HMP Chelmsford, where he'll be on remand until the trial. We don't have a date yet, but I imagine you'll be expected to appear in court, especially after what he did to you.'

Rose grabbed a towel from the toolbox and began wiping her hands. Then, without saying anything, she turned her back on him and moved into the kitchen area. Tomek followed her. To his right, he spotted a massive hole in the wall.

'Did you fall through by accident?' he joked.

Rose pointed to a sledgehammer on the other side of the kitchen floor. 'No, but that bad boy did.'

Standing in what had once been the doorway, Tomek observed the rest of the skeleton of the kitchen. Brown circles littered the floor from spillages over the years. Wires and cables protruded from the walls in the place where the oven and washing machine had once stood. Tools and debris littered the linoleum floor, and there was a large box on the other side of the kitchen.

Rose dropped her towel onto it. Tomek watched it fall onto the box, and then immediately wished he hadn't.

There, hiding beneath the towel, was an item that gave him cause to hold his breath: a welder's mask and black coveralls. The outfit of the mysterious woman from The Nights of Eden parties. The outfit of the woman that Angelica had spent several nights with. The woman who had taken her from Emilia Solveig. Beneath, protruding from the material, was something Tomek recognised instantly. Another invitation from Micky Tatton to The Nights of Eden. Addressed to Angelica.

Tomek opened his mouth, but stuttered.

'Everything all right?' Rose asked.

He stumbled. In his pocket, his phone began to vibrate.

'You...' His thoughts were running away with themselves. 'You said... You said the bathroom was finished? Is it all right if I use it?'

'You haven't even offered me a drink yet,' she replied.

'Ha. Sorry. I...'

'Of course you can. Do you think you can find it?'

The phone stopped ringing.

'Yeah, I should manage.'

Slowly, Tomek shuffled out. As he made his way towards the bathroom, the room, the walls, the floor had all become black, merging into one. His head felt dizzy, light. His pulse pounded in his ears, and for a moment he thought Rose had put the music back on. He felt like he'd been yanked from his body, his limbs moving freely and independently of one another, like he wasn't at the helm.

Eventually, after what had felt like the longest walk in the world, Tomek entered the bathroom and shut the door behind him. She was right. The bathroom was finished. The white tiles on the floor, the porcelain toilet and sink sitting next to one another, the window above it, the bath wedged into the corner, the wicker storage unit in the other corner. It was like stepping into another world. A world that confused and disoriented Tomek further.

Then his phone rang again, pulling him from his thoughts.

He pulled it out and answered.

'It was Rose,' Chey shouted in his ear. 'Rose was the one posting on Angelica's blog from the library. You have to get out of there now. Uniform is on the way.'

Just as Tomek was about to respond, he heard the sound of a door closing.

The front door.

She was escaping!

Tomek chucked his phone into his pocket and threw open the bathroom door.

The light bouncing off the metal hammerhead caught his eye first, and he reacted instinctively, ducking beneath the swing, avoiding the fatal blow to the skull. Rose, wearing her welder's mask, roared as she raised the hammer to bring it down on him again. But he was too quick for her. He reached up for it, grabbed her, and then launched it away from them. The metal tool cascaded through the air and crashed into the wall on the opposite side of the bathroom, creating a large hole. Beneath his grip, Rose used her other hand to punch and claw at his ribs and face. She was surprisingly strong, and her nails tore through the skin on his cheek and neck. Reluctantly, Tomek released his grip on her arm, and as he let go, she wrapped both arms around him and pushed him backwards, nails digging into his flesh. Before he knew it, he was in the bathtub, bashing the back of his head against the wall. Then Rose turned on the water. The stream of water disoriented him, choking him. She held his head under for a few seconds before turning and sprinting away. Using his hands, blinded by the water in his eyes, Tomek found a grip on the side of the tub and pulled himself out. Rose was trying to make a run for it, but Tomek had other plans. He reached out a hand, grabbed her coveralls, wrapped his arms around her waist, encasing her in a bear hug, and lifted her feet off the ground. Rose's arms and legs flailed in the air. Then they caught a purchase on the toilet, and using all the strength in her legs, she pushed him backwards. Together, looking like they were in a scene from *Titanic*, they stumbled backwards, Tomek's upper back crashing into the drywall, carving a large hole. As he fell to the floor, winded and stunned, they were showered in drywall and paint chippings, Rose clambered off him and started towards the exit.

Coming to, his hands running across the floor's surface, he found the hammer. Wrapping his fingers around its hilt, he raised it, took aim, and launched it. The hammer somersaulted through the air until it came into contact with the back of Rose's head and sent her flying into the sink, which crashed under her weight. As her body fell to the floor, the water burst from within the sink and began spraying into the air, quickly covering the floor and walls. Within a few seconds, Tomek caught his breath and staggered towards her on all fours. First, he grabbed the hammer and chucked it into the living room, then he rolled her body over and felt for a pulse.

She was alive. Breathing, but unconscious.

Tomek collapsed to the floor, resting against the side of the bath, as the water from the broken sink pipe continued to douse him. He sat there for a few moments, catching his breath, panting. He turned to look at the destruction their altercation had caused. The broken porcelain on the floor. The puddle of blood from the wound to the back of Rose's head mixing and swirling with the rising water level. The hammer, covered in debris from the drywall behind him. And then he saw it, glistening beneath the light.

Slowly, he clambered to his feet and stepped towards it, holding his ribs and massaging the side of his face.

In the assault, Tomek had gouged a massive hole into the drywall beside the bathtub, and buried inside it was a large plastic Ziplock bag. He pulled it out and observed the contents. Inside were the dress and underwear Angelica had been wearing on the night she'd died. Her mobile phone. A twelve-inch dildo that had been used to rape her. A white angel costume and a pair of wings. A paintbrush still covered in blood. A long, thin plastic tube, and a large tin of paint, covered in dried blood.

Evidence of the murder that had taken place here.

Evidence that Rose had killed Angelica, presumably in this very room, drained her body of blood, raped her, cleansed her, then applied a layer of make-up to her face.

As he continued to look at the bag, the front door to the flat burst open and, shortly after, several officers spilled in. Chey was first to arrive in the bathroom. He came to a sudden stop in the doorframe and observed the scene.

'Is she dead?' he asked bluntly.

'No,' Tomek answered, 'but Angelica is because of her.'

CHAPTER SIXTY-THREE

After two days of intense interviewing and questioning, Rose had finally conceded and told them everything. Ever since she had first laid eyes on her sister-in-law, she had become infatuated with her, obsessed by her beauty and the kindness of her soul. Over the years, that desire and lust had grown, and as she'd felt herself growing apart from Johnny, her feelings had only intensified. But it wasn't until Angelica had told her about The Nights of Eden parties that Rose had found an excuse to take their relationship to the next level. She had stolen an invitation from Angelica's coat one afternoon and used it to gain access to the party. From there, under the guise of looking like a welder, she had approached Angelica, and together the two of them had shared a bed for the night. It had come as a surprise for Angelica to see her sister-in-law there, but it had not bothered her in the slightest. And as a result, their relationship had developed in secret, meeting each month for sex, some time together, and the comfort of one another's company. Angelica had harboured the same intense feeling, Rose had explained, but as soon as she'd found out about the baby, Rose had decided that their relationship couldn't continue. Angelica had lied to her, betrayed her. The baby would change everything, ruin everything, and Rose couldn't tolerate it. If she couldn't have her, nobody could. And so, on the night of Angelica's death, Rose had messaged her on WhatsApp, when she knew she would be intoxicated, picked her up, taken her to the flat, and then killed her. Fortunately, at least in her opinion, she had been given a helping hand by Adam Egglington, who had been successful in slipping Angelica the date rape drug when she hadn't been looking, the effects of which had already started to take hold of her within minutes of their arrival at the flat. The rest of the evening had followed with delicacy and the affection Angelica deserved, Rose had told them.

Tomek was able to piece together the rest, and so stopped watching the live feed in the incident room. He left the room and made his way to his desk, guilt ravaging his body and mind. He was at his desk for a few moments before Victoria called his name from the other side of the office.

'You got a moment?' she asked.

Tomek confirmed he had, then slowly made his way over.

'Take a seat,' Victoria said as he shut the door behind him.

Tomek did as he was told.

'How are you feeling?'

He noticed the softness and sensitivity in her tone.

'I've felt better,' he answered.

'What's troubling you?'

'I almost sent an innocent man to prison.'

Victoria chewed on her bottom lip. 'These things happen,' she said. 'You just need to be grateful that you caught the right person at the right time.'

Tomek saw little consolation in that.

'Do you need any time off?' Victoria asked.

He paused to reflect on that. Time off? To let the thoughts and guilt fester? No, thanks.

'I'll be fine.'

'Well, if you ever need anyone or anything, you know who to speak to.'

'Nick?'

'Fuck you,' she said, stifling a chuckle. '*Me*. I'm happy to talk if you need anything. I'm also here to help you work on the improvements you can make to be a better inspector.'

Tomek's gaze fell to the table. 'About that...' he began. 'I've been doing some thinking.'

About that and everything else.

'And?'

'And I don't think I'm ready to be an inspector. Don't get me wrong, I'm grateful for the opportunity you gave me, but I'll have to pass for now. I nearly put an innocent person in jail, and I don't think I could live with the possibility of making that same mistake again.'

CHAPTER SIXTY-FOUR

Tomek was sitting in the corner of The Fork and Spoon, spinning his pint glass in his hand, staring up at the football on the television. At the bar, two blokes wearing jeans that looked as though they hadn't been washed in years were nursing their drinks slowly, shouting and swearing at the players on the pitch, as though they could hear them from several hundred miles away.

Tomek finished the last of his drink, then made his way to the bar.

'Fucking pass the ball, you cunt!' the man nearest to him yelled. Then a moment later: 'Fucking pass it! You earn a hundred grand a week and you can't pass the fucking ball!'

Tomek ignored him and waited for the owner, Jim, to come over. A few seconds later, he arrived, reaching out for Tomek's glass.

'Same again, mate?'

'Please, Jim.'

Ian took the glass from him, then began pulling his pint. Tomek watched as the thick, yellow liquid slowly rose in the glass, bubbles streaming to the surface.

'Penny for your thoughts?' Jim asked as he set the drink in front of him.

Beside Tomek, the football fan continued to scream profanities at the screen.

'You wouldn't want to know,' he replied, then turned to the space in the pub where the vending machine had once been. 'Unsuccessful business venture, was it?'

'Like you wouldn't believe,' Jim answered. 'I swear to fucking God, I ever catch the fucker who sold it to me, I'll break his fucking kneecaps.'

'Not the sort of thing you admit to a copper, Jim. But I'll let you off this time.'

'You're a copper?' the football fan screeched as he spun the top half of his body towards Tomek.

'Unfortunately so,' Tomek replied. 'Someone somewhere along the line decided it was a good idea to make me one.'

At first, Tomek had been expecting the man to swing for him, or to start an altercation, but the reality was much different. The man set his beer down on the counter, then patted Tomek on the back. 'Nice work. My dad used to work with the dogs in the seventies and eighties. Got a lot of respect for you and the work you do.'

'Cheers,' Tomek replied, feeling slightly dumbfounded.

'You been working on that murder with the young girl in the church?'

'Yeah.'

'I saw you got an arrest. Nice one. Fucking awful what happened to that girl.'

'Thanks,' Tomek said. 'I was the SIO for a time.'

The man held out his hand. It was sweaty and clammy, but Tomek didn't mind.

'Good job. The world could do with a lot more people like you.'

Tomek smiled awkwardly. He didn't know what to say. It wasn't often he received praise, let alone from an outside voice.

A moment later, Jim placed the card machine in front of Tomek.

'Ready when you are,' he said.

As Tomek reached into his wallet for his card, the man stopped him and said, 'This one's on me, all right?'

'No, I couldn't.'

'Nonsense. It's the least I can do.'

At that moment, Tomek felt truly humbled. To have a complete stranger appreciate the work he did, to understand and acknowledge the toll it took on him, was something he'd never experienced before. And after letting the man reach into his pocket and hand some cash across, Tomek stayed at the bar, watching the football with him. He joined in with the man's frustrations at the players' total lack of passing ability, and together they screamed at the television for ten minutes until half time.

Just as the whistle blew, Tomek felt his phone vibrate in his pocket.

He held a finger up to his new friend, apologised, and stepped away. He answered the call without checking the caller ID and held his phone to his ear.

For a few seconds, there was nothing but silence.

Then came the sound of heavy breathing.

Then: 'Hello, Tomek. Why haven't you tried calling me? I've been waiting by my phone for weeks now. How are you? I have a little surprise for you when you get home. It should have arrived in the post today.'

ALSO BY JACK PROBYN

The DS Tomek Bowen Murder Mystery Series:

1) DEATH'S JUSTICE

Southend-on-Sea, Essex: Detective Sergeant Tomek Bowen — driven, dogged, and haunted by the death of his brother — is called to one of the most shocking crime scenes he has ever seen. A man has been ritualistically murdered and dumped in an allotment near the local airport. Early investigations indicate this was a man with a past. A past that earned him many enemies.

Download Death's Justice

2) DEATH'S GRIP

Annabelle Lake thought she recognised the Ford Fiesta waiting outside her school, and the driver in it. She was wrong. Her body is discovered some time later, dangling from a swing in a local playground on Canvey Island.

Download Death's Grip

3) DEATH'S TOUCH

When the fog clears one December morning in Essex, the body of a teenage girl is discovered lying face down in a field. But as soon as the investigation begins, Tomek discovers Lily's death may be linked to a killing spree that has lain dormant for many years — with no one ever being brought to justice for it.

Download Death's Touch

4) DEATH'S KISS

The body of a teenage girl is found face down in the middle of a field. The evidence surrounded her death is scant, until a vital clue uncovers a terrifying serial killer lying in wait...

Download Death's Kiss

5) DEATH'S TASTE

The body of a homeless man is found wedged between the beach huts of Thorpe Bay. But it isn't until the victim's identity is revealed that the town begins to sit up and wonder: who killed him, and why?

Download Death's Taste

The Jake Tanner Crime Thriller Series:

Full-length novels that combine police procedure, organised crime and police corruption.

TOE THE LINE:

A small jeweller's is raided in Guildford High Street and leaves police chasing their tails. Reports suggest that it's The Crimsons, an organised crime group the police have been hunting for years. When the shop owner is kidnapped and a spiked collar is attached to her neck, Jake learns one of his own is involved – a police officer. As Jake follows the group on a wild goose chase, he questions everything he knows about his team. Who can he trust? And is he prepared to find out?

Download Toe the Line

WALK THE LINE:

A couple with a nefarious secret are brutally murdered in their London art gallery. Their bodies cleaned. Their limbs dismembered. And the word LIAR inscribed on the woman's chest. For Jake Tanner it soon becomes apparent this is not a revenge killing. There's a serial killer loose on the streets of Stratford. And the only thing connecting the victims is their name: Jessica. Jake's pushed to his mental limits as he uncovers The Community, an online forum for singles and couples to meet. But there's just one problem: the killer's been waiting for him... and he's hungry for his next kill.

Download Walk the Line

UNDER THE LINE:

DC Jake Tanner thought he'd put the turmoil of the case that nearly killed him behind him. He was wrong. When Danny Cipriano's body is discovered buried in a concrete tomb, Jake's wounds are reopened. But one thing quickly becomes clear. The former leader of The Crimsons knew too much. And somebody wanted him silenced. For good. The only problem is, Jake knows who.

Download Under the Line

CROSS THE LINE:

For years, Henry Matheson has been untouchable, running the drug trade in east London. Until the body of his nearest competitor is discovered burnt to a lamppost in his estate. Gang war gone wrong, or a calculated murder? Only one man is brave enough to stand up to him and find out. But, as Jake Tanner soon learns, Matheson plays dirty. And in the estate there are no rules.

Download Cross the Line

OVER THE LINE:

Months have passed since Henry Matheson was arrested and sent to prison. Months have passed since Henry Matheson, one of east London's most dangerous criminals, was arrested. Since then DC Jake Tanner and the team at Stratford CID have been making sure the case is watertight. But when a sudden and disastrous fraudulent attack decimates Jake's personal finances, he is propelled into the depths of a dark and dangerous underworld, where few resurface.

Download Over the Line

PAST THE LINE:

The Cabal is dead. The Cabal's dead. Or so Jake thought. But when Rupert Haversham, lawyer to the city's underworld, is found dead in his London home, Jake begins to think otherwise. The Cabal's back, and now they're silencing people who know too much. Jake included.

Download Past the Line

❅

The Jake Tanner SO15 Files Series:

Novella length, lightning-quick reads that can be read anywhere. Follow Jake as he joins Counter Terrorism Command in the fight against the worst kind of evil.

THE WOLF:

A cinema under siege. A race to save everyone inside. An impatient detective. Join Jake as he steps into the darkness.

Download *The Wolf*

DARK CHRISTMAS:

The head of a terrorist cell is found dead outside his flat in the early hours of Christmas Eve. What was he doing outside? Why was a suicide vest strapped to his body? And what does the note in his sock have to do with his death?

Download *Dark Christmas*

THE EYE:

The discovery of a bomb factory leaves Jake and the team scrambling for answers. But can they find them in time?

Download *The Eye*

IN HEAVEN AND HELL:

An ominous — and deadly — warning ignites Jake and the team into action. An attack on one of London's landmarks is coming. But where? And when? Failure could be catastrophic.

Download *In Heaven And Hell*

BLACKOUT:

What happens when all the lights in London go out, and all the power switches off? What happens when a city is brought to its knees? Jake Tanner's about to find out. And he's right in the middle of it.

Download *Blackout*

EYE FOR AN EYE:

Revenge is sweet. But not when it's against you. Not when they use your family to get to you. Family is off-limits. And Jake Tanner will do anything to protect his.

Download *Eye For An Eye*

MILE 17:

Every year, thousands of runners and supporters flock to the streets of London to celebrate the London Marathon. Except this year, there won't be anything to ride home about.

Download *Mile 17*

THE LONG WALK:

The happiest day of your life, your wedding day. But when it's a royal wedding, the stakes are much higher. Especially when someone wants to kill the bride.

Download *The Long Walk*

THE ENDGAME:

Jake Tanner hasn't been to a football match in years. But when a terrorist cell attacks his favourite football stadium, killing dozens and injuring hundreds more, Jake is both relieved and appalled — only the day before was he in the same crowds, experiencing the same atmosphere. But now he must put that behind him and focus on finding the people responsible. And fast. Because another attack's coming.

Download *The Endgame*

The Jake Tanner Terror Thriller Series:

Full-length novels, following Jake through Counter-Terrorism Command, where the stakes have never been higher.

STANDSTILL:

The summer of 2017. Jake Tanner's working for SO15, The Metropolitan Police

Service's counter terrorism unit. And a duo of terrorists seize three airport-bound trains. On board are hundreds of kilos of explosives, and thousands of lives. Jake quickly finds himself caught in a cat and mouse race against time to stop the trains from detonating. But what he discovers along the way will change everything.

Download Standstill

FLOOR 68:

1,000 feet in the air, your worst nightmares come true. Charlie Paxman is going to change the world with a deadly virus. His mode of distribution: the top floor of London's tallest landmark, The Shard. But only one man can stop. Jake Tanner. Caught in the wrong place at the wrong time. Trapped inside a tower, Jake finds himself up against an army of steps and an unhinged scientist that threatens to decimate humanity. But can he stop it from happening?

Download Floor 68

JOIN THE VIP CLUB

Your FREE book is waiting for you

Available when you join the VIP Club below

Get your FREE copy of the prequel to the DS Tomek Bowen series now at jackprobynbooks.com when you join my VIP email club.

JOIN THE VIP CLUB

Your FREE book is waiting for you

Available when you join the VIP Club below

Get your FREE copy of the prequel to the DS Tanzi K wave-first novel, independent books soon when you join my VIP email club.

ABOUT THE AUTHOR

Jack Probyn is a British crime writer and the author of the Jake Tanner crime thriller series, set in London.

He currently lives in Surrey with his partner and cat, and is working on a new murder mystery series set in his hometown of Essex.

Don't want to sign up to yet another mailing list? Then you can keep up to date with Jack's new releases by following one of the below accounts. You'll get notified when I've got a new book coming out, without the hassle of having to join my mailing list.

Amazon Author Page "Follow":
    1. Click the link here: https://geni.us/AuthorProfile
    2. Beneath my profile picture is a button that says "Follow"
    3. Click that, and then Amazon will email you with new releases and promos.

BookBub Author Page "Follow":
    1. Similar to the Amazon one above, click the link here: https://www.bookbub.com/authors/jack-probyn
    2. Beside my profile picture is a button that says "Follow"
    3. Click that, and then BookBub will notify you when I have a new release

If you want more up to date information regarding new releases, my writing process, and everything else in between, the best place to be in the know is my Facebook Page. We've got a little community growing over there. Why not be a part of it?

Facebook: https://www.facebook.co.uk/jackprobynbooks

www.ingramcontent.com/pod-product-compliance
Ingram Content Group UK Ltd.
Pitfield, Milton Keynes, MK11 3LW, UK
UKHW041949030625
6215UKWH00017B/139

9 781805 200574